# crystalfire

Published by Kensington Publishing Corporation

# crystalfire

## THE DEMONSLAYERS

## KATE DOUGLAS

ZEBRA BOOKS
KENSINGTON PUBLISHING CORP.
http://www.kensingtonbooks.com

# Chapter 1

The steady *slap, slap, slap* of Taron's sandals echoed off the rough stone walls. He checked his sword, made sure his tunic and pants were properly fastened, and wondered if he'd ever get used to this absurd style of clothing.

After a lifetime in scholarly robes, it was difficult to believe these new designs were more practical, though he had to admit that the pants didn't tangle around his legs the way his robes often had. Of course, he'd rarely had to rush as he rushed now, hurrying down the dark and empty utility tunnel toward the training grounds.

Any other time he would have taken the main passage, but these narrow tunnels, used mostly by the Lemurian Guard, were more practical when one was in a hurry. Besides, there was little risk of being waylaid by any of his fellow scholars. He didn't want to have to explain why he, a well-known scholar and philosopher, was now training some of Lemuria's new Paladins.

He still wasn't quite certain himself.

"Who the nine hells do they think they're kidding?" He would have laughed if it didn't sound so pathetic. Though well-trained in battle strategy and swordsmanship, he was a man who won battles with words, not a sword.

Gods be damned, even his own so-called sentient blade still didn't think enough of his fighting skills to speak to him, but times were changing.

He did have the skills, and he had, after all, volunteered.

After Roland, the new Captain of the Guard twisted his arm.

A flash of blue caught his eye as he rounded a curve in the passage. He jerked to a stop.

It couldn't be . . . could it?

"Willow?" His heart pounded as he flattened his palm against the wall and searched for the elusive blue sparkle. He'd never thought to see that amazing little will-o'-the-wisp again.

He drew his sword and used the light from the crystal blade. "Willow . . . are you there?"

Carefully he searched the narrow passage. She couldn't be . . . but there was always a chance, always . . . A small chip—a bit of crystal embedded in the tunnel wall—reflected swordlight with a flash of blue. *Gods be damned.*

He let out a big breath and sheathed his weapon. "Of course you're not here, are you?" What the nine hells was he thinking? Willow was gone, nothing more than consciousness now, that amazing mind, that beautiful little sprite, stuck inside the body of a stupid dog.

Sighing, remembering Willow, wishing the impossible and feeling like a fool, he continued down the tunnel to the training field.


"Nine hells, woman. Be careful!"

Blinded by sweat, Taron lunged to one side. His foot slipped out from under him on the slick stone floor; he ducked his head and rolled to the left. Shoulder first, he hit the ground hard, a hairsbreadth ahead of the sharp edge of the Paladin's sword. The shimmering crystal blade sliced much too close to his throat.

Lying on his back, gasping for air and absolutely livid, he glared at his opponent. "This is a training exercise, Isra! You're not supposed to try and kill me!"

Isra held out her hand in immediate apology. "I am sorry, Taron. Thank the gods you're so quick! I guess I got a bit caught up in our battle."

"Mock battle, Isra. And gods be damned, but quick had nothing to do with it. I fell on my ass or I'd be a dead man. Please, try to remember I'm one of the good guys." Shaking off his unexpected anger, he took her offered hand.

She tugged and he stood, but she didn't turn him loose. Her full lips lifted into a sexy smile. "That you are, Taron of Libernus." Her voice had gone low and rather husky, and she cocked one dark eyebrow as she studied him with unabashed interest. "You are most definitely one of the good guys."

He glanced at their hands—still linked—and back at her face. She continued to assess him in a most forthright manner. He wasn't quite sure how to react—the average Lemurian woman was not so bold.

Isra, though, was a Paladin. Once a slave in the crystal mines, now she was a soldier in Lemuria's new army of women warriors.

Paladins knew no fear, nor did they lack confidence.

Taron could use a little of that confidence himself, he thought, staring uncomfortably at their linked hands. He'd learned long ago that women were not for him, and he wasn't about to let this one distract him from his scholarly goals.

Isra glanced at their clasped fingers and then raised her head. "Would you, by any chance, be interested in . . ."

*Gods-be-damned, no!* Taron quickly extricated his hand from her grasp. "I'm flattered, Isra, but I'm a scholar. My interests lie elsewhere."

Frowning, she stepped back a pace and stared at him like

he had two heads. What? Didn't the woman believe him when he said he wasn't interested?

Obviously not.

Still staring, she said, "You're well-formed and powerful. You move with a soldier's grace and speed. You're here, training women to fight. Not a very scholarly occupation, is it?"

He shrugged. "We do what we must in times such as these. Once the Paladins are fully trained, I will return to my studies and my solitude."

Laughing softly, she shook her head. Why would she look so confused? It was only the truth, after all. "Are you a celibate?" she asked. "Or is it possible you prefer the company of men?"

His laughter surprised him as much as her question. "No, Isra. I do not prefer the company of men. I am celibate by choice. It's not unusual for a man to choose a life of quiet study over the constant turmoil of politics and warfare—or love."

She grinned at him, still shaking her head.

"Do you think I make light of you?" He honestly didn't know what she thought. He didn't really care, though he did not want her to think him rude. Women had always been, and probably always would be, a mystery to him.

One he had absolutely no interest in solving.

Still smiling, Isra was the one to shrug this time. "I know better, Taron. You are not one to make light of an honest question. I guess it's just not the answer I expected."

"Well, I certainly didn't intend to confuse you, though I'm pleased you realize I would never play you false." Truth be told, she was a lovely young woman, and if he were so inclined, he might be showing interest in Isra the female rather than merely dodging her crystal blade in training.

Isra reached for a cup of water while he turned away and grabbed a towel. Wiping the sweat from his face he tried to think of Isra as a woman, as someone with whom he might want to form a relationship.

He couldn't do it. He saw her as a Paladin and nothing more. It wasn't the Lemurian way to lust after women, and it certainly wasn't his way. Control of what he thought of as his baser instincts, that wild creature buried deep inside, was more than a matter of honor—it was the way he had chosen to live.

It was a choice many of his peers had made, though that so-called "Lemurian way," like many other things in their society, was undergoing a rapid change. For one thing, these strong-willed, intelligent women now training as warriors were not quiet and soft-spoken like their aristocratic counterparts.

No, they were bold beyond measure.

Taron found their attitude refreshing, invigorating, even, though he had no intention of pursuing any of them for romance.

They were much too distracting.

This was different, though, this position as a trainer for the women who'd once been slaves. This was a role that had essentially chosen him—one he found he enjoyed in spite of the risk to life and limb.

Of course, Isra's sentient sword would never have allowed her to actually harm him, which was the only reason they were able to train with their crystal blades. Nor could he blame her powerful strike on demon influence. His people, for now at least, were free of the bastards. None remained who were possessed by demonkind.

Isra—an average-sized woman fully a foot shorter than he and with only a fraction of his reach—had almost taken him down, proving once again that women had the ability to stand as equals beside their men.

One more long-standing Lemurian tradition that had quickly been erased. Like the one that said a woman waited all her life to be chosen by an interested male, so she might then focus her life on making his easier.

Taron had a feeling that particular tradition was already gone. But just as women were now free to flirt, Taron was free to ignore that flirtation. Setting his towel aside and smiling ruefully, he did exactly that, shaking his head over Isra's skill and his own clumsiness.

"You've learned quickly, Isra. I'm going to need more work with Roland if I expect to best any of you in battle, mock or otherwise." He bowed his head in respect. "You have done well. All of the Paladins are doing an amazing job, but you have truly excelled."

A brilliant flash of blue light set him back a step. Again, the image of Willow and her trail of blue crystals entered his thoughts, but only for a split second. A strange voice— a woman's voice—echoed from everywhere, yet from nowhere in particular.

"Taron is right. You have done extremely well, Isra."

Taron was almost certain his heart stood still. He stared at Isra's glowing sword, unwilling to believe what he'd just heard, but there was no denying the truth.

*Impossible. Absolutely impossible.* How could this be? It was too soon—Isra was too new a warrior. He swallowed back a curse, raised his head and focused on the wide-eyed woman.

"Isra. Your blade. It speaks."


Ginny Jones redialed her cousin's number, but the call didn't go through. She stared at her cell phone long enough to register Markus's panic and the blinking icon telling her the battery was going dead. Then she shoved the phone in her pocket, turned around and walked right into the solid wall of red rock.

In seconds she'd passed through the portal at Red Rock

Crossing in Sedona, Arizona, and entered the vortex. She bypassed the tunnel to Bell Rock where the main entrance to Lemuria was located, and took the small portal leading directly from this vortex to the Council of Nine's chancellor's office.

It took mere seconds to step out of Earth's dimension and enter Lemuria's, something that never ceased to amaze her.

She'd have to save the amazement for later. Ready or not, there was another crisis looming, but where the hell was her team? The damned chancellor's office was empty.

"Shit. Where is everyone?" Ginny brushed her hand over her crystal sword, as much from habit as the need to connect to her ever-present companion. After another quick glance about the empty chamber and adjoining rooms, she slipped through the doorway and took off at a full run, heading for the great plaza with her cousin Markus's panic-stricken words echoing in her ears.

*Ginny! Something bad is going on. Animals are acting really weird. I mean really, really weird. Tom the cat's got all those teeth again and he just ate the neighbor's dog. Like chewed him up and swallowed him. And the dog's a Rottweiler. Uh . . . he was a Rottweiler. Ginny? Answer the phone! Where are you?*

Skidding as she rounded a jeweled column, Ginny collided with Alton. Her mate grabbed her arms, steadying her as she gasped for breath.

"Ginny? Sweetheart . . . what's wrong?"

Blowing so hard she couldn't speak, Ginny linked up and telepathically shared Markus's message with Alton.

Hanging on to her arm, Alton spun around and looked out across the great plaza. He called out to a familiar figure near the dais. "Dax! Grab Eddy. See if you can find Daws and Selyn. We need to go to Sedona. Now."

Eddy Marks popped out of one of the council chamber rooms. "What's going on? We were just headed back to

Evergreen to check in with Dad and see how Bumper-Willow's doing."

Ginny shook her head. "There's no time. I just got a message from Markus. It sounds like a full-scale invasion in Sedona. I tried calling him back. He didn't answer, but my battery's really low. I barely got a signal."

Dax, Selyn, and Dawson Buck trotted across the plaza. Ginny waved them over. "Can you guys leave now? We really need to hurry."

Dawson nodded. "We're ready. I need to check on the clinic anyway, make sure my assistant's got everything under control. He's a good vet. Esteban's used to running the place, so if animals are affected again he'll have heard." He checked his blade and then glanced toward the plaza filled with citizens. "Should we tell anyone we're going?"

Alton nodded. "I've contacted Taron. Told him we've got a new demon outbreak in Earth's dimension. I wonder if this is the group Isra saw the demon king sending toward Sedona?"

"It has to be." Ginny took off at a trot toward the council office and the small portal. "We couldn't find any sign of them when we were there a couple days ago, though. Makes me wonder what they've been up to."

Alton shook his head as he pushed the pace. "Nothing good, that's for sure."

He and Ginny led Dax, Eddy, Daws, and Selyn through the door into the chancellor's office. Dawson paused by the portal—the one that led directly to the small vortex at Red Rock Crossing.

"Let's go to my place first," he said. His home was close to the portal. "We can charge our cell phones while you use the landline to try and reach Markus. I'll get in touch with my clinic, see if they've heard anything, but we might want to fan out, cover as much area as we can."

Ginny nodded. "Works for me. Let's go."

They slipped through the portal and entered the vortex at Red Rock Crossing. The entire chamber reeked of sulfur, and Dax stopped everyone with a wave of his hand. "Look. The portal to Abyss. It's open again."

Ginny drew DarkFire. "I've got it." Anxiety rippled across her shoulders as she pointed her sword at the pulsing gateway to hell. A beam of dark light shot from the end of her amethyst blade. Silently she willed DarkFire to hurry. In less than a minute, the small portal was once again sealed. Ginny slipped her sword into the scabbard and set a glamour over the blade.

The brilliant amethyst sword faded from sight.

Dawson was the first to step through the portal out of the vortex and into the waning light of a late October afternoon. The area was empty, the blue sky a welcome change after the caverns of Lemuria.

Ginny took a deep breath of the clean, desert air. No sulfuric stench of demon here, no sense of danger, but Markus had sounded absolutely terrified.

Alert and moving quickly, she followed the others—this amazing band of demonslayers—along the well-marked trail. It led to a shortcut that ran cross-country for a small distance before eventually dropping them into the back side of Dawson's property.

It would be night soon. The perfect time to hunt demons.

Visibly trembling, Isra clutched the hilt of her crystal sword and stared at the shimmering blade. "Why, Taron? I heard her voice, but . . ." Slowly raising her head, Isra stared at him. "I've done nothing to deserve her praise. How can this be?"

The other women in the training room gathered close as Isra's sword shimmered, diamond bright, and pulsing with life.

Once again the blade flashed and the sentience within spoke. The voice was soft and melodic, definitely female. "You will call me FrostFire, Isra. My name will forever be a reminder of the cold that once encased your heart. I speak because I wish to, because it is time. You've had more personal demons to overcome than most, Isra, once a Forgotten One. You turned away from evil. You saved Nica's life. You have fought your own demons to become a stronger, better woman. You've done this, not for personal glory but for Lemuria. We will make a formidable team, you and I."

The glow faded, the blade was once again merely faceted crystal. Isra raised her head and stared at Taron, not as a man she wanted to bed, but as a friend, one who might understand what had just happened. All sense of her earlier flirtation was gone. Tears coursed down her cheeks, but she didn't say a word. Her rapt expression spoke volumes.

Isra's silence was not unexpected. Taron figured if his gods-be-damned sword ever condescended to speak to him, he'd not know what to say, either.

He bowed low to Isra, a heartfelt show of respect.

Respect tainted by his own unfathomable jealousy— a foolish and unwelcome response he quickly buried. "Your sword is correct, Isra. You will make a formidable team. Congratulations to you, and to FrostFire. May your partnership be long and successful."

She nodded, but her attention shifted quickly from Taron to the crystal sword clutched in her hand. Taron turned and walked away as Isra's sisters gathered around her . . . walked away, clasping his own mute weapon in his right hand.

The proof of a warrior's value was in the sentience of his blade. Isra, who'd partnered with a crystal sword for mere days, had already been validated as a warrior, while he, a Lemurian aristocrat who'd carried crystal for millennia, who'd wielded his blade in battle, had not heard a word from his weapon.

If he'd proven himself, his sword would have spoken by now. Would have at least acknowledged him as a demon fighter. What did he lack? What did he need to do? He'd fought demonkind, and fought them bravely, yet obviously it wasn't enough.

Even if he had wanted to romance a woman—and he knew he could choose any of the Forgotten Ones with the odds of a successful outcome—he didn't feel worthy.

His sword had been the one chosen to replicate the crystal blades which now armed those same women, he'd killed demons in battle, had stood bravely against powerful odds.

Still, it had not been enough.

No matter what he did, it was never enough.

He knew he should not be so beholden to anyone or anything for affirmation of his own value, but the truth hurt. He needed to know his blade found him worthy, that he'd earned the respect of the sentience within his crystal sword.

There was no one else. He was a man without a family. His parents were long gone. Alton had been the closest thing to a brother he'd ever known.

Now, Alton had Ginny and a sword that spoke to him. Taron was truly alone for the first time in his life.

Head down, heart heavy, he walked slowly back to his quarters, much too aware of the disconsolate sound of his footsteps as he headed down the long tunnel. His shadow, the dark shape of a powerful warrior bearing a sword, mocked him.

The melodramatic thoughts in his head mocked him even more. Why did this bother him so? Why couldn't he just let it go and get on with his life? *Fool,* he thought. *You act the fool.*

Yet once inside his apartment, he set the sword down on the low table in front of his couch, sat back in the comfortable chair, and stared with unabashed bitterness at the blade.

So much had occurred over the past month, and through

it all, he'd expected the sentience in his crystal sword finally to make itself known. He'd felt as if he was paused on the precipice of history when he and Alton made the decision to free the demonslayers from their cell. He'd risked death, and yet he still believed the choice they'd made that night to defy the Council of Nine's edict would bring about change.

Change for the better of his world and his people. And, in many ways, it had, even though the demon king still lived.

Artigos the Just, a leader they'd long thought dead, had been freed from captivity and now governed Lemuria with his son beside him. The new Council of Nine—one untainted by demonic possession—would be seated in a couple of days. This would be the first council including both women and common folk since the great move to this dimension in the depths of Mount Shasta. The women, those brave Forgotten Ones, were no longer slaves. Now Paladins, they had become honored guardians of Lemuria, ready to usher in a renewed age of strong women warriors.

So many amazing changes in such a short time—unheard of in a world that was slow to embrace change of any kind. But where was Taron of Libernus's place in the new order? What role would he be called upon to play?

If he were called to play any future role at all.

He stared at the sword, running through all that had occurred since that moment just four weeks ago when he and Alton had first spied what they thought were normal humans sitting forlornly in their Lemurian prison cell. Dax and Eddy had looked absolutely pathetic, and the silly dog hadn't been much better.

And Willow. Dear, beautiful little Willow. Unexpected tears stung his eyes when he thought of her. He'd been fascinated with the sprite from the very first moment he saw her. Not even as tall as his smallest finger, she'd stood there in the palm of his hand and actually flirted with him.

The others hadn't noticed, thank the gods, or he'd still be

getting teased, but the little flirt had spoken mind to mind with him and every word had been loaded with teasing innuendo. It should have sounded ridiculous, coming from such a tiny creature, but there'd been something special about the sprite. Something that tugged at his soul and made him smile even now, though inexplicably, his heart was breaking.

How could he grieve so for a creature he hardly knew, one that could never be more to him than a friend? Still, the thought of that perfect little body being eaten by the demon king as the tiny sprite bravely battled evil made Taron's failings even more painfully obvious.

Ginny said Willow was handling it well. Just one more change among many—new life for Willow, new leader for Lemuria, new way of life for a people who preferred to debate a subject to death rather than deal with it.

Taron wished he was as good at dealing with change as Willow appeared to be, but there were just so many changes, so much to do . . . it made his head spin.

He closed his eyes and leaned back against the sofa. Consciously, he slowed his breathing, eased the taut muscles in his shoulders, and hoped the knot in his gut would finally settle.

Nine hells, but what a long month this had been . . . and yet, it felt as if all that was familiar had been upended in the blink of an eye . . . which was quite close to reality for a man with a near-immortal span of years. What was one month in thousands of months? One year in millennia? He drifted, falling deeper and deeper into a sea of calm, relishing the sense of utter relaxation, if only for a moment.

A thought flittered through his mind, that it was probably not the smartest thing, to steal this time for himself . . . sort of like inviting chaos or tempting the gods.

As if merely giving freedom to that thought had opened

a door, a brilliant blast of light flashed brightly across his closed lids.

*Nine hells* . . . Blinking, Taron opened his eyes. Shut them tightly, opened them again and stared.

The entire room glowed. His crystal sword flashed again—blue fire almost blinded him. He blinked and jerked away from the shimmering light, then slowly leaned forward. Heart racing, he gazed, transfixed by the glowing blade. There was a sense of portent about the moment, a feeling that power gathered.

*Tempting the gods, indeed!*

Chills ran along his arms. He rubbed them, barely aware of the act, at least until a voice filled the room. A man's voice, speaking with strength and conviction.

His gods-be-damned crystal blade was actually speaking.

"Nine hells and then some . . ." Taron swallowed back another curse as the voice rang out.

"Taron of Libernus? Prepare. The final battle draws nigh. It is time."

*Holy shit, as Ginny would say . . . time for what?*

He took a deep breath. "I'm listening. What should I do?"

"Go now to Evergreen. Post haste. Time is short."

The glow faded. The blade went silent.

*Evergreen? It wants me to go to Earth's dimension?*

He thought of Alton's brief message, received a short time ago. His friend was probably there now, slipping into Earth's dimension as if it was no big deal. He'd done it often enough over the past few weeks as one of the soldiers on the front lines of the battle against demonkind.

But not Taron. His work had all been here, in Lemuria. Until now. *Time is short.* How short? And why?

Still in shock, Taron ran his fingers over the faceted surface. The crystal felt cool to his touch, though it pulsed with a new sense of life.

His fingers trembled as he stroked the blade. His throat

felt tight. He gazed at the crystal he'd carried for thousands of years, lost in wonder.

He couldn't wait to tell Alton, but his friend was already out of reach, already in Earth's dimension. Well, if Taron followed his blade's orders, he'd be seeing Alton soon. He couldn't wait to tell him his sword had . . . "Nine hells and then some."

Taron burst into laughter. Shoulders shaking, he laughed like a veritable madman, until the tears ran down his cheeks and he knew he looked and sounded like an idiot.

Finally he got himself under control. Wiping his eyes, he stared ruefully at the silent sword. "The least you could have done after all these years," he said, "was tell me your name."

# Chapter 2

The demon stood alone in the foul miasma of Abyss, horned head tilted to one side, all four arms cocked, taloned hands planted firmly against his scaled body. Howls and shrieks and the cries of the damned filled the air.

*Music,* he thought. *Just think of it as music.*

But he remembered the glorious sound of harps, of voices rising in perfect harmony, a celestial choir filling air sweet with the scent of . . . *no, damn it.* That was another life, another man, another world. This was his world and the cacophony that rattled his brain was merely background noise, much like the stench that permeated every nook and cranny of Abyss.

A stench he'd learned to appreciate. And he'd appreciate it a lot more once he got out of here, except someone had closed the blasted portal again. Cursing under his breath, he stared at the freshly melted rock in front of him. This portal had been open mere moments ago. Somehow the bastards had sealed it. Did they know he'd planned to use this one? Impossible, but it would have given him access directly from Abyss to the small portal leading to the Lemurian council chambers.

Growling, he slammed two of his fists against the melted

rock. Shards of stone scattered, but the portal remained closed. *No matter.* He curled his fists and stared dispassionately at the dark green blood seeping from his knuckles.

Fascinating color, green. He wondered if he'd ever get used to bleeding such an obnoxious color. He glared at the melted stone as more dark blood dripped over darker scales and pooled at his clawed feet. *The portal can be reopened. All that matters now is that they die.*

*Kneel, fool.*

He was on his knees before he'd fully registered the command. Like he had a choice?

The powerful voice in his head felt like splinters of glass driving into his brain. *All that matters, fool, is that you succeed. You have failed me three times. Do not fail me again.*

*Shit.* The last thing he wanted to do was draw the Dark Lord's attention. He turned his head, swinging his horned skull slowly to gaze at the black tower of rock almost hidden in the foul vapors behind him. It rose, dark and forbidding over an even more forbidding landscape—the castle where the Lord of the Dark, the one who ruled Abyss, was said to reside.

He couldn't know for certain. No one did. The ruler of this land was an enigma—secretive, entirely unknown to most who dwelled here—and yet there was no doubt in his mind that the creature—whomever and whatever he was— was powerful beyond belief.

More powerful even than the one who ruled over Eden, which was part of the reason he'd chosen this world. Or he would have, maybe . . . if he'd had a choice.

Bowing his head, fighting the urge to curse the bastard even as he knelt before him, the demon acknowledged the other's greater power. *I will not fail, my lord. Failure is not an option.*

*That's a human saying, fool.* The link snapped closed.

*My name is not Fool.* But he said that to himself, quietly, though he had no alternative to offer. At one time he'd had a name. He'd even had a family, long, long ago. Still, no matter how hard he tried, he couldn't remember what his name had been, or who the people were who once had loved him.

He barely remembered his original home, his life in Eden, but that was by choice. When one lived in Abyss, it could be painful recalling life in Paradise. To remember was to wonder if he'd chosen the right course.

Wondering—*doubting*—had no place in his life. Not anymore.

Of course, he really hadn't had much choice—not after the Edenites kicked him out. His own father had . . . no. He would not go there again. He would not remember.

There was no room for second-guessing decisions already made, already acted upon. Slowly he rose, though he couldn't stop himself from glancing over his shoulder once again. He had to be careful, but he could not give in to fear. Fear showed weakness, and weakness of any kind was fatal.

Besides, what was the point of remembering failure? He had a name, though it wasn't one he was quite ready to share with the Dark Lord. It was a name his enemies had given him, the ones who fought his kind with sentient crystal— they had crowned him the demon king. He liked the sound of that. He would soon wear the title openly, as ruler over all of them—over Earth and Lemuria, Atlantis and Eden.

He turned away from the black tower. He would rule over Abyss as well. Let the bastard in that pile of rocks deal with him once he had the power. Once he had the life force of the one who had first owned this body, nothing could stop him.

*Nothing.*

He took a deep breath and filled his lungs with the sulfuric stench of Abyss, inhaling the heavy air with the appreciation of a connoisseur testing the bouquet of a fine wine. His eyes watered and his lungs burned.

He reveled in the pain.

*This is your world, now. So get over it.*

He focused on the dark stone that covered the portal, flexed the thick, ropey muscles of all his arms and held one huge fist in front of his face. Razor-sharp claws extended from the end of each finger, the tips every bit as lethal as the curved horns atop his head.

Damn but he loved this body, the pure functionality of demonform. He loved the powerful muscles and sharp claws, the scaled hide that was impervious to almost anything . . . almost.

If only he could maintain it when he left this dimension, but that wasn't going to happen—not as long as this body's original inhabitant survived.

Dax, the one who called himself *demonslayer*, an ordinary looking man who had once been a demon—*this demon*—clung to enough of his original soul that he still had a link to this body. He, and he alone was the only one standing in the way of complete and utter power—of all glory— to the demon king.

Until he could fully absorb Dax's life force and gather the final remnants of that which connected Dax to this body, he could only maintain a wraith's form in other dimensions without an avatar. Oh, he could pull it off for a short while— given enough demon souls, it was amazing what a guy could do—but that was only temporary.

He wanted this body, all the power, permanently.

And he couldn't have it until he had all of Dax . . .

Growling softly, he focused once again on the sealed portal, but he couldn't keep his mind from going back to the same damned thoughts. After a moment's contemplation, he snarled, curling his lip over curved fangs. Damn those demonslayers and their crystal swords! If not for them, he'd be ruling Earth right now, but they'd been lucky. Too damned lucky.

How in hell's name did they keep managing to save the one among them that he needed?

This time, he'd damned well better succeed. If he failed, he'd lose not only the battle for all worlds in all dimensions, he'd lose everything.

His life would be forfeit. Taken by the Dark Lord as payment for failure. This perfect demonic body and any hope of owning the role he'd already been assigned by those worthless humans and Lemurians, would end.

*Demon king.*

Damn. He really liked the sound of that. How could it be that only his enemies recognized the threat he posed to them and their worlds? Somehow, they knew he was the only one capable of ruling over Earth and Lemuria, maybe even Atlantis. And Eden. How he wanted to rule Eden.

His family had thrown him out. Discarded him like so much trash merely because he was smarter than the rest of them. Stronger. More powerful, more cunning—the perfect one to rule.

They would all be his, once this battle was won.

He glanced over his shoulder, gazing between the second set of thickly muscled arms that erupted from his powerful back in exactly the place where his wings would have grown—if things had been different. If he'd stayed in Eden.

If he'd been as disgustingly pure as the rest of those sniveling souls. The thought sickened him—or was that an unwelcome coil of fear in his belly? Fear that refused to leave when he glanced through the sulfuric mist that was the only atmosphere the creatures of Abyss would ever know, and stared toward the tower where the Lord of the Dark supposedly lived.

After a long moment's contemplation, he turned his attention once again to the sealed portal. There were other gateways. Other doors that would take him out of Abyss.

This time, he needed a plan. He must focus.

Who among the demon hunters was the weakest? Which one could least withstand his power?

There was an older man, father to the woman, but again, it was more difficult to possess a sentient human form. He'd tried on more than one occasion, but the humans had fought him. The effort to overcome a human mind could be exhausting, should he run out of demonic souls to feed his powerful need.

*But what about . . . ?*

An image of that foolish, curly-haired beast they all seemed to love so much popped into his mind. It made no sense—an animal had no value—but for whatever reason, each of the demonslayers deferred to the stupid creature. Taking on a brainless animal's form was simple.

Once the demon hunters knew their beast was threatened, he would have them.

Most importantly, he would have the one he needed most of all. That fool Dax wouldn't be able to ignore the cries of their stupid animal. The demon rubbed all four of his hands together. This was absolutely perfect.

He knew exactly how to make it cry.

With another quick glance at the dark tower, he moved swiftly toward a different section of the stone cliff. The Dark Lord could open these portals at any time, without any effort, but he seemed to enjoy throwing roadblocks before his minions.

Well, this *minion* was tired of such a subservient role. Almost tasting the power of the vortex, he gazed at the swirling mass of energy. This wasn't the portal he'd planned to use, but it would suffice.

With nary a glance toward the one who still ruled Abyss, he slipped through the swirling gateway and entered the vortex. Here he was nothing more than mist, a black, sulfuric cloud, but it appeared that, unlike some of his previous excursions, this time, his mind remained clear, his ability to think and reason and plan was still sound.

He drifted toward the portal that led to Sedona. There were demons aplenty in that small town. Most of the ones he'd sent through the doorway to Mount Shasta had been destroyed, but he'd sensed no endings in Sedona. He should go there first, absorb more souls to power his own. Stir up a bit more death and destruction.

Open a few more portals.

The thought was no more considered than accomplished. He drifted a moment within the Bell Rock vortex. The smell of demonslayer was strong here. He followed the scent to a smaller portal, and, though he had no idea where this one went, he slipped through without hesitation.

There! He'd indirectly reached the small gateway that led straight into the Lemurian council. Interesting. When he'd first thought that was where he wanted to go, the portal had been closed. Now his plans had changed and the damned thing was open.

Fate? He had to wonder. Things happened for a reason, and already his mind was spinning—he smelled demonslayers here, as if they regularly used this gateway between Sedona and Lemuria.

He hadn't realized it had become one of their regular escape routes.

And what would happen should that escape no longer exist? If he could laugh in this form, he would, though he didn't need laughter to seal the portal. One less escape for the fools.

His mist form flashed in a burst of pure energy, all of it

directed at the portal. Rock sizzled and melted and the gateway disappeared entirely. Feeling unaccountably pleased with himself, the demon returned to the main portal at Bell Rock. He was definitely on a roll. The sense of personal power pulsed within his mist form. Spreading across the chamber, he searched the energy vortex, found the main portal to Lemuria and blasted it shut.

The rock glowed and melted into a satisfying smooth, dark wall of stone. See them try and escape now! Reveling in the visceral thrill of omnipotence, he slipped through the portal that had first brought him here, and found himself back in the vortex that led to Mount Shasta.

The one closest to that stupid animal his enemies so loved.

Closing portals was infinitely easier than opening the damned things, but if everything worked out the way he intended, soon nothing would be beyond him. The Dark Lord could open portals with ease—so would he when he was demon king.

He drifted toward the gateway that would take him out of the vortex to the rocky flank of Mount Shasta. Before he could slip through, he paused with all his senses on alert. What caused that strange disturbance in the air? Curious, he slowly drifted toward the dark ceiling, scattered his mist to reduce the sense of demon, and hid himself among the stalactites.

A tall male armed with a crystal blade burst out of the main portal from Lemuria. Long arms, long legs, long, blood-red hair tied back in multiple braids hanging down his back. These damned Lemurians were all tall and beautifully built, though disgustingly interchangeable as far as he could tell.

Nothing unique—same number of arms and legs, no horns, no claws. The red-haired creature paused and sniffed the air. The demon didn't recognize this one, but what else was new? They all looked alike to him. Cursing silently, he held perfectly still, becoming one with the shadows as the man followed his nose, obviously searching for the source of the sulfuric scent.

He paused in front of the portal leading to Sedona, the one the demon had just come through. Then he sniffed the air again and scowled. A moment later, he drew his sword, pointed the blade at the gateway, and gave a command.

Blue flame shimmered along the faceted surface and then leapt from the point of the blade. Within seconds, rock began to glow and melt down the walls of the cavern. After a few minutes, the large portal to Sedona was sealed shut entirely.

But why? The man had saved the demon from having to do it himself, but for what reason had the Lemurian chosen to seal this one? Curious, the demon hovered against the ceiling and watched while the Lemurian marched back across the cavern, gave a final glance toward the Lemurian portal and then slipped through the gateway leading to the slopes of Mount Shasta.

No point in leaving that one open. The demon floated down along the wall and focused on closing the portal to Lemuria. He noticed a slight hesitation as he sent a blast of power toward the swirling gateway. He was going to need to replenish his energy soon—closing portals drew more of it than he'd realized.

But there was plenty to finish the job, and within a few moments, that entire dimension was now cut off from access to this one. Bell Rock was closed, Shasta was closed, the small access point from the other vortex, closed.

This should successfully lock at least the two he needed in the tiny town of Evergreen: that curly-haired beast to use as bait, and the ex-demon who wouldn't be able to ignore her cries of pain, her dire need for a timely rescue.

He did love the way it felt when a plan started coming together. He followed the red-haired Lemurian, crossing through the portal into Earth's dimension, coasting along behind as just one more shadow amid other shadows.

The wind was perfect, sweeping up the mountain. It would keep the scent of sulfur—the sense of demonkind—away from the Lemurian. Everything was in his favor. He could not fail.

He was close—so very close to success.

Full ownership of a fully functional perfect demonform, his for all eternity, as ruler over all worlds in all dimensions. It just didn't get any better.

The sun was beginning to set by the time Taron found the rocky trail leading down the snow-covered side of the mountain. It was an unusual yet exhilarating feeling, to be walking in Earth's dimension with a sense of purpose, the knowledge he was here on a mission.

Of course, it would help if he knew more about the mission, but his sword had been characteristically silent since that one burst of instructions.

He should have expected no less.

His sandal slipped on an icy patch. "Nine hells and then some!" Taron managed to keep his balance, but he watched carefully where he placed his feet. This frozen trail was not designed for sandals, and he wasn't used to walking on uneven ground, not to mention ice.

Nothing here was familiar at all. Even his clothing felt foreign, and he wondered if he would ever become accustomed to the chafe and pull of denim trousers and the tight stretch of a fitted shirt, rather than his loose and flowing Lemurian robes. Even the silly pants and tunic had been more comfortable than these strange clothes, but at least he wouldn't stand out.

He hoped Alton wouldn't mind that he'd borrowed a pair

of his faded blue jeans and a red flannel shirt in order to better blend in with humans. He'd worn his own shoes, a sturdy pair of work sandals, though he wondered now if that wasn't a mistake.

He thought of the boots he'd seen in Alton's room and wished he'd at least tried them on. His feet were freezing. He'd definitely need warmer shoes if he spent much time here.

His sword rested in its scabbard across his back, hidden by a glamour in case he came across any humans on his way down the mountain. He doubted that would happen—it seemed wild and isolated here on the snowy mountainside, and not the sort of place where one would expect to encounter any others.

He had a vague idea where Evergreen was from conversations with Alton, but he wasn't entirely certain, so he set out a call for his friend, leaving the contact open to find any others who might be listening.

*Hey, Taron. It's Darius. What are you doing here?*

*Darius? I'm trying to reach Alton. Where is he? He contacted me and said he's fighting a new demon invasion. I'm here to help.*

*No idea. I haven't seen him or Ginny. Eddy or Dax, either, for that matter. There've been no signs of demons here for days. In fact, Mari and I are taking off in a few minutes to spend a couple of nights on the coast. She's going to show me the ocean!*

*That's great, Darius. Really.*

But if there were no demons here, why in the hell had he been sent to Evergreen? That made no sense at all, though he was pleased for Darius. He had been born after the great move, after the original continent of Lemuria sank beneath the sea in a horrible cataclysm that they had only recently learned was caused by demonkind. Until he'd come to Evergreen, Darius had never seen the sun, never felt the earth beneath his feet.

And tonight Darius would see the ocean . . . Taron stared at the wide-open spaces around him. So, Darius would see the ocean, but that didn't solve Taron's problem. Where in the name of all the gods was Alton? He'd specifically told Taron he was headed to this dimension to fight demons. So why wasn't he answering?

Taron reached out for Darius once again. *I need to find where Eddy Marks lives.*

*No problem. Tell me where you are, and I'll direct you to her father's home.*

The instructions seemed simple enough. Eddy's father would know where to find his daughter and her lover, and they in turn would know how to find Alton . . . but why wasn't Alton answering? He should be close enough and well within contact range.

But then Taron gazed again at the huge sky overhead, at the shadows of mountains in the distance, and realized this dimension was much larger than he'd remembered.

A man could be well away from telepathic range and yet still within the same dimension. Amazing.

At least the portal to Sedona was closed. That small chamber within the vortex had been thick with the stench of demonkind, most likely the demons Isra saw the demon king sending that way just before the invasion of Lemuria. Well, the bastards were stuck there, now. At least they couldn't come back through the portal and attack anyone in Evergreen or Lemuria.

Alton had described Sedona as a beautiful but desolate place. It had been totally uninhabited the last time Taron had been there, when Mount Shasta had erupted many hundreds of years ago and all of Lemuria had relocated until things supposedly had settled down.

Of course, discovering that it had all been a ploy by the demon-possessed Council of Nine to further erode the well-being of Lemurian citizens was something Taron was still coming to terms over. So many lies—his entire life had been lived within a framework of lies.

That was over and done with. There was no point in worrying about all the crap they couldn't change, and if he'd just locked a bunch of demons on the wrong side of a portal and left them stuck in the desert, so be it. Better the mostly uninhabited community of Sedona than Evergreen as a good place to lose a few demons.

Taron continued on in the gathering dusk, following a narrow trail down the mountain that finally dropped below the snow line. It was just as Darius had described, and hopefully, now that he was out of the snow, his feet would thaw out. He'd never felt such cold before. His feet were so cold, it was difficult to keep from stumbling.

Then he looked up, and the colors stretching across the immense horizon took his mind entirely off his frozen toes. The sky was an ever-changing canvas of color—hues unimaginable to one who had spent most of his life in an underground world. He felt inexplicably sad, watching the shift from day into night. All of this lost, because of demonkind.

Generations of people who had never experienced a sunrise or sunset, who had never smelled the clean, fresh scent of pine and cedar, who didn't know what it felt like to hike along a mountain trail while the sky overhead put on a slowly evolving show of unbelievable color.

Maybe someday they'd have the freedom to walk this world openly again, but that wouldn't happen until the demon threat had been neutralized. And that was exactly why he was here.

Why his crystal sword had sent him to Evergreen in northern California.

He ran his hand over the silver pommel and wondered when his weapon would speak to him again. If it ever *would* speak again. Taron quickly descended the mountain, carefully sticking to the trail until it ran into a well-traveled road. Lights twinkled in the distance and lit up what appeared to be a small community seat lower on the mountain's flank. He sat his course for what had to be the town of Evergreen.

His heart rate picked up with each step that took him closer to town. He'd never been this far before, nor spent this much time in Earth's dimension. Not since his childhood on the island continent of Lemuria. He'd stepped out of the vortex and experienced Earth a time or two, but he'd never strayed far from the portal.

This time, screw the rules. He was following his sword's directive, and a sentient sword definitely trumped any law as far as he could tell. Besides, with Artigos the Just now in control of Lemuria, the rules were beginning to change.

So much so, that no one really seemed to know what the rules were anymore. Did it matter?

*Yes. It does.*

He was heading to Evergreen, he was Taron of Libernus, and after many thousands of years by Earth's calendar, his sword had finally spoken to him.

Had spoken and told him to get his butt in gear and hightail it to Evergreen because the final battle drew nigh.

He paused, midstep. *Final battle? Nine hells!*

He'd been so excited to hear his sword's voice at last, he hadn't really considered the portent of the message.

Just whose final battle was coming?

The battle against demonkind?

Or was it his own final battle?

"Well, crap, as Alton's Ginny would say." Taron gazed overhead at the dark blue sky, staring, almost mesmerized, at the stars beginning to flicker in the heavens as day faded into night. He couldn't stop grinning at the absurdity of it all.

A lifetime spent waiting, but for what?

For the chance to die in a battle against demonkind? Not if he could help it. Shrugging off the frisson of fear that tickled along his spine, Taron set his steps once more toward the lights in the distance. So be it. His sword had spoken and he was nothing, if not a man who followed orders.

With that thought planted firmly in mind, he picked up his pace and followed the path toward his own, personal destiny.

And maybe, just maybe—if he lived long enough—he'd even discover his gods-be-damned sword's name.

# Chapter 3

Bumper slept soundly beneath the big square table where a single N-scale steam engine *chug, chug, chugged* along the track, circling the perfect replica of Mount Shasta that was the centerpiece of Ed Marks's model train layout. Willow, as usual, was awake inside the snoozing beast, and she knew what an N-scale train was because Ed had patiently explained it to her.

Now Eddy's father sat on one of the high stools pushed up close to the layout, puttering, as he called it. He could do this for hours, fiddling with the various engines and cars, the toy people and tiny buildings that filled the huge workshop behind his house.

Inside the dog's brain, Willow paced endlessly.

Yeah, it beat being dead, but life inside Bumper was no picnic for a busy will-o'-the-wisp with places to go, people to see, and things to do.

Right now she should be in Sedona, fighting demons with Dax and Eddy. They were her responsibility, but no, Bumper wanted to be here with Ed, sleeping under the table like . . . like a *dog,* for crying out loud!

*I am a dog, Willow. Relax. It's almost dinnertime. I wonder what Ed will have for us tonight?*

*Kibble, Bumper. We get kibble every night. Go back to sleep.*

Bumper sighed, content for the moment. Her eyes closed, her curly blond tail thumped once . . . and Willow thought seriously about screaming.

A few moments later, she sensed Bumper's nose twitching. Probably thought she smelled food. No . . . it was something else. Willow went on alert as, groaning, Bumper rolled to her feet and stared at the door.

Ed continued futzing around with his model trains. Bumper trotted toward the door. Her tail was wagging, though Willow had no sense at all who or what might be out there.

Couldn't be a demon. Bumper hated demons, and if the dog didn't sense them, there weren't any nearby. But someone was coming. Through Bumper's sensitive ears, she heard the soft slap of footsteps. Sandals, not boots or running shoes. The sound was distinctive enough that even a will-o'-the-wisp could tell the difference. Whoever it was, he or she was walking around the back of the house toward the workshop.

Someone taking long, sure strides. At least it didn't sound like anyone was sneaking up on them. That was a good thing, right?

Bumper yipped. Her tail started going ninety miles an hour. Ed raised his head.

Willow asked, *Bumper? Who is it?*

*A friend, a friend, a friend!*

*Well, that's not a lot of help. What friend?*

Bumper ignored her. She was much too busy bouncing around to answer Willow. Too busy showing Ed what a great watchdog she was. Fickle beast.

"Something out there, girl?" Ed set down the caboose he was working on, got up and headed toward the door. Just as he reached for the handle, someone knocked.

"Wonder who that is?" Ed flashed a quick glance at Bumper

and turned the handle. "Demons don't knock," he said, pulling the door open.

The tall Lemurian standing in the doorway would have knocked the breath out of Willow if she'd had any of her own to knock out. *Taron? What are you doing here?*

He sent a quick grin toward Bumper, but he nodded at Ed. "I'm Alton's friend, Taron of Libernus. I've heard of you, Ed Marks."

"And I've heard of you, Taron." Smiling in welcome, Ed stepped back. "Come in. Please, come in. What are you doing here in Evergreen?"

Taron was so tall he had to duck his head to walk through the door. He smiled at Ed, but Willow sensed his attention on Bumper. She wondered if he was interested in the dog or in her, and then she was glad she didn't have a body because she'd be crying about now.

She might have been created by the Edenites to help Dax, but the tall Lemurian with the scarlet braids had caught her attention from the very first moment she saw him in that Lemurian prison cell.

Her crush had been hopeless even then. Now, trapped within Bumper's body, it was nothing more than a terribly sick joke.

Taron glanced in her direction once more. Then he looked away and spoke to Ed. "I'm here because my sword sent me to Evergreen with warnings of a final battle. I fully expected to find Eddy and the others here."

Ed shook his head as he offered Taron a seat on one of the tall stools lined up next to the railroad display. "You won't find them here. I got a quick call from Eddy just a few minutes ago. They're all down in Sedona, chasing after a huge demon invasion. Ginny's cousin called, scared half to death, and told them demons were taking over animals again, and . . ."

"Sedona? They're in Sedona? That can't be." Taron

flopped down on the stool and shook his head, obviously upset about something. "Nine hells. What have I done? I thought only demons were using the portal. I had no idea Dax and Eddy had gone to Sedona." He let out a huge, frustrated sigh. "I sealed the portal before I hiked down the mountain. It will take hours to open it, but I'm here because my sword told me the battle would be in Evergreen, that I had to be here. How will they get back?"

Ed placed a comforting hand on Taron's shoulder. "They'll be fine. There's another gateway that leads directly to the Council of Nine's main office. They'll just use that one and then come back through another portal to Shasta. Let's go on in the house and I can call. They need to know about your sword's warning, too. We'll just let them know what's happened, and . . ."

Bumper leapt to her feet, snarling and growling. Willow felt the dog's hackles go up and pictured all that blond, curly hair standing on end. Bumper's entire body quivered. She stared at the door, glanced at Taron and Ed and then concentrated once again on the door. Her growl rumbled low in her chest.

*Bumper! What is it?*

Bumper snarled and barked, too agitated even to tell Willow what had her so upset.

Willow cast out her thoughts, but she couldn't sense anything out of place. Bumper's demon radar was a lot better than hers, though, and the dog obviously sensed something she didn't like.

Taron leapt to his feet, drew his sword, and spun about, going from frantic Lemurian to powerful warrior in a heartbeat.

He moved closer to the dog, all lethal grace and surging muscle, looking so unbelievably sexy that Willow almost forgot why he'd suddenly gone into warrior mode.

As much as she hated the loss of self when she did this,

she synced her thoughts to Bumper's, drawing herself deep within the dog's mind. Immediately she sensed demonkind, outside the workshop and moving closer.

She shot a warning to Taron. *Demon!*

*I thought so, Willow, and not just any demon. I think I recognize the stench. It's the demon king.* He grasped his sword in both hands and went into a crouch.

A sense of pressure, of growing evil, swept through the workshop. The door bowed out. Wood creaked against the strain. Everything went deathly quiet for less than a heartbeat.

With an ear-shattering boom, the door exploded. Sharp splinters of wood shot across the room. Ed cursed and ducked behind the table. Willow saw him reach for a fire extinguisher as thick, oily black demonic mist billowed through the opening, spread across the floor, and headed straight for Bumper.

Taron lunged for the demon with a powerful two-handed swing. His sword sliced through the sulfuric mist, leaving a trail of blue fire in its path. While a strike like that would have killed a lesser demon, it had no effect at all on this one. The demonic wraith reformed after the blade passed through, boiling and pulsing up into the air until it almost reached the ceiling, then it shot toward Bumper once again.

Ed pulled the pin on the fire extinguisher and blasted a stream of thick foam at the stinking mist, but the stuff went right through the cloud and spread out across the floor.

Snarling and barking, Bumper lunged at the black cloud but Taron caught her by the collar and pulled the feisty mutt back.

*It's after Bumper!* Willow screamed, but she screamed in anger, not fear. She might be nothing more than consciousness at this point, but she still had her powers. Concentrating on the energy swirling about the room, she pulled in all she could and, using Bumper's voice as a conduit, threw a tremendous blast at the demon.

Willow watched through Bumper's eyes as everything appeared to slow to stop-action speed. Bumper howled. Willow's burst of power shot from between the dog's powerful jaws—a thick stream of brilliant blue sparkles, propelled in a shimmering torrent of pure energy.

Taron's blade flashed in the overhead light. He raised his arms and then brought his sword down in a smooth yet deadly arc, slicing neatly through the demonic mist.

His stroke was perfectly timed to Willow's blast.

Combined that way, their power should have worked. Should have killed the demon king except . . . instead of hitting the demon, all that energy collided with the broad side of Taron's crystal blade. Willow couldn't believe what she was seeing, the sparkling blast of power slamming into crystal, exploding in such bizarre slow motion that it was like watching a movie, one frame at a time.

It seemed to take minutes, not the fraction of a second that was actually needed for all of that power—the energy of crystal combined with all that Willow had gathered—to glance off the faceted blade and explode in a multicolored shower of stars.

Stars that ricocheted in all directions, with the bulk of them turning back in a mass of energy both light and dark. Turning back and bathing Bumper in a fiery storm of cold, sparkling light.

Light that turned Willow's world entirely dark.

Taron's sword passed through the demonic mist, trailing a shower of sparks. Cursing, he raised both arms and swung again, but as his blade completed its powerful arc, an unexpected burst of blue sparkles flew out of Bumper's mouth as if shot from a cannon.

Blue sparkles—Willow's unmistakable trademark—bursting forth, slamming into the side of his crystal blade and bouncing off. Taron's curse was lost in a cacophony of horrific sound—the demon's banshee screech and Bumper's single, frantic, high-pitched yelp. A roar of wind as the demon coalesced into a dark cyclonic force, spun into a tiny, tight tornado of demonic mist and shot across the workshop.

Ed screamed.

Only it wasn't Ed—it was all demon, a horrible, harsh demonic shriek of frustration and anger, a powerful cry of unimaginable evil.

Taron spun about with his sword held high, searching for the demon. His sandals hit the slippery foam from Ed's strange weapon and slid out from under him. Flailing his arms, Taron dropped his sword as he fought for his balance. He managed to grab the edge of the worktable and kept from falling on his butt, but he didn't see the demon anywhere.

He took a deep breath, steadied himself.

Ed's fist came out of nowhere and the old man landed a roundhouse punch. He slammed into Taron's jaw with impossible force. Demonic force. The blow lifted Taron off his feet and sent him flying. He sailed over the model train layout, bounced off the wall on the far side of the room, and landed on the floor.

Stars flashed in front of his eyes, almost as if Willow's blue sparkles had followed him. Before his head had cleared completely, Ed raced around the table and leaned over him, still howling like a banshee. Taron blinked. Black spots and bright stars filled his vision.

He willed himself to remain conscious.

*Nine hells and then some* . . . Taron blinked again, tried to focus and wondered if what he saw was real or merely the effect of Ed's tremendous blow. The old man's thinning hair stood on end. His eyes were wide and staring, an incongruous vision with the banshee shrieks coming from his wide-open mouth—a mouth filled with row after row of impossibly sharp teeth.

Then, between one heartbeat and the next, the ear-splitting shrieks stopped. The sound just cut off. Stopped dead.

Taron heard himself breathing.

Heard Ed's deep, ragged breaths. The two of them stared at each other, hearts pounding, lungs heaving. Taron's jaw throbbed. Ed blinked. Then he cackled—a sound of pure evil that segued into another ungodly howl. Shrieking once again, he turned away, jumped entirely over the table with the model train layout and raced out through the splintered door.

In mere seconds, he'd disappeared into the night.

Once again, silence filled the workshop. No sound but the labored rush of Taron's breaths and a steady *chug, chug, chug* as the model train engine slowly made its way around the track.

Taron lay on the floor, sucking in huge gulps of air. Stars still spun before his eyes—definitely not Willow's pretty blue sparkles. He stared straight overhead, trying to figure out which way was up, what had just happened. His head slowly cleared, though the demon's harsh scream still echoed through his skull.

He rolled to his belly and planted both hands on the floor. Slowly he made it to his knees and rocked there a moment before he decided against trying to stand. The floor spun beneath his nose, so he sort of collapsed in a semi-controlled fall to one side that left him sitting on his butt on the workshop floor.

His sword lay on the floor on the other side of the room, half buried in the white foamy stuff from that weird and seemingly ineffectual weapon Ed had used. Taron stared at the foam and tried to figure out what had just happened. Nothing made any sense.

The little engine continued to circle the track.

*Chug, chug, chug* . . .

He couldn't seem to make his mind work and his jaw ached like blazes. He rubbed it carefully with his fingers, surprised to find that it didn't feel broken. Still, something was very wrong. Obviously, the demon had taken over Ed's body, but something else hung there on the fringes of . . .

"Nine hells. Bumper?" Taron shook his head as he tried once again to clear the fog from his brain. He glanced around the cluttered workshop. "Where are you girl? Bumper? Willow?" He tried once more to stand. This time, by grabbing on to the edge of the worktable, he struggled to his feet.

There was a switch in front of him. He flipped it off.

The tiny engine came to an immediate stop. Now where the hell was Bumper? Moving very carefully on legs that didn't quite respond, Taron took shaky steps around the big layout table and retrieved his sword. It was covered in white foam. Carefully he wiped it off on his pants and stuck it in his scabbard.

His head began to clear. Finally.

Someone, somewhere, moaned. He glanced quickly around the room, but there was no sign of Bumper. Ed was gone so it had to be the dog. He heard the sound again. Frowning, Taron dropped carefully to his knees and peered beneath the huge table. There, in the shadows . . .

A hand. Certainly not Bumper's paw, this was a pale, slender hand with long, perfectly shaped nails, palm up, unmoving. The wrist disappeared in the darkness. Taron wrapped his fingers around the hand and tugged. The arm plus another hand and part of a bare arm came into view and he grabbed that hand as well. Tugging slowly, carefully, he pulled until the body attached to the hands slid out from beneath the table.

"Gods-be-damned . . . who the hell . . . ?"

She moaned again, though she wasn't quite conscious. Her

eyelids fluttered. Dark lashes tipped in gold flickered against pale cheeks. Her long, curly blond hair had tangled around one table leg. Carefully he unwound the strands and pulled the woman the rest of the way out from under the table.

She was slim and fair and entirely naked, her body long and lean, her breasts small and firm. Her nipples reminded him of dark coins against her pale skin. Taron slipped his hands beneath her back and legs and, moving slowly and carefully, eased her limp and unresponsive body into his arms and then close against his chest.

His legs were still a bit rubbery, but he managed to stand up smoothly in spite of his burden. His own badly bruised jaw was forgotten as he carried her out of the workshop and across the back lawn to the house. There were a million questions running through his mind. A million questions, but only one answer that mattered right now.

He recognized her. Recognized the perfect line of her jaw, the full, rose-colored lips, the arch to her brows. Recognized her, even as he knew that the woman he held in his arms couldn't possibly exist. Shouldn't exist, not in this form.

How in the nine hells could this beautiful, perfectly sized woman be Willow? He may have seen her up close only once before, when she was a mere slip of a sprite, but he would never forget her face, her beautiful little body, her perfect red lips.

But this was no longer a tiny will-o'-the-wisp, and that body was, after all, gone forever.

The woman he held in his arms was all woman, with skin like silk and a body unlike anything he'd ever seen, impossible or not. She'd fascinated him when he saw her as a sprite, but there was no describing the effect she had on him now.

She was also unconscious and her skin felt like ice, which meant he'd damned well better get his mind working and his priorities straight.

First he needed to get her inside the house and see if he

could find a couch or a bed for her to lie on and a blanket to warm her. Then he had to figure out how to help her, and then what to do with her. Way down on the list was figuring out how to rescue Ed, and getting rid of the demon that appeared to have commandeered Ed's body.

How in the name of the gods was he supposed to do all of this on his own? As he strode across the backyard, Taron sent out a frantic call to Alton. Tried to reach Darius. Called hopefully for Dax.

Nothing. Not a single response.

Okay. He was on his own, at least for now. Somehow, he'd make this work—if he could get inside the gods-be-damned house. He paused at the back door and stared at it a moment. What he wouldn't give for a nice Lemurian energy portal about now. After a moment's pause, he shifted Willow and carefully slung her over one shoulder to free up his hand, so that even with his arms full of unconscious woman and one hand planted firmly on her soft, round butt, Taron managed to figure out how the handle worked. Feeling just a little bit smug, he turned the knob and opened the back door to the house.

*First obstacle overcome.* He carried Willow down a long, dark hallway until he reached a room where a night-light burned. This one had to be Eddy's. He recognized a shirt lying on the bed, one he'd seen her wear before.

The big bed was made up so he laid Willow down on top of the comforter and brushed the tangled hair back from her face. She had felt icy cold when he first picked her up, though she'd lain in his arms as still as death while he carried her into the house. Now her body shivered and trembled as if she were freezing. The tiny pulse at her throat fluttered faster.

He put his hand against her forehead. Her skin still felt like ice. What the nine hells could he do for her? Taron glanced around the room, found a soft knitted blanket tossed over a chair in one corner and carefully covered her. Then he sat down beside her and took one of her hands in his.

Her icy, trembling fingers clutched his hand, as if, at least on some level, she was aware of his presence. She moaned softly and drew her knees up, tucking herself into a fetal position. Why was she so cold?

That single knitted blanket wasn't nearly enough. He hoped Eddy wouldn't mind, but he tugged the blankets back, lifted her again and stuck her beneath the covers. Then he tucked them close around her chilled body and sat down beside her again. He held onto her hand and sat there without a clue what he could do to help. What did humans have for healers? Dawson Buck would know, but he wasn't here.

How the nine hells could he get her warm? The room felt uncomfortably hot to him, so her chills made no sense. But, if he was hot and she was cold . . .

He'd read about using body heat to warm victims of hypothermia, which made the only solution more than obvious. Taron kicked off his sandals, unbuttoned the flannel shirt and took it off. He shoved his jeans down his legs and the stretchy underwear went with them, so he kicked everything off. Then with a prayer to whatever gods might be watching, he slid beneath the blanket and drew her body close to the warmth of his.

She felt like ice, but if he'd had any concern that he was doing the right thing, those worries fled as Willow snuggled close against him, buried her cold nose in the dusting of hair on his chest and sighed. Her tremors seemed to slow and she pressed even closer. Taron wrapped his arms around her, and held her tighter.

He refused to think of the obvious, that she was naked and so was he. That his body was reacting in a manner that was far removed from his intention of merely warming her. No. He searched for and found control, forced himself to relax, reminding himself he held her for one purpose and one purpose only—to warm her. That was all.

So how many times did he have to repeat that stupid command before he actually believed it? Nine hells, what else could he do? He was alone in Evergreen with an unconscious woman who could only be Willow, his friends were all fighting demons in Sedona, and the demon king had taken over the body of a very good man who was now in terrible danger.

He'd panic, except he knew that if he lost it, he might never get it back. He'd never felt so terrified in his life, though it wasn't fear for himself that had his heart thudding in his chest or his lungs clutching at every breath of air. It was fear for a woman who shouldn't be. Fear she might not survive, that she could somehow disappear as quickly as she'd appeared.

No. He would not allow that. He would hold her close, share his body's heat. He would not allow her to disappear. Sighing, he held on to Willow. Focused on the soft rise and fall of her chest against his, on the softness of her skin, the firm globes of her bottom beneath the palm of his hand.

He couldn't help himself—couldn't stop gently rubbing her smooth skin, couldn't avoid the thoughts that pushed against his mind. She'd fascinated him from the very first time he saw her. Fascinated him even more, now. Where had this perfect body come from? Willow had been locked in the mind of that curly-haired mutt. Surviving as pure consciousness, sort of hitchhiking along with Bumper. Now she was whole and beautiful, and somehow he had to make her warm. He would keep her safe.

His fingers tangled in her hair, in the mass of blond curls cascading over her shoulders. He remembered the first time he saw her when she was merely a tiny sprite. She'd looked like a tinier version of the woman he held in his arms now—except she'd had long, straight blond hair.

She was a larger version of that tiny sprite in every way

but her hair—hair that reminded him of something, some-where. He buried his face in her tousled curls and sighed. No matter. She was in his arms, her body was beginning to warm, and he'd find out the answers when she awakened.

She'd been so terribly cold—colder than she could ever remember, but now she was surrounded in the most deli-cious warmth. It had to be a dream. She'd not had any real feelings or physical sensations of any kind for so long—not since the demon king had eaten her body. Thank goodness she'd already escaped from that fragile shell before he actu-ally started chewing.

That would have been truly awful, but she'd practically exploded out of her physical body and shot straight for Bumper, and there she'd remained ever since. Without real sensations or feelings, without actual contact with anything physical.

Until now.

She'd learned to sense what Bumper felt, to see through her eyes and, if she really concentrated, to hear clearly with Bumper's very sensitive ears, but it wasn't the same. Besides, as much as she loved the silly dog, she missed being her own woman, no matter how tiny that woman had been.

She didn't feel tiny anymore, either. How odd. She cast out with her thoughts.

Bumper answered. *Willow? Are you awake?*

*Mmmm? Yeah, I think. Where are you?*

*In you, Willow. I'm scared. What happened?*

*In me? How did that happen?* Willow frowned and tried to remember. They'd been in Ed's workshop and Bumper was napping on the floor. Then Taron had come, and then . . .

The demon king!

Willow's heart was suddenly pounding in her chest and Bumper whined. *Hang on, Bumper. We'll figure this out.*

Willow felt the brush of air across her face and opened her eyes to the pale rays of early morning sunlight coming through a window. Startled, she jerked her head.

"Ouch! What . . . ?"

"Taron?" She turned, eyes wide. Taron stared at her, only he was the same size as she was, and she wasn't looking at him out of Bumper's eyes, which meant . . .

"Eeek!" Scrambling away, she sat up, realized she was naked and grabbed the blankets that had been covering both of them.

She ripped them away from Taron and held them against her breasts, biting back another scream. Or was it a nervous giggle? Whatever—she still slapped a hand over her eyes.

Taron was naked. Oh, good gods was he naked! She peeked out from between her fingers just in time to see him grab the pillow she'd had under her head and slam it down to cover up all those manly parts she'd never once seen on anyone except Dax.

"Are you okay?" Taron peeled her fingers away from her eyes. "Willow? You are Willow, aren't you?"

"I don't know. I mean, yes, I'm Willow, but no . . . I don't know if I'm all right. I'm big! How did I get big?" She sucked in one big breath of air after another, but she couldn't seem to get enough to fill her lungs. Bumper was yammering away in her head, but she had no idea what the dog was saying. All she could hear that made sense was the air rushing in and out of her lungs and a buzzing in her ears, and . . .

Taron pressed his hand against the back of her head and forced her to bend way over until her nose was between her knees. "You're hyperventilating. Take slow, even breaths or you're going to pass out."

*Easy for you to say.*

He laughed. "I heard you. I wondered if you'd still be able to use telepathy. That's it. Slow, even breaths."

He rubbed her neck and back, and there was something

really soothing about the soft stroking of his big hand along her spine. She managed to slow her gasping down to almost normal respiration—at least to what she thought was normal.

How could she possibly know what was normal for a body this size? After a moment, Willow raised her head and took a couple of slow, even breaths. She looked at her arms and legs, wriggled the toes peeking out from beneath the blankets, and stared at Taron, who stared right back at her. "I'm big. I've got a body. A people-sized body. What happened?"

Taron kept rubbing the back of her neck, but he shook his head. "I don't know for sure. It must have something to do with the energy you flung at the demon king interacting with the power from my sword. The combination of the two energies, maybe? Your blast ricocheted off my blade and covered Bumper in a flash of sparks." He shook his head. "I can't find Bumper."

*I'm here, Taron. Here I am. I'm in Willow.*

*Bumper?*

*Hi, Taron. It's me, it's me, it's me!*

*Uh . . . hi, Bumper.*

He stared at Willow. "Bumper's in you now? Did the two of you trade places somehow?" He sat back on his heels and stared at Willow.

She shrugged, but she could *feel* Bumper jumping up and down inside her head—or at least she imagined that's what she felt from the way Bumper was bouncing around in there. "It appears so. Bumper, calm down. Sit, Bumper. Good girl . . . you're fine."

She shook her head, focused on Taron. "Where's Ed?"

Taron's shoulders sagged. "I don't know. The demon got him. I think he was trying to take over Bumper, but when the power exploded he somehow ended up in Ed. We need to find him. I can't reach Dax and Eddy."

"Can't you call them?"

He looked absolutely devastated. "On what, Willow? I don't even know how those things they call cell phones work, much less have one."

She touched his arm. Right now Taron, who always seemed so self-assured, looked badly in need of a bit of encouragement. "There are regular telephones in the house. We just need to find Eddy's number. What about Mari and Darius? I don't know Mari's number but I know where they live."

He shook his head. "They're gone for a couple of days. Let's find one of those telephones. We have to let Eddy know what happened."

A flash of bright light had both of them covering their eyes. "No. Dax must not know the demon has Eddy's father."

"Oh crap." Taron's head popped up and he stared at the source of the light.

Willow followed his gaze. "Who and what was that?"

"My sword. Hang on."

He leaned over, giving her an absolutely delicious view of his backside. As a tiny sprite, she'd never quite appreciated the beauty of a naked male, not the way she could now that she was closer in size. Unfortunately, Taron was leaning over so he could grab his pants off the floor. Before she'd had nearly enough time to study him, he slipped into a pair of knit shorts like the ones Dax wore under his jeans, and padded across the room.

A moment later, he returned with his sword. Willow stared at the glowing blade for a moment. "I didn't think your sword talked yet."

"It didn't. Not until last night when it told me I had to come to Evergreen." He sat on the edge of the bed and placed the sword on the blankets between them. "Okay. Why can't we tell Dax about the demon taking over Eddy's father?"

The sword pulsed and glowed. "Dax is a warrior of great honor, a man filled with power. He will do anything to protect the family of the woman he loves. The demon king wants Dax's life force—his soul, which would give the evil one full control of Dax's demon body. It would belong entirely to the demon, not merely as his avatar. With Dax's powerful life force, the demon king will be impossible to stop. He is now the strongest he has ever been during his forays into Earth's dimension. He must not be allowed near Dax. He must be stopped, or evil will prevail."

Taron shot a quick glance at Willow, but he spoke to his sword. "Okay. So how can we stop him?"

"The human body needs nourishment the way the demon needs demonic souls to survive. The demon knows naught of caring for the human—it wants only demonic souls. There are very few demons left in Evergreen. You must find them and destroy them tonight, before the demon king feeds on their life force. By tomorrow night, without food or sleep, the human body he inhabits will be weaker. Without demon souls to feed his evil side and without nourishment for the human, the demon will be easier to destroy."

Willow focused on the glowing blade. "How do we kill him without hurting Ed?"

The sword flashed a brilliant blast of blue light. "You cannot kill the avatar. That will give the demon more power. You must force the demon out of the human while far enough from the vortex so that he cannot escape to Abyss. Then and only then, can you kill him. Together, you have the power to end him."

The sword dimmed. Taron raised his head and stared at Willow. "Well, that's simple enough. All we have to do is kill all the demons in Evergreen, find the demon king, get him to leave Ed's body without hurting Ed, and then destroy the bastard."

He snapped his fingers, but the look on his face was not at all positive. "Simple, right? Sure . . . no problem."

# Chapter 4

Willow dug through Eddy's dresser drawers and found tiny underpants and soft, warm jeans that looked as if they'd fit her. She'd been in both Eddy and Ginny's rooms often enough while inside Bumper to know how a girl should dress, but she'd never imagined getting a chance like this.

Slipping on the panties, she slid her finger under the elastic and smiled when it popped back into place against her flat belly. Then she pulled the jeans on over her long legs.

She was built a lot like Eddy with long legs and a flat belly and real breasts. Her skin was fair, her hair long and curly and pale blond. She kept looking in the mirror, just to make sure it was really her looking back. She'd discovered her eyes were still as blue as they'd been when she was nothing more than a sprite.

Her face was the same, the shape of her body, the color of her hair, though the curls were definitely Bumper's. Now that was strange—knowing she had a touch of Bumper in her physical makeup as well as Bumper's consciousness lodged in her brain.

She glanced toward the door. Taron was probably pacing a hole in the floor waiting for her, but she didn't want to rush a thing. This body absolutely fascinated her, though it would certainly be a lot more fun dressing it if she weren't so worried about Ed. She kept thinking of him out there, alone and afraid, aware of the evil that controlled his body, but for now, there wasn't a thing they could do. According to Taron's sword, there was nothing to be done until tonight when it was dark and the demons were active.

In the meantime, she had no idea how long she'd get to keep this body, and she didn't want to miss a second of the experience. She was loving the clothes she'd found to wear, even if the pants were a bit tight. She had to sit on the floor to get the jeans on. Then she stood and pulled up the zipper in front. It took her a minute to figure out how the snap worked, but it finally clicked into place.

Willow stopped and stared at herself in the full length mirror on the closet door. Good Lord, but was that really her? All long legs and round butt and breasts like Eddy's. She really liked what she saw. When she'd thought about what it would be like to be a real woman like Eddy or Ginny, this was exactly the way she'd imagined herself.

She slicked her hands down her legs, exploring the texture of the fabric, the feel of smooth muscles underneath. The pants were snug, clinging intimately to her bottom and thighs, but they stretched when she moved and weren't at all uncomfortable. So many times she'd watched Eddy putting on pants like these, and she'd always wondered how it felt.

She'd only worn her little tunic before now, which had been perfect for a sprite, but an outfit like that was not at all appropriate for a demonslayer. Besides, it was long gone.

She was not going to think about it, or the fact it had been eaten by a demon. Yuck. Just the thought of that disgusting creature chomping down on . . . no. She really wasn't going there.

She turned again and checked out her butt in the mirror, the way she'd watched Eddy do. Smoothed her hands over her hips. The pants looked okay, as far as Willow could tell, though she knew she couldn't go out without a shirt of some kind.

Not that she didn't like looking at her naked body. She loved it! It was so . . . so, big. And she had breasts. Not huge breasts. No bigger than Eddy's, but they were still feminine and made her feel like a real woman. She went back to the dresser, tried another drawer, and held up a bra. Eddy sometimes wore these things, but they never looked very comfortable. She set it aside and glanced at the closet. She wanted something to cover her top that would make her feel less . . . well, she wasn't really sure what. Less huge? Less awkward? Less female?

No. That wasn't it. She liked being female. She merely had to get used to being such a large female!

She crossed the room and opened the door to the closet. Something in here might work. But what style, what color? What would give her that extra boost she'd heard Eddy say that women needed? She really wished Eddy were here now. She'd know what Willow should wear, how she should act.

When she was a sprite, a tiny will-o'-the-wisp with gossamer wings and a body all of two inches tall, she'd had more confidence and attitude than she'd managed to summon up yet as a full-sized woman. As much as she loved this body, she still felt like a stranger in it. Sort of ungainly. Awkward, as if her brain wasn't used to moving so much mass.

She missed her wings. Missed the way she could flitter from place to place with merely a thought, though at the same time, she knew she wouldn't trade this woman-sized body for that little one—even with wings—for anything.

It made no sense. Not missing her wings or being a full-sized woman or standing here in front of Eddy's closet wondering what color shirt she should put on with the jeans she'd found in the dresser drawer.

Did the color really matter when evil was afoot?

And a very feminine side of her answered, *Of course it does.*

She grabbed a sapphire blue tank top that she thought might be the same color as her eyes and slipped it on over her head. It fit tight enough that she figured she really didn't need the bra. She'd heard Eddy complain about the things often enough to know she'd rather go without if she could, and these breasts, though definitely feminine, seemed firm enough not to need one.

She shook her torso. Her breasts wobbled, but not too noticeably, and the shirt was tight enough to hold them in place, though they didn't smash down as much as she'd hoped. Sighing, Willow smoothed the soft cotton over her chest and tucked the tail into her pants.

Once again she twirled slowly in front of the mirror. Not too bad, and she did feel a bit more confident, now that she wasn't standing here half naked. Of course, with Bumper whimpering in the background of her mind, she'd felt just a bit off balance all morning—at least since waking up naked in bed with Taron.

Which was flat out stupid, since she'd dreamed of doing exactly that since the first time she'd seen him, but then her dreams had been exactly that—dreams without any hope of ever actually doing what she'd fantasized. Of course, Bumper hadn't been involved then, but now she was, and Willow was no longer the Willow she'd been . . . and it was all just weird.

Much like her life. She shouldn't have existed as a sprite, much less now as a woman, which had made her fantasies safe and fun. For all of eternity in Eden, she'd been nothing more than swamp gas, to put it bluntly. Fairy lights sounded a lot prettier, but there was no point in prettying up the truth—will-o'-the-wisps were swamp gas and that's all she'd been before the Edenites plucked her out of the damp and turned her into Dax's helpmate.

She'd fully expected not to *be* anymore after Dax was

killed by the demon king, but then the Edenites had given Dax immortality and allowed her to live on in Bumper, and while it was frustrating as could be, at least she'd still had her thoughts and her fantasies.

But now . . . now she had to think of things that might actually happen. She had to behave like a real woman—a woman with long arms and legs and full, round breasts, but no wings.

She really missed her wings.

*But you still have your puppy parts. Mine are gone, but you have yours.*

*What? Bumper, what are you talking about?*

*Your puppy parts. Where you grow puppies. I had an operation and mine are gone, but you have yours in this new body. Wouldn't puppies be fun?*

Good gods! That was the last thing she needed. *No, Bumper. Puppies would not be fun. At least not right now.*

Willow felt rather than heard Bumper's sigh, but within a couple of seconds, Bumper had curled up—figuratively speaking—and gone to sleep. One thing about dogs: they definitely lived in the moment. And something else Willow could be absolutely positive about: neither puppies nor babies were a good idea at this particular time in whatever life she had.

"Willow? Did you find something to wear?"

She glanced up and saw the side of Taron's face through the crack in the partially open door. His profile was framed by the long, dark red braid hanging over his shoulder. She loved how it perfectly matched the red plaid of his flannel shirt.

He looked so cute standing there, as if he didn't know whether or not to come in. Then she realized he was afraid to look into the room—afraid she might still be naked. Poor guy. This was probably a bigger adjustment for him than it was for her. "I did," she said. "You can come in now."

He opened the door fully and stepped into the room. He was as tall as Alton, and every bit as lean and graceful. His green eyes twinkled with humor and he moved like a man comfortable in his body. Obviously Taron knew how all his parts worked—he didn't have to think about every move he made, but as he stepped closer, something seemed to unfurl deep in Willow's belly.

What was it about this man?

What was it about this body!

Just looking at Taron appeared to cause all sorts of physical responses, none of which were familiar, though she was almost certain she liked them. She fully intended to figure out what was causing them.

Just not now. Instead, she held her arms wide and turned in a circle. "Do I look okay?" She did love the way Taron watched her. Almost as if she looked like something he wanted to eat, the way Dax looked at Eddy and Alton looked at Ginny.

The way Bumper looked at kibble . . . forget that one.

How could a man's eyes possibly say so much?

He shook his head. "You're beautiful. Absolutely beautiful. I still can't believe you're Willow, except you look exactly as I remember you." He chuckled and moved closer. So close she had to tilt her head back to see his face. He stuck his forefinger into one of the long curls hanging over her shoulder. "Well, I recognize everything but this. It appears Bumper had a bit to do with your hair."

"It's still blond."

He laughed. "So it is." Shaking his head as if the simple move might help him clear his thoughts, Taron stretched the curl out and watched it bounce back. "I keep thinking of the first time I saw you, in that prison cell when you were such a tiny little thing. I never dreamed I'd get to see you as anything other than a beautiful little sprite. I never imagined you like this—a real woman."

His voice dropped. He took a deep breath and, almost as if he were speaking to himself, said, "An absolutely breathtakingly gorgeous real woman."

She wasn't quite certain what to say about that. Was she really beautiful? More important, was she a real woman? Or was she going to turn back into a curly-haired dog? Or even a less-than-two-inches tall sprite? That first little body, the one Taron remembered, had been manufactured by the Edenites specifically to give her a form that would work in Earth's dimension.

She much preferred this one. She took a deep breath and stepped back, putting a little space between her and Taron. When she was close to him, close enough to inhale his scent and feel the warmth of his body, it was much too hard to concentrate.

"What do we do now?" She figured it was smarter to ignore the nice things he said. They might not be true, anyway. She couldn't say for certain that she was a real woman, because she didn't really know, and she wanted to think she was beautiful, but that was a bit too subjective.

Besides, did real women have talking dogs in their heads?

This was much too much to figure out right now, so she went with what she knew. "The sword said we have to kill off any demons before the demon king can absorb their life force, but we can't do that until tonight. Should we look for Ed? Do you have any idea how we're going to find him?"

Taron watched her a moment without speaking, and maybe it was rude not to thank him for his compliments or talk about how she'd turned into a woman, but Willow just wasn't ready to go there. Not now.

He nodded, almost as if he were silently agreeing with her. "I just asked my sword. We definitely have to wait until dark when the demons come out. The blade can't sense the lesser demons until they're actually moving, taking on avatars and leaving whatever kind of trail it is that demons leave. The same goes for Ed. He's probably hiding out right now, someplace where the demon can rest until it's dark and he's able to hunt for other demons for their energy, but even if we were to find him, there's no way we can get the demon to separate from the man. Not until he's weaker, so interrupting his supply of demons to take their life force first is our best bet."

"Okay." Willow nodded, thinking of how they'd gone about this before. "In the past, we had to destroy the avatars before the demon king could get the demonic life force. How can it hunt them on its own?"

"I imagine because it has Ed. Once the demon king gets complete control of Ed's body, he can use it to destroy whatever avatars the lesser demons have taken over. If they're in inanimate objects, he can take the demon's soul, but if he has to kill a living avatar, he'll get the soul of the innocent victim as well as the demonic soul. We can't let that happen. It will give him too much power, make him too strong for us to fight him. We'll have to be prepared tonight."

He reached out once again and ran his fingers through her blond curls. Then he sighed. "It could get very ugly, Willow. It's just the two of us against the demon king."

*Three, Taron. Don't forget me.*

He laughed and Willow's heart lurched in her chest at the wonderful, deep sound he made. "I'm sorry, Bumper. You're right. What was I thinking?"

Then, before Willow knew what he intended, Taron went still. He looked down and stared directly into her eyes. His gaze was so intense it was moderately unsettling, but she couldn't look away.

Then, so slowly she could have easily escaped had she wanted, he leaned close and pressed his lips to hers. She wasn't at all ready for the sensation of his mouth on hers, the soft press of his lips, the warmth—she really had not expected him to kiss her. She'd seen plenty of kisses. You couldn't hang around Eddy and Dax or Ginny and Alton or even Dawson and Selyn and not see kisses, but she'd never had any idea what they felt like.

No wonder everyone did this so often! Kisses were wonderful. Taron's lips were soft and full and moved over hers with a whisper of sensation that made her toes curl. If she actually thought about it, she had no idea what to do. Thank the gods, her body seemed to know. Following her instincts, Willow wrapped her arms around Taron's shoulders and stood up on her toes, curled or not, so she could reach.

The slight movement raked her nipples over his chest, and even though their bodies were separated by his flannel shirt and her cotton tank, she felt a sharp zing of current that raced from those sensitive points. It was lightning—a fiery need that shot from her breasts to her belly. She'd barely gotten past that amazing sensation when she parted her lips at the insistent pressure from his tongue, and the kiss leapt to an entirely new level.

*This is arousal,* she thought. *This is desire.*

*This is why you have your puppy parts!*

*Not now, Bumper.*

Bumper grumbled and went quiet.

Taron groaned. His arms tightened around Willow's waist and one big palm cupped her bottom. She lifted her left leg and wrapped it around his thighs, pulling him close against her, close enough to feel the thick ridge of what had to be an erection pressed tightly against her belly.

She knew about those things, a vague knowledge that must have been part of what the Edenites had given her so that she could function as a living creature and help Dax, but they'd not described how it would feel. Nope. They hadn't gone anywhere near the actual sensations and they'd certainly not given her enough details.

Even if they had, she might not have believed. How could anyone describe this to someone who'd never been kissed?

He surged against her, a hard, fiery brand that felt as if it marked her, even through denim. His other hand came under her bottom and Taron lifted her, pulling her closer to him, aligning her perfectly so that he rubbed himself against whatever it was between her thighs that really needed rubbing.

The sensation was exquisite.

It was unbelievable.

It was driving her absolutely insane!

He was hard where she was soft, her curves fit perfectly into his valleys and vice versa. Amazing. She wanted him. She wanted more, she just flat out wanted. But what, exactly? She'd never stayed in the same room when Dax and Eddy made love. She'd always managed to be far away whenever any of her full-sized friends were intimate with one another, and now she didn't know!

Why hadn't the Edenites given her more information, damn it all? They'd skipped the specifics altogether. Somehow, she'd have to figure it out on her own, though with Taron's help, it shouldn't be too difficult.

He was male. Men knew these things, right?

The forceful, hungry, all-consuming pressure of his mouth against hers abruptly ceased.

Well, damn. It looked as if it wasn't something she was going to learn about now, either.

Taron ended the kiss with a slow slide of his mouth over hers. His retreat seemed to be filled with regret. He pressed his forehead against Willow's, breathing hard but chuckling softly. His hands still cupped her bottom, her legs still wrapped tightly around his waist, and she clung to him, breasts to chest, crotch to belly, but it was obvious the moment had ended.

Taron's sigh rivaled any sound of frustration Bumper could make. "I'm sorry. I had no idea how much I wanted to kiss you, or I would have been able to stop myself before it got so . . ." He glanced at the way he was holding her and grinned. "Intense. That's the word I want. Before it got so intense." He planted a brief kiss on the end of her nose. "I was kissing you with too much feeling before I knew what I was doing."

He frowned, but he really wasn't looking at Willow anymore. It was almost as if he were arguing with himself. Lemurians were known for their love of debate. But now?

He focused on her once again. "I certainly didn't realize how kissing would not be nearly enough, but this is something I'm totally unfamiliar with. Will you accept my apologies, Willow? I believe I was out of line."

She leaned back and glared at him. Her body literally trembled with unmet needs and he was busy having a debate all by himself. Of course, his beautiful green eyes sparkled, and he didn't look as if he regretted kissing her all that much, but what did she know?

"Why?" she demanded. "Why would you want to stop yourself? What was out of line?"

A tiny frown appeared between his brows. "I shouldn't be kissing you like that. Becoming so aroused."

"You don't like being aroused? You didn't like kissing me?"

He leaned his head back and closed his eyes. He had a rueful smile on his face when he said, "Willow, you have no idea."

"Well, of course I don't. I've never been kissed before, but I thought it felt pretty good. You're saying you don't want to do it anymore?"

His eyes flew open. "You've never been kissed? Ever?"

She sighed. "Taron. Think about it. I was less than two inches tall. Then I lived inside a dog. Of course I've never been kissed. Who would have kissed me?"

She unhooked her heels and let her legs slide to the floor.

Taron relaxed his grip on her butt, and draped his hands loosely over her shoulders, but he had a stupid grin on his face.

"I guess I never thought about it. I mean, I just figured that if there were tiny little women, there must be tiny little men."

She shook her head so hard her stupid curls bounced around her face and shoulders. "Maybe you *should* think about it. I was created for Dax. My sole purpose was to help him function in Earth's dimension by gathering enough energy to feed his demonic powers. I started out as a fairy light, otherwise known as swamp gas." She snorted. "Even you must admit, Taron, that there is nothing remotely attractive about the thought of kissing swamp gas."

He laughed at that, a soft, sweet chuckle that made her tummy clench again. Willow sighed. "For awhile, I actually thought I was in love with Dax, but obviously I didn't have a clue what love was, at least not the kind of love that Eddy feels for Dax and he feels for her. Not what Alton and Ginny share. Point being, I didn't exist until Dax existed, at least not as a woman. I was barely sentient before the Edenites turned me into a sprite."

"Oh."

His expression didn't fit his simple statement. No, not when his eyes flashed and his hands tightened on her shoulders. Then he hugged her close against his chest and rested his chin on top of her head. "I don't feel nearly as stupid as I did a moment ago."

"Why would you feel stupid?"

He leaned back and smiled at her. "Because that was my first kiss, too. I've never kissed a woman before."

She frowned at him. "I don't believe you. You knew exactly how to kiss me."

"I'm a scholar, Willow. I study everything, including sex. It's not all that difficult to figure out. It's true. I've never kissed a woman, never even held one in my arms. The closest I've gotten to a woman is swordplay during training."

When she opened her mouth to disagree, he merely smiled and shook his head. "Don't look at me like that." He kissed her nose. "I'm telling you the truth. No kisses, no women. Not ever. For one thing, it's not my way. I think Alton might have been with someone many years ago at some point, though I'm not even sure about that. But for me, life has always been my studies and learning."

He sighed. "And my own inexcusable cowardice."

"Cowardice? Are you saying you're afraid of women?" He certainly didn't seem to be afraid of her, but then Taron had known her when she was barely two inches tall, and maybe . . .

But he was shaking his head. "No, not of women in general. Of falling in love. Of making myself vulnerable. It's a long story . . ."

"I love stories." She cupped his cheek with her hand. "What happened?"

Now he merely looked embarrassed. "I really don't . . ." His lips quirked up in half a grin. "Okay. But don't laugh. It sounds really stupid, but it honestly affected me."

"I promise not to laugh. Too hard." She gave him her cheekiest grin.

He smiled and merely shook his head. "Years ago, when I was still young, when we still lived on the island continent of Lemuria before it fell into the sea, Alton and I attended a fair."

She thought of the only fair she'd ever been to. She'd gone with Eddy and Dax and Alton and Ginny to one in Sedona when she'd been inside Bumper and the demon king had attacked using a huge, angry bull as an avatar. She doubted there'd been demons at Taron's fair, but she remembered good stuff, too. "A fair? Like with contests and games and food—that sort of thing?"

He nodded. "Exactly. We used to have them when I was a boy. And this fair had a fortune teller, a woman who sat in a dark tent with candles burning all about and a huge crystal ball on a stand in front of her. She looked really scary, like an ancient, evil witch, and she told our fortunes."

He shrugged. He still looked more than a little embarrassed, but she waited.

Slowly he shook his head and his eyes were focused on something far away and long ago. "I haven't thought of Alton's fortune for all these years, but the woman said he would become a great warrior and find love in another land far from his home, but that love would return his home to him. Wow. At the time it made no sense, but now . . ."

"She was talking about Ginny and the role she played in helping Alton go back to Lemuria, wasn't she?"

"She must have been." He kissed her lightly. "But that makes my fortune even worse, because it means it might come true, too. What she read for me in the crystal was short and to the point, and it made a powerful impression on me. I made my decision then that I would never fall in love, never allow a woman to love me." He swallowed and looked away, as if he might actually be hearing the old woman's words. "I decided it wasn't worth the risk."

He paused then for so long that Willow prodded him. "What risk, Taron?"

He took a deep breath, as if steadying himself, but he didn't directly answer her question. "She gazed into the crystal for a long time. Then she stared at me, and I still remember how scary she was. She had one brown eye and one blue and a bunch of her teeth were missing. She had to be as old as dirt, and her voice sounded like she spoke from the bottom of a well."

He laughed, but it was an uncomfortable sound that raised chills along Willow's spine. Whatever happened that day had definitely left its mark on the child. A mark that stayed with the man.

"The thing is, Lemurians are almost always physically beautiful people. Our teeth don't fall out, we don't usually shrivel up and look old. We are, for all intents and purposes, almost immortal. This woman was a dried up husk, so unusual that her words carried more weight. It's hard to explain."

"What did she say?"

He gazed directly into her eyes, but it was more than obvious he was back in that dark tent, staring at that really scary woman, and he repeated the fortune she'd told him with an odd, hollow note to his voice.

"You will love but once. With that love, you will experience unimaginable joy and unendurable pain."

"Oh." Willow pulled free of his embrace and rubbed her hands up and down her arms. "That is sort of creepy, isn't it?"

"That's what I thought." He chuckled, but there really wasn't any humor in the sound. "So, I've avoided women my entire life, terrified of falling in love and having to endure all that pain. See? I told you I was a coward."

He pulled her back into his arms and hugged her. "It wasn't all that hard, not falling in love. Things are more rigid in Lemuria than they are here in Earth's dimension. When our continent sank beneath the waves—around the time I grew old enough to realize men and women had such fascinating differences—everything changed. There were many deaths and much turmoil among our people, and since that time, there have always been fewer women than men. Our energy went to building our new home within the mountain. Not as many of our men found mates."

"But I bet if you had looked, you would not have had any trouble finding a woman for yourself." He was so utterly beautiful, she couldn't imagine any woman turning him down, but he was smiling, shaking his head in denial.

"I really am a scholar, Willow. I'll admit I've been curious about sex, but I wasn't ever interested enough in any particular woman to want to work at an actual relationship. Plus, I had that fortune hanging over my head. I still do."

"Enough to keep you from stealing a kiss or two?"

He chuckled, but this time she sensed he meant it. "Things really are different in Lemuria than on Earth. Our women know their worth and generally withhold themselves until marriage. The opportunities for casual sex don't exist as much in our world. At least they haven't in the past, though there are many changes coming. So far, though, it's not been as open or free. Certainly not conducive to much experimenting."

Willow gnawed on her lower lip for a moment. Then she slipped out of his embrace once again. "We're not in Lemuria anymore, Taron. And I'm not asking you to fall in love."

He took a deep breath that expanded his chest and let her know he'd been thinking along the same lines. "I know that, Willow." He rubbed the back of his neck and glanced at the bed.

She felt her heart rate begin to speed up. Her gaze followed Taron's. Her body suddenly felt soft and pliable.

Taron's sword, strapped in the scabbard across his shoulders, flashed. Willow blushed. Did his sword know what they were thinking?

Taron glanced ruefully at Willow. She slapped a hand over her mouth to stop the giggles. "It appears your sword knows, too," she said. "But I think it has other ideas."

Taron's soft chuckle totally ended the moment. "I think you're right. Come."

He held out his hand. She wrapped her fingers in his. His grasp was firm and felt just right. Willow raised her chin and smiled at him.

He smiled back, but he shot one last, longing look at the bed. Then he tugged her toward the door. "We can speak of this later. Right now, we need to eat something, and then we should plot our course of action against the demon king."

*Kibble? Is it time for kibble?*

*No, Bumper. It's time for people food.*

# Chapter 5

West of the town of Sedona, the stench of sulfur lay heavily in the air. Eddy Marks wiped the sweat out of her eyes, leaned back against the side of Dawson Buck's big SUV, and flashed a tired grin at her lover. Dax was so ruggedly handsome he took her breath away. It was hard to imagine him as he'd once been—a creature of shimmering scales and sharp claws, curved horns and razor-sharp fangs.

Once a demon, but a demon no more. He was the man she loved, the one she would love for all eternity. He was also her partner in battle, as sweaty and disheveled from fighting demonkind as she was. She leaned her head against his hard shoulder. "I keep thinking this will get easier, but it's damned hard work."

"You're not kidding." Dax sheathed his sword and gave Eddy what was probably meant to be a quick kiss. A kiss that ended up taking on a life of its own. When they finally separated, he leaned his forehead against hers and sighed. "How is it you always manage to distract me?"

"Just lucky I guess. I'd rather kiss you than kill demons any day. Today has been absolutely exhausting."

"It's always more difficult when the demons take on a live avatar."

Eddy nodded her head against his. That was the truth. They didn't want to injure an innocent host—not only was it wrong, but a dying creature's life force would empower the demons.

Sighing, Eddy leaned back against the SUV and gazed out across the field filled with comatose sheep. Almost the entire flock had been taken over by demonkind. Thank goodness for Dawson's tranquilizer gun—once the animals had fallen asleep, the demons had fled—right into the sharp crystal blades of the demonslayers' swords.

Now the lanky vet moved among the fallen animals, checking to make sure they were breathing okay. Selyn worked quietly beside him—the perfect partner for Dawson, as far as Eddy could tell. Then she turned and gazed at Dax. Just as he was her perfect match. The perfect lover, perfect partner, perfect friend. In fact, life in general would be absolutely perfect if it weren't for the blasted demons.

But then, if not for demons, she wouldn't have Dax, Dawson would never have met Selyn, the Forgotten Ones would still be forgotten, and Alton and Ginny would never have met.

Never have fallen in love. Not be out there, on their own, following up more reports of invading demonkind. Eddy grabbed her cell phone. "I need to check in with Ginny. She and Alton were planning to go by that horse ranch on the other side of Sedona. I thought we'd have heard from them by now."

Dax nodded. "Do that. I'll go help Daws and Selyn." He pushed away from the vehicle and headed across the field.

Nodding, Eddy dialed the number on her cell. She really needed to call her dad, too, but they'd been so darned busy since the first moment they'd arrived in Sedona that she hadn't had time. Ed understood how these things went, though. He'd let her know if he needed her for anything, and right now they had a bigger problem here in Sedona than any of them had imagined.

Ginny's cousin Markus hadn't been kidding when he said they had trouble.

Ginny's terse hello and her immediate segue into their situation yanked Eddy out of her daydreams. "Eddy? You guys okay with the sheep ranch? Got things under control, yet? 'Cause if you do, Alton and I need you here. We're just south of Boynton Canyon on Dry Creek Road, not far from the lodge where we stayed. The horses are fine, but there's a huge flock of birds out here—ravens, I think. I'm positive they're all possessed."

"Crap." Eddy glanced up. Daws, Selyn, and Dax were walking slowly back toward the SUV. Sheep were beginning to stand, shaking their heads, a bit dopey from the tranquilizer, but obviously no longer ruled by demonkind. The stench of sulfur had faded. There weren't any demons left— at least not here. "Ginny, you two hang in there. It looks like we're done here, but it will take us at least twenty minutes to get to you guys."

"Alton and I will meet you at the Boynton Canyon vortex. Eddy, I have a terrible feeling we're dealing with more than just the demons Isra saw headed this way. I'm afraid more of the portals to Abyss are open again. There are just too damned many demons to be coming in through one gateway. We're headed up the trail now to check on this one."

*Crap.* "Be careful." Eddy ended the call and waved at the others. "C'mon," she yelled. "Alton and Ginny need us."

She piled into the back of the SUV with Dax. Daws had the vehicle in motion before the rest of them had their seat belts fastened.

Eddy turned and caught Dax's eye. He was grinning ear to ear, obviously having the time of his life. She thought of socking him. Then she caught Dawson glancing at the two of them in his rearview mirror, blue eyes twinkling, saw the big smile on Selyn's face, and tossed her worries out the window.

This was, after all, what they did, wasn't it? This eclectic little band fought demons: an ex-demon, a veterinarian, an ex-newspaper reporter, a Lemurian Paladin, a Lemurian aristocrat, and an ex-911 operator. As crazy as it sounded, right now they were the soldiers on the front lines—just about all that stood between the people of all worlds in all dimensions, and total subjugation under the rules of hell.

No problem there, right? Why should she worry?

Grinning like an absolute idiot, Eddy settled back in the seat and wondered what kind of mess Ginny and Alton had discovered.

Mouth watering aromas filled the kitchen in Evergreen. Taron stared at the amazing looking and smelling plate of food Willow had set in front of him and realized his mouth was actually watering. "How did you learn to cook?"

Watching her prepare the meal had certainly taken his mind off the uncomfortable discussion they'd been having in the bedroom, though both issues seemed to test his self-control.

He felt as if he was being bombarded with too many sensory pleasures, and Willow wasn't the only one. Right now, it took everything he could muster to wait until she sat across from him with her own plate before digging in to his meal.

"In a way, Ed taught me. I loved to watch him prepare meals. Everyone says he's a wonderful cook, though I never ate anything he made." She picked up her fork and smiled at him. "Go ahead. It's probably not anything like Lemurian food, but I know you can eat it. At least Alton loves all of these things."

"I recognize eggs, but what else is here?" He picked up a strip of some kind of meat that sort of reminded him of a food they served at home and took a bite, then closed his eyes with the absolutely mouthwatering burst of salty flavor.

Never had he tasted anything remotely as good.

Willow grinned. "That's hickory smoked bacon. The pile next to the omelet is fried potatoes with onions and bell peppers. The omelet is made with mushrooms and spinach and fresh garlic. The white stuff inside is called feta cheese, and it's made from sheep's milk. I hope you like it. It's the first meal I've ever cooked."

She took a bite and chewed slowly. Then she flashed him a bright smile. "Oh. And maybe I should mention, other than sharing the taste of kibble and the occasional handout from one of the guys with Bumper, this is also the first food I've ever eaten."

He almost choked on his bite of omelet. Swallowing carefully, he stared at her. "What do you mean, the first food you've ever eaten? Didn't they feed you?"

Her smile had him grinning like a fool, and when she shook her head, all those beautiful blond curls bounced over her shoulders, inviting him to tangle his fingers in the strands. It wasn't easy, but he kept his hands to himself.

"I survived on energy as a sprite. Since I was created to help Dax adjust to life here on Earth, to feed him the energy he needed for his demonic powers, that same energy fed me as well." She shrugged as if it were no big deal. "Then I was inside Bumper and she took care of eating."

She glanced both ways, as if checking to make sure they were all alone. "Don't tell Bumper, but I am not at all fond of kibble."

The dog's voice popped into Taron's head. *I hear you, Willow. I love kibble. It's perfect. It makes me happy. I like eggs. I like bacon. I really like bacon. Eat more bacon, please?*

Laughing, Willow took a strip of bacon and ate it slowly, obviously savoring every bite. Taron heard Bumper's telepathic groans of pleasure. Watching the way Willow enjoyed her meal had him fighting his own need to groan.

He wasn't quite sure how to handle his body's reaction to every single move Willow made. Whether it was chewing or swallowing or glancing his way with a smile. He didn't just see her—he felt her. As if everything she did was directed his way.

Conversation lagged as they focused on eating, though Taron's concentration continued slipping away from the meal and focusing on the woman across the table. As wonderful as the eggs and potatoes and bacon tasted, Willow was the one who had his senses screaming for more. She was the flavor, the texture, the scent he wanted. At the same time, he'd never enjoyed a meal more, and it wasn't just the fact Willow had prepared something so tasty.

He'd never once in his life gone hungry for food, but he wondered now if he'd hungered all his life for what Willow represented. Was it a woman's touch he'd missed? A woman's smile . . . or was it just Willow?

It came to him in a flash of insight that he could easily spend the rest of his life watching Willow. Her smile, and her brilliant blue eyes that were so amazingly expressive. The tilt of her head when she thought about something. The way her lips moved when she spoke, when she chewed . . . but definitely when she smiled.

He loved her smile. Especially when it was directed at him, and thank the gods, but she smiled at him more often than not. He knew he should be planning their next moves and preparing for whatever final battle he'd been warned of. His thoughts slipped away from Willow and he worried about Ed. Just as quickly, though he certainly hoped Ed was okay, he reminded himself there was nothing to be done for Eddy's father until nightfall.

Which left almost an entire day with nothing to do.

Should his conscience be this easily appeased? He thought of that for a moment as he used a piece of toast to scrape the last bits of his omelet off the plate. He popped the last bite into his mouth and sighed. Then he pushed worries about Ed aside, glanced up and caught Willow grinning at him.

"I don't think I've ever enjoyed a meal more than that," he said. "Thank you."

She actually blushed. He'd not expected that from someone as gutsy as Willow. "You're an amazing cook," he added, wondering how far he could push her.

"I think you were just very hungry." She flashed a quick smile his way. Then she concentrated on the empty plate in front of her for a moment, as if she wondered where the food had all gone. With a sharp shake of her head, she stood up, gathered her plate and utensils and carried everything to the sink.

Taron did the same, and again that sense of pure enjoyment he felt just being with Willow flooded his senses—along with the ever-present shadow of guilt. He sent a sharp glance at his weapon lying quietly in the scabbard. If the damned sword was to be believed, there was nothing they could do about Ed until tonight. They had no idea where to look for him in the daytime and hours to go before nightfall.

Again he shoved the guilt aside, and concentrated instead on the way Willow was rinsing her plate. It appeared washing dishes on Earth was the same as in Lemuria, and for some reason the comparison stopped him cold.

Were there really that many differences between Lemurians and humans? And what of Willow? Once a sprite, now a woman. An absolutely beautiful woman, but what was she, really?

And did it matter? Alton had thought Ginny was human and he'd loved her anyway, long before he'd actually discovered she was also part Lemurian, but Taron felt as if so many of the foundations he'd long built his personal beliefs upon were crumbling. Was nothing as he'd believed it? Even the trusted Lemurian council had been proved to be run by demonkind. And a sword that had never deigned to speak a word had ordered him to come to Earth's dimension to fight a battle against demons. Without question, he'd left the only home he'd ever known and come here without any real idea what to expect.

He certainly hadn't expected Willow, which brought him full circle, every bit as confused now as he'd been when he sat down to eat, though as he set his plate on top of Willow's, he knew he'd never enjoyed a meal more in his life. Never had such a wonderful time cleaning up the mess afterward, either, but he'd never had Willow to entertain him.

"I'll wash. You dry." She filled the sink with water and detergent and Taron grabbed a towel out of a drawer Willow pointed to. He paid close attention to everything she did, telling himself it was so he could learn to function here in Earth's dimension.

He'd never realized his capacity for lying to himself. For just a moment, he forced himself to be brutally honest, and he had to admit he would watch Willow doing anything, for whatever reason, just to have the pleasure of studying her, of being close to her. She moved with an innate grace that belied the fact she'd only been in this body for a few hours. She'd been a perfect sprite and now she was proving to be the perfect woman.

And Taron had never wanted anything as much in his entire life as he wanted Willow. That kiss this morning had been the equivalent of setting a match to tinder. His body thrummed with needs he'd never had before and certainly hadn't expected. And while he knew the mechanics of sex, had experienced the unimaginable arousal of that amazing kiss, he'd never dreamed how intense the feelings could be, how much they could rule a man's mind.

It was almost as if there was another side to him, a wild beast that had spent a lifetime slumbering. Willow had awakened that creature, an animal side of Taron that was all about sensation and pleasure, arousal and the baser needs of man.

That other creature was proving to be a difficult soul to rein in. It would be one thing if Willow was the least bit hesitant about making love, but she seemed perfectly willing.

Nine hells, did she seem willing! All during their meal she'd watched him, sneaking glances when she'd obviously not expected him to be looking, except he'd not been able to take his eyes off of her, so he'd caught her, every time.

And now, cleaning up the kitchen after breaking fast, they were both finding every excuse in the world to touch, to brush against an arm, a shoulder . . . a breast.

Dear gods, but her breasts were such amazing things. The women of Lemuria hid theirs beneath their heavy, flowing robes but that brilliant blue shirt Willow had chosen molded itself so closely to those beautiful globes that even the taut points of her nipples were distinctly visible through the fabric.

He must remember to have her wear something more seemly when they left the house tonight. Something that covered her more decently than the garment she'd selected for now.

Like Willow would let him decide how she dressed? That wasn't going to happen, yet he hated the thought of other men seeing what she so freely chose to show him. Hated to think how he would feel, walking beside her, aware of her beauty visible to the world.

Had she selected that tight blue shirt for that effect? Did she wear it now, knowing what it would do to him? Had that been her intent, to keep his body hard and aroused, his mind so scattered he could barely think straight? If so, she'd succeeded much better than she'd probably imagined, because his brain was empty of everything but Willow.

He knew Ed was out there, his body ruled by the demon king. Knew there were lesser demons nearby—demons he and Willow must destroy before the night was over, but now?

Now there was nothing to do at all but wait. Wait and kill time. So, how would they spend the coming hours?

They couldn't tell Eddy about her father. She and Dax would be here in a heartbeat, and the risk was much too great. If the demon king were to finally succeed in claiming Dax's life force, his power would be insurmountable, if Taron's sword were to be believed.

Crystal swords did not lie. No one knew how they gained the information they chose to share, but there was no instance of a sentient sword ever misleading the one they served. Taron had to believe his blade was telling him the truth. After all these years, he had to trust the mind behind the voice.

Stupid sword. Giving him bits and pieces of information and yet still not divulging its name. Of course, he could have gotten sentience well-versed in snark, like Alton's sword. At least HellFire seemed to have started behaving as a good crystal sword should, but why couldn't things be a little less complicated?

He turned his mind from things he could not change and watched something every bit as confusing. Willow. Would he ever know what made a woman tick? She excited him doing something as simple as wiping down the counter and hanging the damp towel on a rack. Then she turned and leaned against the stove, cocked one hip in a very suggestive manner, and smiled at him. She didn't say a word. Didn't wink, didn't gesture with her hands. She merely smiled and waited, leaving whatever decision was to be made up to him.

His brain turned to mush. The only thing he understood was that gods-be-damned old woman and her prophecy. The words rolled through his mind, and her voice was as scary in memory as it had been in real life. He thought of how the words she'd spoken about Alton had come true, how she'd turned away from his closest friend and settled that unnerving gaze on him. He could still see her—one blue eye, one brown—as she spoke the words that had forever changed his life.

*Unimaginable joy. Unendurable pain.* He'd love to experience the joy, but he wasn't about to set himself up for the pain.

He truly was a coward—one able to admit that even Willow, as beautiful as she was, as smart and sweet and brave, wasn't worth unendurable pain.

He'd seen pain firsthand, watched his mother waste away and die after his father was killed fighting in the demon wars. She'd given up on life, which had been bad enough, but the one thing he'd never forgiven her for was that she'd given up on her only child.

If not for Alton's friendship and the occasional hug from Alton's mother, Taron would have been entirely alone. He knew what unendurable pain did to people. Knew what it had done to his mother. He might be a coward, but there was no way in the nine hells he'd go seeking something so awful.

All he had to do was lock his heart away. Remember that love was not for him, and everything would be fine. Besides, he doubted Willow wanted love any more than he did. This chance at life was so new for her, the opportunity to experience the world as a real woman, that the last thing she'd want would be a man trying to control her and hold her close.

Of course, he reasoned that didn't mean she wasn't interested in experiencing as much as she could, that she didn't want to know what sex was like. It was something they could learn about together.

As long as he didn't fall in love, he'd be okay. What was the risk of that? They'd only known each other a short time. Love took much longer to grow, and it suddenly came to him—since he'd never been in love, it shouldn't be a problem.

Obviously, he was one of those men incapable of such deep feelings.

They had hours to go before nightfall. Hours when they should prepare for the hunt tonight, which meant looking over maps of the city, and figuring out where to hunt for demonkind.

Getting some rest . . .

His thoughts drifted once again toward the big bed in that

empty bedroom. They'd definitely need to get some sleep before going out tonight. He didn't think Eddy would mind if they used her bed. Again.

His body tightened and his breath caught in his throat. *To rest. Merely to rest.*

Willow shoved away from the stove and took a step toward him. "I can practically see the little wheels in your brain spinning, Taron. You know and I know that if we don't do something about this . . ." She waved her hands as if she were searching for words.

He didn't have to ask her what words she needed. They were right there, big as life in front of them. He stared at the floor. He truly was a coward.

She sighed. "If we don't do something about the curiosity that's making both of us just a little bit crazy, it's going to be what Eddy calls the elephant in the parlor when we should really be concentrating on fighting demons and rescuing Ed."

He raised his head, looked up and realized he was staring directly into Willow's beautiful blue eyes. She was right. She was also a much braver person than he could ever hope to be.

He wondered where she'd found the backbone to speak her mind, the strength to say what she thought without worrying how it would sound, who it might offend. Then he thought of her newness, the fact that she was a fresh creature without the lifelong inhibitions and baggage that battered so many lives.

Was it bravery or innocence that gave Willow courage? Whatever—he would wish for either, knowing full well he'd never truly be free of all the things that had made him the man he was. That kept him from being the man he should be.

His sword flashed. He waited, but the blade didn't speak. Was that flash of light disapproval he sensed? Most likely. What had he ever done to earn anyone's approval? Did it really matter? Now that was a thought. Maybe it was time to stop worrying about approval or what he was afraid of. Maybe it was time to take the lead, for once in his life.

A tiny yet familiar voice in the back of his mind suggested this might be the wrong time to be making such a huge decision.

For now, for this time, Taron chose to ignore the voice of reason. He'd been reasonable his entire life, and what had it gotten him?

*Nothing.*

Slowly, he removed the scabbard and set it on the kitchen counter. The blade remained dull and lifeless, as if rebuking him with its silence. He stared at it a moment. Nothing changed. He turned and once again caught Willow's steady, blue-eyed gaze focused on his face. He gazed back and weighed his crystal sword's disapproval over Willow's invitation.

He almost laughed at the foolish comparison. Turning away from the silent sword, he took Willow's hand and led her, unresisting, into the bedroom.

# Chapter 6

Blinking slowly, the demon king stared into the shadows through inferior human eyes. He'd taken refuge in this abandoned building once before, the first time he came to Earth's dimension with a mind so scrambled he'd been unable to plan, to think beyond anything other than taking on an avatar.

He'd been capable of little more than causing chaos, but he'd begun to evolve, to grow and regain the brilliant mind he feared he'd lost forever. This time he had no need of stone statues or inanimate objects, though he'd grown quite attached to the huge gargoyle that had been his first form in this dimension.

He'd almost brought the beast to life, but the gargoyle now lay shattered on the mountainside, nothing more than a pile of crumbled stone, destroyed by that bitch who dared challenge him.

Things definitely had changed. His mind, for one thing. Finally he'd made the journey from Abyss to Earth without losing the intelligence that made him superior to others. His mind was every bit as clear as it had been when he was still in Eden, as powerful as when he'd first entered Abyss. There were no limits.

Not anymore. He no longer needed to confine his search

for an avatar to something of the earth. Nor was he limited to dumb creatures. He stretched out his human arms, gazed at his long human legs. He had full control, though he hadn't believed such a thing possible. It must be proof his power was growing, not waning. This body should do him well, though it was not as strong as he'd hoped.

Not as mobile as that four-legged beast would have been.

Damn the Lemurian and his crystal sword!

However, he sensed that this one was even more beloved by those fools who called themselves demonslayers. Soon they would come in search of this man, prepared to risk all to save his worthless life. And he would kill them all. Every single one.

Except for the one he had to have.

*Dax.* Dax who still held title to that demonform he wanted.

He turned his gaze toward a broken window and stared at the brilliant sunlight streaming in through the gap in the filthy glass. Just a few more hours and he would go in search of demonkind and gorge himself on their life force. A few more hours until night fell and those lesser demons came awake.

Once he'd fed, he would be ready. When Dax appeared to fight for this human's mortal soul, the demon king would prevail. How he loved the sound of that!

There was something he didn't understand, though, and that was why? Dax had obviously been a demon, more powerful than most if his demonform was any indication, and yet he'd given it up. It made no sense. Why would any creature with that much strength and intelligence forsake the chance for even more power? Dax had traded it all for a puny human body and a miserable life.

And to think that fool was the only one standing between he who would be the demon king and his chance for eternal rule.

His fingers clenched, his body hardened with a dark rush of unexpected arousal. Absolute power. There was no other joy as intense, as defining. He could barely contain himself. Could not wait for the amazing rush of satisfaction he would feel when he not only took Dax's life force for his own, but also the lives of all the others who called themselves demonslayers.

Just a few more hours, a few demonic souls, and he would be ready. He would be strong—truly invincible.

Then nothing could stop him. Nothing at all.


Something was terribly wrong. Ed tried to wake up, but he felt as if he were crawling to the surface of something absolutely evil, and there was nothing but darkness. He tried to open his eyes, but he had no control. Somehow, he knew he wasn't alone, just as he knew he wasn't dead. At least, not entirely.

He was alive but not. Something horrible had happened, but he had no idea what it was.

Was Eddy okay? What about Bumper? And that young man who'd come . . . Taron? Where was Taron? Ed pushed, fighting against the weight of another's consciousness, but it was like swimming upstream in a river of thick, sulfuric muck. Disgusting. Wrong.

No matter. As long as Eddy and Dax were okay. That mattered. That and nothing else. He could think of nothing else, not with this pressure holding him captive. He fought against the other, the sense of something pressing him back into the corners of his mind, but he had nothing to fight with. No power, no strength. Only the knowledge that some *thing* was inside him, controlling him.

It had no name, no substance, but it existed. Existed inside Ed Marks. It was evil, and it was wrong, but he had no power to make it go away.

He turned his thoughts to Eddy. His daughter was strong and she fought evil. Eddy could help him. She was the only one. He reached out, searching for her mind, for her crystal clear thoughts. She was out there, somewhere, and he would find her.

# Chapter 7

Taron couldn't get that phrase out of his head. *The elephant in the parlor.* Unfortunately, it made perfect sense and described the direction of his thoughts exactly. There were so many things he should be thinking of right now, but it was as if his brain had stopped working entirely. As if the only thing he saw, the only thing he could think of, the only thing—*period*—was that gods-be-damned elephant.

Otherwise known as making love to Willow.

How could he imagine something he'd never actually done? How could he know to the very depths of his soul, how wonderful it would feel?

All those jokes about men thinking with their *other* head suddenly made perfect sense. He'd never allowed himself the freedom to consider sex, and as a scholar and philosopher intent on learning, he'd kept all those potential desires entirely under control.

Now that he knew he could turn that control loose, he felt as if he'd freed a beast that might devour him. Hunger gnawed at him, but it wasn't a need for food that had his cock hard and his balls aching. He'd never even noticed the beast before, never given himself permission to feel, to desire, to give in to the desperate arousal that felt like an uncaged wild thing clawing at his soul. Pressure built, twisting and turning the quiet scholar into something totally alien, something entirely apart from the man he'd always thought himself to be.

Following Willow into the bedroom with her fingers loosely tangled in his, he fought the almost painful need to grab her now, to tear the clothes from her lithe body and take her. It was suddenly so easy, so perfectly natural to imagine her naked, her body warm and inviting, her lips once again kissing his.

The strange thing of it was, his rational self wanted to gaze at her beauty and appreciate the sensuality inherent in her amazing innocence.

The beast wanted none of that. He wanted Willow.

So far, Taron had managed to hang on to his control, but his grasp was tenuous, his ability to keep his wild side caged growing weaker with each step he took.

Just walking behind Willow was killing him. That perfect heart-shaped bottom, the way the denim fit her lush curves and hugged her tiny waist . . . the man imagined his hands spanning that waist, his lips against the smooth contours of her flank, the way her warmth would call to him. Hold him close.

The beast thought of sweat and heat, of biting and marking her as his, only his. It wanted the chance to drive deep inside her welcoming body, to bring her to a screaming climax, to take whatever veneer of civilization she'd spun about herself and shred it. He wanted to take her to the very brink of sanity, to make her insane with the pleasure of their joining.

He refused to think of Willow the woman. Willow the one who made him laugh, who'd cooked his breakfast, who teased him and flirted with him and worried about him. No, this was all about sex, about satisfying his curiosity, about finally discovering what the big mystery was all about.

It was all about giving his wilder nature the freedom to take what it wanted. If he let that civilized self in, if the one who truly enjoyed Willow as a woman were allowed to surface, he faced more questions than he could answer. More pain than any man or beast should ever have to endure.

*Unendurable pain.*

Which left him hungering for her perfect body, aching to spear his hands into the thick fall of blond curls covering her shoulders, wanting to kiss and lick his way over and around her breasts—breasts that curved perfectly beneath the sapphire blue top clinging to her like a second skin.

Those thoughts were not only apropos to the moment, they were safe. At least they were safe for him. The beast would be appeased and Taron could walk away, heart intact. In a way they'd be working as a team—Taron and his wild side, two very separate entities.

His breath was coming in short, choppy gasps and his heart rate sped up with each step he took. He was hard, erect, and aching inside these denim pants. That was something that never happened to a man who valued control over all things.

He made a conscious decision then, and shoved the man aside. There was no need here for the one who followed rules. Hadn't Willow given him permission to lose control? He hoped so, because it was getting harder to think, to make sense of what he was doing here, alone in this room with the most beautiful woman he'd ever seen in his life.

Beautiful, sweet, smart, loving, and kind. No. He couldn't let himself think about all her wonderful qualities. That way led to madness and to something even more dangerous—to love. He was not going there. No way was he risking his heart.

Of course not. It wasn't necessary.

The beast didn't have to love. It only wanted satisfaction. Wasn't it Willow's suggestion, that they come in here and appease their curiosity—without any declarations of love, without any strings?

Well, he'd never been so curious about anything in his

life. Not until Willow had mentioned that gods-be-damned elephant. Not until she'd invited that other side of him out to play. That side was here, now, and he was growing tired of all this foolish internal debate.

The scholar was the one who wouldn't shut up.

*So be quiet, already! Before you screw this up.*

This unbelievable opportunity. A chance to make love to a beautiful woman without the risks, without the need to commit, without love. A chance to appease his curiosity.

That's all this was. All it could ever be.

*So get over it. Quit thinking about it. Just think about Willow and what she looks like naked. Think about her breasts and her perfect butt and those long, long legs, and quit worrying about all the rest.*

Yeah. Right. He could do this.

She let go of his hand, walked across the room and paused beside the bed. Then she turned her head, glanced over her shoulder and grinned at him, and it was so damned obvious she didn't have a clue what was going on inside his head, what was happening to the civilized side of the man she knew.

She folded her arms over her chest, but her smile never wavered. "I have no idea what comes next, though I imagine it has something to do with taking off our clothes."

He couldn't respond, couldn't make his voice work the way it should. He was afraid if he tried to speak, all that would come out was a snarl. He felt like someone had tied a band around his body and pulled it tight. His lungs couldn't expand, his heart couldn't beat, and if his cock got any harder, the thing was going to explode.

The beast loved this. The scholar was very confused. He'd lived a life of control, an ascetic existence as the scholar he thought himself to be. A philosopher didn't allow his body to control his mind. No, a Lemurian philosopher, a student of the mind, controlled his body. Needs and desires were contained, emotions held in reserve for the more powerful philosophical debates and arguments one was expected to participate in.

The beast practically snarled. *Forget philosophy*. He had absolutely no desire to debate anything. There was no argument here. Not now. Willow wanted this. The wild side of Taron wanted this. Hell, even the scholar wanted to get laid.

Willow took a step closer. Her long, slim fingers slid over his chest. He sucked in a breath. Didn't know what to do with his hands. How to rein in the unbelievable lust that felt like an untamed beast trying to get free.

She reached for the top button on his shirt and slipped it through the hole and he stopped breathing. Then she went to the next one, and the next, while his heart stuttered in his chest. He sucked in a jagged breath, and then another, shivering with blind and desperate need.

He shed all semblance of control as easily as he shed his clothing. When she finished undoing the final button and tugged his shirt out of his pants, he shoved it off his shoulders and grabbed both of her wrists. "Let me," he said, amazed his voice actually sounded almost normal.

She looked at him with wide, blue eyes. Her lips parted and he sensed a combination of fear and arousal in her, one beating at the other, as if she had no idea what creature he'd become. He gentled his grasp and turned her wrists free, slipped his hands beneath her blue shirt and felt the warmth of skin like silk beneath the cotton. Then he wrapped his hands around her torso and rubbed his thumbs along the line of her lower ribs.

He ached with wanting her, with the strength it took to touch her gently. Lust bludgeoned his mind, but his hands touched her with feather-light caresses.

She leaned close and kissed him. Soft, warm lips brushed

over his and he shivered as desire flamed out of control. Groaning against her mouth, he fought his nature and forced himself to move slowly as he cautiously peeled the tightly fitted shirt off her body.

He bared her breasts and once again forgot to breathe. Willow gazed at him for so long he almost forgot what he was doing. Wasn't staring at her perfect breasts the prize? A shiver ran up his spine and snapped his brain into gear. He finished undressing her then, tugging the shirt up and over her head.

She slipped her arms free as he held onto the tank top. Then she shook her head, sending her loose curls tumbling all about her shoulders. Taron reached up, searching through her tousled hair like a blind man, using his fingers to separate the curls, but his fingers got sidetracked in all that gorgeous hair and his attention wandered as he fell into yet another sensual pleasure he'd never imagined. Lost in the tangles and springy curls, he looked down and stared at her breasts, at the smooth, round curves, the dark nipples with their pebbled tips standing so erect. His breath caught.

Too much. It was all too much, and yet he knew it would never be enough. He wasn't certain what made him lean forward and draw the nipple over her heart between his lips, but it was the most natural thing in the world to suckle her like a babe, to use his tongue to tease the very tip, to nibble with the sharp edges of his teeth.

Willow arched against him, pushing her breast against his mouth. All that silky, warm skin, and he wanted to bury himself in her warmth, taste every inch of her body, find the softest places, the warmest. He read her body language with instincts he'd never tapped, knew she told him with her sighs and the soft twists bringing her closer, how much she loved what he did to her. And for the first time in his long, barren life, he, a man of learning and study, a man who treasured knowledge of all kinds, had absolutely no practical idea of how to proceed.

No instructions, no training . . . nothing but his most basic animal instincts—the ones he'd locked away forever, the same instincts now telling him to suckle her breasts, to kiss her full lips, to touch her glorious body and make love to her.

He thought he'd sent the scholar away, but once again he surfaced. The beast practically snarled. Didn't that idiot realize how much better it was to shut down that part of his mind, the part that wanted to question Willow's reactions and his own desires? Who wanted the guy around who would stop in the midst of a kiss to study the effect it had on his heart rate, or hesitate before touching her body in a most intimate manner?

Thank the gods the animal in him still existed. This was not a time to question what might or might not be seemly, and that thought alone almost brought the beast to laughter. There was nothing seemly about sex. It was the male animal at its most primitive level, and Taron's beast was discovering just how much it loved those base desires.

Even so, animal or man, he was learning as he went. Remembering what Willow seemed to like best, what worked and what didn't.

She was tall, though not nearly as tall as Taron. The height difference made it awkward. Standing here, leaning down to suckle her breasts, made it utterly impossible to lick and kiss and taste those other places calling to him. At least that was easy enough to remedy. He turned her free, slipped his hands beneath her shoulders and thighs, picked her up as if she weighed nothing at all, and stretched her out on the bed.

She smiled up at him, all lazy and knowing, and his beast wanted to laugh. She still had no idea what she'd unleashed, still thought she knew everything she needed to know, though how she could possibly think she knew more about the act of sex than he did made no sense. None at all.

Didn't she understand basic animal instincts? So far, he was almost positive she didn't recognize the other side of him, the one who was making love to her.

Of course, women made no sense to him, either. They never had, so why the nine hells did he suddenly expect to understand Willow? The concept of actually figuring her out almost had him laughing out loud as he reached for the fastener on her pants and, after a moment fumbling with the unfamiliar equipment, managed to unsnap and unzip her jeans.

Even the beast had trouble with things like zippers and snaps. Dear gods, but he was so far over the top he could hardly function. That damned adult kept popping back into his mind, the one who still needed to figure out what was going on here, while the one who was getting ready to crawl on top of Willow and bury himself deep inside would rather figure it all out by touch.

Still, it probably wasn't a good idea to laugh at a woman when you were busy trying to undress her. At least her tight pants slipped off easier than he'd expected, and laughter was the last thing on his mind when he finally tugged them over her feet and realized there was nothing left to hide her but a tiny scrap of lace.

This time he did growl. The low snarl that slipped out appeared to appeal to Willow. She watched him as he stared at her, at the bit of fabric covering her feminine mound that was somehow even sexier than if she'd been naked, and when he made that low, needy sound, she licked her lips and the muscles across her flat belly rippled. He'd seen her naked just hours ago, but he'd not reacted as he did now, not felt the thrumming in his veins or the pain in his balls.

Of course, then the beast hadn't been awakened. Then he'd seen her as someone who needed him, a young woman who shouldn't exist, who was unconscious and cold and required his help to protect her, to keep her warm.

He'd warmed her. Dear gods had he warmed her, but that's when his motives had gotten somewhat tangled, when he'd first realized there was another side to the scholar. That was the first moment he'd recognized the wild side he'd kept buried all his life, because things had gotten pretty hot for him as well.

What had begun with a scholar's fascination for the feel of her sleek length against him, the sweet scent of her hair, the sensation of their bodies so closely aligned, had quickly taken on a life of its own. He'd maintained control. It hadn't been easy, but he'd not allowed himself to think beyond the fact that she needed him to help her.

Now, the tables had turned. Taron needed Willow. Desired her more than he'd ever desired anything or anyone in his life. He was shaking from head to foot by the time he stepped back from the bed, unfastened his jeans, and lowered the zipper. He was so hard, so erect, it was difficult to drag the zipper down over the thick length of his erection, harder still to pull his pants off over rigid muscles, to step out of the jeans and the cotton knit shorts.

Willow stared at him without any pretense at all. Didn't she have any idea what it did to him, how his body reacted when she looked at him this way? Her eyes were wide, her lips parted. The intriguing scent wrapping around him had to be Willow's arousal. It made him even harder, needier than before.

He paused for a moment, for one last frantic reminder, attempted to remind himself he was a man of reason. A scholar. He did not need, did not want what he should not have.

That other part of him, the wild part, rose up in frustrated denial. He had to know. Now. Needed to feel. Needed to experience life before the chance was forever lost.

He thought of Isra's unspoken invitation, of how easy it had been to turn her down. He'd not felt any desire at all for her, a beautiful young woman who'd so obviously wanted him.

There was no way he could turn down the invitation in Willow's eyes. No reason to deny himself what she so freely offered. What he was so willing to take.

He leaned over the bed, placed his hands on either side of her shoulders and slid one knee between her legs. His other foot remained on the floor, anchoring him. He stared at her for what felt like forever and was probably less than a heart-beat. She gazed back at him, so sweet, so utterly trusting, it felt like a punch to the gut.

Everything inside Taron came to a complete halt. His heart stopped, his breathing stopped in the very act of drawing a breath. The beast knew. Somehow, even with the blood pounding in his ears and his body so hard he was clawing for release, the wild creature inside knew he couldn't take her alone. No, that other side of him had to be here, too. The gentle scholar, the one who questioned every move, who denied himself pleasure in all things.

That guy, too. Both sides of him, whole and complete. It was almost as if he felt the two halves come together, joining with an audible *click* as if separate parts were snapping into place.

He kissed her, both sides of him, once again claiming her lips, tasting her mouth, delving deep to tangle his tongue with hers, running the tip over her perfect teeth, across the roof of her mouth.

Kissed her with the full knowledge of his passion and the untamed creature that wanted to take her and keep her as his own, kissed her with the restraint of a man unwilling to frighten such a perfectly innocent, trusting soul.

She kissed him back without restraint, unafraid, tasting him, exploring with her mouth while her body slowly writhed against the bed, silently eloquent in her need. He left a row of tiny kisses along her jaw, the line of her throat. Followed the sharp jut of her collarbone and trailed kisses over her ribs. Her breasts were too perfect to ignore, and he laved those with his tongue, his lips, even nipping at the hard tips with his teeth.

He ached. His balls, his cock, the pit of his gut. Ached with need, with wanting something he'd never known. Yet as urgently as he wanted her, for the very fact this was new and wonderful and unexplored, he didn't want to rush.

He had no idea what to expect, but he wasn't about to hurry something along he might never have a chance to do again. This was, after all, about satisfying curiosity. Once satisfied, they'd have no reason to repeat, but he wasn't going to worry about that now. Now he was willing to make the most of this one amazing opportunity, but just let the scholar try and keep him away from Willow again.

He would discover just how hard it was to cage a wild thing. Willow arched her hips, inviting him closer, but he wasn't through exploring. She moaned.

"More," she whispered. "I want more."

Taron chuckled and nuzzled the tender underside of her breast. "I'm a philosopher, Willow. For every question, I must find an answer." He teased her nipple with his tongue. "If I have answers, I need to know the questions." Then he put all teasing aside, raised his head and stared into her guileless blue eyes. "There is so much I need to know. So much I want to experience. Let me explore, please?"

She growled. That was the only way to describe it, but it was Willow, not Bumper making that noise, and he loved it. He took the sound as a *yes*, trailed kisses across her flat belly and nipped the tender skin of her inner thigh. She had tight, blond curls between her legs, and he nuzzled those, drawn by her scent, by the promise of all the pleasures he knew those tight curls had to be hiding.

He knelt between her legs and spread them wider, even more curious now. Her scent aroused him beyond rational thought. He glanced up and caught her frown, but she didn't question him as he lifted her legs and draped them over his forearms. He felt as if both sides of him shared this experience, the part of him that was in touch with the instincts he'd denied for so long, and the one who needed to know everything.

When he leaned close and drew her scent deep into his lungs, it was the most natural thing in the world to put his mouth on her, to use his tongue and lips to taste her unique flavors.

It was just as natural to follow his instincts to arouse her, to make her somehow feel the same powerful needs that had his heart hammering in his chest and his cock swollen high and hard against his belly. He had no idea how he knew to do the things he did, but the knowledge was there. The desire to lick deep between her velvety folds, to find that tiny nub at the top and gently concentrate his attention there.

As devoid of passion as Lemurians had become over so many centuries, he was amazed the instincts had even survived, amazed that the beast still existed, but he wasn't about to question something that felt so unbelievably right.

He licked, unable to avoid analyzing the taste, the texture, the scent. He wanted more, but he didn't want to stop, either. So much was beginning to make sense to him—the things he'd heard the soldiers say about sex, the whispered comments, the jokes. It was only the working class that ever discussed anything so ribald as sex, though many among the aristocracy were mated for life.

He'd always wondered what it was that held couples together for a lifetime. Now he knew.

Willow whimpered and he licked harder, changing the

speed, the depth, the approach. That tiny knot between her thighs seemed to bring the most response, and he worked it carefully with his lips and tongue.

Sensing that she skated on the edge of orgasm, he carefully kneaded the round globes of her bottom as he made love to her with his mouth. She flooded him with moisture, a sweet release that had him growling deep in his chest.

This was the precursor of her climax. He knew it with a sure sense of what Willow was feeling, what her scattered thoughts were telling him. He thought of connecting telepathically, but it didn't seem right, to intrude on what had to be for Willow as much a journey of discovery as it was for him, but he didn't hesitate to absorb the thoughts spilling out of her open mind.

Part of him was insisting he enter her then, that he finally ease the pain of his own amazingly sensitive erection, but the purity of this moment, of this chance to share Willow's very first climax was more than he could bear to waste.

In this, the scholar won.

He'd pleasured himself on occasion, when he was younger, when his body was ripe with the hormones of youth, but not for many years had he felt the need. He'd buried all those desires, all those physical needs he'd come to see as weaknesses, as he pursued more scholarly interests.

And while he'd been merely existing without living, he'd also managed to avoid any risk of falling in love.

What a damned, pompous fool he'd been. He'd lied to himself his entire life, and he'd allowed fear to rule him. But he hadn't known. Hadn't realized what he was missing.

But part of him had known. That other side, the more primitive creature he'd contained for most of his life, had known. But now that wild, almost feral beast, was free. Under control to a certain extent, but free to remind Taron of what he'd missed by chaining such a powerful part of himself.

This was utterly amazing, this sense of desire building between his heart and his soul, all fed by the needs of his body, by the chance to experience Willow's tastes, her scent, her feminine textures.

This was the thing he should have been learning about, discussing with his fellows, exploring in whatever manner he could. This act, these sensations—they were the things that drove men to greater heights. Sex had to be more important than he'd been told, a necessary life-experience he'd never understood.

Because he hadn't asked. Hadn't wanted to learn, to know.

Again, he thought . . . *what a fool I've been.*

He wrapped his lips around that tiny nubbin, knowing full well that this would take Willow over the edge. At the same time he managed to wrap his arms around her legs and reach the soft, wet opening to her sex. Stroking with his thumbs, he brushed gently against her outer lips, suckled and licked and felt her body surge against his mouth, felt the clenching of her muscles, heard the cry as it crossed her lips.

Burying his face between her legs, he brought her over the top, felt her shivering, trembling, rippling release as her body arched against his grasp, as her rich flavors filled his senses. Then he slowly eased her down the other side, licking, sucking, touching, until her legs hung limply over his forearms and her breath no longer rushed noisily from her lungs.

Only then did he carefully set her legs back on the bed and move over her. He wrapped his hand around his thick length and pressed gently at the damp and swollen lips of her sex. She opened her eyes and gazed at him, blinking slowly. Then she smiled, carefully parted her thighs, and invited him to enter.

*Taron! Willow's still got puppy parts. Are you sure you want to make puppies?*

"Nine hells and then some. Bumper? What the hell are you

talking about?" Startled out of his sexual haze, he sat back on his heels and glared at Willow. He'd entirely forgotten about the blasted dog! His erect penis thumped against his belly, his balls ached, and suddenly he had a gods-be-damned dog talking about puppies?

Then he realized Willow looked as shocked as he felt.

"I forgot about the dog," he said.

"I forgot about the puppy parts." Willow raised up on her elbows. "I know there's something Dax and Eddy do to prevent babies. Look in that drawer."

He glanced at the small table beside the bed, leaned over Willow, and tugged on the drawer. "There's just a box of little packages in here."

"Good. Eddy calls them condoms. Take one out and put it on that."

She pointed at his penis, which wasn't nearly as impressive as it had been a moment ago. He pulled out a small packet and carefully tore it across the top. "What do I do with this?"

"You use it to cover yourself before you put it in me. It catches the stuff that makes puppies . . . uhm, babies." Laughing now, she sat up and took it out of his hand.

He handed it over. His hands were shaking, but it wasn't from laughter. Far from it.

"Here." She smiled. "I'll do it."

This wasn't going at all the way he'd expected, but when Willow wrapped her fingers around him, he surged back to full size almost immediately. She placed the clear disk over his unbelievably sensitive tip and slowly rolled it down to sheath him in what looked like a clear film of some kind.

She used both hands to stroke his full length, smoothing the film over his erection. He groaned and his cock jerked in her grasp. He took a deep, controlling breath and tried to spend a moment observing what she'd just done to him.

He was, after all, a scholar. And hadn't Alton mentioned using something like this? He'd have to ask him, if he could figure out a way to bring up such a thing in conversation. He couldn't recall ever once discussing anything of a sexual nature with Alton, even when they'd been boys.

Something else to consider. He raised his head and looked into Willow's blue eyes. "Now what?"

She smiled, that secretive smile that had to be something instinctive for women. Then she lay back down and spread her legs. "Now you do what you were doing before, except we don't worry about puppies. And Bumper? I would advise you to take a nap."

Without waiting to see if Bumper complied or not, Taron positioned himself over Willow once again. This time, he used his fingers to open her, pressed the tip of his erection against her soft petals and slowly pressed forward.

And quickly stopped. "There's a barrier there. I wasn't thinking, Willow. You're a virgin. Completely untried. This will hurt you."

"Then do it quickly so it doesn't hurt for as long."

He stared at her, at the smile on her face and shook his head. "Are you sure? We can wait."

She tilted her head and then pushed herself up on her elbows where she studied him as if he were a bug on the wall. "And how long do we wait? It will still hurt the first time, right? Now, Taron. We do it now. I thought you were through acting the coward."

"I am," he said, somewhat embarrassed that she'd reminded him. The beast reared its head before Taron had a chance to consider what he was about to do. He tilted his hips forward and in one quick thrust, buried himself completely. Willow gasped and clutched his arms with both hands.

Taron held perfectly still, amazed by what he'd just done. By the amazing sensations he was suddenly feeling.

Willow took a couple of deep breaths and then seemed

to relax. "Go ahead," she said. "It hurts, but I know it's got to get better."

He forgot about how good it felt and stared at Willow. Frowning, he asked, "How do you know that?"

"That's obvious." She looked at him as if he lacked the brain cells necessary to function. "Do you think everyone would be doing it all the time if it always hurt?"

"No, Willow." Chuckling, he leaned close and kissed her. "I imagine you're right." Slowly he pulled out, then slipped back in just as carefully. Her inner muscles rippled along his full length and his entire body tightened. She raised her hips, giving him better access. He didn't want to think about access or technique or anything else. Nothing but how good this felt.

How right. He felt that strange side of him pushing at his mind, the wild creature he'd not known until now. That beast that preferred acting to thinking.

There was a lot to be said for such an approach at times.

This was most definitely one of those times. He moved his hips forward, pushing deep into Willow's warmth, pulled back, and then pushed forward again. Then again, and again, building up speed, reveling in the sweet friction as he filled her over and over. Willow lifted to him, meeting him on each thrust. She wrapped her legs around his waist and clutched his shoulders with both hands, clinging to him, holding him close.

Each thrust felt better than the one before, each rippling pulse as her inner muscles tightened around him, pulled him deep, held him as he drew back for another surge forward—each better than the last, until he didn't think he could contain the joy, the amazing pleasure, the sense of joining she gave him.

Her eyes were closed but she smiled, and he wondered where she was, what she thought and saw as they did this amazing dance, as their bodies connected and they each discovered an ability to experience sensations neither of them had felt before, to be part of such an amazing act of trust.

To be this close, this connected to another person. It was utterly unbelievable. Indescribable, though he knew he would never of tire trying to find the right words.

The wild side reared its head and told him to stop thinking of words, but this time, the scholar beat him back. It was too important to just feel—he had to understand what they did.

Finally he was experiencing something that had always been beyond reach. Without any risk at all. This was truly joyful. Unimaginably joyful, but safe. He wasn't in love. They were just having a really great time, enjoying an amazing experience that was new to both of them.

He felt her body clench tighter. Her muscles rippled spasmodically around his erection and he felt the first stirrings of her climax, but this time he felt it from the inside, and it was indescribable. There was an unexpected tightening in the small of his back, a sensation as if he'd gotten an electrical shock that ran from his spine to his balls, down the length of his cock.

It happened so fast, was so unexpected, that when Willow's orgasm wrapped itself around him, he'd not known he was going to come at the same time. He felt the heat of his climax boil up and out of his balls, felt the tight clench of muscle and the rush of his ejaculate as it raced the length of his cock and exploded into the tip of the sheath.

The shout that burst out of him surprised Taron. He'd not expected to make any noise, not realized exactly how it would feel when his climax hit, literally exploding through his body with a force unlike anything he'd ever experienced.

But he shouted like a fool and blamed the beast, that uninhibited creature he'd only just met. Then his arms turned to jelly and he collapsed on top of poor Willow, who, for some reason, didn't seem to mind at all that she had a near-comatose Lemurian lying full out over her body.

Her breasts were smashed beneath his chest, her tousled hair tickled his nose and he was still buried deep inside her warm channel, still pulsing with the last vestiges of his orgasm. She'd wrapped her arms around him the moment he landed, and the sensation of being hugged inside and out was a most amazing experience.

Her muscles clenched and rippled over his full length, and it was utterly exquisite. He'd never felt anything like this. Nothing else had ever come close—so wonderful he didn't even try to move.

Willow seemed to be able to breathe. At least she was still hugging him. She certainly wasn't trying to push him off.

He'd move. Later. When he got his strength back.

Her vaginal muscles tightened around him in a slow, almost hypnotic rhythm. He found himself clenching his own muscles in response, realized he was becoming aroused once again.

Was that possible?

It must be, though he was almost certain he couldn't use the same condom again. Slowly, carefully, he withdrew from Willow's warmth. She mumbled a soft protest as he rolled away from her and walked the short distance to the bathroom where he disposed of the condom. Then he went back to the bed, dug out another one and covered himself.

He was already hard. Willow looked like she was almost asleep, but he didn't think she'd mind, not if her orgasm had felt as delightful as his.

Taron knelt between her legs again. Willow opened her eyes, smiled and spread her legs wider. Chuckling softly, Taron slipped between her buttery folds. This time he would make it last. This time he'd be ready for his orgasm so that it wouldn't sneak up on him and surprise him like that first one had.

This time. And if not this time, maybe the time after, or the next. What had he been thinking, telling himself they'd do this only once? He really was a fool. An idiot. An absolute idiot.

Did it really matter?

He gazed into Willow's beautiful blue eyes. She watched him with a lazy, sated expression, one he knew he could bring back to full arousal.

It really didn't matter if he was a fool. At least, Willow didn't seem to care. No. It didn't matter at all as, once again, he found that amazing rhythm.

And again he took that simple journey toward unimaginable joy.

# Chapter 8

Dawson wheeled the big SUV into the parking lot at the trailhead to the Boynton Canyon vortex. Ginny's rental Yukon was the only car in the small lot. There was no sign of Ginny or Alton, but the sky was filled with ravens, silently circling overhead like a slowly spinning tornado.

The four of them got out of the vehicle and stared at the huge flock of birds. Dawson pushed his baseball cap back from his eyes. "That's really weird. Ravens rarely circle so quietly. They tend to be pretty vocal."

"Normal ravens, maybe."

Eddy looked too tired even to smile as she said it. They'd been up for hours dealing with this latest invasion of demonkind. All of them were exhausted, but Eddy was right.

There was nothing at all normal about the flock circling against the brilliant blue of the Arizona sky—a flock that appeared to be growing. Not only did the birds move in a steady, silent pattern, but there was a sense of evil so pervasive it was impossible to ignore.

A shiver ran along Dawson's spine. He glanced at Dax. "Any sign of Alton or Ginny?"

Dax shook his head. "I imagine they're inside the vortex. I can't feel them anywhere out here."

Eddy nodded in agreement. "It's not far. Let's go."

She checked her sword, turned away, and headed toward the trailhead while Dawson locked up the car. Selyn waited for him, and the two of them walked together behind Eddy and Dax.

Daws kept glancing over his shoulder at the ravens, but the silent birds took no notice of the four of them climbing the trail to the vortex. He needed to call his assistant. Esteban Romero had noticed the odd animal behavior before, enough that Dawson had convinced the others they needed to tell the assistant vet exactly what was going on.

It hadn't been hard to convince the man they had a problem—not after Dawson showed him how to suck up demons as they escaped from their caged hosts, using his shop vacuum and plastic bags.

Now though, Dawson needed to check in with him and discover if he was still seeing as many possessed animals as he'd taken in a couple of days ago. There had to be an end to the influx of demons. Isra had counted a huge number of them directed through the portal by the demon king, but Dawson and the others had killed hundreds over the past couple of days.

There had to be another open portal.

Dax paused before a solid wall of red rock. He shaded his eyes with his hands and stared once again at the circling ravens. After a moment he turned away. "They don't appear to be going anywhere. In fact, I have a strong feeling they're waiting for something. C'mon." He walked straight into the rock. Eddy followed.

Dawson gazed at the solid wall of stone and wondered if he'd ever get used to seeing that—people just walking right through solid rock as if it didn't exist.

No. There was no way in hell he'd ever believe his eyes. He'd do it without question, but it was one of those things you just had to accept on faith.

He glanced at the woman beside him. He'd accept energy portals the same way he accepted Selyn's love. If he really thought about it, about how perfect she was, how impossible it was that anyone like her would love someone like him, he'd know it couldn't be true. Just like walking into solid rock, he'd have to accept it on faith alone—accept the fact she loved him for whatever reason, and count himself the luckiest bastard alive.

She gazed at him out of those gorgeous blue eyes and took hold of his hand. He couldn't help himself. He leaned in close and kissed her. "I love you," he said, because he loved saying the words and meaning them with every beat of his heart. Loved knowing she believed him and loved him right back.

Loved the dreamy look she got on her face whenever he reminded Selyn just how much he loved her, but before she could answer, he stepped past her and walked directly into the cliff.

Some words didn't need an answer. Some feelings went too deep, were too powerful to question, but Selyn was smiling broadly as she followed him, as the two of them passed through what looked like solid stone, into the vortex.

Just like that. His scientifically trained mind said it couldn't be done. The little kid science geek who still appeared to rule his world merely grinned at the fact it was proof all things were possible.

All things, including Selyn's love.

"Hey, Alton." The Lemurian nodded in response to Dawson's greeting. He and Ginny were standing just inside the cavern, while Dax and Eddy waited against the wall to their left. Ginny faced the back wall with her sword, DarkFire, held in both hands. Dawson and Selyn stepped to one side so that Ginny would have plenty of room to work.

"We figured you two were in here." Dawson wrapped his arm around Selyn's waist and the two of them stood beside Dax and Eddy, watching Ginny's amazing sword do its job.

Dark purple fire shot from DarkFire's amethyst blade and spread over a glowing red portal. The stench of sulfur filled the small cavern, but there was no sign of live demons.

Eddy asked, "How many were there?"

Alton glanced at Ginny before answering. "At least two dozen inside the cavern, but we have no idea how many might have come through before we got here, how many escaped through the portal to the outside. As soon as we finish here, we need to check the other portals. If this one's been reopened, odds are the others have as well."

Dawson nodded toward the gateway that led out of the cavern. "What about the ravens? You guys were right. They certainly aren't acting very raven-like. How can we catch them?"

"I don't think that's going to be a problem." Ginny lowered DarkFire. The sword no longer gleamed with purple fire, and the portal to Abyss was melted shut. Again. "DarkFire says they're waiting for all of us to show up together. They're massing to attack." She sighed, obviously ready to fold. "You guys ready?"

"The question is," Dax asked, laughing, "are you?"

Ginny punched his shoulder. "Well, if your big, blond buddy wouldn't keep me awake half the night . . ."

"Me?" Alton leaned over and kissed the top of her head. "You're blaming me?"

"Gotta blame someone." Ginny tugged his hand, wrapped her fingers around his and kissed him. "I guess this is what comes of too many years of not getting laid." She laughed. "For both of us. And I'm not complaining . . ."

Alton kissed her again. Then he gently cupped her face in his big hand. "In my opinion, it was worth going all those years without because I finally got you."

Then, as if he'd not just said something so intimate and sweet it left Ginny standing there with a bemused grin on her face, he reached into his scabbard and withdrew HellFire. "I think we're all as ready as we're going to be. C'mon."

The others quickly unsheathed their swords, but the mood had definitely changed. Crystal flashed within the small cavern. A sense of purpose Dawson had quickly learned to recognize as a combination of their own readiness for battle along with that of the intelligence behind their swords filled the air.

He'd quickly learned the sentience within each blade was more than a disembodied voice, more than the flash of power. Their swords housed the living souls of warriors.

Knowing he had such a powerful ally gave Dawson courage such as he'd never felt in his life, and Selyn's love gave him the most tangible reason to fight he could ever imagine.

Whatever he did, he did for her.

He took her hand, squeezed her fingers. *Are you ready? I am.*

Together, with swords drawn, they followed the others through the portal—a single step that took each of them out of one dimension and into another as they exited on the other side.

It was like marching into hell.

Shrieks and howls and the stench of sulfur filled the air.

Daws looked up. "Holy shit." He grabbed Selyn and moved away from the rock face, but he kept his gaze locked on the sky. Where there had been hundreds of ravens only moments ago, there were now thousands of birds of every imaginable species. Hawks and pigeons, blackbirds and sparrows. Ducks and geese, crows and more ravens.

The noise grew louder, the stench of sulfur stronger. Dawson and the others found their fighting positions as if they'd choreographed each step, moving smoothly into a defensive circle.

Side by side, back to back, they stood in an open area and waited.

"Remember," Dax said. "We cannot harm the avatars."

"I'll bring them down," Ginny said. "DarkFire will render them unconscious without harming them, but you guys have to take care of the demons."

No one questioned what she said. Ginny's sword among all of them showed powers unique to its amethyst blade. A woman once known as Daria—her mind filled with a wealth of memories and experience—was the sentience within Ginny's sword.

Daria, called DarkFire, enabled Ginny to accomplish things none of the others could do, things, it appeared, that included knocking demon-possessed birds out of the sky without harming them.

At least, that's what Dawson was hoping.

"Here they come!" Selyn's shout had them quickly tightening their positions. Alton took Ginny's back as she stepped away from the others and held DarkFire high. The birds spun out of their whirlpool of flight and streaked toward the ground like a single shrieking, screaming feathered beast.

Ginny's blade began to glow. A brilliant flash of dark light shot from the tip and Ginny swung her sword in a wide arc.

Purple light hung in the sky, a transparent shield of shimmering amethyst that covered the six of them. Banshee howls grew louder, closer, as the birds spun out of the sky and flashed toward the arc of light. The first few hit the shield. Their squawks and screams abruptly died as they broke through the barrier and tumbled lightly to the ground.

"Now!"

Dax leapt forward and slashed at the black mist that exploded from the first birds to fall. Careful not to step on any of the stunned birds, he spun and swung in a shower of sparks.

Dawson and Selyn took their stand on the other side of Ginny. As the birds crossed through DarkFire's light, their bodies went limp, their rate of descent slowed, and they tumbled through the shield. The demons immediately tried to escape their suddenly worthless hosts, but Dax and Eddy, Selyn, Alton, and Dawson moved in a macabre dance, finding their rhythm, reaching out for the fleeing black mist with their deadly crystal blades.

They shouted their victories as hundreds of demons turned from black, oily wraiths to nothing more than sparks and stench and dust as they died.

Birds huddled in dazed groups on the rocky ground.

Ginny turned, moving DarkFire's beam of purple light as more and more birds continued to attack. Many veered away before reaching the shimmering barrier, but many others flew into it.

Those that passed through, passed out. They dropped to the ground and their demons fled, but none escaped.

Dawson's arm grew tired and he watched Ginny with growing concern. Her arms trembled with the effort of holding her crystal sword, yet the birds continued to attack. They'd all been exhausted when the battle began, but never before had they fought so many.

"Ginny? Are you okay?"

"Yeah, Daws. I think so."

He didn't think she sounded all that okay.

Alton had been watching her as well. He sheathed Hell-Fire, moved close to Ginny and stood behind her. Then he wrapped his hands around Ginny's and helped her hold DarkFire high.

Dawson slashed his blade through another demon. He glanced up and caught Dax looking his way. Pointing to his blade, he asked, "Do these things ever run out of energy?"

"I hope not. This is the most prolonged battle I've been in. A test if there is to be one."

"Great." Dawson stepped over a pile of dazed birds and caught a demon as it shot out of a downed eagle. The raptor sat on the ground and stared with dazed eyes, but at least it was unharmed.

The demon died in a flash of smelly sparks.

Birds were beginning to recover, regaining consciousness once their demons were gone. Dawson noticed dozens of them moving out from under the shield, waddling away and taking flight. Even as they left, more attacked.

Ginny'd been right. There was something well beyond Isra's reported demon sighting going on here. Even more than Markus had reported. More demons than Dawson had ever seen at any one time, in any single place. Once again he slashed his blade through a thick burst of oily, black mist. Once again he watched as sparks faded to stinking smoke.

Another demon burst out of yet another dazed bird, a duck this time that landed almost at his feet. He raised his sword with an arm almost too tired to obey, and killed yet another of the wraiths. As the crystal sword completed its arc, he lowered his trembling arm and wondered how many of the portals to Abyss had been reopened.

How long could they continue to fight an enemy that never seemed to run out of combatants, no matter how many they killed?


Willow blinked and then squinted at the bright shaft of light coming through the bedroom window—light that was gently filtered through red . . . *hair*?

Well, that explained the reason it was so hard to breathe. Taron was still sprawled across her body. His long, red hair had somehow come undone and covered her face in a soft blanket of silken strands. His head rested on the pillow beside hers, and one big palm covered her left breast.

She clenched her inner muscles and felt his cock swell in response. "No," she said, laughing.

He raised his head and blinked owlishly, his green eyes hazy, his lips as swollen from her kisses as her mouth felt from his.

"No, what?" He leaned close and kissed her.

"No more sex. Not now."

He grinned at her, a slow, lazy smile that sent a spark of pure lust racing through her body. Lust that settled somewhere between her legs, right around that spot that was beginning to stretch in reaction to his growing length and girth. "Are you absolutely certain?"

He glanced toward the window and blinked as sunlight caught him. "It's not dark yet."

"It's late afternoon. We've been asleep all day." She pushed at his shoulders in a futile attempt to move him off of her.

"I don't remember sleeping all that much. I think we were . . ." He tilted his hips forward.

She moaned. How could he keep pulling this response from her? She'd lost track of how many times they'd made love. Had sex. Whatever he wanted to call it.

Taron wasn't kidding when he said he was a coward. There was no way this guy would ever fall in love. Not with that fortune teller's prediction weighing so heavily on his mind. She'd sensed it in him, the fear that he might care for Willow more than he should.

No matter. She'd never expected the chance to have even this much of a real life. Hoping for the one she loved to love her in return was probably too much to ask.

She remembered how Eddy had fought loving Dax. Knowing Dax would be gone at the end of one week had hung over the two of them from the first day they met, but it hadn't stopped them.

Knowing Taron could never allow himself to love her wasn't going to stop Willow, either. As if she had a choice . . .

He kissed her again. Goodness, but she loved the way his mouth felt against hers. Loved the look in his eyes, the taste of his lips, the feelings his kisses kindled deep inside. There wasn't a choice, really. No choice at all as the tip of his tongue swept over her lips and then tangled with her tongue. Sighing against his mouth, she gave in to desire, and more.

She gave in to the powerful feelings she had for this man, in spite of his flaws. She refused to fear what they had. Refused to give him the power to frighten her away from something that felt so perfect.

Taron of Libernus could hide from love all he wanted, but he couldn't stop Willow from loving him. Nope. She was a real woman now, with a real woman's desires.

A woman's needs, and they were needs that Taron appeared capable of filling quite well. All except that very important one, she thought. The emotional one. Just then, his fingers found the curve of her breast and she arched uncontrollably toward his touch. He bit down on her nipple, none too gently, and she groaned, shivering with the rush of sensation that coursed from her breast to her womb. Her thoughts scrambled with the explosion of pleasure.

He was everywhere, kissing her, nibbling and biting, and licks of fire had her writhing and twisting, begging for more. Begging for everything except what she really wanted, really needed. Oh damn, but everything would be so perfect if he weren't so afraid of love, but he'd been upfront from the beginning. She couldn't ask him to give what he'd already admitted was impossible.

As he filled her once more, as their bodies surged together in a most perfect dance, the two of them as perfectly matched as any two lovers could be, her real woman-sized heart broke a little more. She wondered—a bit hopelessly—if she might not be able to love enough for both of them.

No. She knew, without any doubt, that would never be enough.

"It's going to be dark soon."

Taron glanced up from his meal and realized Willow no

longer sat across from him. She stood at the counter and peered out the window above the kitchen sink. "Then you need to eat," he said. "We should be out there now, searching for Ed."

She turned and studied him for a moment. She'd changed today. Something in her appearance was different from the woman she'd been this morning. Had sex changed her? Was there something physical that happened to a woman after she made love—no—after she had sex?

Love was not going to be part of their relationship. He'd promised Willow, and he'd promised himself. Taron might be a coward, but he was also a man of his word.

Willow, though . . . what was it? This morning she'd looked like a sprite in a woman's body. Now, she looked like she was all woman. Her eyes studied him as if she knew things Taron would never understand. It made him uneasy, to find himself under such close scrutiny from a woman with whom he'd been intimate.

From a woman who now dominated his thoughts, took his breath away, and, if he wasn't really careful, could easily steal his heart.

He felt strange. More settled and yet, in some ways, more frightened than he'd ever been in his life. Fighting demonkind hadn't scared him this much. Willow was . . . amazing. Looking at her made his chest feel tight. Made it hard to concentrate.

They might have diffused the power of the elephant in the parlor, but something else had taken its place. Was he the one who had changed? Was this what his sword had objected to? Did the blade know that intimacy with Willow could somehow change more than merely the dynamics between the two of them? That it would change Taron?

If only he knew what it was. When he looked at Willow, he felt stronger. More determined, as if there was nothing he could not accomplish, no demon too powerful to fight.

And yet his feelings for her unmanned him, and the prophecy teased the edges of his mind.

He shoved it away. He didn't love Willow. He wouldn't love her, and that was the one thing that had definitely changed. It wasn't his own heart he worried about anymore. He no longer feared for his own peace of mind. He'd thought a lot about the prophecy as he'd lain beside Willow in that wonderful period of post-coital bliss.

Unendurable pain could mean only one thing—if he loved her, he would lose her. That was a risk Taron wasn't willing to take.

Only now he wasn't worried about the foolish risk to his own heart—it was the risk to Willow that was unacceptable. Suffering unendurable pain meant he would still be alive to suffer—but the only thing that could cause such pain would be if something terrible happened to Willow.

He would not love her. He could never put Willow's life at risk for such a selfish reason as love.

He sealed his feelings away. He could do this. He was Lemurian. They'd learned millennia ago to suffer in silence.

Willow nodded and sighed. "I know."

He started. Had she heard his convoluted thoughts? His heart settled back to its normal rate as she went on.

"I'm not very hungry, though. Anyway, I'm trying to think of where we should look for Ed. The only place I could come up with is the old library building. That's where the demon used to hang out during the day, when he was using a stone gargoyle as an avatar. It's an old building, abandoned now, but I imagine there's a way a demon could get inside, and if a demon can get in, so can we."

She walked back to the table, sat across from him, and stared at her plate. When she finally raised her head, she was smiling. "At least it's a place to start, right?"

He nodded. "After we take care of the rest of the demons.

That's the first order of business—getting rid of the demon king's energy source."

"I'm worried about Ed." She gnawed on her lower lip for a minute and stared toward the window. "I know we need to take care of the lesser demons first, but I guess I just want to know he's all right."

Taron merely shrugged. As if anyone possessed by a powerful demon could be all right, but he didn't need to say it. Willow knew the danger. She knew more about all of this than he did, had more experience actually fighting demons than he could claim, but this probably wasn't the best time to remind her of that, of the two of them, she was the more qualified to call herself a demonslayer.

He worried about her, about the effect sex might have had on her. She'd definitely changed, and that perfect smile of hers looked almost brittle. He hoped the two of them hadn't made a horrible mistake, but there was really no way to know.

None at all.

It was already too late to undo what they'd done. And when Taron thought back to the day he'd spent with Willow in his arms, with his body buried in hers, he knew there was nothing in this world or any other that could make him want to change what he'd finally experienced. What the two of them had shared.

Nothing at all.

# Chapter 9

The sun was slipping below the western horizon by the time Willow and Taron left Ed's house. They stepped out on the front porch and Willow took a deep breath of the pine-scented air. "It's so beautiful here. Peaceful. It's hard to imagine the terrible threats we've faced, the number of demons we've fought in this little town."

Taron didn't answer. In fact, he seemed a bit distracted. She wondered if he was thinking about the day they'd just spent, about all the new things both of them had experienced. She'd had to force herself to stop reliving every touch, every kiss, every sensation. Now that she knew what she and Taron were capable of doing together, she knew she'd never get enough of making love—just as she'd never get enough of him.

Except he'd been adamant about this being a one-time-only experience—though they'd definitely done it more than once! She figured he must have lumped all the times they'd made love into one event. That had to be a male way of looking at things, but as far as Taron was concerned, it had merely been a chance to satisfy their curiosity. It most definitely was not something they were going to do again, according to Taron. The risks were too great, he'd said. The danger of falling in love wasn't worth the pleasure they found with one another.

He'd certainly spent a lot of time trying to convince himself of something that Willow thought was absolutely stupid. She'd wanted to tell him about Eddy and Dax, how they'd been brave enough to fall in love even knowing Dax would be gone after seven days. They hadn't let it stop them, but then she realized how selfish that was.

She wasn't the one facing unendurable pain. She couldn't ask Taron to just put himself out there, knowing it would end badly. That wasn't fair at all.

Still, she wished they could talk about it. Maybe tonight. They had a long walk if they went all the way to the cemetery, or even just into town to check on the old library building.

She sighed and gazed about the quiet neighborhood. It was hard to look at the beautiful old homes and the huge, stately trees and imagine demons invading, but the risk was higher now than it had been in days.

Even harder to realize that Ed Marks had been possessed and was out there even now with his body under demon control. At least it was almost dark. Demons would be stirring soon and they could finally do something about what had happened to Ed.

"Hey! You two. What are you doing in Ed's house?"

She glanced up. Damn. That grumpy old man who lived across the street was yelling at them.

She knew Mr. Puccini, or at least Bumper did. He wouldn't have a clue who she was, and the man was a certified pain in the butt, according to Eddy. Willow plastered a big smile on her face and waved at him.

"What're you kids doing in Ed's house? Where's Ed?" He leaned out over his front porch railing and glowered at them.

Taron glanced at Willow. "Who the nine hells is he?"

Willow grabbed his hand and squeezed his fingers. *Don't*

*worry. Just leave it to me.* "Hello." She stepped off Ed's porch, dragging Taron across the street along with her.

*Make sure your sword's hidden,* she said. "Hello. You must be Mr. Puccini. Ed told us about you."

The man's eyebrows shot up. "What'd he tell ya?"

Willow smiled, turned on the charm and kept walking. She stopped on the sidewalk in front of the man's house with Taron beside her. "He said you've been neighbors since Eddy was little, that you keep an eye on his place whenever he's away."

Mr. Puccini grunted. Willow kept smiling. "Ed had to leave rather quickly last night, but he'll be back in a couple of days. I'm Willow and this is my friend, Taron. We're staying at the house while Ed's gone."

"He never needed a house sitter before."

Willow slanted a fairly overblown glance to her right and then her left before gazing directly at the old man. Eddy was right—he really was grumpy. And suspicious, too, but she couldn't blame him. She lowered her voice and looked directly at him when she said, "You know what's been going on, Mr. Puccini. There have been some really strange things happening in town. Ed wasn't comfortable leaving his home unguarded."

Mr. Puccini folded his arms across his chest. "I don't blame him for that, but I don't understand Ed, bringing all these new people in to our neighborhood. How do you know him?"

"We're friends of Eddy's." She smiled again, but the old fart was obviously still suspicious.

"That's what I was afraid of. She's a nice girl, but she knows too many weirdos." He glared at both of them and grunted again, but before he could say anything, Taron raised his hands and passed them in front of Mr. Puccini's face.

His eyes glazed over. After a moment he smiled like a serene little cherub. Nodding slowly, he said, "It's good of you to watch the place for Ed. I'm sure he really appreciates it."

Taron stuffed his hands in his pockets. "He does, Mr. Puccini, and we're glad to help him. You have a good evening."

Still smiling, the old guy waved them off. Taron grabbed Willow's hand, and this time he was the one dragging her down the street.

Once they'd put a few houses between them and the neighbor, she laughed. "I forgot about that cool Lemurian mind trick. Alton already used it on Mr. Puccini a couple of times."

Taron slowed his steps. "He did? I'm glad you told me. It loses effectiveness over time if you reuse it on the same person. We may need to zap him again in a couple of days."

Willow tilted her head and stared at Taron for a long moment. "We may not have to worry about it in a couple of days. If the demon king is still alive, it will probably mean we've lost."

"Don't even say it."

Taron grabbed her hand and held on tightly. He was right, though. They didn't need to borrow trouble.

They already had more than enough.

Willow headed down the quiet street as if she knew exactly where she was headed. Taron tugged her to a stop. "Any idea where we're going?"

"Yes, actually. To the cemetery first, if our job is to destroy demons tonight. Demons seem to be drawn to the place. Something about all the ceramic statues, I imagine, but we need to find out where the lesser demons are hanging out, since they'll attract the demon king. Your sword said it's more important that we find them first, before the demon king does."

"How are we going to find them? This is a big world. It's not enclosed the way Lemuria is. They could be anywhere."

Willow let out a big breath. "I'm hoping Bumper and I can still sense them. She was good at it."

"Well . . ."

*I'm still good at it, Taron. I'm paying attention, and Willow's nose is pretty good. Not as good as mine but . . .*

"See? Even Bumper recognizes that she's not going to have her animal senses. You're working with a human nose." And it was such a perfect nose, set just above those perfect lips, and . . .

"Powered by Bumper's doggy brain," Willow said, "and she is a very smart dog, right, Bumper?"

*I am, Willow. I really am. Honest, Taron. Don't worry.*

"See? C'mon, Taron. Relax. We'll be fine."

"Yeah, right." He held on to Willow's hand because he honestly couldn't stop touching her, and they continued along the street. He wore one of Ed's caps on his head that Willow said would help hide the dark red color of his hair. He hadn't realized it wasn't a natural color for humans. At least Alton's clothing helped him blend in, and as the night grew darker, his hair didn't stand out quite as much.

He didn't want to worry about how he looked. Didn't want to worry about demons or the demon king. He had enough to worry about with the beautiful blonde hanging on to his hand.

What in the nine hells was he going to do about Willow? They'd made love all day long, but instead of getting her out of his system, instead of satisfying his curiosity, he wanted her more than ever. He'd never been driven by his libido before, but it sure seemed to be in charge now. It was as if there'd been a part of him caged all these years, but now that wild creature was finally free, and there was no putting him back inside.

All he could think of was Willow naked.

He had that amazing visual so stuck in his mind that he couldn't have shaken it loose if he'd wanted to.

He did not want to lose it. Not the memory of Willow with her head thrown back and her body arched, her nipples tight with arousal, her thick blond hair in tumbled curls about her naked shoulders. He still saw her with her lips parted and eyes closed as her body trembled in orgasm.

He wanted Willow's wet heat surrounding him, her inner muscles rippling along his hard length and her heels digging into his butt as she surged against him, all warm and willing woman. Wanted it so much he had to force himself to continue walking, to concentrate on the real reason they were here.

He'd always been so single-minded. He'd never before had a problem concentrating on the issue at hand. He should be thinking of demons, of how he and Willow could possibly defeat the demon king. How they were going to rescue Ed. He shouldn't have thoughts of a naked Willow filling his head. Shouldn't be worrying what would happen the next time they slept with each other—or didn't.

The next time they crawled into bed together. He'd told her they wouldn't have sex again, and he'd meant it. At least until the words had left his mouth. Sex was the last thing he should be thinking about right now. The future of all worlds was at stake, and all he could think of was Willow.

Willow naked. Willow kissing his mouth, her hands wrapped around his cock, her eyes shining with need. The demon king was somewhere nearby and his long-silent sword had finally spoken and said just enough to scare the crap out of him, and what was he thinking?

That he wanted to turn around, go back to Ed's house and make love to the woman holding his hand.

Being told it was time to prepare for a final battle wasn't the way to inspire a guy's confidence, so why was he telling himself that sex with Willow was more important than saving the world from demonkind?

That was what he should be worried about. Demons and upcoming battles and whether or not he and Willow were going to be able to rescue Ed Marks, not whether or not he'd get Willow naked, whether or not he could somehow justify making love to her again.

And again.

Suddenly Willow stopped and held a finger to her lips. *Do you smell that? Sulfur. Bumper agrees. There are demons nearby.*

They'd left the quiet neighborhood and he hadn't even noticed. His first time in a town in Earth's dimension and he wasn't paying any attention at all. He needed to be focused on the job at hand, for now, anyway. Nine hells, what had happened to his analytical mind?

He squeezed Willow's hand so she'd think he'd been paying closer attention. *Any idea where?*

Gazing about, he realized they were walking along the main street through town. Small shops lined the road, but it was the dinner hour and most businesses appeared closed for the night.

Willow didn't answer him. Instead, she took his hand and tugged Taron toward a small store with a sign that read EVERGREEN HARDWARE AND GARDEN.

There was a display behind an iron fence that drew her attention—birdbaths and concrete planters and stone animals of all shapes and sizes. Taron stared at the figurines and then turned to Willow. "I don't see anything different. What are you . . . ?"

"Shh." Again with the finger over her lips. "Look at their eyes," she whispered. "What do you see?"

How in the nine hells had he missed this? The scent of sulfur in the air had been the first clue, but the plain, gray stone figurines had glowing eyes. There was life behind them—demonic life. He glanced at the tall fence locking the public out and the creatures in. "What now?"

"I want to try something."

Willow held her hands out and pointed her long, slender

fingers at the creatures. Taron thought of Dax, with fire and ice shooting out of his fingertips, but this wasn't quite the same.

Willow shot blue sparkles. The same little blue sparkles that had trailed along behind her when she flew about as a tiny sprite poured from her fingertips. They didn't damage the figurine, but they must have really pissed off the demon inside.

Black, oily mist shot out of a stone cat and headed right for Willow. Taron drew his sword and caught the wraith with his crystal blade. It disappeared in a small flash of light and a whole lot of stink.

"Perfect." Willow glanced to either side. So did Taron. He didn't see anyone around, but in a town this small, it was like they just rolled up the streets at dusk. Willow shot sparkles at the second stone statue, and then the next.

Taron caught every demon. There were seven altogether. Willow turned around with a huge grin on her face, held her fingers up and blew on the tips, as if putting out flames.

Taron couldn't help himself. He shoved his sword in his scabbard, grabbed Willow around the waist and kissed her.

She kissed him back. The moment their lips met, her body seemed to melt against his, her arms wrapped around his shoulders, and the kiss went from simple congratulations to absolute combustion.

Taron's mouth moved over hers with a practiced ease that totally shocked him. He'd never kissed a woman until Willow, and now it felt like the most natural thing in the world to taste her lips, to tangle his tongue with hers, to groan into her mouth when she nipped his lower lip with her sharp teeth.

He lost himself in the feel of her mouth on his, the taste and texture of lips and tongue and teeth. He could have stood here on the sidewalk, kissing, for the rest of the night.

It was Willow who came to her senses first. She ended it slowly, teasingly, and it was all Taron could do not to whimper.

Then he realized exactly what the two of them had just accomplished . . . and he wasn't thinking of the kiss. Grabbing her hand, he held it up with her fingers spread wide.

"How did you know that would work? Where did the sparkles come from, and why did they run the demon out of the avatar?" He pressed his forehead to hers, breathing fast and trying really hard to regain control. Talking helped. It had to.

"I didn't." She curled her fingers around his. "I hoped it would. Your sword said that together we would have the power to destroy the demon king. I couldn't imagine what kind of power I might have, and then I remembered my sparkles."

Taron held up their linked hands and stared at her fingertips. "But what do they do? Where do they come from?"

Laughing, she shook her head. "I have no idea. They just sort of tickled and buzzed in my fingertips and then there they were. I don't think they hurt anything. They just made the demons really mad. Did you see how they came right at us?"

"I did. It was amazing." Taron glanced over his shoulder and checked the glamour on his sword. It was well disguised. "So your sparkles and my sword are all that stand between us and the demon king?"

Willow nodded.

"Why does that give me so little confidence?"

Willow tugged his hand and pulled him along the sidewalk. "Maybe because you're a logical mathematician, and none of this adds up?"

He laughed. What else could he do? "Ya think?"

One thing definitely added up. He'd just discovered that, logical mathematician or not, it was difficult to walk with a full-blown erection in tight pants.

Willow shrugged and kept walking, but she was smiling. The tension between them had eased. He'd kissed her and they'd both enjoyed it and yet they'd still stopped in time.

At least Willow had stopped them. Taron wasn't so certain he could have ended that on his own. At least his arousal was beginning to subside. Now they just needed to worry about the demons. And the demon king. And saving Ed Marks, and not letting Eddy find out her father was possessed, and keeping Dax away from all of this.

Impossible? Damn, but he hoped not.

But he was holding Willow's hand and they were walking along a quiet street in a beautiful little town in Earth's dimension, and at this moment, all things felt possible. The stars were coming out and he'd never felt so free in his life.

He wasn't about to consider those other feelings thrumming in his veins, filling his heart to bursting. No. One thing at a time, and the most important thing now was fighting demons.

He put his other concerns aside. It was the Lemurian way, after all. He would work on his argument, consider all the facts, and deal with it when he was ready.

If only he could be like Willow. She merely accepted, dealt, and moved on. He glanced at their hands, at the perfect way their fingers linked, and knew that moving on was already impossible.

He had a feeling he was going to pay for that unimaginable joy he'd experienced all throughout the day, that he felt even now. He didn't mind, as long as he was the one who paid. No matter what, he had to protect Willow. If that meant leaving her when this battle was over, he would do exactly that, but he refused to put her life at risk.

Already he knew that he could endure any pain, except one that hurt her. She squeezed his fingers and glanced at him. There was a question in her eyes, and he knew she must sense his worry. Carefully he locked his concerns inside.

And then he swore, to any and all gods who listened, that he would keep her safe.

# Chapter 10

No one said a word as Dawson drove away from Boynton Canyon. Everyone seemed a little bit numb after that wild fight outside the vortex. Now, though, shadows stretched across the desert landscape. If not for the tension radiating from everyone in the vehicle, Selyn would have thoroughly enjoyed the ride.

She'd never imagined seeing any of this—not after a lifetime of captivity deep in the Lemurian crystal mines. The Arizona desert was breathtaking, though she hoped that Dawson would one day be able to follow through on his promise to show her the ocean.

She'd heard about it from her mother so many years ago, and the concept of water stretching for as far as the eye could see, of dolphins dancing, and sunlight sparkling off the waves was well beyond her imagination.

For now, the beauty of the desert would have to do. She wasn't sure if she loved dawning or nightfall best, but already the colors were beginning to change with the coming of night. The sky had lost its brilliant blue and was shifting to shades of peach and orange, and the shadows gave the huge, red rock formations a ghostly appearance.

If only she didn't view this natural perfection through the

dark threat of demonkind hanging over all of it. That was more than enough to ruin anyone's day.

Eddy leaned forward. "Daws, why don't you head toward the vortex at Red Rock Crossing? I know there's no doorway to Abyss there and it's out of the way, but I've got a weird feeling about it. Besides, we can check Bell Rock from there and then move on to the one by the airport."

"Works for me." Daws glanced at Selyn and smiled. *You okay, sweetheart? You're awfully quiet.*

*As long as I'm with you.* She settled back in her seat and watched the red rocks speed by. It was still beautiful.

Even the threat of demonkind couldn't change that.

Eddy tried calling her dad again, and once again the answering machine picked up. She'd even tried his cell phone, but since he rarely remembered to carry the damned thing, she wasn't surprised to get the recorded message.

It wasn't even turned on. Fat lot of good that did. She was edgy and uncomfortable and her brain wouldn't stop buzzing. Something was going on but she couldn't tell what. She had a weird feeling, like a bubble was about to burst, as if there was just a bit too much pressure all around, and something had to give.

Ginny had fallen asleep the minute she and Alton got in the car. All of them were hanging by a thread. Even Dax was quieter than usual, but the fight they'd just waged at Boynton Canyon had been beyond anything any of them had ever seen.

There'd been no end to the possessed birds. An unbelievable barrage of every kind of bird imaginable coming at them in a mindless attack—but for what purpose? The demons had died, the birds had survived, and then, as suddenly as the attack began, it had ended.

The sky had been full of circling, diving birds of every

species native to the area. Then nothing. Where had they gone, and why? What had the attack accomplished?

She glanced about her, at Alton and Ginny in the back, Dax beside her and Dawson and Selyn in front. They all looked like hell. Was that the goal? To wear them down to the point where they couldn't fight back? The number of demons appeared to be endless—was this fight going to be one of attrition?

And where the hell was her father? Shivers ran along Eddy's spine. Dax wrapped an arm around her and hugged her close, sharing his warmth.

Sharing strength. She hoped they had enough to last. So many things felt terribly wrong, Eddy wasn't sure what to worry about next.

"We're here."

Dawson pulled into the parking lot at Red Rock Crossing. There was still enough light to see the trail, and their swords would show them the way if they returned after dark.

Eddy climbed slowly out of the SUV. Ginny was yawning, Alton got out and stretched, and even Dax looked a bit haggard. Of course, they'd gone almost nonstop for a month, now, ever since the night she'd found Dax in her potting shed.

Had it only been a month?

Dax leaned close and kissed the top of her head. "It has," he said. "It's been exactly a month since you found me."

"You're snooping in my head." She kissed him. As much as she'd felt it would be weird to share thoughts, Eddy realized it was wonderful to have someone who understood what was spinning around in her brain. Especially someone who loved her as much as Dax.

"I am," he said. "I do." He kissed her again. "I love what happens in there, especially when it concerns me. C'mon."

He took her hand and they followed the others. Dawson and Selyn led the way with Alton and Ginny right behind. Shadows spilled across the red cliffs and the sky had taken on a dark blue color tinged with pale shades of peach and yellow.

As beautiful as sunsets usually were, this one seemed off, as if the sunlight were filtered through a dark lens. Eddy shook off the sense of something out of sync and concentrated on the rocky trail. They reached the portal. Ginny and Alton were the first to step through.

Ginny had drawn DarkFire—her blade was the only one that would show the demons' true shapes, which made it hard for the foul things to hide in the shadows. The strange light shining from Ginny's blade meant Eddy and Dax stepped into a cave that reminded her of a cheesy bar with black lights overhead.

DarkFire's odd amethyst light had everything glowing—but there was no sign of demonkind. Eddy and Dax scouted the small cavern. It looked fine, but Eddy couldn't ignore the strange tingling sensation that wouldn't leave her alone.

"Eddy?"

She turned at Selyn's soft question. "What? Do you see something?"

"It's what I don't see. Isn't there supposed to be a portal here? I thought this vortex had one that led to the council chambers in Lemuria, but I can't find it."

"What?" Eddy spun around and stared at the wall. It was shadowed and dark, and there was no sign of the swirling energy that signified a portal. She drew DemonSlayer and held the blade aloft. Light spilled over the wall, illuminating melted stone.

"Shit. It's gone." She stepped close to the wall and ran her fingers over the cold, smooth rock. "Someone's sealed it. But who?"

Alton ran his fingers over the rock. "It wasn't done with one of our swords. The rock melts differently when we close them with swordfire. This is almost as if it caught a single but powerful blast."

Dawson stared over Eddy's shoulder. "Could demons do this?"

"Possibly a very powerful demon." Alton kept running his fingers over the rock, as if rubbing it might somehow bring the portal back. "But why?"

Eddy glanced at Dax and then turned to Dawson. "Well, it does close off an escape route. We need to get to Bell Rock and see what's going on there. There aren't any new portals to Abyss here, are there?"

"I'm still checking." Ginny held DarkFire high and went over the walls and ceiling. "Doesn't look like it, though DarkFire says she senses the stench of demonkind here. It must be really faint. I can't smell it at all."

The sense of something about to blow had Eddy almost running down the tunnel for the portal to Bell Rock. "C'mon. I don't have a good feeling about this at all."

They slipped through the portal and entered the large cavern that marked the Bell Rock vortex. This was the Grand Central Station of Arizona portals, as far as Eddy could tell.

Or it had been. "What's going on?" She checked the portal to Mount Shasta, but it was nothing more than melted rock.

"The main entry to Lemuria's been closed, too. It almost appears to have been done by swordfire. I'm not really sure, but that doesn't make any sense at all." Alton looked up from the far side of the cavern. "Is anything else open?"

"You know what this means, don't you?" Ginny pointed DarkFire to all parts of the cavern, illuminating every crevice, crook, and cranny. "We're trapped here. We can still move around within Sedona, but everything else has been sealed. Can you tell who did it?"

Alton studied the walls while Eddy went to the main portal that opened to the outside. She stepped through, noticed nothing amiss, and returned. The other five were gathered in the center of the cavern. "What's going on?"

Alton shook his head. "The portal to Lemuria was closed

in a manner I can't determine, which leads me to believe it was done by a demon, but HellFire says the one between here and Mount Shasta was closed by crystal. He's not sure who, though. I don't understand it."

Eddy rubbed her arms. The sense of evil, of foreboding had grown stronger. "I can't reach my dad. I've been trying to call him for a couple of hours, but there's no one there. We can't even go there and check on him. Not with all the portals shut."

Dax slipped an arm around her waist. "He's got to be okay, Eddy. He's probably out in the workshop. You know he spends hours out there, and if the trains are running, he won't hear the phone."

"I know. I'm still worried, Dax. Something just feels wrong." She glanced at the others and caught Selyn studying her with an odd expression. Eddy frowned.

Selyn sighed, as if she wasn't sure she should say what she was thinking. "I know I've never met your father, and I am very new to this business of hunting demons, but I can't imagine your father being out of touch with you on purpose. In the short time I've known you, he's always maintained close contact. Does he have any friends you can call, some-one who can tell you if he's okay?"

"He does. I'll see if I can get hold of Mari and Darius, or even Mari's parents. If not, there's always the grump across the street." Lordy, but she hated the idea of asking Mr. Puccini for anything, but desperate times and all that. "Thanks, Selyn. That's an excellent idea. I can get the numbers I need once we're back at Daw's house."

"Good." Alton sheathed his sword. "We have to check on the vortex at the airport, and then all of us need a good night's sleep. Tomorrow I'll start working on reopening the portal to Shasta. I don't like feeling trapped here. We can't access Lemuria, either. If we could, I might be able to connect with Taron. He could at least let us know what's going on."

* * *

They stood in the darkness outside the vortex near the airport. Alton glanced at Ginny. She had a look of pure determination on her face, but he could tell that, especially after the last battle, she was running on little more than nerves alone.

The sense of demonkind was strong here, the air thick with the stench of sulfur, though they'd not seen any actual demons while walking between the parking area and the portal.

Of course, after dark the damned things were difficult to see. Black mist had a way of disappearing much too easily into dark shadows.

"How should we do this?" He addressed all of them, but Alton's eyes were on Ginny. DarkFire's unique power had made Ginny the natural leader of their group. She'd taken the responsibility without regard to her own safety. It was what she was destined to do, and none of them questioned her decisions.

"This portal is really too small for all of us to go in at once if we have to fight, but DarkFire can show us where the demons are hiding and if there are any others hanging out inside, so I'll go in first." She sighed and wiped her hand over her eyes. "Damn it all, but I'm positive this sucker's going to be full of demons. It's obvious the portal to Abyss has been reopened."

"No shit, Sherlock."

The moment the words left her mouth, Eddy glanced up and caught Ginny's eye. They both exploded in giggles.

The others looked at one another and then at the two women as if they were absolutely nuts. Alton bit back a grin and folded his arms across his chest. He focused his most superior expression on Eddy. "Eddy, that really doesn't sound like the sort of thing a warrior with a crystal sword would say."

She glanced his way, bit her lips, and then lost it again.

Selyn frowned and nudged Dawson. "Who is this Sherlock?"

Dawson looked at Ginny, who was laughing so hard she was practically doubled over. "Our exalted leader's going to have to explain that one in detail, but essentially it means that what Ginny said was more than obvious."

"Ah." Selyn nodded, unsheathing her sword. "I see. It was human humor. You can be such an odd race." She moved closer to the portal. "Ginny? We're ready when you are."

Ginny took a deep breath and flashed a big smile at Selyn. "Yes, Ma'am. Selyn, why don't you and Daws and Alton come in with me. That way Eddy and Dax can keep an eye on the outside and zap any demons that try to escape." She smirked at Eddy. "And it also separates the two of us, which is probably a good tactical move."

Eddy was still chuckling when Ginny went through the portal first with DarkFire held high. Alton was glad he was right on her heels, because the place was so full of demons, their sulfuric stench made it hard to breathe.

Ginny slipped to one side and illuminated the entire cavern. Selyn and Dawson paused in the entry. Startled and obviously finding it hard to believe what he was seeing, Dawson ducked as a dark wraith shot across the small cavern and headed for the portal. Selyn caught it with her crystal blade.

"Thank you." He kissed her quickly and shook his head. "Holy shit, Ginny." He was staring at the walls and ceiling where demons glistened in all their shapes and sizes, in full display beneath the black light from Ginny's blade.

The variety alone was pretty overwhelming.

"Pretty impressive, eh?" Alton swung his blade along the wall, incinerating dozens of wraiths. Their banshee screams were so loud they were practically deafening. Alton had to shout to make himself heard. "Daws, why don't you see if you can close the portal. It's probably the same one we closed once before. Look up there." He pointed up with his blade.

"It was hidden in among those stalactites, unless they've built an entirely new one."

Daws leaned back and looked up, using his crystal blade to illuminate the ceiling. "I see it." He ducked as a mass of demons boiled out and down through the portal. "Crap. At least now we know where they've been coming from."

Alton didn't answer. He was too busy scraping demons away from the walls and watching them flash and die beneath his crystal blade. Selyn was doing the same thing on the far wall, while Ginny kept the area illuminated. Howls and screams echoed off the walls and the air was thick with sulfur.

Eddy poked her head in through the portal and then stepped fully inside during a bit of a lull in the noise. She took a quick glance around the small cavern. "Everything okay? We've killed a few outside, but there aren't too many."

She ducked as a wraith flew by. Selyn cut it down with her blade while Eddy looked up at the portal Dawson was in the process of sealing. "Wow . . . at least now we know where a lot of them were probably coming from. This one and Boynton. I'll tell Dax." She cocked her head to one side and frowned, as if she heard something over the banshee cries. Then she disappeared into the wall.

Dawson turned and flashed a smile at Ginny as Eddy slipped through the portal and disappeared. "Do you ever get used to that?"

"Nope. Especially when I'm actually walking through rock, because I know it's dead wrong." She laughed and focused the beam from DarkFire as she searched for more demons.

Daws held DemonsDeath with both hands. A powerful stream of blue fire shot from the tip of the crystal blade, covering the portal to Abyss with brilliant ripples of energy. The demons within the cavern grew more agitated as they realized the gateway was closing. The screams and howls were deafening, the stench almost suffocating. Alton continued scraping demons from the walls and killing them, while Selyn worked the area close to the portal.

The stench grew thicker, the screams and howls of dying demons more intense, even as their numbers dwindled.

"I think I've got it." Dawson lowered his sword.

Alton stepped across the cavern and gazed up into the shadows. He held his sword overhead so he could get a better look at the melted rock. The portal was definitely sealed.

Once the portal was closed, they finished up in a couple of minutes. Ginny sheathed DarkFire and glanced about the cavern. "Hopefully that will hold for awhile." She yawned. "I need some sleep. You guys ready to go back?"

Alton grabbed her arm. "As long as we can stop for hamburgers and French fries along the way."

"Are you ever not hungry?"

Alton plastered an innocent expression on his face and shook his head. Laughing, Ginny led them all through the portal.

Dax waited outside. He glanced from one to the other, frowning. "Where's Eddy?"

Alton shot a quick glance at Ginny and then stared at Dax. "With you. She came in and checked to see if all was okay, stayed less than a minute, then she left."

Eyes wide, Dax shook his head. "No. She stepped through to speak with you, but she never returned. I thought she stayed to fight demons." He stared at the cliff where the portal remained hidden in the rock, shot a terrified glance at Alton and then rushed through the portal. A moment later he returned.

"She's not there. Not here. Where the hell is she? Alton, she's gone. Where can she be?"


If he could describe the sense of regaining consciousness, Ed figured he would compare this experience to swimming upstream in sewage. The stench was disgusting, the sense of evil permeating every cell in his body enough to make him retch.

He couldn't really see and had no actual feeling in his arms or legs, mainly because he wasn't the one actually controlling them. His heartbeat was all wrong, as if it labored against something that was trying to force a different cadence out of the damned muscle. His lungs worked, but the knowledge that something other than his own brain was controlling things made all of his senses feel wrong.

Everything was wrong, but he fought the powerful desire to slip back into that private corner of his brain where he'd been hiding. Somehow, he had to figure out what the hell was going on. But how, with no sense of time, no feeling of where he was, of when it was?

He thought of Dax trying to describe the void, but Dax had only said there was nothing there. No time, no sense, no smell, no feeling.

Wherever Ed was, it definitely smelled bad. He fought against the pressure to go back into hiding deep within his own mind. Something was trying to control him—had been controlling him, but for some reason it appeared to be weakening.

He tried to see what was going on, and then realized he couldn't see because it was night. Blinking his eyes felt very odd, as if he were blinking someone else's eyes, thinking with someone else's brain.

He glanced down at his body—same legs, same arms. He held out his hand and turned it palm up, palm down. He still wore his gold wedding band, even after all these years.

It was definitely his body, but he wasn't in here alone.

So who was in here with him? And how did he know this?

And where the hell was he? He had a vague memory of waking up once before with sunlight streaming through a broken window but now he was outside and it was night. He'd been walking. He was almost certain he'd been walking, but when his mind had begun to clear, he'd stopped.

Whoever was trying to control him wasn't happy with that at all. Something wanted him to keep moving. But why? And where was he going?

Slowly he looked around. The moon wasn't up yet, but the night was crystal clear and the stars cast a bit of light. Enough that he recognized the shapes of headstones.

*It's the cemetery. I know this place. I know it . . .*

Could he be dead? Was he buried somewhere nearby? Could one of these headstones be his? He almost laughed. Wouldn't it be funny if he actually turned out to be a ghost? All those years of trying to convince Eddy that ghosts really existed . . . wouldn't it be fun—just show up and say *Hi, I'm a ghost . . . a visitor from beyond the veil.*

Except he wasn't ready to die and he didn't have to prove anything to Eddy anymore. Not since she'd fallen in love with Dax, a man who'd started life as a demon. Who'd have thought his perfectly pragmatic daughter would end up with an immortal lover? At least now she didn't think her old man was a complete nutcase.

So, what was he? Because he wasn't just Ed Marks anymore. No, he was someone else, too. Someone evil and utterly disgusting—someone who wanted him to keep going, to walk farther into the cemetery, to go beyond the newer, more manicured graves on the perimeter.

He leaned over and picked up a stout piece of wood. Held it in his right hand and stared at it. No. This wouldn't work.

Work for what? And why the hell had he picked it up?

He tossed the wood to the ground and shuffled toward the small caretaker's shed. There was a lock on the door, but he tried to open it anyway. There was a sense that whoever was in his head didn't understand the concept of locked doors.

He grabbed the handle and pulled.

There was a horrific noise, a sound of metal tearing. The

handle pulled out of the metal door—just ripped right through the aluminum—and the door hung crazily on bent hinges. Ed stared at the latch still clutched in his hand.

How the hell did he do that?

Before he thought to answer the question, he was moving forward, into the dark shed. He reached for a thick handle leaning against one wall and picked up a huge pickax.

The handle was wood, but the iron pick was solid and deadly. Somehow, he knew this would work.

But for what?

As he walked out of the shed, he stared at the twisted door. Ed Marks was in great shape for a guy in his late sixties, but there was no way he could have ripped that door off the hinges, no way he'd be strong enough to pull the handle right out of the metal.

Except he'd just done it.

Confused, he let his body go wherever that other mind directed him. He walked through more rows of newer headstones, still proceeding toward the older part of the cemetery. Trees grew thick here, and the shadows made it more difficult to see, but that other mind running the show seemed to know where he was going.

At least his feet did. Ed struggled to maintain control of whatever thoughts he was hanging on to. He had a sense that the one who controlled him was growing weaker. That would explain his ability to surface now. He'd been held down by the entity in control of his mind, but it couldn't afford the energy now to keep him totally subjugated.

He paused in front of an old grave. There was a tiny cherub on top of the granite stone. Ed stared at the statue.

It glared at him out of eyes that glowed a sickly shade of green. Even as befuddled as his mind was right now, Ed recognized demonkind when he saw the signs, so he didn't fight it a bit when his arm lifted the heavy pickax and swung. The iron point connected with the stone cherub.

It shattered and the demon inside shrieked as pieces of the ruined cherub fell to the ground. A thick, oily mist seeped from the broken pieces of stone. It hovered for a moment, a dark and stinking wraith.

Ed opened his jaws wide and inhaled, and the power of his lungs drew the disgusting creature into his mouth.

He swallowed. The human part of him wanted to vomit.

The demon part chortled.

Ed lifted up the pickax and walked to the next small statue, this time an angel with glowing eyes. He tried not to lift the ax, fought the need to swing it, did not want to release the demon hiding within its stone avatar.

But whatever ruled his body—and it had to be demonic—had gained strength from that first demon soul. It shoved Ed back, shoved the last shreds of his consciousness down into the dark corners where he'd been held prisoner.

He hovered there a moment, struggling to hang on to whatever threads of himself existed, and in that brief moment, he sensed Eddy. Dear God, he didn't want her to know what had happened! She'd want to come and help him, and that wouldn't do.

He used his last bit of self, the slender threads of consciousness that had once been Ed Marks to push her away. *Run Eddy! Go! Go away!* Her startled cry sounded so close she might have been beside him.

*Dad? Dad, where are you?*

He felt a huge surge of power. Not his. Evil. Focused and aware. Very, very aware. Whatever it was, it reached for Eddy. He felt it, pushed with everything he had and tried to stop it.

Failed.

Eddy disappeared, along with Ed's grasp on the world. Everything recognizable slipped away, buried in the disgusting sense of demon flowing over him like thick, black sludge. He was almost certain he heard demonic laughter, felt a new surge of power. Not his. Not anymore. Vaguely aware of Ed, of the man he once was, he swung his ax. It came down on the angel and he saw the thing shatter into a million pieces.

Once more he felt the pressure in his lungs as he inhaled yet another demon. Fought a vague desire to retch. And then, as before, his sense of himself as Ed Marks, his fear for Eddy, his knowledge of reality, all winked out.

# Chapter 11

Taron wished he had some way to contact Alton, but they'd not had any luck finding a phone number for Ginny and it appeared Mari's parents—who might have known it—were out of town. Maybe they went to see the ocean with Mari and Darius.

He knew he could talk to Alton and explain the necessity of keeping Dax away from here, though with the portal closed, there was no way for Alton to get to Evergreen, unless of course they were able to go to Lemuria first and then come here.

It was all a moot point, though, without a way to make contact. Which meant he and Willow were on their own.

He held her hand as they walked, and the connection was oddly soothing. As if the mere feel of her hand in his gave him strength. Her touch reminded him of the necessity of prevailing in whatever final battle awaited them. He had to win. There was no way he could fail, because failure could mean the end of Willow. Somehow, he knew, should demonkind win, a creature of Eden would have no place in this world.

Of course, neither would he. At least not as anything beyond a source of energy for demonkind. He didn't even want to think of what that would entail, but it couldn't be good.

With those thoughts weighing him down, he continued on,

holding tightly to Willow's hand as they walked along the streets of the small, quiet town. Neither of them spoke, but it was a comfortable silence. The occasional vehicle passed by, and he wanted to stop and study them, to see what it was that made them move so quickly, but the sky was growing dark and the sense they must be somewhere soon was pressing.

The moon hadn't come up yet, but as the night grew darker, street lights and the occasional porch light from homes along the way came on and made it possible for them to see.

"I want to check this building out, okay?"

Willow tugged him toward a dark wreck of a building in the middle of town. Built all of stone, Taron at first thought it looked unfinished. Then he noticed the wood boarding up windows and the weathered look of the stone and realized it was a derelict remnant of another time. It must have once been a beautiful structure, with statues of some sort at either corner. Two barren pedestals were all that remained.

Willow headed around to the back side of the building. There was a locked set of doors that appeared to cover an opening into the basement. The rest of the building looked solid, though there were a couple of broken windows here at the back. Only one was partially barricaded with wood. Wires hung loose from an open panel near a barred door.

"What is this place?" Taron ran his hand over the rough stone exterior.

"It was a library building. Eddy said it's been condemned because it doesn't meet safety requirements. The town can't afford to fix it, but they don't want to tear it down, either."

"Libraries are important. You'd think they'd find the money." He studied the solid old structure and tried to imagine when it had been new.

Willow shook her head. "There's still a library, but in a newer building. It's just this old building that's a wreck. Come on. I don't sense the demon king here, though Bumper says she can smell faint hints of his presence. I imagine he stayed here during the day."

"Is this where he hid before?"

She pointed to one of the empty platforms almost lost in the shadows. "In plain sight. He took over the stone gargoyle that used to sit up there. It was the one that ate my sprite body and killed Dax."

She said it so lightly, but the image sickened him. "Where is the gargoyle now?"

Willow's smile took on an unexpected twist. "It's a pile of rocks on the side of the mountain. The bastard got what he deserved. I'm only sorry Eddy wasn't able to finish him off."

"Me, too." As Taron followed Willow down the street, he thought of that battle on the mountainside. Alton had told him about it. They'd all wished Eddy had been successful, though she'd accomplished more than either Dax or Alton. Still, if the demon king had died that night, they wouldn't be in this fix, trying to find Eddy's father and stop the demon who was controlling Ed's body.

But that wasn't fair, either. Eddy had done more than any woman of Lemuria would have even attempted. She'd done more than he, a supposed warrior of Lemuria could imagine. He thought of the final battle Alton had described and wondered how brave he would be should the demon king come after him. Not brave enough, he feared, though somehow he had to find enough backbone to stand up to the beast.

Dax had given his life. Alton had almost been killed and Willow's body had been eaten. All of them had shown great courage. Taron glanced at their linked hands, the way his fingers and Willow's interlocked, and felt as if he should apologize for holding hers.

What good was he as a warrior? How could he possibly fight a demon that had grown stronger with each day that passed, one that—weeks ago—had already been powerful enough to stop Alton and Dax and Willow?

A faint sound caught his attention. "Did you hear that?"

Willow shook her head. Bumper's voice popped into his mind.

*I did. It came from the cemetery. I'm almost sure that was the shriek of a demon.*

"This way." Willow tightened her grasp on his fingers and pulled him toward the faint sounds of demonkind. She stretched out her long legs and picked up the pace. Taron broke into a trot to keep up with her.

He heard a loud noise, as if many machines were running. It grew louder as they ran along the dark road, and he could see lights up ahead, moving quickly back and forth.

"What is that?"

"The freeway. Part of the Earth's transportation system. Those are vehicles traveling north and south along the road. The same as the cars you've seen here in town, but they're moving a lot faster and there are more of them. The traffic runs night and day—it's how people here travel great distances."

Again he wished he could stop and watch, but this was obviously not the time. This was truly a fascinating world and he hoped the day would come when he could spend more time observing, but Willow was tugging his hand and running up a roadway that crossed over the freeway.

He felt a strong compulsion to unsheathe his sword, so he pulled it out. The blade glowed, and somehow he knew the blade was aware that demons were close.

Another shriek echoed through the night, much closer this time. Why weren't people coming outside to investigate? Did they have no sense of curiosity over these strange sounds? He glanced at Willow. She walked quickly now, focused on the road ahead.

He tugged her hand without slowing her down. "How have you kept the demon invasion from the humans living here? Don't they wonder at the strange sounds, the cries of demonkind?"

She glanced his way but kept moving forward. "Alton has kept a compulsion over much of the town. The citizens think they're hearing the cries of birds in the night, and the damage has been blamed on vandals. No one has been harmed by demonkind—at least not yet. I think Ed is the first human to be possessed in this town, and it took the demon king to manage that."

A flash of light caught Taron's attention. "Look!" They both paused at the top of the road that crossed over the freeway. Another light flashed. "What is that?"

"Crap." Willow grabbed his hand and dragged him down the other side of the road. "That's the cemetery. I think the demon king is munching on demon souls."


She'd never been a screamer, but Eddy figured now might be as good a time as any to start. Where the hell was she? There was no up, no down, no sense of her body, no light no dark. Nothing.

Just her mind, spinning in terrified circles that went nowhere fast. *Dax? Sweetheart? Where are you? Are you there Dax?*

Nothing. Oh, crap. Double crap. She felt like she was going to hyperventilate, but she didn't seem to be breathing, so how the hell could that happen?

Her brain was buzzing, like she was going to implode if she didn't, somehow, find somewhere to anchor herself . . . figuratively speaking, of course. How do you anchor nothing that's obviously nowhere?

She'd stepped through the portal, talked to Alton and Ginny, Selyn and Dawson, and they were doing fine. Killing demons, closing the portal to Abyss, no problem.

Just an average day in the craziness her life had become.

Then, just before she returned, she could have sworn she heard her father's voice. In her head, saying her name, except his telepathy wasn't all that great and there was absolutely no way he could reach her in Sedona when he was in Evergreen.

Something had felt wrong, but at the same time, she'd known it was him. And, like any daughter would, she'd tried calling to him. She'd been in the process of popping back through the portal, but it had been pure instinct to respond to that familiar voice.

So of course she'd called to her dad, except he hadn't answered—and she hadn't ended up where she'd planned.

She'd had a vague sense of something pushing her, but that didn't make sense. How could anything push her while she was passing through a portal? Could she be trapped in the vortex? Somehow caught in the wall of rock they so easily stepped through—even though it should be impossible, right? No one could walk through rock, except she'd been doing it like it was no big deal, just walking right through energy portals like they actually existed, when everyone knew they couldn't possibly be real.

Doing the impossible on faith.

Oh, shit. This was so not a good thing.

She was afraid she was going to hyperventilate again, except she wasn't breathing so that, at least, was one thing she probably didn't have to worry about.

Crap. How could she exist without breathing? Without seeing or feeling or tasting? Without a body. Is this what it was like for Willow, stuck in Bumper now for the past three weeks? For the rest of her life?

Damn, but she had a whole new respect for Willow. That brave, funny little sprite had adjusted awfully fast to what had to be a living hell.

Eddy didn't see herself adjusting to this situation very well at all.

*Dad? Are you here, Dad? I know I heard you! Daddy!*

Breathe in, breathe out, breathe in, breathe . . . no. No

breathing. Oh, this was so not good. She needed to calm down and think. Start with simple things. Normal things.

She concentrated on toes and fingers. Nothing.

Tried blinking her eyes.

Nothing.

Shit. What did she expect? There was nothing remotely normal about her life anymore. She was sleeping with— hell, she was in love with—an ex-demon, fighting a demon invasion in two different dimensions and carrying a crystal sword that talked to her. Normal? What a joke that was.

Carrying a crystal sword. She'd had it with her when, well, when whatever had happened, happened. Frantic, she called out for her sword. *DemonSlayer? Can you hear me?*

*I am here, Eddy.*

*Oh, shit. Ohshitohshitohshit.* She never thought she'd be so happy to hear a familiar voice. *Thank goodness. Are you okay? Where are we? What happened?*

*I'm not sure. We have no substance. We are merely consciousness. I do not know where your body is, nor my blade.*

That really wasn't what she wanted to hear. Eddy took a deep breath, figuratively speaking. *Okay. So that's what we know we don't have. What do we know that's a positive thing?*

*Well, Eddy . . . it's not so positive, but I have a feeling we're in the void.*

*Dax's void? The same place where he was exiled?*

*I believe so.*

*But how? We just stepped through the portal—I've been in and out of that portal before, but this time we ended up here. Did you sense anything when it happened? Was the demon king involved?*

*I don't know, but that's not to say he wasn't, merely that I did not sense his presence. I'm almost positive I heard your father speak . . .*

*Me too! I was calling out to Dad and then* wham! *I was suddenly here, which is pretty much nowhere.*

*That is the essence of the void. It is nowhere. Without form or substance or any true location. No time, no . . .*

*Uh . . . DemonSlayer? I really don't want to hear any more of that. Think positive. Use some action verbs. What can we do? How can we get out of here?*

It felt as if she waited forever for DemonSlayer's answer. When it came, it was definitely not what Eddy wanted to hear.

*I don't know, Eddy. I honestly don't know.*


"Dax? You have to eat something."

Ginny sat down beside him on the top step in front of Dawson's house and put a sandwich in his hand. He stared at the thick slices of bread filled with leftover roast and wondered why she thought he could possibly eat while Eddy was missing.

She put an arm around his shoulders and hugged him as if he were a child in need of comfort. He should feel insulted, shouldn't he? But it felt too good to complain.

Maybe he was nothing more than a child. He certainly needed something to comfort him. He needed Eddy.

"We'll find her," Ginny said. Her voice broke, and he hoped she wouldn't cry. If she started crying, he'd probably cry, too. He didn't want to lose control. It was too frightening. He'd lost Eddy.

"But if you don't eat," and he realized Ginny was still speaking to him, "you won't be in any shape to help her. Please? For Eddy's sake?"

He nodded and took a bite of the sandwich. Staying strong made sense. Being ready for whatever was needed of him, but what if they didn't find her? What if she was lost forever? He was an immortal and so was Eddy.

Forever wasn't merely a word.

He could not survive forever without Eddy Marks. He

didn't know if he could survive a single night without her. She was his world, his sole reason for existing.

He took another bite. Usually he loved to eat. As a demon he'd never had anything remotely like the kinds of meals he routinely ate in Earth's dimension, but as he chewed, Dax realized that each bite tasted like cardboard.

He could barely swallow.

All he could do was worry about Eddy. Had demonkind taken her? It was as if she'd just winked out of existence. There wasn't a trace of her in the portal and they'd checked all the other vortexes in the area, just in case she'd somehow slipped through the wrong one or gotten caught in some sort of energy flux or a dimensional warp.

Nothing. No sign of Eddy. No sign of her sword. Even DemonSlayer had disappeared. The really odd thing, though, was that all their portals to either Evergreen or Lemuria were sealed, as well. Which meant that, for now at least, they were trapped here in Sedona.

That was okay. He wasn't going anywhere until he had Eddy back. He took another bite of the sandwich. What was he missing? Where in the nine hells could she be?

Ginny didn't say anything while he ate, which was good. He needed to think. Eddy couldn't just disappear. Things like that couldn't happen, could they?

Ginny handed him a cold beer to go with his sandwich, and he drank that down without really tasting it, but his mind was still spinning. What was he missing? Eddy was gone. So was her sword, which meant that, hopefully, she wasn't entirely alone. DemonSlayer was probably with her.

DemonSlayer! He turned around to Ginny. "Our swords can communicate with one another much more effectively than we can. Wherever Eddy is, DemonSlayer is with her. We need to see if our blades can make contact with Eddy's."

Ginny leapt to her feet. "I knew food would help."

He grabbed her hand and she hauled him up. "Actually," he said, "I think it was the beer."

"Whatever." She shoved the door open and Dax followed her into the front room. "Hey guys. Grab your swords and come out here. Dax has an idea."

He reached for DemonFire, pulled it out of the scabbard, and set the blade on the low coffee table in front of the couch. He had to clear his throat, which felt unnaturally tight, to say anything at all, but he couldn't look at anyone. Not if he intended to maintain any composure at all. "Let's just hope the idea has merit," he said. Then he made the mistake of glancing up, of looking at the others.

They looked at him with eyes full of hope, but wasn't that all they had right now? Hope? This had to work.

*Because if it doesn't,* he thought, *I have nothing else. No other ideas, no way to find her.* His heart actually ached, and he felt like weeping, but that wouldn't bring Eddy back.

Once again he called to her, just as he'd called since the moment he realized she was missing. *Eddy? Eddy, why in the hell don't you answer me? Where are you? I love you, Eddy. Come back.*

"That is just freaky." Willow slid down the berm that bordered the cemetery until she was out of sight, just in case anyone on the other side might be watching. She rolled over on her back and stared at the stars overhead.

Taron scooted down beside her. "What? The way he's smashing the statues?"

She shook her head. "No, the fact that it's Ed Marks doing the smashing, but he's not really Ed. Ed's the sweetest man you could ever meet. He's kind and loving and he adores Eddy, so it's just horrible to see him like this—smashing the avatars and then inhaling the demons. That's how the demon king did it when he was a gargoyle—he'd wait for us to destroy the avatars and then he snagged as many of the escaped demons as he could and he just sort of inhaled them. Each one made him stronger."

"That was a stone avatar, though. This time he's got a human avatar. According to my sword, the human body will grow weaker without food."

"I don't think it matters." She had to keep in mind that she actually had more experience fighting demons than Taron or his sword. He might be bigger and physically stronger, but Willow had been on the front lines with Dax since the very beginning. "We have to stop him before he kills Ed, because I don't think it matters if Ed is dead or alive. Think about it— if the demon king grows strong enough, he could animate Ed's body even if Ed dies. If he can make a stone gargoyle fly, he could certainly make a corpse walk."

She really didn't want to think about that. Poor Ed!

Taron grasped his sword. "Sword? Can we stop him?"

The blade didn't respond. Taron cursed softly under his breath.

"Why do you call it 'sword?' Doesn't your blade have a name?"

"I'm sure it does."

He sounded somewhat disgusted, which didn't make sense. All of the warriors she knew loved the sentience within their crystal blades. They trusted them with their lives, after all.

Taron glared at the weapon. "However, my weapon has not informed me what his name is."

"That's ridiculous." Willow touched her fingers to the blade. The crystal softly glowed. "What is your name? If we are to defeat this enemy, we have to work together. You're not making this any easier for Taron."

The blade shimmered softly. "It is not my place to make things easier for Taron. Fighting demonkind is difficult work."

"Great. Like I don't realize that already?" Taron gazed at

Willow and shook his head. "Alton got snark . . . wonder what you would call this?"

Willow didn't know whether to laugh or cry. The fate of all worlds at stake, and she was dealing with not one but two male egos. It really didn't seem fair.

She glared at the blade. "Enough already. We have no time for such foolishness. Your name, please?"

The light along the faceted blade pulsed. Probably the crystal sword version of a long-suffering sigh.

"I am CrystalFire, named for the swords replicated in my image, created in the heart of Mother Crystal."

Taron muttered, "Swords we could probably use about now."

"What's 'Mother Crystal?'" Willow stared at the softly glowing sword.

"The cave?" Taron shook his head. "Remember where we fought the demon king? There's a whole series of caves, all formed from different kinds of crystals. You were in the diamond cave where I replicated the swords."

"And where the spirits of the departed warriors live. I remember!" Willow stared at the shimmering crystalline blade. "What can you tell us, CrystalFire? What do you know about this demon and his avatar?"

The sword pulsed and then continued. "This demon grows more powerful with the life force of each lesser demon it consumes. If we have any hope of saving the human, we must attack now."

"Any ideas how we're going to do that and not end up dead?"

Taron's question sort of hung there. The sword didn't answer. Willow heard the sound of ceramic shattering, and knew another avatar had been destroyed, another demon soul consumed.

More power for the demon king. Less chance of Ed's

survival. An idea popped into her head. Now why hadn't she thought of this before?

"CrystalFire? I can draw energy and shoot it from my fingers as power. Is there any way for me to share that energy with you? Can you use the energy I collect to charge your fire and make it hotter or stronger?"

The sword pulsed and shimmered. Taron gazed at Willow, but she couldn't tell what he was thinking. Maybe he thought she was just nuts, but they had to help Ed. She'd loved Ed from the first moment she met him, and he was Eddy's father. She hated to think what it would do to Eddy if they couldn't save him.

"Draw forth your power and send it to me. If I open myself to your energy, it might work."

Did CrystalFire actually sound hopeful? It was so hard to tell with a sentient sword, and so far she wasn't all that impressed with Taron's. But Willow sat up, folded her legs comfortably, closed her eyes, and held her hands out. She felt the energy coming to her, just as it had when she was tiny. She'd missed the sense of power rushing into her body, the pressure of the huge charge as it built up inside.

She felt Bumper stirring, and wondered if she felt it as well. *It's okay, Bumper. This won't hurt you.*

*It tickles!*

*Tickling is okay. Just relax.*

It felt as if Bumper were running in excited circles inside her head. Willow blocked the dog and concentrated on the power building inside. "CrystalFire? Do I need to touch you to share the energy?"

"That would be impractical in battle. See if you can send it directly to the blade."

She held her hands out and pointed her fingers at the crystal blade. Closed her eyes, concentrated on the crystal sword, and *pushed* the power toward the faceted blade.

"Gods be damned."

Her eyes flashed open at Taron's soft curse. He sounded almost awestruck. When she looked at the crystal blade, Willow knew why.

The blade vibrated, awash in a blinding silver light. "It worked!" Giddy with success, Willow glanced at Taron. "Can you feel it?"

"Amazing. It feels as if it could fight without me even holding on."

The crash of breaking ceramic echoed in the night. A banshee cry raised chills, and then immediately ended on a sharp note. Willow leapt to her feet. "Now. We have to do this before he gets any stronger."

Taron nodded. With CrystalFire held high, he and Willow leapt over the low berm and raced through the dark cemetery. The glow from the sword lit their path between the silent graves. They headed toward a long row of trees barely visible in the darkness. Newer graves gave way to older, more intricate sites. Flat stones flush with the grass gave way to upright markers, polished granite segued into old, carved headstones and large crypts. Little fences surrounded some—everything from stone to wire to rusting iron.

Light flickered up ahead. The stench of sulfur grew thicker, stronger, until it was almost suffocating.

Another demon howled. Another shriek abruptly ended.

Taron held his hand up for silence and then slipped behind a large, stone crypt. Willow stuck close, ready to draw more power as needed. Her fingers actually tingled with the need to fight, to do something to stop the demon and save Ed, but the night was silent for now.

No. It wasn't. The soft rasp of labored breathing on the far side of the crypt had to be Ed.

He didn't sound good. Slowly Willow slipped around the back of the crypt until she could see Ed. Almost lost in dark shadows, he was barely visible. It appeared he grasped a heavy ax in one hand, but he leaned on it, as if it were a cane and he needed its support to remain upright.

He was an older man. Not at all frail, but certainly not in any shape to house a demon intent on taking over the world. Plus, Willow had to believe that Ed was fighting this horrible thing with all his will. That alone would exhaust any man.

CrystalFire shimmered and Ed turned in their direction.

The light from Taron's sword illuminated Ed's face, and Willow gasped. His eyes glowed a dark, unholy red. Saliva ran down his chin, and there was blood on his hands from myriad cuts and scrapes. He stared at her and shrieked, but it was not Ed Marks looking at her.

No, she felt as if she stared into the eyes of Abyss.

# Chapter 12

It was painful to see Ed this way, yet in his face, that dear, familiar face, Willow saw the same glowing eyes she remembered from the gargoyle, the same look of evil.

Taron touched her shoulder. "Stay back. I don't want to worry about you when I'm swinging this thing."

Like she didn't know that? Men! Still, Willow managed to place one hand on his arm without saying anything insulting. "Be careful, Taron. You don't have to worry about harming Ed. The sword won't let you, and if the demon king knows that, it could put you in danger. Let me try zapping him with sparkles first. It might not run the demon out of his avatar like it did with the others, but it could at least confuse him."

He stared at her a moment. "I don't want you to get hurt, Willow. I'm afraid . . ."

She shook her head. "We don't have time to be afraid. I'll zap him, you see if you can slap him with the flat side of the blade. That's what Dax and Alton do to drive demons out of live avatars. Watch out for that pickax, though. It's deadly."

Taron leaned in close and kissed her. At that moment, Ed screamed, swung the ax over his head and ran straight at them. Willow spun around and shot a flood of blue sparkles pointblank into Ed's face.

He obviously hadn't expected anything like that. The blast of blue energy hit him full on, even though he tried to duck. With a loud shriek, he tripped over the pickax and fell face down. Taron rushed forward and slapped Ed across the shoulders with the flat of the blade. Silver sparks flew and the air sizzled with energy.

The demon inside Ed howled, but he didn't come flying out of the man the way Willow had hoped. Instead, Ed crab-walked away from Taron's blade on all fours, still shrieking. Then, moving like a marionette with a few missing strings, he popped disjointedly to his feet, bent down, and reached for the pickax. Bloodied fingers wrapped around the wooden handle. He brought it up in a powerful overhead swing, still shrieking that banshee wail, and went straight for Willow.

She backed up, tripped over the raised border marking a burial site and went down hard. The air knocked out of her lungs with a loud *whoosh*, but she rolled to one side just in time as she hit the ground. Ed buried the point of the pickax in the dirt mere inches from her thigh. As he struggled to pull the ax free, Willow rolled again, until she'd put a headstone between herself and Ed.

Taron swung his sword again and connected with Ed's arm, striking hard with the flat of his blade. Energy flared. The air crackled around both Taron and Ed, and for a brief moment the contact of blade to arm held Ed immobile. He struggled against the force, still shrieking, before he finally broke away.

He turned and red fire shot from those banshee eyes. Then he shrieked at Taron, spun around, and headed directly for Willow. Again he raised the heavy pickax and swung it over his head. Willow jumped from behind the headstone, pointed all ten fingers at Ed and shot another huge blast of sparkles.

They caught him right in the chest. He dropped the ax and slapped both hands over his heart, still shrieking. His eyes flashed red and spittle flew from his mouth. Taron came in from behind and swung CrystalFire in a deadly arc, but Ed spun out of reach. He stood there, gasping for breath, staring at both of them out of glowing red eyes.

For a moment, for the briefest instant, the red faded and the glow disappeared. Willow was almost sure she caught a glimpse of Ed—of the wonderful man she knew behind those dark brown eyes. She felt terror, remorse, and undeniable fear.

Then he straightened and shook his head. The red glow flashed from his eyes and he turned away and ran. Within seconds he'd disappeared into the darkness.

Blinking, drawing in huge gasps of air, Willow sat down on the headstone. Her fingertips burned from the blasts of energy and she felt totally depleted, much as she had in those earlier battles when she'd fought beside Dax.

If she still had her wings, she knew they'd be drooping.

Slowly, Taron sheathed his sword. He stopped just in front of her, and his head hung low. "It didn't work," he said.

"Actually, it did." Willow reached for his hand and wrapped her fingers around his. As hot as hers were, his felt like ice. "There are still demons here. Bumper can smell them, but the demon king is gone for now, so he's not hunting them. We might not have saved Ed or driven the demon king out, but he's obviously regrouping. Those demons that are still here? They're demons that the demon king won't be able to feed on. Not if we get them first."

Taron slowly nodded and glanced about the dark cemetery. "I hadn't thought of that, but you're right." His smile slowly spread, and Willow's heart melted.

He was, without a doubt, the most wonderful, most handsome man she'd ever seen. He held out his arm. "Will you join me?"

Laughing softly, Willow stood up and curtsied. "Delighted," she said, as if he'd asked her to dance. And she wondered how she knew about dancing, and where the response had come from. Unless she still had the same ability as she'd had as a tiny will-o'-the-wisp, when she'd been charged with gathering the information Dax would need to survive in this different dimension.

She'd never quite figured out how that worked, though she'd always seemed to know what she needed in order to help Dax get along as a believable human. She was still trying to figure it all out when Taron swept her into a tight embrace, leaned in close and kissed her. She hadn't been expecting it— he seemed to pick the oddest times to claim her mouth.

She kissed him back, but she took control and ended it. Taron merely shrugged and backed away. She had a feeling he'd merely given her that small victory. Then she took a deep breath and switched gears.

"Okay, Bumper. Where are the little bastards?"

*Straight ahead there's one inside the stone angel. And over there on your left, I sense one in the carved bird. C'mon, Taron. Bring CrystalFire. We have work.*

"Why do I feel as if everyone's giving me orders?"

Willow laughed and grabbed Taron's hand. "Maybe because we are?"

She risked a quick glance at their linked hands, and didn't even attempt to bite back the huge grin that split her face. She'd just helped run off the demon king with those fingers. It felt really, really good.

Now, all they had to do was figure out a way to get rid of him for good without harming Ed. She knew they could do it. She glanced at Taron and drew a sense of strength from him. Yes. They could do it. Somehow. She just had to have faith.

Dax stared at the blades, all five of them arranged on the long, low table in front of Dawson's couch. There should be six. Eddy should be here, along with her sword, but she was gone and so was DemonSlayer.

He still couldn't believe she was missing. They'd never been separated—not since he'd died and then been reborn. He'd promised her then they'd always be together, but now . . .

Crap. Staring at the blades, he felt lost and uncertain, as if his anchor were missing. The one who held him to this world, this life. The one who kept him from the darkness he sometimes still feared might be part of his soul.

The soul of a man who was once a demon.

Could one ever totally walk away from his beginnings? From what he'd been born to, from the life he'd embraced since time began? Eddy had helped him hold on to this new life. Eddy was the one who gave him the courage to survive as something other than demonkind.

With any luck, their swords would bring Eddy back.

Shimmering across the wooden tabletop with the blue fire of pure diamond were his DemonFire, Alton's HellFire, Dawson's DemonsDeath and Selyn's StarFire. Ginny's beautiful amethyst blade, DarkFire, lay in the center.

They'd arranged the blades like a fan with the points touching.

Dax raised his head and caught Ginny watching him. Thank goodness she didn't look at him with pity. He couldn't take pity right now. He needed her resolve, and Ginny had that in spades. He nodded, acknowledging her unspoken request. "Have DarkFire take the lead. Does she understand what we're asking?"

The amethyst blade pulsed. Ginny ran her fingers over the shimmering facets. "DarkFire? Eddy and DemonSlayer, with the spirit of Selyn's mother, Elda, are lost. We've tried to contact Eddy without any luck. Wherever she is, she's beyond our reach. Can you try to connect with DemonSlayer and help us find them?"

She glanced at Dax and then at her sword. "We're hoping you have better luck than we've had. We thought that maybe, if you shared your energy, it might . . ." She let out a huge, frustrated sigh. "We want to bring them home. Please try and find them."

All of the blades glowed, but none spoke. Ginny stared at them for a moment and then raised her head and looked at Dax.

Her eyes had always fascinated him. Now he found himself caught in the steady gaze of what Alton called Ginny's "tiger's eyes." Eyes that let him gaze directly into her heart, into her soul. He knew without asking that she was devastated by Eddy's loss, but Ginny wasn't about to let it stop her. She was strong and resilient—every inch the tiger.

"DarkFire says it may take awhile, Dax. We'll have to be patient as they search. They can't always cross dimensions, though DarkFire is hoping that, with their energy combined, they'll have better luck."

He sighed. Waiting was never easy. He wasn't sure why, but he had a horrible feeling Eddy had somehow stumbled or been pushed into the void—and the feeling kept growing. He thought of all the time he'd spent in that place that was nothing at all, and he wondered, if that was where Eddy had ended up, how would she handle it? How did a woman who was always planning or doing—or at least thinking about planning and doing—exist in a vacuum?

He pictured her, how she was at night, often talking in her sleep, her body restless, her eyes flickering behind closed lashes.

Sometimes he would wake her from uneasy dreams and they would make love—slow and easy, their bodies coming together in the way of lovers who knew each other so well. It was so hard to realize they'd only been together for a month, not when they'd both lived lifetimes over the past four weeks.

It wasn't a lifetime he could imagine losing.

He and Eddy were perfectly matched as friends, as part-ners, as lovers—at times hot and passionate, but often making love so slow and easy, as if they had all the time in the world, touching and stroking, finding that perfect rhythm until both of them tumbled into orgasm and then into restful sleep.

His body ached with missing her. She'd only been gone for a couple of hours, yet he yearned for her with a pain that might have festered for a lifetime. He hated feeling so useless—unable to do anything but sit here and stare at the shimmer-ing blades.

He wished there were some way he could add his own power to their search.

He ran his fingers over the phoenix tattooed on his chest. Where he'd once carried a colorful snake that was supposed to guard his powers—something that went horribly wrong when a demon's curse turned those powers against him—he now wore the phoenix and its sign of rebirth.

What good was rebirth if the one he loved died?

He couldn't think of that. Refused to consider something so drastic, so horrible, so he went back to worrying about Eddy.

If that was where she'd gone, the silence of the void would drive her nuts.

Just as the silence here, in Dawson Buck's living room, was making him crazy. He stood up, startling the others. "I have to go outside. I can't stay in here. Tell me the minute you hear anything, okay?"

Alton stood and rested his big hand on Dax's shoulder. "Do you want company?"

He shook his head. "No." He laughed, a short, sharp bark that definitely lacked humor. "I may go run a few laps around the pasture. I need to burn off some nervous energy."

"You need to sleep." Alton glanced at the others. "We all

do. We're exhausted—every one of us is at the end of our strength."

Dax nodded in agreement. "Later. I'll be in later. I just . . ." He sighed. "I need to go outside."

Turning quickly away, he walked across the room and out onto the front porch. He didn't want to fall apart in there. Not in front of his friends. They were upset enough by Eddy's disappearance. The last thing they needed was to witness his loss of control, and Dax knew he was very close to losing it.

He leaned against a post in front of the house and listened to the sounds of the night. Crickets chirped, and he heard what had to be an owl nearby. Dawson had pointed one out to him, with its huge yellow eyes and the tufts of feathers atop its head that looked like little horns.

Which, of course, made him think of demons and Eddy and what in the hell could have happened. He'd watched her step through the portal, and then he'd waited. There was always the sense of her going away when she crossed through an energy portal—that mental connection that was so much a part of them was severed by the dimensional change.

Had this separation felt any different? He tried to remember, but nothing had seemed out of place, so he'd not noticed anything different.

Except she hadn't returned. She was out there, somewhere. They'd searched the portals, tried pausing in the midst and had no luck. You were either on one side or the other—there really wasn't a middle to those things—almost as if the portals themselves were two dimensional, not three.

*Eddy? Where the hell are you, Eddy?*

It could only be the void. Had to be. Where else could she have gone without a trace? He didn't remember sliding down the pole. Didn't recall sitting on the front porch with his head in his hands, sobbing like a child.

Couldn't recall ever feeling so lost, so entirely alone as he did at this moment. She completed him. She was his soul, his reason for everything. For fighting demonkind, for getting up every morning and facing a new day in this strange new world, each day filled with more battles and more risks.

He'd not counted on risking Eddy. His own life wasn't important. Not like hers.

He sensed movement and hoped whoever it was would just go away. He should have known better. Alton sat down beside him and threw an arm over his shoulders.

Dax didn't try and move away. He knew Alton needed this connection every bit as much as he did, and he could deny it all he wanted, but Dax truly appreciated Alton's offer of comfort.

He knew the man loved Eddy as if she were part of his family, and in many ways, she was. They were all family, connected by the common desire to fight demonkind, but it was even more than that.

This body that was now his had belonged to a soldier—a brave man who had stormed the beaches at Normandy during one of Earth's great wars. Dax had been with the man as he relived that fight, and he'd learned much about the strength of comrades in arms, the bond that connected those who risked death together.

It was blood shared in battle, a tensile strength more powerful than any genetic connection. No, the family he had now was unlike anything he could ever have imagined . . . before.

They loved one another, and they'd come together to form an unbreakable bond. It was stronger than any ties based on blood relationships—this was a brotherhood built on love and trust, on the knowledge that someone in the group would always have your back.

Only this brotherhood was strengthened by the women

who were so much a part of the whole. Ginny and Selyn . . . and Eddy Marks. Dear gods, he needed her.

Needed each and every one of them, but Eddy most of all.

He and Alton had fought side by side—with each other, with Eddy, and with every other person inside the house. They were more than friends, more than family, though that's how they thought of themselves—as a family.

And family didn't let other members suffer alone. Knowing someone shared his pain made it easier to bear. Easier to think through the options, maybe figure out a way to find Eddy.

"They're still searching," Alton said, interrupting Dax's convoluted thoughts. "We'll find her. Nine hells, man . . . I'm so sorry."

Dax turned and gazed into his best friend's green eyes. "I know we will. Thank you. You've reminded me why I should never give up hope."

Alton gave him a very tired smile. "And how did I manage that?"

"By coming out here and reminding me I'm not the only one worried about Eddy. As individuals we're each pretty tough, but as a group we can't be beaten. I believe that with all my heart."

"Good. Then that means you'll come inside, eat some of the dinner that Dawson's putting on the table, and then get some sleep. Our swords will keep searching, but we need to rest if we're going to be any good to anyone."

Dax nodded. "Ginny already fed me, you know. Made me eat a sandwich."

"So you'll eat another one. C'mon."

Dax grabbed the tail of his shirt and wiped his eyes. Then he stood, grabbed Alton's hand, and tugged him to his feet. They stood for a moment, each looking at the other.

Chuckling softly, Dax said, "I'm thinking that if I don't listen to you, and Eddy finds out, she'll kick my butt."

Alton laughed softly as Dax opened the door. "There is

that," he said. Then he led the way inside with Dax following close behind.

The swords still glowed on the low table. Their Lemurian and human partners had moved to the dining room to eat. No one mentioned Dax's red eyes or the husky sound to his voice, and that was a good thing.

It meant they understood, that they felt the same way. They understood his grief and his fear, and they shared his resolve.

It meant they were all going to do whatever they could, no matter the risk, to find the woman he loved.

# Chapter 13

Dawn was near. At least that appeared to be the source of light on the eastern horizon—it must herald the coming of the sun. He'd missed sunrise his first morning here. Taron leaned against the twisted oak at the edge of the cemetery and gazed at the multi-hued sky. His very first dawning in this dimension in many thousands of years. Awakening beside a full-sized Willow yesterday morning had taken priority. Even now, with the colors spreading overhead, Willow drew his gaze, away from the multi-hued atmosphere. He watched as she made a final pass along the edge of the older graves, checking each small statue, pausing and then moving on to the next. As tired as he was, Taron knew she had to be ready to fold, and yet she still moved with such grace and beauty, as if to music. They'd spent hours killing demons—more than they'd expected to find hiding amid the small statues and ceramic figurines decorating the hundreds of graves, yet Willow never faltered. What kept them going, what motivated them, was the realization that the demon king could have easily absorbed enough power from the many demons hiding here to repel any foe.

Taron had a feeling that the damned creature might not have needed an avatar if he'd been allowed to feed without interference. Then what would have happened to Ed?

Willow paused in front of him and sighed. "Bumper doesn't sense any more demons and neither do I. Let's go home." She stood on her toes and kissed him.

He closed his eyes and kissed her back, and it was all he could do not to take her in his arms and hold her tightly enough to hang on to her forever. What an amazing woman! She'd fought bravely last night and then, for hours after, she'd worked beside him to find every last demonic soul hiding here among the graves.

He forced himself to end the kiss, and it was almost painful, pulling away. "We can't do this, you know. We need to stop, no matter how good it feels."

She didn't say a word, but she didn't push for more, either. He wished he knew what she was thinking. At least he'd stayed entirely in control. It wasn't easy. Not with Willow smiling up at him with those beautiful blue eyes and now, with her slightly pouty, just kissed mouth mere inches from his.

"Let's go," he said. He kissed her nose and tried to give her a casual grin. That wasn't easy, either. Not when he wanted so much more. "I need food and a shower." He took her hand, smiled at her, and tugged lightly so that she'd follow.

"I need you."

*Well, nine hells and then some.*

She dropped that little bombshell as if it were nothing at all. He stood there, blindsided, with his mouth hanging open like a damned fool, but Willow merely winked and turned away as if she'd said nothing mind blowing at all.

Bemused, Taron followed. How in the hell had he lost control of the situation so quickly?

And how was it that a woman who had only been a real woman for a matter of hours could so quickly figure out how to use all those womanly secrets he'd heard of?

Gods be damned, but it did put the male portion of a population at a distinct disadvantage. Musing over the many things he had yet to learn, Taron followed Willow through the quiet streets of pre-dawn Evergreen, alert to the threat of demonkind, but even more powerfully aware of the subtle threat of the woman ahead.

Aware as well, that this was one threat he'd have to fight. The risk was too great, the consequences too dear. Yet no matter what he told himself, his desire and his need grew stronger every moment he spent with her. She was absolutely fascinating and definitely forbidden, and gods-be-damned, but he wanted her as well.

Actually, as much as she loved rattling his cage, and as much as she wanted to get up close and personal with the sexy Lemurian following behind, Willow knew the fight against demons came first, and she really had to take a detour by the old library building.

If the demon king had gone there to hide out, they might have a good chance of taking him down in the light of day, now that he'd gone without the energy he'd hoped to gain last night.

They'd discovered that demon powers were noticeably weaker when the sun was shining, and sunrise wasn't all that far off. The eastern sky was well beyond the gun-metal gray of predawn, brightening now in glowing shades of red and orange, purple and gold.

Lights glowed brightly through windows of the houses they passed, and the sound of traffic rushing by on the interstate had grown steadily louder. Time was passing, a new day dawning.

Ed had been possessed by the demon king for almost thirty-six hours. How long could he last and still retain his humanity? Willow had been almost certain she'd seen hints of Ed last night, a brief glance of the man she'd known since she'd first entered Earth's dimension with Dax just one short month ago. Then, just as quickly as he'd surfaced, he'd disappeared again beneath the evil that was the demon king.

She glanced at Taron. "Come with me. I want to check on the library. Just in case . . ."

"Do you think he's gone back there?"

She shook her head. "We'll never know if we don't stop and look." She didn't wait for his answer. One thing Willow had learned watching Eddie and Ginnie was to think something through and then act. If you waited for others to make up their minds, opportunity could be lost.

With a man like Taron who loved to question everything, it could easily be lost forever. She shot him a quick look and picked up her pace. He followed without question, though she knew the questions were all lined up in nice, neat rows, somewhere in that brilliant scholar's mind of his, just waiting.

The image that popped into her head had her fighting a smile. He wouldn't understand at all what she found so funny.

She took a side street that brought them directly to the back of the library building. It appeared even more desolate in the early morning, lacking the soft shadows that came with the muted light of evening. It felt as abandoned as it appeared, but she went to the back anyway, to the double doors that led into the cellar.

"Do you think he might be in here?" Taron grabbed the handle on one of the doors.

Willow shook her head. "I don't know. I don't really sense anything, do you?"

He didn't answer, but he tugged. The door didn't budge. "I think it's locked. Any other ways to get in?"

"I'll check." Willow walked slowly around the perimeter of the big building. She spotted a couple of broken windows, but they were too small to allow Ed inside. By the time she'd gone all the way and circled back to Taron, he was talking to a sheriff's deputy who didn't appear very happy to see strangers snooping around his town's abandoned library so early in the morning.

She thought the man looked familiar. *Bumper? Do you recognize the guy in the uniform?*

*Deputy Milton Bradford. He's a friend of Eddy's.*

*I thought so. Good girl! Thanks.*

Pasting a smile on her face, Willow walked up with her hand out. "Deputy Bradford! Good morning. How are you?"

He spun around and stared at her. "Do I know . . . ?"

"I'm Eddy Marks's friend, Willow. This is another friend of hers from college. Meet Taron. I was just showing him the old library." Still smiling, she grinned at Taron as he shook hands with the deputy. "Taron's an architect. I wanted him to see this gorgeous old building. Don't you think it would be just perfect to fix up for the community?"

Milton scratched his head and stared at Taron. "Why didn't you just say something? You coulda told me what you were doing."

Taron merely shrugged and smiled at Willow. "Well, you know how it is," he said. *Willow? Just how is it?*

She bit back a laugh as the deputy nodded and said, "True. You even mention anything to the wrong people and the story's all over town. I can get the keys if you'd like to see inside."

"Thank you." Willow put a hand on Taron's shoulder. *Not now. If Ed's in there we'd have way too many questions to answer.*

"I'll remember that," Taron said. "Willow just wanted me to get a quick look at the building's exterior before the sun was fully up. Shadows, you know. The lighting."

Again, the deputy nodded. "I understand. If you need to get in, just stop by the sheriff's substation. It's at the south end of Lassen Boulevard."

He glanced at the sky. The colors had gone from pale pink to blood red over the past couple of minutes. "Looks like we might be in for a storm." He turned and grinned at Willow. "You know the old saying, 'red sky at dawning, sailor take warning.'"

Willow grinned and nodded like she knew what he was talking about. And she did, kind of. There was a similar saying in Eden.

*Red sky at dawn. Good weather's gone.* Or the other old one that she really hoped wasn't valid. *Red sun on the rise. Beware, take care, or someone dies.*

Bumper's perky voice popped into her somber thoughts. *Maybe it'll be the demon king.*

*Let's hope so.*

The deputy tipped his cap and headed back to his car. Willow let out a deep sigh of relief. Taron cocked one eyebrow and stared at her. "Architect?"

She shrugged. "It was all I could think of. What did he say?"

"Before or after he threatened to arrest me? I'm glad you knew who he was. I wasn't sure if Alton had used compulsions on him before, so I didn't know if they'd still work."

"He has, actually. A number of times. You need to thank Bumper. I don't really know him. I mean, I recognized him, but I couldn't remember his name. Bumper did, though. She's better at names than I am. Thanks, girl!"

*I did good, didn't I Willow? I smell demon here. Do you? I smell Ed, too, but not really strong. I think it's from him hiding here yesterday. I don't think they're in the cellar. I wonder where they went? I hope Ed's okay. He's nice to me. He always gives me kibble. I love kibble, Willow. Could you taste some kibble for me?*

She loved Bumper. Really she did, but the dog was going to drive her absolutely nuts. "How about bacon and eggs instead, Bumper? We've got plenty at the house. Ed must have just made a trip to the store, because the refrigerator is full of goodies."

*I like bacon, Willow. Let's go cook bacon.*

"Bumper says bacon's okay." Willow grabbed Taron's hand. "I need to eat, shower, and sleep, in that order."

Taron slipped an arm around her waist and pulled her close. She suddenly found herself staring directly into those gorgeous emerald green eyes of his.

"Are you sure that's all you need?"

He was going to kiss her. She was absolutely positive, and just thinking of the way his mouth would feel on hers had her going all weak in the knees, all soft and warm and welcoming in another part of her anatomy. She blinked, lost in a sensual haze that was growing thicker by the second.

He hovered there, his lips mere inches from hers, but reality intruded. She shook her head, a short, sharp jerk that broke the spell. "Yes," she said, speaking with as much firm conviction as she could force into that one word. Of course, it was conviction she didn't feel at all with Taron so close, his lips almost touching hers, his arm a firm anchor holding her still. "That's all I need. And you, Taron, need to make up your mind. You know how I feel."

She managed to grab hold of his hand, lift his arm away from her waist, and walk away. He followed, but she heard his soft chuckle and knew he was well aware how much she'd wanted his kiss. She glanced over her shoulder. "You can't have it both ways, Taron. To kiss or not to kiss . . . that really is the question."

She quickly turned forward, but she didn't miss the frown that crossed his features. Damn him, though. What did he want from her? For a guy who'd never had anything to do with women, he'd certainly figured out how to keep her off balance while keeping her attention. Unfortunately, he didn't have a clue how to hold onto her. No idea at all.

Mainly because he obviously didn't have a clue what he wanted. First he thought they could have sex without entanglements, but even with her lack of experience Willow was certain that never worked. Then he didn't want to touch her at all, but he couldn't seem to keep his hands to himself, which left it to Willow.

He chose that moment to grab her hand and hold it tightly as they walked. So much for keeping him at arm's length, though it did appear it was going to be up to her. Not easy when she'd already told him what she wanted.

It didn't really matter though, did it? They had to get their priorities straight. Ed was out there, probably terrified and even in pain. He didn't seem to be here, so there wasn't much they could do until nightfall, but at least they'd kept the demon from gaining more strength. With any luck, tonight would be the night they stopped him.

*Luck.* Was all of this really based on luck? She looked down at the way Taron's fingers linked so perfectly with hers. Then she raised her head and found herself staring into brilliant green eyes that seemed to ask more questions than Willow knew how to answer.

Taron just sighed and smiled at her, but he walked steadily beside her without complaint. Like he knew that, no matter what Willow said, he was still going to get his way.

And she knew he was right.

Even though he'd told her that sex was a one time deal, she had no doubt she was going to end up in that big bed with him, naked and compliant, falling even deeper in love with a man who would never love her back.

What was she going to do with him?

Even more important, what was Taron going to do about her?

Now that was the question she'd love to see answered. And maybe that was the way she needed to look at this. Smiling, Willow tugged lightly and picked up the pace. They really needed to get something to eat and a few hours sleep.

*Ed, hang on. We'll get you out of this.*

Or die trying.

She glanced once again at the eastern sky and the huge,

rugged shape of Mount Shasta looming over the town. The sun was almost up and the sky had turned to dark crimson.

Red spilled out of the sky and spread over the snow-covered mountain. Willow shivered. It looked exactly like fresh blood covering the pristine slope.

*Eddy? Are you awake?*

*I think so. It's hard to tell the difference between waking and sleeping, DemonSlayer.*

*I guess that's right. I've been a spirit for so long, it's almost all I remember.*

*Am I dead?*

*I don't believe you are. You know when you die. I was aware of death. When I died, I didn't go to the void. I went to Mother Crystal.*

*Who's that?*

*The crystal caverns where Taron replicated swords for the Forgotten Ones. They're alive. They are one and She is the heart of Lemuria. We call her Mother Crystal. When a brave and honorable warrior dies, that warrior's spirit goes back to Mother Crystal's womb to await rebirth.*

Eddy thought laughter. There was no way to make the sound. *That's all well and good for Lemurian warriors. I'm human.*

*Not anymore. You are immortal and you carry crystal. When you die, you'll be reborn just as I was.*

Oh, crap. This time she was certain she made the sound of laughing. She was almost certain she heard herself snort. *You mean I'll get stuck as partners with some idiot like you have? How can you stand me? I'm not so sure I want that.*

There was a long pause. When DemonSlayer spoke, she was most definitely not teasing. *I would never choose to serve an idiot. Don't insult both of us, Eddy.*

*I'm sorry. Really, Elda. I do apologize. I'm scared. I say stupid things when I'm afraid.* She sighed, paused, and then switched gears. *You woke me. Was there something you wanted?*

At least the voice of DemonSlayer, who had been Selyn's mother, Elda, sounded mollified. *Try and link with me. I sense contact, but my ability to receive in the void is very weak. I need your help.*

*How?*

*Open your mind and push. Give me your energy.*

How in the hell? But she did what DemonSlayer asked and immediately sensed a burst of energy moving out of her and into something else. Hopefully into DemonSlayer's consciousness.

Time seemed to pass, but there was no way of knowing how much. Eddy waited. She let her thoughts float, open and accepting. Tried to imagine Dax floating like this for so many years, nothing but consciousness, a mind without form.

How had he managed it without going utterly insane?

*Eddy?*

*DemonSlayer! Who was it? Who was trying to communicate? Did you hear them?*

*DarkFire has reached me. It took the combined power of all five of our companions' blades, but we made brief contact. Dax is devastated by your disappearance. They did not know where you were, but now they do. They'll figure out a way to bring us safely home. I sent a message from you to Dax. I told him you love him. I hope I did not overstep my bounds.*

*Thank you. No. You did not overstep. I do love him, and I miss him so much! But now what?*

*We wait. Contact has been made. If they found us once, they will find us again.*

*Dax!* I'm here, she thought. *Please find me. I love you. I need you.* She said it over and over again as if her plea were her mantra, but DemonSlayer's voice had faded away and

Eddy's thoughts were merely her own. Finally, she stopped, but she floated on in a formless sea, all alone, an insubstantial, inconsequential bit of nothing in the ultimate scheme of things.

She wondered what was going on with everyone. Was her father okay? She worried about him, about that very brief yet powerful sense of connection to him that she'd felt. Was he all right, or had something awful happened?

She'd tried to contact him without any luck before she got sucked into the void. She'd called a number of times—he always answered the phone when she was away. Always.

Except when she'd tried to call him today. Or was it yesterday? A week ago? Dax had said that time did not exist in the void, so she had no idea how long she'd been trapped here. How long since she'd last spoken with her father.

Where was he? She knew Dax was okay. Maybe it was time to concentrate on finding her father.

Dax stared at the fading glimmer of purple light shimmering along the amethyst blade and hated the fact he'd been right.

Eddy was in the void.

DarkFire had made contact with DemonSlayer. Eddy was okay, but how in the hell had she ended up in the void? At least they knew she and DemonSlayer were alive, but they were trapped in a place where they didn't belong.

How was he going to get them back?

Dax shuddered. His imagination was running overtime, and he rubbed his hands over his arms to drive away the sense of something crawling over his skin. He'd spent way too much time in the void and that experience would forever haunt him.

How in the hell was Eddy coping? She was life and action, color and song, her mind and body in constant motion. What would the total sensory depravation of the void do to one like Eddy?

HellFire shimmered and everyone's attention immediately went to Alton's sword.

"Mother Crystal is the only hope. Only she can bring Eddy and DemonSlayer back."

Dax stared at Alton. "Who the hell is Mother Crystal?"

Alton shook his head. "Haven't got a clue. HellFire?"

Once again Alton's blade came to life. "The crystal caves where Taron and his blade labored are sentient. They are the heart and soul of Lemuria. They are one, and She is called Mother Crystal. She is the womb where the souls of all brave and true warriors rest and await rebirth within a sentient sword. We must go there, to the source of power, and ask her to bring Eddy Marks and DemonSlayer home."

Light faded from the crystalline facets and silence filled the large room. Finally Alton stood. "I'll get to work on the portal to Lemuria. Ginny, can you help me? We need to open them anyway, but if the crystal caves are the only way to get Eddy back, that's where we have to go."

Dax stood. "How long will it take?"

"It's easier to seal one shut than it is to open the gods-be-damned things. At least a couple of hours, though with Ginny and DarkFire helping, it might not take as long."

"Is there anything I can do?" Dax grabbed DemonFire off the table and sheathed the sword.

Dawson stepped closer. "Selyn and I are planning to patrol the other portals, to make sure none of the ones to Abyss have been reopened." He sheathed DemonsDeath as Selyn reached for StarFire. "Dax, why don't you come with us? Alton can reach us telepathically as soon as he's got a working portal."

Dax nodded. He had no idea how to open a portal and would only get in the way. It wasn't the answer he wanted, but it would have to suffice. He had to do something. Had to keep busy or he'd go insane with worry. Eddy was out there, alone in a place that could only be described as nowhere. As nothing. She'd have no sense of anything beyond her own thoughts.

This was the existence she'd saved him from—an existence that was little more than a living death—and there was nothing he could do to help her right now. Sick at heart, frustrated beyond words, he turned to Alton. "Good luck, my friend. Please hurry. I . . ." He sighed. There was nothing to say. Nothing at all that would make anything better.

Alton threw his arms around Dax and hugged him. "I know. We'll hurry. Listen for our call and be ready. We're going to the main portal at Bell Rock. It takes the same time to open a small one as a large one, and that gateway gives us a more direct route to the caves. Ginny? You ready?"

She nodded, stood on her toes, and gave Dax a quick kiss on the cheek before she followed Alton out the door. Dax watched the big Yukon peel out of the driveway, and a fleeting thought popped into his head. Why did they still rent that dumb SUV?

All of them still acted as if who and what they were was only temporary. A rented car, a borrowed room here with Dawson, a sense of danger their constant companion. Would life ever settle down? Would this war against demonkind never end?

Would he ever hold Eddy in his arms again?

"C'mon, Dax. Let's go."

Dawson stood by the door with the keys in his hand. Selyn had already gone outside to the SUV and waited in the backseat.

"Looks like I'm riding shotgun," he said, attempting a lightness he didn't feel. "Where are we headed first?"

Dawson walked out with Dax right behind him, but he paused on the step. "Boynton Canyon. After that we'll check

Red Rock Crossing. We'll go to the Airport vortex last, since that's the last one we sealed."

"The one where we lost Eddy."

Dawson didn't answer. He merely nodded and quickly turned away. Dax followed him out to the car, but his mind was spinning and his heart felt like a lead weight in his chest. How had they lost her? How could she possibly have disappeared between one moment and the next?

Did it matter? No. All that mattered was finding Eddy and bringing her back. Dax got into Dawson's SUV and slammed the door shut behind him. The sun was already well above the red rocks and birds sang as if they faced another perfect day.

He fastened the seat belt and tried to relax as Dawson backed up, turned around, and headed down the long driveway. How could everything look so beautiful? So absolutely normal?

It felt wrong. So totally wrong for the world to keep spinning when his own reality was twisted and lost in despair. When the true love of his life was lost. Alone, probably frightened, and lost in the void.

He sent a prayer to whichever gods watched over demon-slayers. There had to be one, somewhere, didn't there?

# Chapter 14

Hiding here in the shadows had taken the last of his strength, but at least the bitch hadn't found him. He'd been worried when she made that loop around the building, but it appeared he'd once again outsmarted the idiots. Let them look in the cellar all they wanted. He rather preferred it here in the attic where he had a view of the town and the stupid humans who lived here.

So oblivious—they had no idea their lives were about to change forever. He sighed and found a spot in one dark corner where he could spend the day resting. He'd not planned on having to conserve energy quite as carefully, but the bastards had definitely screwed up his energy source. All those wonderful demon souls wasted. Not merely sent to the void, but actually dead and gone. Forever.

He shuddered, thinking of the finality of that final death. He needed that damned demonslayer's life force or the same future awaited him as well.

No. He would not even think of such an end. He would think, instead, of how he might reevaluate his plans to ensure success. He'd not consumed nearly enough demons last night, and he was actually tired. What was it with this human body? It appeared to have needs he didn't understand, but it only had to last one more night—two at the most.

He'd expected Dax to appear before now. The ex-demon no longer had his woman to worry about. Now that had been a brilliant move—catching her at precisely the right moment as she passed through the energy vortex. What were the odds of the father connecting to the daughter at the only time when she could be mentally pushed out of the portal and into the void, using the power of the vortex?

It was about time something went his way.

He sighed and tried to find a comfortable position, but the floor was damned hard and this body's sensory input was letting him know it preferred comfort. He spied an old chair against one wall, a long, low couch that would give him a more comfortable place to rest. Shoving himself to his feet, he limped across the uneven floor.

There was a bunch of crap piled on the chair, but he knocked everything off with a sweep of his arm. Dust flew. He sneezed. That was certainly a new experience. Sneezing. He wiped his face with one filthy sleeve and then slowly lay down on the lumpy couch. It took him a bit of squirming to find a position that was moderately comfortable. Demons didn't really sleep, but it appeared this human needed rest. He could animate it with his own power, but he hated to waste any energy he'd be unable to replace. So be it. He needed to be strong. Dax was certain to show up tonight, and he'd be waiting.

Lying back on the dusty couch, he closed his eyes. He sensed the human stirring in the back of his mind, but the man was much too weak to manipulate this body on his own.

The physical shell was next to worthless at this point, but as an avatar it would have to do for the short time that he needed one. Even if the damned thing died, he could still use it. It would take a bit more energy—energy he really didn't have to waste—but the payoff would be worth it. He held up his hand and stared at it. Covered in scrapes and small cuts, it bled sluggishly, as if the ability to heal had been compromised.

How did these creatures survive with such easily damaged bodies? He thought about his demonform—the powerful legs, the four muscular arms and the talons and fangs and hard scales. Soon, it would be his forever. He could dump this worthless piece of crap and rule with the perfect body of a demon god.

Patience. He had to have patience. Dax would be here tonight. He was positive the ex-demon's disgusting sense of honor would draw him to rescue the human. Once he had Dax . . .

His eyes slipped shut, his body stilled, though a smile played about his lips. Just a few hours. That was all he needed. A few hours to rest and regain his strength, and then he would have more than he needed—and he'd have it forever.

With that thought in mind, he let go of the last threads of consciousness and the darkness settled in around him.


The demon let go and Ed's consciousness burst into life. It was his fault! His fault that Eddy was somehow trapped in the same place where Dax had languished for so long, where Eddy's ex-demon had feared he would end up after his work on Earth ended.

Now how in the hell was Ed going to get his daughter out of the void? He'd waited for what felt like hours for the damned creature to sleep, but finally he'd felt the shift in power when the demon's mind faded into darkness—faded and left Ed almost alone in his ruined body.

But what the hell could he do? He couldn't go anywhere. His physical self was an absolute mess. According to the demon's mind, it had "seriously degraded" over the past hours. Now that was an understatement as far as Ed could tell, but he didn't mind. He'd not been allowed to eat or sleep since the demon had taken control, thank goodness. As much as he hated the thought of life ending, with any luck the body that had housed Ed Marks for almost seven decades would die, making it harder for the creature to harm Eddy or Dax.

Without an avatar, the demon would be forced back to Abyss. Enough of the demon's thoughts bled over into Ed's mind when the creature was thinking. He knew what was coming—knew that the goal was to steal Dax's life force.

He also knew that the demon figured he could still use Ed's body, even if it was dead. Not if Ed Marks had anything to do with it, but how could he fight an entity like the demon king?

What in heaven's name could he do? How could he protect Eddy and Dax? Damn, but he loved Dax like his own son, and Ed knew if he had to die, Dax was the perfect one to take care of his baby girl for all eternity. If he'd chosen a man for Eddy, he couldn't have done any better than Dax.

The poor boy must be frantic by now—Eddy lost in the void and her father just lost. Did they even know what had happened to him? He'd not talked to Eddy the day he was taken. His only contact since—that brief mental link—was what got her into this damned mess.

Lying there in the filthy attic, he thought of the things he wished he could say. Words he would speak if he had the chance, and he poured his heart and soul into the thoughts that would haunt him forever.

*Eddy? Eddy, I wish you could hear me. I'm so sorry, sweetie. If I hadn't called out to you when I did, the demon never would have found you, never would have had the ability to shove you out of the portal and into the void.*

*He somehow used the power of the vortex. I wish I knew how to help. I wish I could tell you how proud I am of you, how much I love you, but it might be too late. For what it's worth, I have always been so proud of you and so glad you're my daughter. Your mom was proud, too, and she loved you so much.*

He sensed a pulse, as if a heart beat nearby. Then Eddy's voice burst into his thoughts.

*Dad? I can hear you! Where are you? I'm in the void, that place Dax talked about. I'm here with DemonSlayer. Why is it too late? What's happened to you? Can you hear me?*

Eddy? He wasn't just imagining her. Fate wouldn't be that cruel . . . couldn't be. Ed focused his thoughts and tried to pinpoint the source of that familiar voice. *I hear you, sweetie.* He hoped the demon wouldn't notice the tears running down his face. Hoped the bastard wouldn't wake up for a long, long time. *Talk to me, Eddy. Tell me what you know. Maybe we can help each other.*

Willow stepped out of the shower, toweled dry, and grabbed Eddy's old bathrobe off the hook by the door. She brushed her hair back and twisted it into a ponytail that she tied up with a bright red scrunchy.

She stared at herself in the mirror and wondered how she could already have such dark circles under her eyes. For all intents and purposes, those eyes were only two days old.

*Bumper? I'm sorry I didn't make bacon for you. I'm just too tired.*

*Me, too, Willow. Don't worry, though. It's okay.*

Of course, Bumper's long, shuddering sigh was a reminder that it wasn't entirely okay, but Willow refused to feel guilty about not cooking breakfast. Cereal and fruit were just fine.

Besides, Taron seemed to expect her to cook for him, and she wasn't about to fall into that role. She knew exactly what Lemurian men expected of their women.

Not this girl. She wanted to be just like Eddy and Ginny. Strong women—brave and self-assured. Confident and tough as any of the men.

Thank goodness she had a couple of really good role

models, or she might be sucked in by that feeling to put her own needs and wants aside so she could take care of her man.

Even if he wasn't really her man.

To all nine hells with it! She was tired and her brain did not need to spin in circles over things that she couldn't change. The only person she had control over was Willow. Taron would have to make up his own mind.

Willow welcomed love. She might not know very much, but she was certain she was strong enough to fall in love even knowing it couldn't work. Not when the object of that love was a hard-headed Lemurian.

She marched out of the bathroom accompanied by a billowing cloud of steam and her own sense of righteous anger. Walked across the room to the bed, prepared to tell Taron he was going to have to stay on his side. She was tired and she needed her sleep—what she didn't need was any more confusion than she already felt.

Taron was sound asleep. He'd unbraided his hair and it spread out over the pillow in a scarlet fan of pure silk. She stood there, staring at him, and felt all her powerful convictions wavering.

Truth be told, she'd fallen in love with him the first time she saw him deep in that Lemurian prison cell, so it was a little too late to decide now that she wasn't going to love the guy. She slipped the robe off her shoulders and stood there entirely naked, watching him sleep, and the truth continued to beat at her thoughts.

Finally, she accepted the inevitable and crawled into bed beside him. She lay there for a moment, propped up on one elbow, staring at him. He slept so deeply he showed absolutely no awareness of her at all.

Something she might as well accept. She'd fallen in love with a flawed man, one unwilling to take a chance on her or on love. As disappointing as that was, it was his choice, not hers, to take the coward's way out.

Feeling equally brave and miserable, she lay there a moment longer absorbing the heat from his body, the soft sounds of his steady breathing, the mere fact he lay beside her. *I can't change how you feel about me, Taron of Libernus, but I can be true to the way I feel about you.*

With that thought firmly established, she relaxed against the mattress and closed her eyes. For however many days she had, she was going to stay true. So what if he refused to see what was right there in front of him? That was Taron's problem. She wasn't about to make it hers.


She had no idea her thoughts were as clear as ink on a printed page. No idea how much it hurt to see himself through her innocent eyes. Taron lay quietly beside Willow, listening to the sound of her soft breathing, aching inside. Wanting her with a combination of arousal and need, pain and fear, and lust and a pure and simple love that went beyond explanation.

And of all those feelings, those needs of his, the simplest was the most difficult of all. He loved her, and by loving Willow, he'd damned her.

Both his heart and body had betrayed him. He'd been intrigued by her from the beginning, but once she'd gained her size, he'd forced himself to see her as a beautiful experiment. A chance to experience something he'd heard of but never really desired for himself.

He knew humans were different, that even the Edenites understood love in its purest form, but many Lemurians had chosen differently. They'd known there were not enough women and had pulled themselves out of the marriage pool—essentially choosing, as Taron had chosen, lives of study and self-improvement. They considered themselves above physical and emotional connections.

What fools. What damned fools, and he was the biggest

fool of all. He'd actually believed the load of crap he'd fed himself, that he could be a scholar and a philosopher, a student of life by placing himself above those other needs. How in the nine hells could any man expect to understand that which he'd never truly experienced?

Now he understood the light he'd seen in Alton's eyes when he spoke of Ginny. He knew why Gaia was willing to stand beside Artigos the Younger, even though he'd failed her worse than he'd failed their people.

Love. They knew what love was, while he, a man who honored learning, who believed one had to be above those simpler needs, had failed the one who mattered most.

He'd fallen in love with Willow, and by doing that, he'd condemned her. Even now, as he fought every instinct he had, every sense of desire that told him to hold her now, to make love to her and let her know he meant it, even as he fought his deepest desires, he knew he was going to lose.

It was too late, and he was too weak.

He would make love to her again because he had no other choice. He would tell her he loved her, because to ignore those feelings building inside him would be to continue a lie.

And then, somehow, he had to figure out how to protect her. How to keep her from reaping the horrible fate that had been predicted so long ago.

It was going to happen tonight. He knew, somehow, that everything was locked together—saving Ed, beating the demon king, loving Willow. The "final battle" that Crystal-Fire had warned him of was coming.

He just wished he knew where he fit into all of this. Wished his sword didn't have such a low opinion of him that the damned thing only spoke when it absolutely had to.

He wished Alton were around. He could use the advice of a friend. A friend who'd actually been there—who'd fallen in love, and understood the pain that could come from the most wonderful emotion a man could experience.

He raised up on one elbow and watched Willow sleep. She smiled and turned to him, snuggling close against his chest. Giving in to exhaustion, no longer quite certain how to fight the feelings growing stronger by the second, or even if he should, Taron lay down beside her once again, pulled her into his arms and drifted away.

Alton glanced up as the portal on the far side of the chamber shimmered. Dawson, Selyn, and Dax stepped through from the Sedona side and headed straight for the Lemurian gateway.

"Are you done?"

Dax looked like hell. Alton couldn't imagine what it must feel like, to have the one he loved so totally lost to him. "I haven't tested it yet, but yeah, I think we're done." He glanced at Ginny. "Why don't you see what DarkFire has to say?"

She nodded, but it was obvious the strain was telling on his woman, too. She and Eddy had been best friends since they were children. Eddy's disappearance was tearing Ginny apart.

Without any preamble, Ginny unsheathed DarkFire and thrust her sword into the swirling energy that was the new portal to Lemuria.

At least he hoped that was where it led. A moment later, she pulled the sword back through. "DarkFire? What's the verdict?"

"I could hear the golden veil up ahead. The passageway is clear. Everything appears to be working perfectly."

The golden veil was a rather noisy illusion marking the boundary between Lemuria and the portals to other dimensions. Alton let out a breath he hadn't realized he'd been holding. He'd opened portals just a couple of times in the past, so he wasn't really comfortable without testing the gateway to make sure it went where it was supposed to.

Only Lemurians in all their national hubris would choose the illusion of a waterfall of molten gold to mark the gateway to their world. If DarkFire sensed the golden veil, it meant he'd created a proper portal that went where it was supposed to go. It was time. He adjusted his grasp on HellFire and glanced over his shoulder. "Dawson? Do you need to contact your assistant before we go?"

"No. He knows he's in charge of the clinic until further notice." Dawson slung an arm over Selyn's shoulders. "Now that he understands what's going on, he's perfectly okay with running the show on the home front. He'll tell me if any more animals show up with signs of possession. Said he'd leave messages on my cell phone, so I'm ready if you guys are."

"Dax?"

Eddy's ex-demon shot a quick glance in Alton's direction that could probably freeze that illusory gold. "Right," Alton said. "Let's go."

He slipped through the portal with the others following close behind, and reached out for Taron the moment they were inside the Lemurian dimension. It was second nature to call his closest friend, but for some reason, Taron didn't answer.

Next he called out for Roland, once a trusted sergeant and now the new captain of the Lemurian Guard. *Hey, Roland! Everything okay here?*

*Alton! Yes. Paladins and guardsmen are doing joint training today. Do you need me for anything? I can break away if I must.*

*Thanks, but for now we're okay. Ginny, Daws, Selyn, Dax, and I are headed to the crystal caves. Eddy's been taken, Roland. Appears she's lost in the void and we've learned the entity in the caves might help.*

There was a long silence. He tried to imagine the look on Roland's face while he puzzled whether or not Alton had lost a marble or two.

*Entity? In the crystal caves? Are you certain you don't need my help?*

*Thanks, Roland, but not right now. I'll explain later, but yes, an entity we knew nothing about. Mother Crystal. Ask your sword who she is—you might get an answer. I'll contact you when I know more. No need to worry my grandfather or father at this point.*

Acknowledging Roland's agreement, he closed the connection and continued with the others along the main tunnel. Taron's lack of an answer was disturbing. Where the hell could he be that he'd not hear and respond?

After a short walk they reached the small portal that led to the tunnels in the lower levels. Alton paused for a moment, but there was no need to hesitate. Everyone was obviously anxious to proceed. They slipped through without comment and headed down the long stairs that eventually led to the level where the Forgotten Ones had been held as slaves.

Alton wondered what Selyn thought as she walked freely through the same passages where she'd lived and worked her entire life—where she'd been imprisoned as a slave until just a little over a week ago.

Now Selyn was a Paladin, one of the new women warriors of Lemuria. The huge machinery she'd once worked on was silent, the drills shut down, the fires in the smelting works no longer burning. Alton's grandfather had plans, though, to make use of these mines. He'd spoken eloquently of reopening the diamond and rare gems mines and the precious metal refineries with paid labor—jobs that would give Lemurian citizens a purpose and a new economy.

Selyn and her sister slaves certainly had not been paid for their work, though they'd been rewarded, in a way, when they'd each received a crystal sword. Already some of the blades were sentient—full partners to the new Paladins of Lemuria.

But Selyn remained quiet as they passed through the mining level and moved beyond, deeper into Lemuria than any had gone before Taron's amazing journey to replicate swords for the Forgotten Ones.

Where in the nine hells was Taron? His friend was an anchor in his life—a solid and trustworthy companion who had never failed in any endeavor he'd set out to achieve. At least not until he'd been faced with convincing a council ruled by demonkind that it must go forth and hunt demons.

If they'd only known what they were truly up against! Taron had done his very best—he was a man who deserved much more recognition than he'd gotten so far. He'd been willing to give everything to the fight against demonkind, and yet he'd remained in the background—a foot soldier whose bravery and determination had been tested time and again.

Not once had he been found wanting.

When this was all over, they really needed to sit down together over a glass of good ale and figure out exactly what had happened over the past month.

Now that would be a conversation to remember!

Alton's thoughts jumped from event to event as the five of them continued on, practically running down the stairs that took them ever deeper into the mountain. So much had occurred—so many changes in a world that had essentially gone unchanged for thousands of years.

Subtle changes in his surroundings, in the changing texture of the stone around them, the sense of having gone into a world totally unlike any other filled him with more questions. Once this was over, their best minds would have to learn more about this world of theirs. Minds now unfettered by the insidious pressure of demon control.

Even now, Alton and the others had no idea if they were still within the Lemurian dimension when they traveled to these lower levels. Had they moved on to yet another world altogether? He didn't know, yet everything about these deep tunnels and passageways felt alien, and they'd crossed through enough portals to have slipped from one dimension to another.

Strange yet tiny animals lived in the shadows. Eyeless salamanders and blind frogs. Small glowing worms moved slowly over etched stone, and in some areas, iridescent lichens covered the walls. There was an odd feeling of immense pressure, and yet the air here was clear and it was easier to breathe than he would have expected at such a great depth.

They'd traveled far very quickly and already had reached the area where only Taron's scratch marks in the stone walls of the tunnels guided them. Their only light was the occasional patch of lichen and the steady shimmer of Alton's and Dax's crystal swords.

The rough scrape of boots over an even rougher floor echoed off the walls, and the harsh sound of their breathing seemed overly loud. No one had spoken for close to an hour—they moved quickly and saved their breath for the journey—until Dawson caught up to Alton and clapped him on the shoulder.

"I thought I was through climbing down into this cavern, but I'm beginning to wonder if maybe we shouldn't just install an elevator."

Alton burst out laughing. Only Dawson . . . "Not a bad idea, Daws, though the trip's not so hard coming down. That climb back up though . . . now that one's a killer."

"Maybe a direct portal," Selyn said. "It would be nice to pop between levels without all these stairs."

Dax merely grunted. "I have a whole new sense of danger with these portals we so easily use. I never dreamed we could go into one and not come out."

Alton glanced over his shoulder. "We'll find her, Dax. No matter what, we'll bring Eddy back, though I can't believe that what happened to her was an accident. I've never heard of anyone not coming out of a portal. Something or someone did something to shove her into the void, but I have to believe that if she can be sent into it, she can be taken out of it."

Dax merely grunted.

Alton couldn't imagine the pain his friend must be feeling. Didn't want to. "She's one of us," he said, making eye contact with Dax. "Eddy's the best of us. We won't lose her."

Dax gave a sharp jerk of his head, but he said nothing more. The way had become narrower, the ground more uneven, and it took full concentration to keep up the pace without stumbling. Alton recognized more of Taron's marks on the walls and knew they drew close. He sensed anticipation in HellFire and wondered if the others noticed any change in their blades.

Ginny picked up his errant thought. "Even with DarkFire sheathed, I feel something. Not at all the way it was when we battled the demon king. That was a sense of dread. DarkFire seems excited about coming this way."

"I agree." Alton reached for Ginny with his free hand. She clasped his fingers, and her solid grasp reminded him once again just how lucky a man he was.

"Sheathe your swords." Dawson moved ahead of Alton. "I think I see the glow of crystal ahead."

"Really? Will the crystal cast light without candles or glow sticks?" Alton stuck HellFire in his scabbard, dousing the blade's crystal light. Dax did the same with DemonFire.

"It appears so."

Selyn's soft comment had all of them blinking in wonder. A brilliant blue-white glow shimmered along the passage ahead. They raced down the tunnel, through the broad opening into the first of the crystal caves.

This one glowed with an inner light they'd not seen before. Even the ruby altar where Taron had replicated the swords, the altar that had only glowed, according to Taron, when the ruby sword of Artigos the Just had appeared, was shimmering from deep inside in all its blood-red glory.

They walked into the center of the cavern, one that was nothing more than a giant geode with a curved ceiling and walls studded with huge diamonds. However, instead of light reflecting off the facets from an outside source, the entire cavern glowed from within.

"It wasn't like this before." Eyes wide and sparkling in the unusual light, Ginny still hung on to Alton's hand. She stood beside him, head lifted, staring as if mesmerized by the glimmering, shimmering crystals overhead and all around. "This feels alive. I sense the spirits of warriors here, both men and women. Before, I thought only the warrior women, the mothers of the Forgotten Ones were here, but it's all of them. Every single one who ever fought and died bravely for Lemuria. Every warrior who lived a life of honor—they're here. All of them."

She pulled DarkFire out of the scabbard and held the blade high. A brilliant beam of purple light shot from the blade and bathed the crystalline walls, striking a bell-like tone, a ringing note of purest crystal.

Ginny spoke to her sword as fire raced along the blade and sparks flew from the very tip. "You came directly from life in Lemuria to service in my sword, Daria of DarkFire. Did you ever have the chance to meet with your companions?"

Soft laughter seemed to echo all around. "When I am in your sword, I am also part of Mother Crystal. I am She, and She is all of us. Here, though, close to her heart, we are stronger. We are bound by our love and our honor, and we are bound to the soul of DemonSlayer. Elda and Eddy shall be saved."

"How? How and when?"

Dax's control had obviously snapped. He stomped forward, aggressive and angry, his demand a harsh snarl rubbed raw with grief. Alton reached out to stop him, but Dax brushed his hand away and spoke directly to Ginny's blade. "How can we get Eddy back?"

"Hold, demon."

Dax jerked to a halt and turned, searching for the source of the powerful command. Alton clung to Ginny's hand and did the same. Dawson and Selyn drew close, each with their swords drawn.

"Anger does not serve you here, demon. Sheathe your swords, warriors."

Dawson and Selyn slowly shoved their blades back inside their scabbards. Ginny sheathed DarkFire. Then she turned and, with raised eyebrows, stared at Alton. *Mother Crystal? Ya think?*

Selyn stepped forward and clasped Dax's hand, lending support. Calming him. Ginny turned Alton loose and put her arm around the ex-demon's waist. Dax's entire body trembled. Rage poured off of him in waves. It took what felt like a very long time for him to gain control.

No one tried to rush him. None spoke. Alton moved to stand behind Dax. He gently rested his hands on Dax's shoulders and offered what support he could. Tension had his friend's body drawn tight beneath his palms, shivering with the strain of curbing and containing his emotions.

Dawson stood to one side with arms folded across his chest, but it was obvious he was there for Dax, ready and willing to do whatever he could to protect his friend.

Finally Dax shuddered and then released a long pent-up breath. He bowed his head, but when he spoke, it was with a voice strained and taut with emotion. "My apologies, my lady, but I wish to correct a misnomer. I am no longer a demon. I have worked very hard to earn the title *demonslayer*."

A soft ripple of light across the curved ceiling was the only response. Dax drew his sword. "The fact I carry DemonFire should attest to my honor. I am demon no more." He looked to each of the ones standing beside him, reached up and pressed his hand over Alton's on his right shoulder. "My friends, honorable warriors all, stand beside me with the same request. One of our band has been taken from us. Somehow, Eddy Marks has been trapped in the void—she and the blade DemonSlayer with the spirit of Elda. Can you save them? Will you help us?"

Again, light rippled across the room. Alton squeezed Dax's shoulders, but all of them waited, standing in place, hoping for a miracle.

The light continued to ripple, faster and faster as if the energy within the crystal worked through Dax's request. The inner walls glowed even brighter and a low hum filled the cavern.

Still they waited. They'd come this far. There was nowhere else they knew to search. There was nothing more any of them could do but wait.

# Chapter 15

Willow awoke to a most unexpected sensation, as if she were wrapped in a cocoon of living heat. Slowly she catalogued the sensations—the soft thud of a heart beating against her ear, the tickle of warm breath lifting her hair.

Comforted by a familiar scent, the knowledge that she was wrapped in the arms of one she loved, Willow snuggled close and rubbed her cheek against what could only be the soft crimson pelt covering Taron's chest.

She'd found that patch of hair unbelievably erotic from the first time she saw him naked—the perfect pattern of deepest red spilling across his otherwise smooth bronze skin. Where Alton was very fair skinned with silvery blond hair, Taron was darker—a warm, bronzed shade that set off his emerald green eyes and that gorgeous crimson mane.

Willow had no idea how she'd ended up in his lap and she really shouldn't allow this, not after all the things he'd said about not getting involved, but it felt too good, and she'd already decided she couldn't change Taron—Willow could only be true to herself.

Well, herself truly loved being held and she wasn't about to ask him to set her aside. At least not now.

He nuzzled the top of her head and kissed her forehead. "Are you awake?"

"I am now." She arched her back and stretched within his embrace. Opened her eyes and realized she was staring so closely into his beautiful green eyes that she saw two sets. She blinked and backed away, bringing him into focus.

He leaned against pillows piled high against the headboard and held her. One arm supported her back; the other curved beneath her thighs. His hands were clasped against her hip, fitting her into the perfect cradle of his body. And right there, pressed tightly against her bottom, was irrefutable evidence that he was more than a little interested in her.

That hard length of him gave her a depth of raw courage she hadn't expected and really wasn't quite certain how to use. At least it gave her the strength to look him directly in the eye and ask without any hint of emotion, "Why are you holding me?"

"I had to." He sighed and kissed her nose this time. "I wanted to talk to you. I figure this way you can't escape."

"That tells me, if you expect me to try and escape, that I'm not going to like whatever you intend to say."

He shrugged. Then he leaned his head against the pillows and closed his eyes. "I don't know. Maybe you will, maybe you won't. I used to think I was becoming an expert on everything, but I really don't know anymore. In fact, I've learned I don't really know much about anything."

She ran her fingers over his bare shoulder and thought about that for a moment. "I thought you were a scholar," she said. "A man whose goal in life is to know all there is to know."

He sighed, raised his head and studied her for a moment. The arrogance she'd often associated with him was missing. Instead, he looked a little bit lost, a whole lot confused.

"Another lesson I've learned is that one doesn't always achieve all their goals. And sometimes, a man comes to the realization that the goals he has pursued for a lifetime are wrong." He stared beyond her, as if unwilling to meet her steady gaze. "He decides those long-held goals were all a terrible mistake. A monumental waste of precious time."

"I imagine that could be quiet discouraging."

He actually snorted. Shaking his head, chuckling softly, he said, "Willow, my love, you don't know the half of it." Then he tightened his arms around her and held her closer. "We need to talk, but I don't want to let go of you. I want to make love to you, but I'm afraid I've ruined any chance you'll ever want me to touch you again. It's not easy to admit I've been a complete ass."

Now, this was a definite improvement. "You might be surprised at how far an apology will go. Especially if it's entirely sincere."

"Is that right?" He smiled this time, reminding her once again how handsome he was. How perfect. "I'm definitely sincere. I really don't know where to begin, how to fix what I've probably broken."

She sighed. "I don't know anymore either, Taron. I'm not certain what's right and what's not. What matters and what doesn't. I know that we have to save Ed. I know we have a battle to fight and a demon that wants to end us, but I'm selfish enough to want to settle things in my own life, too. This life is so new to me, so precious. I don't want to miss a thing. Is that so wrong?"

He shook his head. "There's nothing else we can do right now. We'll need to search for Ed tonight, once the demon is active again. I have no idea where he is right now and our swords haven't had any luck finding him. As far as the battle, I have a feeling the demon will come to us. I don't think we're going to have to search very hard for him."

She touched fingertips to his jaw and stared directly into

those mesmerizing green eyes. "All well said and true, but are we merely justifying our actions?"

He laughed. He actually laughed at her! Willow pulled back and glared at him. "I'm being serious. Why are you laughing?"

"Because you, my dear, sound more like the scholar and I am sounding like a spoiled child. Are we justifying our actions? I honestly don't know anymore. As I told you—I've come to the realization that I don't know much of anything. That a lot of the things I believed aren't true. They aren't real."

She cupped her hand against his jaw and thought for a moment of what he'd said. "What is, Taron? What is real?"

Touching his forehead to hers, he whispered, "You are, Willow. You're as real as anything I've ever known. I'm through acting like a jerk. I promise to do better, to be better." He laughed and rolled his head side to side against hers. "When I figure out how, that is."

Okay. She could give him some major points on that one. He was right. He had been acting like a jerk, but damn it all, he was her jerk. "You were afraid," she said, excusing him. "Fear is valid."

He nodded and leaned back once again. "Not always. Not when it becomes an excuse. Not when it's entirely selfish. At first, it was all about me. I was afraid for myself. Afraid that if I fell in love I would suffer, and I didn't want that. I defined the word coward because I wasn't willing to take the risk."

He was quiet for so long, she finally prodded him. "What changed?"

His soft chuckle definitely lacked humor. "You. We made love and I tried to tell myself it was just sex, that we were both merely satisfying our curiosity, but I was dead wrong. It was so much more than that. You're so much more. When I finally pulled myself out of that world of denial I was hiding in, I realized it was already too late, that I loved you, and that I'd made a horrible mistake."

Her blood ran cold at the serious sound of his words. At the way he tightened his grasp on her body. "I don't understand. Why is loving me a mistake if you're no longer afraid of the fortune?"

"I'm still terrified of the fortune, Willow, but for a different reason. Remember what I told you? What the fortune teller said to me? That I would know unimaginable joy, and unendurable pain. I've already discovered joy beyond anything I'd ever dreamed. You give me that joy, Willow. Your love, your touch. Everything about you gave me joy then and continues to give me joy, and I knew then that the only thing that could cause unendurable pain was losing you. The risk isn't to me, Willow. It's you."

She leaned against him and thought about that for a moment. "So you fear that losing me will cause you pain?"

Shaking his head in denial he said, "Forget about me. This is all about you. The only way I could ever lose you is if you turn back into a tiny sprite, end up stuck in Bumper again, or if you die, because I'm not giving you up. Don't you see? None of those options is acceptable."

"So fearing something that might or might not happen, you will deny yourself the joy of whatever you can have now? That won't work, Taron. At least it won't work for me. Why would I want to live half a life because I'm afraid of dying, of ending before I'm ready? Every second I exist is an unexpected gift. Everything is new and something I never imagined I'd know or feel. If I knew for certain that I only had hours left, I'd still want to love you. I'd want to experience everything. I'd want to know all I could about love, I'd want to feel every sensation and every emotion, experience everything—even the heartbreak. If life is going to be cut short, why waste a second of it? That doesn't make sense."

He pulled her even closer and covered her mouth with

his, but the kiss was much too brief as far as Willow was concerned.

Before she could complain, he laughed again. "How is it, Willow, that a woman who started out as swamp gas got so damned smart?"

"For one thing, I was very perceptive swamp gas in Eden, and for another, an extremely observant will-o'-the-wisp once I got to Earth." She tilted her head and kissed his chin. "I watched Eddy Marks make the decision to love Dax, even though he was supposed to be gone by the end of the week. She said she would rather know love with him for a few short days, than never love him at all."

"And now she has him forever." Taron released her to brush the thick curls back from her face. He began untangling her hair from the scrunchy she'd slept in, almost as if he were afraid to meet her gaze. "Not everyone gets a happy ending, Willow. Real life isn't like that."

Freed now of his tight embrace, she turned until she straddled his thighs, and looped both arms over his shoulders. "Taron, you're such a man."

"Of course I am. What do you mean?" He lifted his hands away from her head and dropped the scrunchy to one side. Only then did he meet her gaze.

"I mean, Taron, I'm not going to think of endings. Right now, I'm only interested in beginnings. Can you try that? Concentrate on beginnings for a change?"

He lifted his hips beneath her, and she felt the thick, hard length of him brushing those sensitive points between her legs. "I think I can do that, though it's merely one of the things I'm planning to concentrate on, if that's okay with you."

She leaned forward and kissed him. By the time they broke apart, Willow didn't think she'd be able to concentrate on a darned thing.

* * *

*Dad! Where are you? I hear you! How can you talk to me?*

He wasn't sure if he should tell her, but Ed had always been honest with his daughter, even when she thought he was nuts. Of course, ever since Eddy'd found a wounded ex-demon and a tiny will-o'-the-wisp trailing blue sparkles in her potting shed, she'd been a whole lot more open about accepting the unacceptable.

She certainly didn't tease him anymore. At least not about his belief in Lemurians or vortexes or magic. He wasn't certain if that was a good or a bad thing. Life had been way simpler before Dax showed up, before they'd met Alton the Lemurian, and before they'd all gotten messed up in this unbelievable battle that threatened to tip the balance forever between good and evil—in the wrong direction.

Still, there was no reason to lie to her. There was never a good reason to lie, so he'd play his cards the way he always did and give it to her straight—as much as he hated upsetting her. But damn, this was a weird place and it was hard to talk to Eddy without seeing her face, picturing her expressions. Hugging his little girl who was suddenly a grown up woman with grown up problems. Where in God's name had the time gone?

He sighed. *Well, I'm not exactly certain, and I don't quite know how to explain this. Eddy, the demon king seems to have taken over my body. I know he's controlling me. It's pretty bad, especially when I'm aware of what he's forcing me to do. A lot of the time it's like I've just gone to sleep, though. I guess my consciousness gets buried under his and I haven't got a clue what he's up to. Right now, I think he's resting and my mind is free—or as free as a possessed person's mind can be.*

The silence lasted much too long. *Eddy? Sweetheart? You there?*

*Yeah. I'm here, Dad. Wow . . . we're both up shit creek without the proverbial paddle, aren't we?*

Laughter, it appeared, did not translate well in the void, but Ed knew that if he could grin, he would. Leave it to Eddy to nail the crux of the matter. *Yep, sweetie. I guess you could say that. Is there anything we can do to get you out?*

*DemonSlayer says she's working on something. She's mentioned getting help from Mother Crystal. I'm not certain who that is, though DemonSlayer says she's the entity of the crystal caves where Taron replicated the swords. How can I find you so I can tell you what I find out? And where are you now? Your physical body. Do you have any idea where the demon king has got you stashed?*

*Right now we're in the attic of the old library building, but I don't know what his plans are for tonight. It's still daytime here. I think he wants Dax for some reason, so if you can talk to your man, make sure he doesn't come anywhere close to Evergreen. Taron is here and I'm not sure, but I think Willow has a full-sized body. I trust them to try and save me if they can, but it's all very confusing. I don't know how to tell you to find me, Eddy. When the demon king is aware, I'm not. In fact, I sense him waking up now. When he's alert, I can't . . .*

His voice just disappeared, which meant the demon must be awake, but there was so much to assimilate and so many questions Eddy still had to ask.

*Dad? Where are you?* She waited, but there was nothing. No sound. No sensation. Nothing at all. A vast nothing that could have filled a universe and gone on forever, or it might have been encompassed inside a single atom.

How did one define the void?

She was really glad she couldn't cry in the void—her emotions were muted, her thoughts limited to the words she could speak and somehow hear within her mind.

Because she knew, without a doubt, that if it were at all

possible she'd be screaming right now. Screaming and sobbing and acting totally out of control.

How was her father coping? He'd sounded so much like himself, telling her he'd been possessed, like it was just one of those things. Poor Dad! She tried to imagine what it must be like, sharing your body with something as disgusting as the demon king.

If she had a body, she'd probably be throwing up right now. It made her sick to think of something so awful. Dad was such a good man. Kind and loving, smart and funny, and just flat out wonderful. It wasn't fair.

But life wasn't always fair, either. If life were fair, she'd be with Dax right now, fighting demons. Not stuck here in the middle of nothing, hoping like hell someone would figure out how to get her out of here—wherever here was.

What did Dad say about Willow? That she had a real woman's body? But where was Bumper, and how did Willow get big? In fact, how did she get out of Bumper? At least Dad said Taron was with her. That was good. Taron was smart. He was strong and good. He'd know what to do, and if anyone could figure out how to help her father, Taron was one of the best to give it a shot.

She wanted her own body back! Her dad needed her. Dax was probably frantic by now. And what about Alton and Ginny, and Dawson and Selyn? Were they okay? They had to be because their swords had worked together to contact DemonSlayer. Knowing they were safe had become her anchor, her link to sanity. If they were safe, they'd do everything in their power to rescue her, to bring both her and DemonSlayer home.

Now though, there was nothing to do but wait. Wait and dream and hope the time would pass quickly until she was out of here. She floated within her consciousness, thankful to have retained at least that much of the woman she'd been before she'd been snatched into the void. She understood now what Dax had said about saving up memories for the time when he expected to be stuck here forever.

Thank goodness she had her memories. Beautiful memories of loving Dax, and all the dreams they'd made together. Strong memories of her father and the pride he'd felt for her. He was such a good dad, raising a daughter without a mother. That couldn't have been easy, but he must have done a fantastic job, because she realized her mind was filled with wonderful memories. Memories of friendships savored, challenges met, fears overcome.

She would overcome this as well. Eddy Marks was not a quitter, not one to give in or give up. DemonSlayer had told her to hang on, and hang on she would. For however long it took.

What was time, after all, when one was lost in an endless void with a heart and mind filled with wonderful memories?

It sucked, that's what. Sucked big time. Memories were terrific, but she wanted life. She wanted Dax, and she really wanted out of here.

# Chapter 16

Alton knelt at the edge of the clear, cold creek running through the crystal cave and, using both hands, scooped a drink of water into his mouth. Light continued to ripple through the thousands of diamonds covering the walls and ceiling of the crystal cave, a hypnotic pattern driving a low, throbbing pulse, a subtle yet clear reminder of a beating heart.

Ginny, Dawson, and Selyn sat near the ruby altar, tired but alert and waiting. Dax paced a consistent pattern across the cavern floor, over and back. He'd crossed it over and over again as he walked off the nervous energy that obviously had to go somewhere. His impatience was a palpable force in the glimmering cavern, his frustration building with each step he took.

Alton felt it as if Dax's pain were his own. He sat back on his heels and watched his friend. Dax had stripped off his shirt and tossed it over the ruby altar. His arms, chest, and back glistened with sweat and his powerful body was primed for action. The colorful tattoo of the phoenix covering his chest and belly appeared ready to fly right off his body. The demonslayer looked capable of killing with his bare hands.

Alton figured the poor guy must be ready to explode by now. Dax had inherited the body of a soldier, one who'd learned to trust in his own physical strength, a man used to wielding power and fighting for those he loved. Alton was convinced he'd acquired much of the original man's personality traits as well.

This inactivity, the inability to do anything concrete to save Eddy while they waited for an unknown entity to feed them information she may or may not be able to produce, had to be killing him.

As Dax spun around to make another pass across the cavern, Alton's eyes were drawn again to the phoenix tattoo. It was impossible to ignore—the damned thing looked alive. The symbol of rebirth had appeared on Dax's chest the night the demon king, in the guise of a huge stone gargoyle come to life, had killed him. Alton would never forget his sense of loss, kneeling there beside Dax's broken body, knowing that his dear friend had died fighting evil. They'd all given up hope of ever seeing him alive again—all except Eddy.

She'd been the only one to believe, and though she'd mourned his death, she'd been convinced Dax had truly earned his place in Paradise, and she'd not given him up. Her love and loyalty and steadfast resolve had paid off—she'd been the first to sense Dax's return to life. Alton would never forget the sight of that tattoo when Eddy had opened Dax's shirt, and instead of the cursed snake etched into his skin, they'd all seen the glowing colors of the phoenix, rising from the ashes of Dax's death.

At first, Eddy thought the tattoo meant he'd achieved his goal of Paradise. Then Dax opened his eyes, and they'd all witnessed the miracle of his return from the dead.

Now, that same tattoo appeared to breathe in rhythm with the living pulse of the crystal cavern, independent of Dax's harsh breaths. Slowly, watching the art on his friend's body pulse with its own life, Alton rose to his feet. He walked across the cavern and stopped Dax in midstep.

He pressed his hand to Dax's right shoulder, over the

screaming beak on the phoenix. "Do you feel this thing, Dax? Does this tattoo of yours have independent life . . . the same as that snake?"

Dax paused, frowning. "The phoenix?" He glanced at his chest, ran his fingers over the brilliantly inked bird. It rose in blues and greens and brilliant red out of a fiery cloud of orange and red flames that licked over his belly. The broad wings spread across his pectoral muscles and covered most of his chest, while the long, curling tail feathers disappeared beneath the waistband of his jeans. "I never feel it. Not the way I felt the snake. There's no evil taint with this art, no sense of life, either. This is just there—it's supposed to hold my demon powers, but those are part of me now. The phoenix is mostly a reminder, I think, of my new life."

Shaking his head, not quite as certain of what he thought he'd seen, Alton pulled his hand away. "For a minute there, I thought it looked almost like it was breathing on its own. Must be the weird light in here, but . . ." He shrugged. There was something he couldn't quite put a finger on. "Why do I feel there might be more to this phoenix of yours than mere art?"

The cavern pulsed with brilliant light. "Because there must be, Lemurian. There must be more if we are to save Eddy Marks. The phoenix is the key."

Dax went absolutely still. Then he glanced at the others, but he was still trailing his fingers over the tattoo. Taking a deep breath, he let it out and, in a voice that was almost frighteningly calm, asked, "What do you mean, my lady?"

"I have found Eddy Marks. She is safe within the void, but I do not know how to save her. Not yet."

Dax's fingers latched on to Alton's forearm with crushing strength. "Explain. Please."

"She is in the void, her consciousness paired with Demon-Slayer's, as is the way of sentient sword and warrior. But her body is gone, just as DemonSlayer's physical sword is gone. The sword we can replicate, but for Eddy Marks . . . without her physical shell, she cannot exist on this plane . . . though she could always return as the sentience in a crystal sword. She is, after all, a warrior."

Alton grabbed Dax as he felt his friend's legs give out. He helped him sit on the hard floor of the cavern. Dax's face had gone ashen, his expression that of a man who has lost everything.

Dax took a series of deep, harsh breaths. Impotent anger scored each word. "She is not dead. Not destined to exist as a blade. Eddy Marks is immortal, and she is mine." He took a long, deep breath and held it a moment before letting it out, but his eyes sparkled with tears not yet shed.

He bowed his head. "Is there no way?" Then he lifted his head and stared at the shimmering crystals, but the look of hopelessness on his face hit Alton like a blow.

Light rippled across the cavern in a subtle dance. Mother Crystal's voice was somehow warmer, more charged with feeling than before. "There is always hope, warrior. Have patience. I must consider this."

The light within the cavern dimmed, though the sense of the entity remained powerful. Alton knelt beside Dax. "Have faith, my friend. Don't give up. Remember this—Eddy never quit on you. Even as your body grew cold, she believed. She was the only one of us who knew you'd come back, and she was right."

"But how . . . ?" Dax shook his head, wrapped his arms around his legs, and rested his forehead on his raised knees. "How can she come back if there's no body to come back to? It's impossible."

Alton sat on the ground beside him. Selyn, Ginny, and Dawson joined them. Selyn knelt behind Dax, wrapped her arms around his bowed shoulders and rested her cheek against the back of his head. She held him like that for a long moment before she spoke.

"I've learned that nothing is impossible, Dax. Nothing. As

long as you believe there's a chance, that chance exists. I knew Dawson was dead, but I couldn't mourn him. I refused to believe he was gone. I loved him so much and I wanted him back. He was returned to me by the strength of his sword, but I believe my love for him helped, just as I believe Eddy will come back to you. Because your love is powerful."

Ginny sat close beside Dax, looking absolutely ferocious as she glared at the shimmering crystal walls. "I agree. She's immortal and she's my best friend. Eddy wouldn't dare ditch me now." She leaned her head against his shoulder and smiled softly. "Besides, she loves you too much ever to leave you. Have faith, Dax."

Dawson knelt in front of him. "Dax, you and I share something that no one else here can truly understand. What Selyn said. We've both died, and we've both been brought back. It was love that saved us, the power inherent in that love. You love Eddy. We all do, so there's a lot of that power right here in this cave. Plus we've got sentient crystal on our side and Mother Crystal searching for an answer. Do as she says and have patience. We'll all be here for you, and I promise you, we'll get her back."

Dax nodded. At least he was listening, though it was impossible to tell if he believed anything he heard. Light continued to pulse around them. Instead of a heartbeat, Alton was almost certain he heard the whispered voices of many hundreds of souls. Something was happening, something important, though he had no idea what it was.

He sat close beside Dax and offered what comfort he could. Selyn still hugged Dax from behind. Ginny sat close against his other side and Dawson had stood once again and was a stalwart force keeping watch over all of them.

There was no tighter knit group of warriors, no stronger love. Alton figured he'd have to do as he'd preached to Dax— have patience. And faith. There was no doubt in his mind— this was going to take a lot of faith.

* * *

This time, Taron was the one to break their kiss. Gently, and with heartbreaking regret. He had so much to atone for. Was it too late? He cupped Willow's face in both his hands and stared into her clear blue eyes. She gazed steadily at him and she was so beautiful, so gods-be-damned pure, he knew that it was up to him to fix things. Now.

If he could.

There would be no going back. Not if they went forward this time. Not if they made love with their minds totally open to the truth of the emotions both of them felt.

Willow had been honest from the beginning. Only days old as a full-sized woman, she'd shown more heart and soul, more maturity and conscience than he, a Lemurian many thousands of years old, could ever understand. She'd been as curious as he was, but she'd been upfront about everything she felt, everything she wanted. He hadn't. He'd been lying to Willow as much as he'd lied to himself.

Saying one thing, doing another. Bouncing back and forth like a child's bouncy ball. Talk about cowardice! It wasn't the fortune teller's fault he'd been afraid to face the truth.

It was his own failure as a man of honor.

No more. He couldn't deny his heart any longer without living a lie, and even though he'd been able to keep lying to himself, he couldn't lie to Willow. Never again. She looked at him so directly, so honestly, that he felt like a complete ass.

Who the hell did he think he was fooling when he told himself they could spend any time together at all and not fall in love? Willow'd known from the beginning he was playing her false.

He'd long been known as a skilled debater. The problem was, he'd never realized the effect his well-honed skills would have on his own ability to make decisions.

But it appeared the time for inner debate had ended.

Willow covered his hands with hers and lifted them away from her face. She pressed his hands to her thighs—palms down—which made it even harder for him to concentrate. Her thighs, after all, gave him a direct pathway to all those feminine secrets hidden at their apex, but Willow patted the backs of both his hands, tilted her head, and gave him one of *those* looks.

He figured that must mean she wanted him to leave his hands where she'd put them. Okay. He stared at their hands, hers still covering his. He could do this. Maybe. Except he made the mistake of raising his head again, looking up from hands to her—really looking, this time—and she was entirely naked, straddling him with all that glorious blond hair cascading over her shoulders and curling over the tips of her breasts. Naked and sleek and so beautiful she made him ache.

And the feel of her! Dear gods, the way she felt wherever they connected. He was almost preternaturally aware of the smooth skin of her inner thighs pressed against his flanks, of the way her downy-soft blond curls tickled the hard root of his penis, and her smooth bottom trapped the full length of his erection beneath her slight weight.

Sweat beaded his brow and he felt that inner beast stirring. Sensed the rising need that ignored his more civilized self, and gods-be-damned, but he had to admire the guy. At least he knew what he wanted, and didn't hesitate to go after it.

Taron glanced again at their hands, but when he raised his eyes he looked directly at her perfect breasts, and that made him harder, needier than he'd been only moments ago, but Willow wanted something from him, and the beast had better watch his manners, at least until Taron figured out what Willow wanted.

She watched him still, and it was all he could do to return her steady gaze without twitching and moving, without adjusting the way their bodies met—so close, but not nearly close enough.

Even that fiery kiss they'd shared hadn't stirred him as much as her steady, assessing stare.

What in the nine hells was she thinking?

She didn't leave him wondering for long. Glancing down, as if to reassure herself his hands were still where she'd put them, Willow folded her arms across her chest. That, of course, had the effect of barely covering her nipples while forcing her breasts up and forward, ensuring that his brain would quit functioning altogether.

If she was trying to affect a businesslike pose, the effect was lost on him altogether. He couldn't get his mind off the points where they connected—her warm sex against his stiff erection, her smooth thighs over his hard flanks. He felt a sensory overload coming on, and Willow was just gearing up to talk.

Talking was quickly becoming the last thing on his mind.

She wriggled her butt, as if she were trying to get more comfortable. Taron bit back a groan. Did she have any idea what she was doing to him?

Impossible. She'd been a woman for such a short time. Even Willow couldn't fully comprehend how precarious his control was right now, how hard it was for him to concentrate, to hold the wild side of himself at bay. Even for a scholar who'd long eschewed anything remotely similar to a naked woman straddling his crotch, this position they both held was really not conducive to an adult conversation.

Unfortunately, it didn't appear that was going to stop her.

"So. What now, Taron of Libernus?" Willow raised an eyebrow and pinned him with her steady gaze. "I think, as Eddy would say, the ball is in your court." She leaned forward and planted both hands on his chest. Her breasts swung forward. His eyes almost crossed, following those perfect nipples. "And no more kissing until you figure out exactly what you want."

He stared at her breasts a moment longer, at least until he finally dredged up the strength to raise his eyes. Then his vision was filled once again with that tangled mass of curls falling across her shoulders and curling around the tips of her breasts, at the sparkle in her blue eyes and the firm tilt to her chin. This woman was no pushover. She was everything he could ever imagine wanting or needing, and she was right.

The ball was in his court, and he knew, without a doubt that only a coward would pass up a chance at love. Only a coward would ignore what was so generously offered, so freely given.

He was tired of playing the coward. And gods-be-damned, but he wanted Willow.

He met her gaze without wavering. Kept his hands exactly where she'd placed them. "I want you," he said. "Without barriers or boundaries. I want to love you for as long as we have. If you'll have me. If you're willing to take a chance on a guy who obviously doesn't have a clue what women really want or need."

Her smile would have lit the darkest night. She reached for his hands, brought them up and placed his palms firmly over the full curve of her breasts. "I never let you go, Taron. I've only been waiting for you to figure out what. You. Really. Wanted."

He nodded. "I think I've got it." Then he closed his fingers around her breasts and gently pinched both nipples. She sighed and arched her back, and he knew that, no matter what fate might think it had in store, he would hang on to her, protect her, and keep her.

"No one," he whispered as she closed the small gap between them. "No one will ever take you away from me."


She'd never been so terrified in her life. Willow couldn't believe she'd actually given Taron an ultimatum. Even more unbelievable, it appeared to have worked.

Leaning close, she pressed her lips to his, sighing when

his hands slipped along her sides and around her back. He cupped her bottom, kneading the sensitive skin with his big hands, lifting her until the thick length of him slipped close against her damp folds.

All it would take was a tiny little adjustment on her part, just a lift of her hips, a bit of a tilt like this, and . . .

*Puppy parts, Willow! Don't forget the puppy parts. Taron, be careful!*

*Bumper! What* . . . She collapsed against Taron's chest, giggling uncontrollably. Taron cursed. Bumper had the good sense to shut up.

Willow thought she heard Taron fumbling with the drawer beside the table and then the now familiar sound of the packet tearing, but she was wiping the tears from her eyes and giggling so hard she wasn't really certain what he was doing.

Finally, gasping for breath, Willow raised her head and looked into icy green eyes totally devoid of any sense of humor. Taron held the tiny clear disk in one large hand, but he didn't look the least bit pleased about the interruption.

Willow leaned over and grabbed a tissue from a box on the table beside the bed to wipe her eyes. Finally, with her giggles under control, she slipped back on his legs almost to his knees.

"Here. Give that to me." She held out her hand. Taron slapped the condom against her palm.

"Don't look so grumpy. Bumper's right, you know."

"I'm not grumpy." He glared at her. Then she could tell he'd thought about how he sounded, and the corner of his mouth twitched.

"You're sure about that?" She rose up on her knees, leaned over his belly and kissed him. "You taste grumpy."

"Do not."

"Do too."

"Well . . . maybe a little." He ran a finger along her cheek. "Bumper's timing is horrible."

"Bumper's timing was perfect." She turned her head and nipped his finger. "I'm not ready for puppies."

That, at least, got a smile out of him. "I don't think I'll ever be ready for puppies." Then his expression changed and he stared at her for the longest time before softly adding, "But babies? Maybe some day. If we're lucky."

That one sort of knocked the breath out of her. She sat very still and studied him—the wide green eyes, the clear bronzed skin, sharp cheekbones and long, straight nose. And that mouth . . . she really loved his mouth. He truly would make beautiful babies. Her answer caught in her throat. "Really? You're sure?"

He nodded his head and brushed his fingers through her tangled hair, tugging it. "Yeah. I'm sure. But it's not easy for Lemurians. We don't make a lot of babies."

Willow shrugged. "I'm not a Lemurian. And Bumper says I've got my puppy parts." A nervous giggle slipped out.

Taron looped his arms over her shoulders and grinned at her. Willow got the feeling he really liked what he was look-ing at, but then, so did she. She'd been attracted to the man from the very first time she saw him, when all she could do was look and dream because she was nothing more than a tiny sprite.

He was so tall, his smooth muscles perfectly defined, and that long, silky red hair falling over his shoulders and pool-ing on the bed beside his hips, the brilliant green eyes and that perfect mouth made a most attractive package. One that truly appealed to her. He would never be a forceful leader like Alton, or a powerful warrior like Dax. No, Taron was different, his mind constantly analyzing and questioning, his skills as a warrior a subtle blend of self-deprecating humor and pure athleticism.

He was gentle and good and kind, and sometimes so unsure of himself he made Willow feel as if she were the more experienced of the two of them. And maybe, in life, she was.

Taron had spent all his years in Lemuria studying life. Willow, in one short month, had lived it.

Taron lifted her chin with his fingertip, interrupting her slowly spinning thoughts. "Where's Bumper now? Doesn't it bother you to know there's a dog watching everything we do?"

His question centered her, and Willow gave him her widest smile. "Not when she's looking out for me. We should not have forgotten this." She held up the condom before she carefully placed the soft disk over the broad crown of his penis and just as carefully rolled the sheath down over the full length of him. He was so silky and yet hard at the same time, and his entire body seemed to quiver with her touch.

"There. Be glad that Eddy and Dax have these, or the question of whether or not we were going to make love wouldn't even be coming up."

She knew by the look on his face he hadn't even thought along those lines. It might not be an easy thing for Lemurians to make babies, but she had absolutely no idea what she was. Not human, not Lemurian, and she wasn't anything like the Edenites.

All she knew for certain, if Bumper could be believed, was that she still had her puppy parts. Other than that, Willow figured she was absolutely unique as far as sentient beings went.

Not too many women could say they started out as swamp gas.

Not the most romantic beginning, but she wasn't going to complain. Not when that weird beginning had led to her being here in the little town of Evergreen, in bed with a handsome man, stroking that most wonderful part of him and preparing to make love.

If she actually thought about it, the entire scenario was impossible. How could someone like Taron actually love a girl like her? How could she even exist? It was truly amazing. Completely unbelievable, but Willow continued stroking the sheath down over Taron's erection and decided she wasn't going to worry about her good fortune for another minute. Instead, she searched her mind for Bumper and found her sleeping.

Then she raised her head and looked into Taron's eyes, and found them looking right back at her. He reached for her as she leaned close to him, and everything sort of clicked, just the way it had the day before.

Had it only been one day ago? Taron ran his fingers over her shoulder, pulled her close, and slowly, so very slowly, rolled her over onto her back. He settled himself between her legs and planted his elbows on either side of her body. She lay there, looking up at him, at the smile on his face and the twinkle in his eyes and just knew.

She was meant for this man. Fated from the very beginning, and today, right now, this moment merely sealed the bargain. It might be their only day together; it could be the beginning of a lifetime. She refused to think of all that could go wrong.

Bumper lived in the moment, and that wasn't such a bad thing, not when the world was falling apart all around them.

Taron's soft lips found her breast and Willow almost came undone. He flicked his tongue over the sensitive tip, and she forgot all about the world falling apart and concentrated instead on not coming apart herself.

How did he do this to her? The slightest touch and she was gone. How could he know how to touch her so perfectly, how to make her body respond to his as if she'd always needed him, always loved him?

One of his hands traced the length of her torso and trailed across her belly. She arched closer, whimpering with a sudden onslaught of need as he ran his fingers through the tight curls between her legs.

One long finger slipped between her folds where she was already wet and sensitive beyond belief. She jerked and gasped as he softly rubbed back and forth, the thick tip of his finger sliding so easily through her buttery cleft. He went deeper each time and yet still managed to find that perfect spot that sent shock waves from her crotch to her womb and back again.

Whimpering, she raised her knees, lifted her hips, and tried to direct his touch with her suddenly frantic motions. He released her nipple, planted a kiss on the underside of her right breast and then concentrated on the other one, but all the time his mouth was pleasuring her so perfectly, his fingers were driving her wild.

What happened to all that wonderful control she'd been so proud of? Right now, Taron of Libernus was in charge, and he played her like a master. Who would have guessed that he'd done this for the first time only yesterday?

He'd already grown adept at finding her pleasure points and making her totally nuts, but what had she done for him?

The thought no sooner entered her mind than Willow slipped a hand along his side, trailed her fingers across his hip and then slowly and carefully walked them over his groin.

When she found his thick length, he jerked. She clasped him tightly and slowly stroked. He groaned. His fingers stilled on her as she continued to move her hand up and down his shaft.

"Okay," he said, and his voice sounded strained. "Enough of that."

She kissed his chest. "I was just getting started."

He laughed and moved between her legs. "Any more and I'll be finishing. Without you."

"Ah." She spread her legs and, still holding on to him, directed the tip toward her sex.

He pressed forward, so thick and hard she wondered how he'd fit so well the day before, but she lifted her hips and he rocked his, and suddenly he was in and her body welcomed him with rippling, clenching muscles and a sense of emotion that burst from her heart and her mind—emotion she never could have imagined before now.

Holding himself above her with his hands planted at either side of her face, Taron gazed at her with eyes gone all soft and dreamy. "I love you, Willow. We'll beat whatever fate has in store. You're mine, and I'm not letting you go."

"Good," she said. Just that one word, but it encompassed everything she felt. Taron was good. This thing they were doing was good. All of it, both of them . . . all good.

Then she rocked her hips, driving him deep and feeling her climax build. Tiny shocks of sensation, growing, building one upon the other. She forced herself to open her eyes, to focus on the brilliant green of Taron's.

He watched her, and his look was one of feral pleasure and absolute need. Of lust and passion and the tenderness of love. When lightning struck, his eyes went wide and bright, and when Willow finally flew from that amazing precipice, she didn't fly alone. With a cry that was both a challenge and a promise, she took Taron with her. In the heat and power of the moment, she branded him. Marked him forever, and claimed him, heart and soul.

# Chapter 17

He lay there on the dusty couch in the attic of the decrepit building where he'd taken refuge, staring into shadows filled with cobwebs, pondering his next move. The visual that came to him, though, was that glorious moment in the crystal caves when he'd held Dax close, when he'd felt the strength and life pour out of the man, into him.

Power. There'd been so much power.

And then it was gone. He wanted that power back. Wanted all of it, but his thoughts kept moving inward, touching on the frail consciousness of the human. Had he erred in choosing this weak avatar? It lived, but barely. Soon it would take even more energy to function in this dimension.

The Dark Lord had not tried to contact him, so that was good. There was still time to make this plan work, though he'd faced more problems than he'd expected.

This body, for one. There was no power here. He raised one arm and stared at the hand. Soft. It was all so soft and easily injured. Much too easy to kill.

He was a predator, housed in the body of prey.

He deserved better. He would have better.

He would have Dax. His life force, his soul.

So where was the bastard?

His mind wandered. It took so much energy to think clearly, and there was no more energy to be had here in Evergreen. He'd sent out his summons to demonkind—they should have come to him, but none had responded.

That damned Lemurian and the woman who was something other than human, other than Lemurian . . . the two of them had somehow managed to destroy every single demon. He'd sent more than enough on ahead, to be here and feed him as he needed their strength, but he hadn't counted on every damned one of them getting wiped off the face of the planet.

Which left him in a bit of an unexpected quandary—he was running low on energy. He could return to Abyss for more, except that would mean abandoning this body which was the bait he needed to draw Dax to him.

He only had need of it for a few more hours.

Unfortunately, though the body was weak and frail, the man himself had shown amazing strength of will, fighting possession every step of the way. It was draining what little energy was left in reserve. A few more hours might be all he had, before he couldn't hang on to the human's body any longer. Without the avatar, he would be forced back to Abyss.

Not an option, not with the Dark Lord's threat hanging over his head. The demon glanced out the window through Ed Marks's eyes and thought the day looked much darker than it had only moments ago. Could it be nightfall already? Slowly he crawled off the couch and shuffled across the dusty attic floor. The window was filthy, but he rubbed a bit of the glass clear so he could peer outside.

It was dark and gray and raining, but the darkness wasn't nightfall—it was merely from the thick layer of clouds. He stood there a moment and watched the water falling out of the sky. He still had a few more hours until sundown.

Moving this body after dark took less energy, and he

didn't run as great a risk of being caught by humans. There was no point in taking foolish chances. Not now.

So what was his next step? What if Dax didn't show up? What if the fool didn't come after him?

He gazed through the falling rain in the direction of the quiet neighborhoods east of town. Not all that far off was the house where Dax stayed when he was here in Evergreen. They'd fought there once before, when he'd used the stone gargoyle as his avatar. When he'd almost managed to bring that creature to life. What a sense of power that had given him! Of course, that was before he'd found the demonform, the one he truly deserved. Before he knew the importance of Dax's life force.

He wondered if Dax was at that house now?

Maybe it was time to find out. Once it was fully dark.

Decision made, he turned away from the window and headed slowly back to the couch for a few more hours' rest. If Dax wasn't going to come to him, he would just have to go in search of Dax. Besides, going on the offense would give him the upper hand. There was nothing wrong with that.

He lay there on the lumpy couch in the dark and filthy attic of the abandoned library, and laughed out loud. He was strong enough to last for one more night. Strong enough to take on Dax.

Something clicked into place. Why hadn't he realized . . . he sat up, alert, his body shivering with a sudden burst of excitement. Why not? If he could steal Dax's life force, what was to keep him from taking the same from other humans? Why must it only be demons whose souls he stole?

Still chuckling softly, he lay down and closed his eyes, but his mind wouldn't stop spinning. Humans . . . they had a powerful life force. Why hadn't he known this before? Humans should work. Had the Dark Lord somehow hidden this knowledge from him? No matter. He knew it now. Knew he needed to be strong. Alert and ready.

Tonight he was going hunting.

Now that was interesting. Ed heard the demon's thoughts as clearly as if he'd been chatting with Eddy in the void. What could that mean? He'd even been aware of laughter. That was just weird, hearing laughter coming out of his mouth that wasn't his. He wondered what was going on, why things felt different.

The creature wasn't fighting him right now, either. Generally, when Ed tried to surface while the demon was awake, the demon forced him down, pushing so hard he had to retreat to the safety of his subconscious mind. In fact, it had ended his last conversation with Eddy with hardly any warning at all.

Was the demon growing tired? Or was Ed's body finally giving out?

Ed thought about that for a bit with a certain amount of sadness. Even though he knew it was probably for the best, he wasn't ready to die, especially since Dax had convinced those Edenites to fix his bum hip. Heck, he'd been moving around like a man half his age for the past couple of weeks, and he'd thoroughly enjoyed not hurting for a change.

He couldn't really feel his body at all now, which made him wonder if the demon had just about used it up. As far as he knew, he hadn't had anything to eat or drink since he'd been taken over, which meant stuff was going to start shutting down before too long.

A sixty-eight year old human didn't exist for long on the souls of demons, but maybe he didn't need to eat or drink when he was possessed. He certainly didn't feel hungry or thirsty. No, he just felt extremely pissed off.

This was his body and his town, and the bastard was after

his loved ones. He was the reason Eddy was trapped in the void, wherever and whatever that was. At least he knew she was safe while she was there. He wasn't sure why he knew that, but he just did, damn it.

He searched for the demon's thoughts, but the creature had retreated into whatever place it went when it rested. Ed stewed for a moment longer.

Then he went in search of Eddy.

*Dad? Where'd you go? We were talking and you just . . .*

*Yeah. Sorry, sweetie. The demon woke up and pulled me back. He's asleep again. You okay?*

*I think so. I don't know how long I've been here. I have no sense of time passing. DemonSlayer's been quiet, but I think it's because she's working on trying to get us out of here. Are you okay?*

He certainly wasn't going to tell her the complete truth, but it wasn't really a lie. Not entirely. He didn't want her any more worried than she already was. *I'm fine. Pissed off, but fine.*

*Yeah. I know what you mean. I'm worried about Dax. He must be frantic by now. He's not real good at waiting for things to happen.*

*Don't you worry about Dax. He's a big boy, and worrying about you is keeping him away from here. This demon wants his life force. Remember how you told me he almost sucked it out of Dax in the crystal caves?*

*That was so scary.*

*I bet it was. Well, that's what this bastard is hoping for again. He wants another shot at your man. Wants to take everything he's got and own it. That happens, all bets are off and the bad guys win, so we can't let Dax anywhere near him.*

*Do you know why? How come he's after Dax?*

*Dax was right when he said it had something to do with the body this demon wants for himself. He's chosen Dax's old demon body. I've picked up his thoughts, and he thinks it was the most powerful demon body in Abyss outside of their big boss, someone he calls the Dark Lord or the Lord of the Dark. Something melodramatic like that. Anyway, as long as Dax lives, there's just enough demon left in him that he's still attached to the body, which keeps this demon king wannabe from gaining full control.*

*I didn't think there was any demon left in Dax. I thought he was kidding me when he said there was some still there.*

*There's enough to keep all of us safe, so don't you worry about it.* He wished he could laugh. Wished he could reassure his little girl with a hug or a smile, but . . . *You know how you women are . . . you all want the bad boy.*

*Yeah. I guess you're right. I really love that part of him. He's so sexy when he lets the demon out to play.*

*No, no, no! I don't want those details, Eddy. You keep those between you and your man.*

What'd the kids call it? TMI? Too much information?

*Okay, Dad. So the demon needs Dax or he can't really keep that body. That's good to know. I just wish I knew how long it was going to take them to get me out of here.*

*Hang tight, sweetie. Dax loves you. He won't let you down.*

"Alton of Artigos!"

Alton popped to his feet, sword drawn. He'd nodded off, but it appeared a command from Mother Crystal could wake even a sleeping Lemurian.

"M'lady?" He sheathed his sword as the others stood beside him.

"Fetch Artigos the Just and his ruby blade. We have a plan to bring Eddy Marks back from the void."

Dax grabbed his arm. "I'll go."

Alton shook his head. "We'll both go."

Crystalline light flashed. "No. Dax must remain. Ginny Jones and DarkFire as well. Make speed, Alton of Artigos.

Time grows short before Eddy Marks is forever lost to the endless darkness of the void."

"Shit."

Dax spun away and continued cursing. Alton leaned over and kissed Ginny. "I'll hurry. Will you be okay?"

"Go. Yes. We're fine. Just get your grandfather back here."

He shot one last, worried glance at Dax and then took off at a steady trot for the upper levels. He hoped he could maintain the pace—he hadn't been kidding when he'd said the climb back up was a killer.

By the time he slipped through the last portal to the main level of Lemurian society less than an hour later, his lungs were practically bursting and his body dripped sweat. Alton knew he'd just broken his own record for the trip. He sent out a call for his grandfather.

Artigos the Just answered within seconds. *Where are you? What's wrong?*

*Eddy Marks has been lost in the void. We need you and DemonsBane in the crystal caves. Mother Crystal is going to try and bring her back.*

*Mother Crystal? She's revealed herself to you?*

*You know of her?*

*Who do you think kept me in books and gossip all the years I was held prisoner?*

He thought about that for a moment. He'd wondered where all those books had come from. His grandfather's shelves had been loaded with books and magazines, not only from Earth's dimension, but other places he'd not recognized. *Grandfather, when this is all over, we need to talk.*

*That we do, Alton. I'm almost there. DemonsBane is leading me to you.*

Alton heard footsteps just seconds later. He turned and saw his grandfather striding down the hallway, dressed in loose pants and a tunic top. The clothing, cut and sewn from his traditional robes, appeared to be the new daily uniform of Lemuria, but even in such casual garb, Artigos the Just carried himself with the natural grace of a born leader.

A leader Alton had helped to reclaim his position in the new Lemuria. A vital, spirited Lemuria, bursting with new energy, alive with fresh hope. Not only were their worthless robes giving way to more practical fashion, their entire society was suddenly energized with Artigos the Just at the helm. After thousands of years of subversive demonic rule, the true soul of Lemuria had finally begun to emerge.

"Grandfather. Thank you for coming so quickly." Alton stepped forward with his hand outstretched, but Artigos pulled him into a tight, emotional embrace.

Just as quickly, he stepped back with both hands on Alton's shoulders. "What's happened to your friend? How did she end up in the void?"

"She disappeared while slipping through a portal. We're not sure how, but we think the demon king managed to divert her into the void."

Artigos nodded and moved quickly toward the portal leading to the lower levels. "Tell me as we go. How did you know to find Mother Crystal? She tends to keep a very low profile."

Alton laughed as he followed his grandfather down the first set of stairs. "You're not kidding. I'd not heard of her before. HellFire was the one to send us to her. How do you know of her?"

Artigos glanced over his shoulder. "When one is locked away with one's own thoughts for millennia, those thoughts can easily become the avenue to insanity. Mother Crystal took pity on me. We began with small conversations, with what you might call mind games. Then one day a scroll appeared, and then another, and eventually books and even magazines. At first, they were rare and difficult for her to come by, but this modern Earth has many books."

"I wondered where you got those. I knew they weren't all

Lemurian, but I couldn't imagine the guards bringing them to you."

"Mother Crystal saved my sanity."

"I'm glad." Alton thought of all those years his grandfather had been a prisoner. How vital a man he was today, and how vitally important to the future of Lemuria. "Now let's just hope she can save Eddy's life."

Eddy's father had disappeared once again, his voice cutting off almost in midsentence, just as it had before. But he'd also mentioned that he'd sensed the demon king stirring again. That must have been what dragged him away.

Still, something felt different, which was odd in and of itself, since feelings and the void didn't seem to go together. Eddy opened her consciousness as completely as she could, searching for whatever had caught her attention.

Something else was out there, some sense of life other than her own.

And just like her, it didn't belong.

*They* didn't belong. Now, how could she know there was more than one of whatever she sensed? How strange.

*Hello? Anyone there?*

Silence, but still the sense of something near.

*Hello? Answer me. Who are you?*

She waited, but no one spoke. Frustrated, Eddy called on her blade. *DemonSlayer? Are you there?*

*I'm here, Eddy.*

*Is there someone else in the void?*

*The void is filled with souls. Unlike ours, most of them belong here.*

*What of the ones who don't? Why do I sense there might be others like me?*

*There are no others like you. You are human made immortal. I believe you are the only one like yourself in the void.*

*Then who am I sensing? Not really human, but not animals or demons. They don't speak, but somehow I feel them. Who can they be? The feeling grows stronger.*

*Ah! I know of whom you speak. They must be the souls of the sons of the women warriors.*

*The sons? I thought they only had daughters. The women who became the Forgotten Ones.*

*Most of them did, but some gave birth to baby boys. Boys who did not fit the demons' plans.*

*Oh. Dear God! The wardens didn't kill babies, did they?*

*No. The demons wanted them to, but the wardens could not be forced to murder their own children. They took them to Mother Crystal who sent them here, into the void, for safekeeping.*

Neither heaven nor hell, Eddy thought. *What can we do to help them? We can't leave them here for eternity. How many are there?*

*Only twelve. Twelve baby boys who have barely known life.*

*This could complicate things, couldn't it?*

*Not necessarily. I will ask Mother Crystal. She might have an idea.*

*Do that. Please.*

Twelve baby boys, born and sentenced to an eternity of waiting. It made her feel petty and small, to think she'd been so impatient. She'd only been here a matter of hours if her father's account of time were correct.

Not really certain if they could understand or not, Eddy sent out a message of sorts. *Stay close to me and hold on. Help is coming.*

And then she hoped she'd not told them a lie.

# Chapter 18

Taron stood in front of the window, buttoning his warm flannel shirt as he stared at the gray, threatening skies. So beautiful, the way the clouds boiled overhead, their shapes an ever-shifting pattern across the sky. He didn't think he could ever grow tired of such a beautiful, dramatic sight.

The snow-covered peak of the big mountain was lost in the clouds, but he could still feel its presence. Having lived within its depths for so long, it was an odd sensation to stand outside and know he was still so close, standing here on its sloping flank.

Lemuria might be in another dimension, but the power that was Mount Shasta crossed all dimensions. The energy vortex here was actually weaker than it was within Lemuria, yet it still held sway over this entire region.

It would be a fascinating subject to study. Someday, though he found it difficult to ever see himself in his old role of scholar and philosopher. So much had changed . . . and the biggest change of all was just coming out of the shower.

He turned away from the window as Willow stepped into the room. He'd showered while she still slept, but now she walked from the bathroom into the bedroom accompanied by her own swirling cloud. Steam billowed out around her, framing her as if she had stepped out of one of those rain-clouds overhead, and it was a struggle not to cross the room and grab her up in his arms, throw her on the bed and make love to her once again.

He didn't think she'd like that. He remembered her making some silly comment about not being able to walk if they didn't stop for awhile.

He really didn't care if he never walked again, as long as he had Willow beside him in bed. Or beneath him. Or his new favorite position with Willow on top.

She sauntered across the room, stopped directly in front of him and stood on her toes to kiss his mouth. He felt her smile against his lips. Drew a deep breath of her scent.

"I can see what you're thinking," she said, "and the answer is no. Not now. It'll be dark soon." She turned away with a seductive sway of her hips and let the towel fall to one side.

He groaned as she dragged the towel behind her on her way to the closet. "One look at you and I know I've created a monster."

She turned, giving him a perfect profile of firm breasts, slightly curved belly, and perfectly rounded bottom. "You?" She dropped the towel and in two quick steps was once again standing in front of him, naked and damp from her shower, her hair hanging in wet curls over her shoulders and breasts. "You've created a monster? I think not."

She kissed him and then pulled away before he could hold her. He let his arms drop to his sides, but he clenched his fists in frustration even as he agreed with her. "You're right. You're too perfect to be a monster. Maybe it's me." He growled deep in his throat as he took a step closer to her, accepting that his entire life had changed because of this woman.

But his first impulse, to tease her and make light of the powerful emotions he could barely contain, faded away, overcome by the simple truth he couldn't hide. Not from Willow, and most definitely not from himself.

With his hands clenched at his sides, he stood over her, looked down into her beautiful, guileless blue eyes, and said exactly what was in his heart. "I love you, Willow. I love you so much it hurts. So much it scares me to death, and I hate to think of what might happen tonight."

The laughter left her eyes. She grabbed both his hands and sighed as his fingers slowly relaxed and tangled with hers. "Oh, Taron, I love you, too. But I plan to keep loving you for a long, long time. Don't let your fears make that stupid fortune a self-fulfilling prophecy. We're going out there to save Ed and we're going to get rid of the demon once and for all. And then we're going to spend the rest of our lives learning all there is to know about being in love."

"I like the sound of that."

She smiled, held his hands to her lips and kissed his knuckles. Then she set him loose and turned back to the dresser again. He watched with an entirely new sense of pure, male pleasure while she made her choices from Eddy's clothing and carefully dressed.

She'd picked out tiny black panties and a matching camisole top that hugged every curve. Then she added a dark blue turtleneck sweater and black jeans, black socks and black leather boots. In that outfit, she'd just about disappear in the darkness if not for the blond hair.

Except she pulled a knit cap out of the dresser and stuck it on her head, tucking all that gorgeous hair up inside.

"Practical, but I'm really going to miss seeing your hair."

Laughing, she whipped the cap off. "I just wanted to see if it would work. I don't plan to wear it until later." She stood there a moment and stared at herself in the mirror. After a moment, she rubbed her hands over her arms. "Taron? Do you feel any different tonight?"

"Different?" He crossed the room, stood behind her with his arms looped lightly around her middle, and studied the two of them in the full length mirror. As tall as she was, he was still so much taller, so much larger. And yet, between the two of them, Willow was stronger in so many ways.

"How so? In what way do you feel different?"

She shook her head. "I'm not sure. It's like I'm buzzing. Eddy says she gets that way if she drinks too much of Ed's coffee. Like she's got to do something to burn off the energy or she'll explode. I sort of feel like that. It's hard to describe."

"Have you been storing up blue sparkles?" He laughed when he said it, but then Willow slipped out of his embrace and pointed her fingers at the middle of the room.

"I don't know. I hadn't even thought of that."

She closed her eyes and Taron felt a slight change in the air pressure in the room. An instant later, a huge blast of sparkles exploded from Willow's fingertips. Willow let loose with a short, sharp shriek of surprise. The mass of blue fire shot across the room, rolled up the wall and licked at the ceiling. Then the sparkles gently dissipated and faded from sight.

Taron stared at the wall and then spun around to stare at Willow, speechless. Then he looked more closely at the dark smudge streaking across the wallpaper. "What the nine hells was that?"

Eyes wide, Willow ran across the room and dragged her fingers over the wall. When she held up her hand, her fingertips were covered in black. "It's soot. I burned Eddy's wall! My sparkles have never done anything like that before. What happened?"

Taron stared at the dark smudge on the wall and then grabbed her hand and looked just as closely at her smudged fingertips. "I don't know, but I'll bet that could really piss off the demon king."

"You're not kidding. Could I somehow be getting stronger?"

"Maybe. But why?"

Suddenly she raised her head and grinned at him. "I think it's you. Because you love me."

He laughed. "That's a bit farfetched. How could that make a difference?"

She shook her head in complete denial. "I don't know how I know, but I do. I can feel it," she thumped her chest with her fist, "here. When you weren't admitting how you felt, maybe you created some sort of barrier between me and my sparkles. It's gone now. I can feel the energy." She tilted her chin and gave him a cheeky grin. "It's quite literally at my fingertips."

She kissed him, and this time it wasn't a quick peck. This time she lingered, making love to his mouth the way he'd made love to her all throughout the day.

When she finally pulled away, both of them were breathing hard. "Okay," she said. "Maybe that wasn't a good idea."

He laughed. "I thought it was a great idea."

"You would. Not now. We need to get something to eat."

"Are you sure?" He cast a quick glance at the freshly made bed.

"I'm sure. Now."

He could hardly understand her through her laughter. As much as he loved the sound of Willow laughing, he wasn't sure he liked the idea that she was probably near hysterics because of his forlorn expression.

He wanted her. Wanted the soft slide of her body against his, the taste of her on his lips, the hot, rhythmic contractions of her feminine sheath grasping him like a tight fist. And after he imagined every way to feel her, to taste and hold her, he let himself think of the other parts of Willow he'd already grown to love. Her wonderful way of seeing the world, her laughter, her sense of humor, her purity. She was a grown woman without any baggage, without a past to mar the way she saw the future. Everything for Willow was fresh and new, and that innocence was something she shared without reservation.

She was giving Taron the chance to see everything through her eyes, and he felt reborn. And then, like an insidious burst of darkness, Taron saw what might be. If he were to lose Willow, if he somehow lost her fresh and perfect doorway into life, he would have no reason to live. Her death would be the end of him. He bit back a curse as reality slapped him awake and he shot back into the moment.

Willow was still chuckling when she turned away and headed for the kitchen. Taron shoved his fears aside as he followed her down the hallway, and the last bits of darkness disappeared when he picked up Bumper's excited thoughts.

*Bacon, Willow? Are you going to fix me bacon? I love bacon. You didn't make it this morning. Will you make it now? Please, Willow?*

*No, Bumper. No bacon.*

Sighing almost as dramatically as Bumper, Taron added his thoughts. *Are you absolutely sure?*

Willow was still grinning when he caught up to her in the kitchen. She turned and planted a big kiss on his mouth, and the last of the shadows vanished. Willow was right. Don't borrow trouble. Do like Bumper and live for the moment.

It went entirely against his nature, but he was damned well going to try.

Willow ended their kiss and was suddenly all business as she pulled two big steaks out of the freezer and stuck them in the microwave to defrost. "This is better than bacon. I promise."

He was almost certain he sensed Bumper's excited leaps for joy. *It is, Taron. You'll like steak. It's good, Taron. Trust me. I love steak. Ed lets me taste it. Will you let me taste steak, Taron?*

"Settle down, Bumper." He glanced up in time to catch

Willow rolling her eyes. "I have this image of her bouncing up and down with her tail going like crazy."

Laughing, Willow tangled both hands in her hair and tugged. "You should feel it from my perspective."

He relaxed even more as he watched her prepare dinner. She was so comfortable with all the different appliances. They had similar things in Lemuria, but he'd never grown all that adept at using them. Single men often took their meals in the various cafeterias or merely reheated simple things in their rooms. Tonight Willow baked potatoes in the microwave and she made a big salad while the steaks cooked under the broiler. Taron set the table, but he kept his eyes on Willow as she did everything with an economy of movement and an undeniable grace.

Proudly, she sat down at the table, taking the seat across from Taron. Her brilliant smile told him exactly how pleased she was with herself for creating such a beautiful meal.

Taron lifted his glass of wine. "To you and your amazing skills," he said, though he wasn't thinking entirely of her cooking.

Willow sipped her wine, but her gaze was pinned to Taron. "Eat," he said. "Don't let it grow cold." Of course, he hadn't taken a bite, either.

Finally Willow dug into her meal and Taron ate as well. It tasted every bit as good as it looked, but the food on his plate wasn't what made this dinner so special. It was the woman sitting across from him, the knowledge that he'd made love to her most of the day and wanted her even now. It was the comfortable way they teased one another and talked about nothing. It was everything and nothing in particular, and Taron wanted to capture the moment. Wanted to save this day and this evening for all time.

Every experience today had been unique, every touch, every kiss. He'd never felt this way about anyone in his entire life, but it was even more than that. He realized he'd never before felt this way about himself, either. He'd been wrong when he told Willow he didn't feel any different.

He didn't merely feel different—he *was* different. She'd changed him in more ways than he could possibly name.

Barely forty-eight hours in her presence, and neither he nor the life he led would ever be the same again.


Alton was a few steps ahead when he led Artigos the Just into the crystal cave. His grandfather paused just inside the huge cavern and then, without any warning, dropped reverently to his knees.

Alton turned just in time to see him kneel, unsheathe his sword, and lay DemonsBane on the ground. Ignoring the curious eyes of the others standing inside the cavern, Artigos folded his arms across his chest and bowed his head. "Mother Crystal, all honor to you, and my heartfelt thanks for your care. I have long hoped to have the opportunity to come to you in person as a free man and offer to you both my loyalty as your servant, and my heartfelt thanks for your care."

Crystals flashed and the soft sound of beautiful feminine laughter flowed across the cavern. "Rise, Artigos, my old friend. It is good to see you free at last, leading your people as you should have been doing all those long years."

"Thank you." He dipped his head. "Your servant, always."

Would wonders never cease? Alton held out his hand to his grandfather. Artigos grasped it firmly and stood, sheathing DemonsBane as he rose. Then he turned and flashed a brilliant smile at his grandson.

"If Mother Crystal were flesh and blood, I would take her as my consort and share with her the leadership of our world. And if she were willing, I would take her to my bed and keep her there, sated and content for as long as I could hold her."

Alton's mouth dropped open. He had no words. None at all.

His grandfather laughed and slapped him on the back. "Shut your mouth, grandson, and don't look so shocked. Though I've never seen her, I have loved the woman I imagine behind that glorious voice for all these long years. She has been my friend, a constant presence speaking words of wisdom in my mind, and she will always remain the anchor holding my heart. She's starred in my fantasies through the long, dark nights, and offered me counsel throughout all the days of my captivity. Should you have any doubt that I have loved her all these many years?"

"Grandfather, I will admit that there are very few things you ever say that don't leave me amazed, but that probably tops the list. Until HellFire spoke, I never knew Mother Crystal existed."

Artigos shook his head slowly, as if the thought of that unrequited love were one more burden he would have to bear. "It's true, Alton. She is as real as you and I, and I have loved her for millennia. I will always love and honor her." He winked at Alton. "And I will forever want the lady in my bed."

Soft laughter rippled about the huge room. "Be careful what you wish for, Artigos the Just. One day I might surprise you."

Artigos glanced at Alton with raised brows. Alton just shook his head and tried not to laugh. His grandmother had died long before Lemuria sank beneath the sea, and his grandfather had been alone for much of his life. Still, he assumed Mother Crystal, a demigoddess, after all, was merely joking.

Wasn't she?

Artigos had to think the same. "You have done much for us, Mother Crystal," his grandfather said. "Thank you for giving an old man hope." Then he straightened and was once again the leader, the ruler of an entire people. "My grandson tells me now that we have an even greater favor to ask."

"Aye, 'tis true, but this is a favor I was not certain I could grant. My power is great, though I am not omnipotent. However, Eddy Marks is a powerful warrior, willing to give everything in the fight against the demon scourge, and demonkind must be stopped. She has been favored as are few humans with the gift of immortality, and even more important, she carries crystal, which eternally links her to me. We can't afford to lose either Eddy Marks or DemonSlayer. The Dark Lord has grown overly confident of late, which might be the key to his downfall. He is beginning to believe himself above the need for balance and he works his evil ways through one who is a traitor to his own blood, the one you call the demon king. Even now, that one has taken over the body of Eddy Marks's father. Ed Marks is possessed by evil, but he fights the demon bravely."

Dax had been standing quietly to one side, but he spun about and stared at Alton. "Ed? Ed's been taken? We have to help him. We . . ."

"No." Crystal shimmered and glowed brightly. "You are needed here. All of you are needed here. As I said, we must do everything we can to bring Eddy Marks back. I am not entirely positive we will succeed, but if you are willing, I say we attempt the impossible this day."

Dax nodded his head. "Anything, my lady. I will do whatever is needed, whatever is in my power to bring Eddy back." The way he stood, with his arms folded across his chest, his chin thrust forward and determination in his eyes told Alton more than his words. Dax wasn't speaking lightly. He would gladly give his own life if he could trade it for Eddy's safety. But what of her father?

"What about Ed?" Alton glanced at Dax, but he spoke to the entity. "Is it too late for us to help him?"

Crystal glowed and Mother Crystal's voice seemed to come from everywhere at once. "Taron of Libernus is in

Evergreen. He and Willow will meet the demon in battle. Much depends on their success."

Dawson shot a questioning glance at Alton. "But Willow's inside a dog. How can she fight demons?"

Once again, soft laughter rippled across the huge cavern. "Don't underestimate Willow. She is a most amazing creature and proof to me that all things are possible. Important proof to have when one is prepared to attempt something that's not only impossible, but could be quite dangerous. Dax?"

Dax snapped to attention, looking every part the soldier. Still bare-chested with his scabbard strapped to his back, he folded his arms across his chest, covering much of the colorful phoenix tattoo. "Yes, my lady?"

"Are you willing to risk all for the life of your lady love?"

He nodded. "Yes, my lady. There is no sacrifice too great. Eddy is my life. Without her, my life has no value and there is no reason to continue."

"Actually, my brave warrior, there is every reason, but I will take your words as your pledge made before these witnesses, and I honor your bravery. Remove your sword and sheath, as well as the heavy trousers you wear. Lie upon the ruby altar."

He nodded his compliance without question, unbuckled his scabbard with the crystal sword inside, and handed it to Alton. As he took the weapon, Alton caught Dax's gaze and held it for a long moment.

Dax was his brother, as close to him as Taron, a man he'd known all of his life. He'd known Dax for merely one month, but during these past few weeks, fighting side by side, facing demonkind as brothers in arms, they'd forged an unbreakable bond. Alton loved Eddy, but he loved Dax every bit as much. He wasn't willing to lose either of them. "You're sure?"

Dax slowly shook his head. "It's all right, my friend. I choose this freely, no matter what happens. If it goes wrong for me, tell Eddy how much I love her. That I will always love her."

"You know I will. Be safe."

Dax nodded. "I'll do my best. Alton . . ." He sighed and shrugged one shoulder. "I have no other choice."

"I know." Alton felt the connection between them, a powerful link through the weight of the scabbard and the living crystal blade tucked within. "I would make the same decision if I were in your sandals. The gods be with you. Both you and Eddy. Come back safely."

"We'll do our best." He flashed a cocky grin at Alton and then, following the entity's instructions, slipped off his boots and socks, and peeled his jeans down his legs. Wearing nothing but the black knit boxers Eddy had bought for him, Dax walked to the ruby altar and stretched out on the blood-red, crystalline surface.

It hurt Alton to see him lying there. Dax looked too much like a living sacrifice.

"Ginny Jones, draw DarkFire. Artigos the Just, draw DemonsBane."

Each did as instructed. Alton, Selyn, and Dawson stood to one side. Alton wondered if the others felt the sense of power within the cave the way he did. The walls seemed to vibrate as if they pulsed with life. Mother Crystal's voice came from everywhere and from nowhere. It filled the room, echoed from each crystal and raised gooseflesh over Alton's arms and along his spine.

"Selyn of Elda's line, Dawson Buck, and Alton of Artigos, remove StarFire, DemonsDeath, HellFire, and DemonFire from their scabbards. Place each sword on the ground at the head of the altar. Then stand beside Dax; touch him, share your life force with him. Ginny Jones and Artigos the Just, give the light from your blades to the phoenix. Share the power, even as the phoenix flies. If all goes as planned, as the phoenix rises from the ashes of its own destruction, so shall Eddy Marks rise from the void."

Without question, Alton, Selyn, and Dawson placed their crystal swords along with Dax's DemonFire on the ground below the end of the altar where Dax rested his head. Then they each lined up along his left side. Dawson wrapped his hands around Dax's ankle and calf; Selyn placed her hands on his thigh and waist. Alton clasped Dax's shoulder and arm, so that each of them held on, skin to skin.

Alton glanced down and looked directly into Dax's dark brown eyes. He was entirely calm and there was absolutely no sign of fear on his face. It came to Alton then, between one heartbeat and the next, that Dax truly was willing to give his life to bring Eddy back. He had no fear because he didn't care what he had to go through or whether or not he survived. Not as long as Eddy lived.

Alton gave Dax's shoulder an encouraging squeeze, and concentrated on sharing whatever he could with his friend. Ginny and his grandfather stood on the other side of the altar and aimed their swords at the tattoo on Dax's chest. Dark purple light shot forth from Ginny's blade while a blood-red beam blasted from Artigos's DemonsBane.

The beams of light met in the very center of the phoenix. The moment the brilliant glow touched the tattoo, Dax jerked and his back spasmed into a full arc. His lips tightened in a grimace, but no sound escaped.

Alton held on. He tried to hold Dax down to the table, but whatever force had caught him was stronger than Alton's Lemurian strength. The sense of power grew until the entire cavern hummed with it. The hum grew louder, pulsing and gaining a rhythm until it sounded as if a heart beat within the crystal walls. The light inside the crystals covering the walls and ceiling dimmed even as they pulsed with life, and Alton felt his energy being drawn through his fingers, pulled from every part of his body into Dax.

No . . . not Dax. It went to the phoenix tattoo.

The phoenix glowed beneath DarkFire's light. The brilliant colors took on an unnatural fluorescence, so bright they hurt his eyes, but he couldn't look away. The red light from his grandfather's blade covered Dax's entire torso, spreading out from the point where it met the glow of Ginny's sword, covering and containing the light from DarkFire.

Dax stayed locked in a powerful spasm, his back bowed, the muscles in his body rigid. Tendons stretched taut from his shoulders to his neck and his hands tightened convulsively over the edges of the ruby altar. Veins bulged along his arms and across his forehead. A dark flush covered his body from head to foot.

He made no sound. His eyes were closed, his lips remained twisted in a painful rictus. Whatever locked him so tightly held the others as well. Alton knew that even had he wanted, he could not have lifted his hands from Dax's shoulder or arm.

Even as his body was locked in stasis, his mind was clear, his brain cataloging everything that happened, every nuance, every sound, every sensation. They were locked together, the four of them, while Ginny and Artigos stood as if transfixed, holding their weapons on Dax, bathing him in what felt like the same power they used to seal a portal or kill a demon.

The only thing that moved was the phoenix. The feathers rippled with life and inked flames licked across Dax's belly. Alton was reminded of the cursed snake, the way it had writhed over Dax's torso as it tried to turn the ex-demon's powers against him. That had been a foul and loathsome thing. Poisonous, striking against Dax with its ivory fangs, it had truly been a cursed creature intent on killing.

Now though, there was no sense of evil, no fear that the phoenix intended to harm Dax. The brightly colored bird was bursting with purpose and filled with life.

One wing lifted a tiny bit, and then the other, slight, gentle tugs as colorful art pulled away from warm, living flesh. The skin beneath the ink was clear and healthy, not the bloody wound the snake had left when it tried to separate itself from Dax's skin. No, the phoenix was lifting itself free, feather by feather, carefully releasing one at a time. Gently, ever so gently with the greatest care.

The sound in the cavern grew, and the thrumming of a beating heart was joined by an angelic choir, a beautiful blend of men's and women's voices singing in perfect harmony. Moving up and down the scale without words, it grew in volume from the faintest musical hum until it became a powerful song, a rhythmic chant in a language Alton had never heard before.

Even though the words were unfamiliar, he was almost certain he understood their meaning. This was a song of power, of life, and he was positive the intent was to share and give strength.

The light in the crystals caught and held the beat with the chanting voices until the entire cavern was alive with song, with the sense of all the warriors who had passed, those whose souls resided here within these crystal walls.

Time lost meaning but the song continued, growing in strength, in power, in life. After a while, Dax's body relaxed a bit and he lay back upon the altar, but still the phoenix struggled to free itself. Finally, the long neck began to undulate, until, twisting and turning, the bird pulled its head free from Dax's shoulder.

It lifted its beak and the eyes were bright with intelligence as it stared at the faces surrounding Dax. Alton heard Selyn's soft gasp and Dawson's whispered curse. Transfixed, Alton stared at the bird as it studied each one of them before returning to its business of pulling free.

Slowly it tugged and pulled, twisting and writhing over

Dax's muscular belly and chest, lifting itself, feather by feather, away from its living canvas.

Like a moth escaping its chrysalis, the phoenix forced itself into a standing position and slowly straightened its wings. Once they were fully extended, the phoenix slowly waved them back and forth until they took on form and shape, growing from a two-dimensional drawing to fully functional, three-dimensional wings. They were bigger than Alton had imagined, spreading well beyond the width of Dax's body. Cool feathers brushed Alton's arm.

Impossible, and yet there was no denying what he saw, what he felt. Dax lay perfectly still, held in stasis by whatever this was that was taking place, and though his muscles remained rigid, he didn't appear to be in pain.

Alton realized he was growing weaker as his life force spilled into the phoenix. His legs had begun to shake; his hands trembled, but still he gave what he could, sharing freely. He realized he was praying, begging the gods he'd never truly believed in, asking them to return Eddy, to protect Dax.

The bird was almost entirely free, now. Its talons remained fixed against Dax's taut belly, and the tail feathers, all the brilliant blues and greens, reds and yellows of the rainbow, were still partially trapped beneath the waistband of Dax's knit boxer shorts. The bird turned and stared at its trapped tail. It jerked its body, but the feathers were well and truly stuck.

Finally, using its sharp beak, the phoenix leaned over, grabbed its tail feathers and tugged. They slipped just a fraction of the way free. He tugged again, and then again until he finally pulled them out from under the elastic waistband. Long and silky, they draped over Dax's thigh and curled against Selyn's hand.

Alton caught her eye for just a second, saw the utter amazement in her expression, but he jerked his attention back to the bird as the phoenix shook himself, ruffling all his feathers. Then he pulled both his feet free of Dax's belly and fluffed his feathers in such a comical fashion, looking so much like a long-necked, brightly colored barnyard rooster getting ready to crow, that Alton almost laughed.

Entirely free now, the phoenix raised its head and looked around. It stared directly at Alton and opened its beak wide, stretched its neck, and flapped its wings.

The chanting grew louder. Lights flashed from crystal to crystal in a dizzying display racing from walls to ceiling and back again. Dax opened his eyes and watched the bird. The impossible creature turned and focused on him, leaned in close and breathed into his mouth. Then it took a couple of steps across Dax's belly and stuck its head up through the clear red glow from DemonsBane's blade, almost as if it were testing the air.

A white mist floated out of the walls, breaking free from the shimmering crystals and gathering overhead. Alton thought of the spirits of the fallen warriors and how they'd looked when Dax had fought the demon king here in this same cavern. It appeared those same spirits were showing themselves again. They swirled faster and faster, spinning until the mist flowed into a tight circle, a small cyclone just over their heads. The chanting grew louder. The sense of power, the growing pressure within the cavern reached explosive levels.

The bird gazed once more at Dax, dipped its head as if acknowledging him, and then leapt into the air with a triumphant cry. The sound it made was of crystal chiming against crystal, the clear tone of a bell heralding something wonderful. Its wings spread wide and gloriously long tail feathers trailed behind. It headed straight up, aiming directly for the center of the swirling mist, lifting into the air on long, strong thrusts of its powerful wings.

As if they'd choreographed the move, Ginny and Artigos

shifted their blades and caught the phoenix in a burst of purple and red light.

The chanting ended on a single note.

Beak spread wide in a beautiful scream that was the sound of shattered crystal and ringing bells, the phoenix exploded into brilliant flames. The mist overhead coalesced into a single arrow point that shot into the midst of the boiling inferno. Not an ash fell. There was no stench of burned feathers, no smoke. Nothing but a mere second of whirling, white-hot mist and flames.

Then there was nothing left at all.

Stunned silence filled the crystal chamber. Alton blinked. He couldn't believe what he'd just seen, yet he had to believe it had happened the way it was supposed to.

He didn't move. Neither did the others, though he was aware of Ginny and his grandfather removing their scabbards and setting them aside. Taking their swords and placing them with the others on the ground at the head of the altar. Then they were standing on Dax's other side, with their hands pressed to his body.

Sharing their life force as Alton and the others shared theirs. Silently, they stood there, connected by touch through Dax's powerful body.

Alton lost track of time, lost all sense of self. He was merely a part of the whole, linked through touch, through love and the age-old power of crystal. He searched for a sense of Eddy, for anything that would tell him she was close, that whatever they had just witnessed had somehow brought her back, but there was no way to tell if they'd reached her or not.

No way to know if they'd succeeded.

He was merely one of six who had become one with his grandfather, Ginny, Dawson, Selyn, and Dax, all of them breathing as one. Their life force shared and combined, their lungs drawing the same air, their hearts beating in sync.

Six as one. Each an individual, yet each a part of the

whole. The sound of a single heartbeat, rising and falling, slowing and then speeding up, filled the chamber. The rush of a single set of lungs. The sense of a single mind.

Six as one. One as six.

The heartbeat stuttered, stopped, and then started again. Steady this time, and even stronger. Lungs filled with life-giving air, the mind welcomed another.

Suddenly, so smoothly he hardly recognized the transition, Alton was one of seven. Seven hearts beating as one. Seven minds in sync. Seven.

And then, before he could question this obviously important event, everything went dark.

# Chapter 19

It seemed to have gotten dark much earlier tonight, but the clouds had obscured the sun for most of the day, and Taron figured that must explain the fact the street lights in the quiet neighborhood were already flickering to life.

"Where should we start our hunt?" Carefully he dried the last dish and put it up in the cupboard with the others.

Willow paused in the midst of wiping down the counter and cocked her head. She frowned and let out a big sigh. "I have a feeling you were right, earlier, when you said the demon king would probably come hunting for us. Turn the light off."

He didn't question her as he flicked the switch on the wall beside him. Willow walked over to the kitchen window and stared into the darkness. Bumper's low growl, even delivered telepathically, sent chills along his spine.

"What do you sense? Is he out there?"

Willow shook her head. "I don't sense anything, but Bumper's really uneasy."

"Bumper? What is it?" He draped the wet towel over the counter and joined Willow beside the window. "Bumper?"

*Sorry, Taron. I don't know. Something's out there. I thought it was Ed but it's not Ed. Then I thought it was the demon king, but it's not him either, but since he's inside Ed, I have a feeling that's what I sense. And he's not that close, but he is definitely out there.*

Taron kissed Willow's cheek. "Wait here. I'm going to take a quick look, but keep those sparkles handy."

She nodded, turned, and quickly kissed him back. Taron went out the door that opened into the garage. He knew it would give him enough cover to slip around the house from the backyard.

The air was chilly, though not too cold, and the wind had died down to barely a whisper. The rain had stopped, at least for now. There was a sense of expectation about the evening. As he moved quietly through the darkness, he wondered if a bigger storm might be brewing.

There had, after all, been that blood-red sunrise this morning, and while it had rained, the storm had been a gentle one. Not nearly enough to explain the odd sense of anxiety that had dogged him for the last couple of hours.

Taron walked around the side of the garage and carefully opened the yard gate, staying to the shadows as he moved to the front of the house. He paused, partially hidden in a large shrub at the corner, and listened.

The neighborhood was still, but he waited, opening his senses to the sounds of the evening. Someone down the street had their television on too loud—he'd watched the machine a bit at Ed's house and discovered that, as fascinating as it was, it was also a monumental waste of time.

Willow loved it. She said television gave her a view into human's lives, but Taron wasn't so sure it was a valid picture. None of the humans he'd met so far took any of the medications that were constantly on the screen. If he took television at face value, he'd have to assume that everyone in this dimension was sexually impotent and had trouble sleeping and growing hair.

So far, he didn't think that was the case.

A man's voice caught his attention. He slipped through the heavy shrubbery until he could get closer to the street. It sounded like Ed's neighbor, Mr. Puccini, and he was obviously agitated about something.

Staying to the shadows, Taron quietly ran halfway down the block until he was far enough away from the streetlight. He crossed the street in darkness and then slowly worked his way back toward Mr. Puccini's house.

The old man was up on his front porch, partially hidden behind one of the posts. Whoever he was talking to was still down at the yard level, but they were obviously focused on each other and not paying any attention to Taron.

He moved closer, until he was hidden beside the porch in complete shadow, only a few feet from the two men.

"I tell you, Ed, you look like hell. What are those kids doing to you? And don't tell me they're good kids. You were fine until Eddy started bringing those oddball friends of hers around."

*Nine hells.*

Ed, or what was left of the poor man, merely growled out an incomprehensible reply. The stench of sulfur was overwhelming, but Taron couldn't very well attack the demon with Ed's neighbor standing so close. He edged around the porch where he could get a better view of Ed.

Mr. Puccini was right—he did look like hell. His skin was sallow and drawn and his arms and hands were covered with numerous cuts and scratches. His hair stood on end and it was obvious he'd not eaten in the past couple of days. Taron wondered how long Ed could survive like this. His body was being used up by the demon.

*Willow? Can you hear me?*

*Taron! I was getting worried. Where are you?*

*Hiding beside Mr. Puccini's porch. Ed's here and he looks awful. He's still possessed. We need to go after the demon*

*king if we're going to save Eddy's dad, but I don't want the
old neighbor involved. Any ideas?*

*I can walk over and interrupt them. Somehow get the old
man inside his house.*

*That might work. No! Wait . . .*

Ed stopped talking. His body seemed to go rigid.

"Ed? What's wrong?" Mr. Puccini moved down the stairs
from his spot on the porch and reached for his friend.

Ed let out a banshee cry and leapt forward. He grabbed
the old man in a tight bear hug. The misty outline of the
demon king burst out of Ed and surrounded Mr. Puccini,
clinging to him like plastic wrap, encasing and silencing his
sharp scream in the seething dark demon mist.

Taron jumped out from behind the porch and swung
CrystalFire. The flat of the blade connected with the demon
mist, but all it did was send worthless sparks into the air.

The old man's struggles were weakening. His head fell
back, though his mouth was still open in a silent scream of
what had to be either terror or pain or both. Taron used the
flat of his blade against Ed's body again, striking him across
the shoulders, but he didn't even react to the blow.

Taron was afraid to hit him harder. He didn't want to hurt
Ed or the old neighbor, but how to stop the demon? And
what the nine hells was the creature doing?

Willow skidded to a stop beside him, held out her hands
and shot a blast of fiery blue sparkles at the demon mist covering Mr. Puccini. A startled howl split the night and the
oily, black mist pulled back. It disappeared into Ed's body,
sucked back inside in less than a heartbeat.

Once the demon mist freed the old man, Mr. Puccini fell
to the ground. Taron knelt beside him while Willow blasted
her blue fire at Ed, but this time her sparkles rolled harmlessly off his body.

The demon king turned as if it were going to attack. Taron
jumped up and raised his sword as Ed stared at first Willow

and then Taron and then back at Willow. Then, with a scream, Ed turned and sped away, racing into the darkness much faster than any human should be able to run.

Taron knelt once again beside the old man and touched his fingers to the big artery at his neck. His eyes were shut, his lips blue. "He's alive, but barely."

"I'm going inside to call nine-one-one."

"What's that?" Taron glanced up from checking on the man's pulse.

"That's a number you call when you need help. Ginny used to answer the calls in her job. She told me about it. We're going to call, and then we need to get out of here before anyone comes."

Taron nodded, but he stayed with the old man. At least Mr. Puccini was breathing regularly, but he seemed terribly weak, and he looked almost as if he'd physically shrunk in size. Before he had time to figure it out, Willow was back outside. "C'mon. Into the shadows before we're caught here. There's no way to explain what's happened."

"Nine hells, Willow. Even I'm not sure what just happened."

"Hush." Finger to her lips, Willow slipped around the side of the house and ran silently down the street to a shadowed area where the two of them could cross the street safely. In less than a minute they were back at Ed's house.

Sirens screamed not far away.

Willow and Taron slipped inside the garage just as a police car and an ambulance pulled up across the street. Taron grabbed Willow's hand and dragged her inside the kitchen where they could watch through the dark window.

Paramedics were kneeling over Mr. Puccini, who still appeared to be unconscious. Taron wondered what story the old man would give the doctors when he finally came to, but that was out of his control. He couldn't fix everything.

Nine hells . . . he couldn't fix anything. Sighing, he turned away from the window and gazed at Willow. "Okay. Now tell me what just happened."

She just shook her head. "I'm not positive, but I think the demon king stole Mr. Puccini's life force. Not all of it, but enough to knock him out. Sucked it out of him just the way he'd steal it from a demon."

"I was afraid that's what happened. Grab a coat. We need to go after him. He's got to be stopped tonight, before he gets any stronger." He stared at Willow. "Before he kills anyone."

"I know." Willow dragged her fingers through her tousled hair. "We have to catch him, Taron. Now that he's figured out how to do that, there'll be no stopping him. No one will be safe."

She turned away and walked over to the back door, grabbed a black leather jacket off the coat rack and tossed it to him. "This is Alton's, so it should fit you." Then she slipped on a black coat that must have been Eddy's, and tucked her blond hair up inside the black, knit watch cap she'd tried on earlier.

Dressed all in black, she'd blend in well with the shadows. As would he. Willow had found another cap just like hers as well as a pair of dark running shoes of Alton's that fit just fine. With the dark blue jeans and the black leather jacket, he'd be difficult to spot at night. Tying his red hair back in a single tail, Taron tucked it down inside the coat, pulled the black watch cap over his head and donned his scabbard and sword.

"Ready?"

Willow nodded. She fastened a small pack around her waist and stuck a couple of water bottles and some energy bars in it. "I don't think he's gone back toward town. Bumper is still uneasy—she thinks he's headed for the portal."

"Up the mountain? That's the only portal around here, isn't it?" Taron adjusted his scabbard and checked to make sure his sword was in reach.

"It's the only one I know of. It makes sense—I bet he's

figured out that Dax isn't here, and if taking Dax's life force is the demon king's ultimate goal, he's going to have to go looking for him."

"Do you think he'll try to go to Sedona? The portal's shut, but I imagine he could open it."

"Not if we can stop him first." She flashed him a bright grin and headed out the back door.

Taron turned out the lights and followed on her heels. His heart thudded in his chest, but it wasn't fear that had him wound so tight. It was adrenaline. Excitement, pure and simple. The hunt was on, and there was only one acceptable conclusion.

Dax crawled out of a deep sea of thick, warm ooze. He felt no fear, no sense of anything other than a need to find the surface so that he could breathe deeply once more of fresh, clean, air. His body seemed unaccountably sluggish, as if the stuff he swam through clasped his arms and legs, clung to his chest, covered his face.

Finally he broke through, but there was no sense of joy or achievement—no, it was merely something he had to do if he wanted to breathe again, and he did. He'd grown accustomed to breathing since he'd gotten this human body, so he took slow, steady breaths, not gulping for air or panicking even though there'd not been a chance to draw a breath for so long.

Breathing was merely something he needed to do to stay alive, so he did it. Once he realized his lungs were working all right, he thought about opening his eyes. The ooze was gone, and he ran his fingers over his chest. Something seemed different, though it wasn't so much in the way he felt as what he sensed. No matter. It didn't feel as if it were all that important.

So he opened his eyes, blinked against the soft light of crystal. Reached out with his mind and couldn't find the one who was always there. "Eddy?" He shoved himself into a sitting position, but that made everything spin. Still blinking, he slowly shook his head to clear his thoughts. The room seemed to spin even more, but he fought the desire to lie back down, to sleep.

Why didn't Eddy answer? He took a few deep breaths and called out. "Eddy? Are you here?"

Nothing. He glanced about, still feeling out of step and disoriented. Alton lay on the ground beside the altar. His fingers were clasped in Ginny's and the two appeared to be deeply asleep. Dawson and Selyn slept as well, their hands tightly linked.

Artigos the Just had fallen beside his grandson. One arm stretched out, the fingers spread wide as if he reached for his blade, but he didn't appear to be in any distress. Dax planted his hands on the edge of the ruby altar, holding himself upright, and studied each of his companions.

Why were they lying so still? And what the hell was he doing on the damned altar? He tried to remember what they'd been up to, but everything was murky. He stared at his friends, waiting for something to make sense.

After a moment he relaxed. Their chests rose and fell the way they should. Everyone was alive. That was good. Maybe they were as exhausted as he felt. He glanced at the ruby altar and fought a powerful desire to lie back down to sleep some more. He couldn't remember ever feeling so weak, so unbelievably tired. He ran his hand over his chest, absentmindedly rubbing the phoenix tattoo.

As he remembered. His mind flooded with an overwhelming fear for Eddy, with need. With the final moments before he blacked out—the whisper of feathers across his chest, the strange sense of the tattoo pulling carefully away from his skin, and the final, brilliant flash of fire as the phoenix spread its wings; as it leapt into the air. He winced, remembering the awesome sight of the magical bird rising up and bursting into flames.

Just before it disappeared in a flash of cold fire.

He glanced at his chest, expecting to see the colorfully inked bird that had appeared on his skin the night he died. The phoenix rising from the flames, signifying his rebirth.

"Nine hells and then some."

Alton's favorite curse seemed totally apropos.

His chest was bare and the phoenix tattoo was gone.


She ached all over. Her head, her arms, her legs. Even her butt ached. She was afraid to open her eyes, convinced they'd ache, too, but not knowing was worse than the pain.

There'd been no pain in the void. No sense of Eddy Marks beyond the simple thoughts within her conscious mind. Pain likely meant her situation had changed and she was no longer in the void, but was it a good change or a bad one?

*Why don't you open your eyes and check, you frickin' coward? Well, yeah. Maybe.*

She could do this. Slowly, carefully, Eddy opened her eyes, squinting against the light. Her first thought was that it seemed as if a thousand candles burned. Blinking, Eddy forced herself to focus and realized she was lying on her back on the hard ground, looking at diamonds. Thousands upon thousands of diamonds, glimmering and shimmering from the inside out, covering the walls and ceiling of . . .

"The crystal cave?" She rubbed her eyes with both hands and looked again. Definitely the crystal cave. She even recognized the crystal sconces carved into the walls where Taron had placed his glow sticks.

The sconces were empty, but the cave still glowed. That was unusual. She was lying on the ground, close beside the little creek that meandered across one end of the huge cavern. She remembered it, now. Remembered how clear and cold the water had tasted. Her throat burned with thirst, so she rolled to her belly and got up on her hands and knees, crawled just a couple of feet and dipped her face in the icy water.

Sucking it up through parched lips, she drank her fill. The water cleared her head and took away most of the pain, and she wondered if the achiness had merely been her body's reaction to not having any sensation at all for such a long time.

However long it had been.

She sat back on her heels, suddenly aware of two important things—she was stark naked, and she wasn't alone. In fact, if she wasn't mistaken, the soft curse she'd just heard had been Dax! She spun around so quickly she almost fell on her butt, caught herself, and gazed around the cavern.

The place where she'd awakened lay in shadows, but the ruby altar was bathed in brilliant crystal fire . . . and Dax was sitting on the edge of the altar, rubbing his hand across his chest!

"Dax? Dax! I'm here."

"Eddy?" His head popped up and turned this way and that as he swept the cavern with his gaze, twisting in all directions to find her.

"Over here. By the creek." She struggled to her feet, but it was hard to hold her balance and she quickly sat back down. "Oomph. Sorry . . . I can't . . ."

But he was already off the altar and racing awkwardly across the space between them. Dax, who was usually so smooth and graceful, running as if his legs would barely hold him up. And for whatever reason, he was wearing nothing but his cotton boxers and there was something else, something different, but . . .

"Dear gods, Eddy. My love, my sweet, sweet Eddy. I thought I'd lost you forever."

He was on his knees beside her and his arms went around her and nothing else mattered. It was Dax and she'd feared he'd never hold her again, but he was warm and alive and hers. Definitely hers, and though she never cried, not ever, Eddy clung to him, sobbing uncontrollably and probably getting snot all over his chest, but she didn't care. She'd thought she was trapped in the void forever. Thought she'd never feel him holding her again, and he felt so good. This felt so good.

He kissed her—kissed her lips, her eyes, her forehead. Covered her face with kisses and she couldn't believe it, but Dax was sobbing with her, crying as hard as she was. He held her so close she felt as if she could just crawl right inside his skin and stay there forever.

She sensed movement and soft exclamations, but she couldn't stop crying and damn it all, but she was bare-assed and she was almost certain one of the voices she heard was Alton's grandfather, and wasn't that just the stupidest thing, to be worried about not having any clothes on when she could have been dead.

"Here, Eddy. Wow, girl . . . talk about making an entrance."

She glanced up, and Ginny was there, grinning like a damned fool, and handing her a man's shirt. Eddy managed to quit sobbing long enough to nod her thanks, and Dax helped her put the shirt on. It was his. It smelled of him and she wanted to bury her nose in the soft flannel and inhale forever, but there was no need to. Not really. Not with the real thing holding her with one arm while he buttoned the front of the shirt for her.

It was big enough to cover halfway down her thighs, and she finally got her crying under control well enough to gaze over Dax's shoulder and see who all was here in the cave with her.

Alton and Ginny, Dawson and Selyn, and Alton's grandfather, all of them looking like they'd had one hell of a rough night, but standing there with huge grins on their faces.

She suddenly realized something was missing. "Demon-Slayer?"

"Elda's here. My mother . . . your sword is here, Eddy."

Selyn was back by the altar, kneeling beside the swords. She cleared her throat in an obvious attempt to gather her emotions. It had to be difficult for Selyn, knowing her mother, the sentience in Eddy's sword, had been lost in the void as well. "DemonSlayer is right here with the others," she said, smiling now as she caressed the silver pommel. "She's been replicated perfectly. Even your scabbard is the same."

"Oh, wow . . ." Eddy swallowed and shifted until she was sitting in Dax's lap. No way was she going to leave his embrace. Not for at least a thousand years. "What happened? I was stuck in the void and then I woke up here."

"Mother Crystal," Alton said.

"The phoenix," Dax said, speaking over Alton.

"What?" She glanced from one to the other. "What did Mother Crystal do? What phoenix?"

Dax grabbed her hand and placed it against his chest, and that's when she realized what had changed. The phoenix tattoo, that beautiful, magical tattoo that appeared the night he died, was gone. He nodded his head when she gasped.

"Mother Crystal somehow took part of the life force of each of us along with that of the warriors' spirits here in the cavern, gave it to the phoenix and turned him free."

Ginny grabbed Eddy's hand. "You should have seen it. The tat just pulled right off of Dax's chest and flew into the air."

Selyn had joined them. She interrupted with a shake of her head. "And then you and Lord Artigos blew the poor bird to pieces with your swords."

"What?" Eddy stared at Selyn and then at the chancellor. "You killed it?" Her voice squeaked on the last word.

"The phoenix has to die to be reborn." Artigos fastened his scabbard over his back as he spoke. "Somehow, it appears that the same bird that gave Dax a new life gave you life as well."

Frowning, Eddy glanced from Artigos to Dax and then at Ginny. "But I wasn't dead."

Dax sighed. "Your body was. Only your consciousness

survived. Sort of like what happened to Willow when the demon ate her body. At least she had Bumper. Mother Crystal wasn't sure how she was going to get you out without a body for you."

"She mentioned something about you coming back as the consciousness of a crystal sword." Dawson flashed a cheeky grin at Dax. "But this guy nixed that idea."

Dax hugged her close and kissed her again. "The idea of snuggling with cold crystal just didn't do a thing for me."

Eddy placed a soft kiss on his chin and then snuggled as close as she could get. It still hadn't entirely soaked in, but they were standing here telling her she could have died—probably would have died—if they hadn't all given her a part of themselves. No wonder everyone looked so wasted.

"Thank you. All of you. It was so scary, so alone. Except . . . oh shit! How could I forget! Dad! He's been possessed by the demon king. We've got to help him." She struggled to push herself out of Dax's lap.

Then more memories slammed into her mind. Her father's warning. She turned and looked into Dax's dark brown eyes. "Dad came to me in the void. He's been taken over by the demon king, and somehow he was able to communicate with me for short periods of time. The demon wants you, Dax. It needs your life force in order to hang on to that demon body that was yours."

Dax nodded. "Mother Crystal told us. I can't risk fighting the demon king. He's almost taken me on more than one occasion, but there's no reason Alton and Ginny or Selyn and Dawson can't go to help Taron free your . . ."

The crystal walls shimmered so brightly that Eddy pressed her face against Dax's chest to protect her eyes.

"There is every reason, warrior."

Eddy popped back up and stared at Dax. "Mother Crystal?"

He nodded, as the woman's voice continued speaking. The sound of her was like the clearest bell . . . just like crystal.

"You have all been drained of your life force almost to the point of death. Replicating an immortal body is not quite the same as replicating crystal. The weakness you feel will stay with you for at least another day. You cannot go into battle, as you have no power to draw upon. Your swords are equally depleted, their force drawn every bit as low. You must rest, or you will die."

Oh, crap. Eddy gazed around her, at the faces of her friends and finally realized the risk they'd taken to save her life. "I had no idea." But there was something else. Something that mattered more than her own life, more, even, than her father's.

She slowly untangled herself from Dax's arms and carefully stood up, though she was glad Dax held on to her hand, bracing her. "Mother Crystal, I thank you for what you've done for me. I thank my friends as well, but I still have one more request."

Soft laughter rippled across the crystals. "I know of the boon you seek, Eddy Marks. There are now, as we speak, twelve childless Lemurian women who have yearned for babies of their own—twelve women who will discover themselves with child over the next fortnight. Each of the lost boys will be born into a loving family, their lives, once interrupted, now allowed to continue."

Eddy felt the tears on her cheeks before she even realized she was weeping. Her knees gave out and she went down, but Dax caught her as she fell. "Thank you," she whispered. "Thank you more than I can say."

Selyn clutched at Eddy's hand. "The lost boys? You found the spirits of our brothers, the sons of the Women Warriors?"

"I did. They've been in the void all this time. The wardens were told to kill any boy babies that were born, but they fought the demons' orders and brought them here to the crystal caves. Mother Crystal sent them into the void for safekeeping."

Now it was Selyn who cried. Eddy pulled her into a warm hug and held her tight. Dawson was right behind her with his arms around both of them. A few moments later, Selyn raised her head. "We have known there were baby boys and always wondered what happened to them. How did you find them?"

Eddy shook her head. "I don't know. They found me. Demon-Slayer said they were attracted to me for some reason, but I could sense their souls. They were just as lost as I was."

# Chapter 20

Eddy thought of those twelve baby boys, the fact they'd been trapped since birth within the void. They'd known nothing of life, but now they finally had a chance. She felt good about that, but she couldn't rest until her father was safe.

She sighed and leaned against Dax. "I'm so worried about Dad. He said the demon king was growing weak because Taron and Willow had managed to kill all the demons around Evergreen. There was nothing for the demon to feed on, but Dad sounded like he was growing weaker, too."

"I didn't know Willow had the power to kill demons." Dax rubbed his chin over Eddy's head.

Eddy shook her head. "According to Dad, she's got a woman's body. He doesn't know what happened to Bumper, but Willow's big, like us."

Alton sat down, hard, and burst out laughing. The others slowly crumpled to the ground as well, so weak they'd given up trying to stand, but Alton's laughter was so heartfelt it was contagious. They were all chuckling by the time the big Lemurian got himself under control.

"What's so funny?" Artigos stared at Alton until his grandson took a couple of deep breaths, wiped his eyes, and grinned at his grandfather.

"Taron, that's what. He was absolutely fascinated by Willow the first time he saw her." He smiled at Eddy. "Remember? That was in the prison cell the night you and Dax got arrested."

"I remember." Eddy turned to Artigos. "Willow was a tiny sprite then, about two inches tall, and Taron couldn't take his eyes off her."

"Exactly," Alton said. "I gave him a bad time about her the last time we were together. He made a joke about me giving up my freedom for Ginny, and I teased him about never finding a woman. He said the only one he'd ever been interested in was now stuck inside a curly-haired dog. I wonder how well he's dealing with a full-sized version?"

"I'm trying to imagine Willow as a full-sized woman." Selyn leaned back against Dawson. "She was one tough lady even when she was stuck inside the dog. I have a feeling Taron has his hands full."

"Let's just hope the demon king has his hands full. Taron and Willow are the only chance my dad has." Eddy sighed and then crawled out of Dax's lap. "We need to go to the upper levels and get something to eat so we can build our strength back." She held out her hand and tugged Dax to his feet. "And you need some pants."

He leaned over and kissed her. "It was a small sacrifice, giving up my pants to get you back, sweetie."

Alton walked across the cavern, grabbed Dax's jeans off the floor and tossed them to him. "You can have them back. Eddy's right, big guy. I've seen enough of your butt to last me a lifetime."

The guys teased each other as Dax dressed. Eddy turned away and faced the crystal wall. "Mother Crystal?"

"Yes, Eddy."

"Thank you. Thank you so much."

"No, thank you, Eddy. Take care climbing out of here, eat well, and regain your strength. I will do what I can to help your father, but Taron and Willow are his best chance."

Eddy didn't know what else to say. She felt as if her mind and heart had been overloaded with too much emotion, too much fear, too much joy. Dax walked over and handed DemonSlayer to her. She looped the scabbard over her shoulder and fastened the buckles across the front.

The others were waiting. As they turned toward the entrance, Alton's grandfather paused and looked back at the glowing cave. "Good-bye, Mother Crystal. Take care, and thank you." He tipped her a quick salute. "I'm going to be waiting, you know."

"And with any luck, you won't be disappointed, Artigos. Take care. Have patience, and please . . . keep yourself safe."

Eddy thought the chancellor looked terribly depressed when they left. She wondered if Alton knew what was going on, but she was almost certain she'd also detected a sad and wistful quality to Mother Crystal's words.

Glancing over her shoulder as they moved through the arched passage into the tunnel beyond, she paused a moment to stare at the crystal cave that she now knew was so much more than she'd first realized. The glow was fading from the crystals, and she thought of the ageless spirit of Mother Crystal. Eternity spent as a spirit within the crystal caves.

She couldn't help but compare it to the short time she'd been trapped in the void, and it made her heart ache. There was something between Artigos and Mother Crystal, but it appeared even more hopeless than she'd felt, alone and frightened in the void. She linked her fingers through Dax's and held on tight.

Some day, she was going to have to tell him what she'd discovered—that no matter how wonderful those memories were that she'd taken into the void, nothing beat the real thing.

Slipping out through a partially opened window, he left the woman sleeping in her own bed in the dark room without any memory of having provided a meal for a demon. With little more than a thought he was back outside, shifting in and out of mist form without any problem at all.

Amazing. This human body could turn to mist and reform in an instant. He'd never realized that, with enough living energy, he would have so much power. It had taken a human body to show him he could draw the life force from other humans.

How come he hadn't known that before?

He stared at the small farmhouse he'd just left. She'd wake up with a bad headache and spend a rather listless day, but he'd allowed her to live. Something told him that a trail of dead bodies might create a problem he wasn't prepared to deal with.

At least not yet. One day, though . . . one day there would be no limits to what he could do. She'd been his fifth tonight, if he counted that little man near Ed's house. What now? He'd gotten close enough to the house to realize Dax wasn't there. Not in Evergreen at all.

Did Dax even know his friend's body had been . . . hmm. What was the proper word? *Utilized? Borrowed? Usurped?* Sated, he turned away from the house and headed up the mountain. Whatever he called it, this was not what he'd planned. Not at all.

Where in the hell was Dax? He wanted the demonform, not this puny human body. It was beginning to degrade and he wasn't sure how to repair it. There was still a spark of life, but once that was gone, he'd have nothing more than a lifeless avatar like those silly statues the lesser demons seemed to prefer.

To rule all worlds, he needed a body fit for a king. It waited for him—that perfect demon's form—but he couldn't claim it without the final spark, the ultimate connection that rested somewhere deep inside Dax.

So where in the name of Abyss was the bastard?

He stared at the mountain rising into the clouds above him. It was a long hike, but he was strong now. Practically invincible, in spite of this dying form.

Already it was little more than the walking dead. A strange noise burst out of him and he slapped a hand over his mouth to cut off the harsh cackle. Laughter? Yes, the avatar knew laughter. It wouldn't do to let anyone hear him now. Not when success was so close, but the image was too funny for words.

Maybe the idea of a dead man walking would bring Dax to him. How would he react, to discover his beloved woman's father was nothing more than the undead—rotting flesh in motion?

The image had a certain appeal to it. Disgusting, but still appealing. With that visual in mind, he began the long trudge up the hill. He could do it in mist form, but there was always the chance of the body repairing itself during the change. He couldn't risk that. Didn't want it looking better.

No . . . the uglier it got, the better it would suit his needs. He'd find Dax. And then he'd let him see what dear old Ed was fast becoming.

Of course, he couldn't wait too long, or Dax might not recognize the man. Timing. It was all about timing. He walked quickly, one foot in front of the other, and the power inside seemed to grow with each step.

Had he taken on too much life force?

Never. You could never have too much of a good thing, though it might not hurt to release a bit of the pressure.

He pointed his hands at a tall pine and *pushed*.

A burst of energy shot from his fingertips. The tree exploded, and huge splinters of shattered pine shot in all directions. Chortling softly, the demon who was Ed Marks smiled at his fingers and their amazing new ability. Then he tucked his hands in his pockets and continued climbing the mountain.

"What was that?" Willow pointed at a bright flare blossoming through the forest on the hillside far above them.

Taron saw the flash of light, heard the sharp crack of an explosion, but he couldn't pinpoint the source through the trees. A minute later, the slight stink of sulfur drifted on the breeze. He turned and glanced at Willow.

She nodded. "If that's him, he's gotten a lot stronger."

He felt a hard knot form in his gut. "I wonder if he's killed anyone? Now that he's figured out how to take the life force from humans, what's to stop him?"

"Us, hopefully." Shaking her head, Willow took off, heading toward the explosion. "If we still can. Whatever he's doing, he's definitely gaining strength."

Taron used CrystalFire's glow to light their path and as he followed the trail up the side of the mountain, he wondered if that was all his sentient sword would ever be good for. The damned blade had maintained silence for most of the day.

Was it mad at him because of his relationship with Willow, the fact he'd finally given in and admitted how he felt? He was really going to be disappointed if that was the case. Here they were, facing a final battle with a demon that could tip the ultimate balance between good and evil, and his damned sword was wallowing in some kind of jealous snit. It made no sense.

In fact, CrystalFire hadn't done anything at all the way he'd expected a sentient sword to act. It was even worse than HellFire's snark, though Alton's blade had finally decided to show a little respect. He'd been downright civil the last time Taron heard him speak.

He certainly wasn't getting any civility from CrystalFire. At least the damned blade made a good flashlight. The blue-white glow emanating from the crystalline blade lit up the forest all around them, so bright it was like hiking within their own bubble of daylight.

The night had grown even darker now that the sun was fully down beyond the horizon. Wind swirled in all directions and clouds continued to gather. The rain had stopped, but Taron knew more was coming. They'd turned on the television long enough to catch the evening news, and a bigger storm was predicted for later tonight.

He hadn't experienced weather in so long, Taron had forgotten what an incoming storm felt like, but the changing pressure added to a sense of dread that wouldn't lift. Anxiety had become a living, breathing force. Chills raced along his spine at every sound in the night. His heart pounded and he had to consciously relax muscles that continued to tense up.

He wondered if Willow felt it. Instead, he said, "Bumper's been quiet for a long time. Any word from her?"

Willow sighed. "She's really uneasy. In fact, she was driving me nuts, whimpering and whining." She rubbed her hands over her arms, as if warding off a chill. "I told her to settle down and be quiet."

Taron chuckled. "You mean she's minding you?"

"Sort of." Willow's dry comment had an edge to it. Taron decided she was as affected by the weather as he was. "She quit whimpering," Willow added. "She's supposed to be listening for the sound of footsteps."

Taron chuckled at Willow's tone. "I'd love to hear footsteps about now—like from a few fellow demonslayers. Doesn't it seem odd to you that we've not heard a word from Alton or Dax? That Eddy hasn't tried to contact us? I thought she'd be checking on her dad by now."

Willow glanced his way. "I know. She's never gone this long without calling her father, or at least checking in to make sure Bumper was okay. I don't know what to make of it. We haven't heard from Darius and Mari again, either. I know they were going to the coast, but they've been gone for two nights."

"I tried to reach Darius earlier. He's still not close enough to hear my call. They're probably still at the ocean."

Willow paused and wrapped her arms around herself. "It's unsettling, feeling so cut off from everyone. I keep getting a strange feeling about it, the fact it's just you and me and the demon."

He watched her for a moment and felt more of Willow's uneasiness affecting his own growing anxiety. "I know. It's like we're pieces in some cosmic game of chess, with no idea who's making the moves. I wish I could explain it better, but . . ." He shrugged. Willow just nodded.

"If it's chess, we're nothing but pawns."

"I'm certainly not feeling like much of a knight."

Willow's eyes sparkled. "You know chess? Ed taught me to play."

He grunted. "Lemurians invented chess." Then he tightened his grasp on his sword. "CrystalFire? You warned me of a final battle. Is it coming tonight? What more do you know?"

The blade shimmered but remained silent. Taron glared at the worthless sword in his hand and wanted to toss the damned thing. Anger surged, hard and hot and his muscles clenched, but then he raised his head and shifted his glance toward Willow.

There was no ignoring the twinkle in her eyes. He looked once more at his blade, at his knuckles gone white from the force of his grasp, and suddenly he was laughing.

Just laughing like a damned fool. The absurdity of the situation hit him like a punch to the gut. Here he was, chasing down a demon on the sides of Mount Shasta, accompanied by a sword that wouldn't speak to him, and a beautiful woman who was really nothing more than swamp gas.

And she was so much more, and just so beautiful with the

wisps of golden hair peeking out around the edges of the dark knit cap and her eyes twinkling in CrystalFire's light, that he laughed even harder. Finally he got himself under control and grinned at her. "No," he said, even though she hadn't said a word. "I really don't want to know what you're thinking."

"I was afraid of that." She covered her mouth, stifling a giggle. "But I'm going to tell you anyway."

"Gee, thanks."

"I'm wondering if CrystalFire's holding a grudge."

"What?" He glanced at the sword in his hand. "Why?"

Willow's voice softened and she ran her fingers along the crystalline blade. Ripples of light followed her touch and it made Taron think of the way Bumper had loved to be petted. "We don't know who CrystalFire was, other than the fact he was a brave warrior, or he never would have become the sentience in your blade. Think of what his life has been—a soldier stuck in a philosopher's sword. No hope of battle, no chance to do what soldiers do. I bet he spent a lot of time stuck in a closet."

Taron suddenly saw his sword with a new eye. "You're right. Soldiers fight. He's had very few chances to engage in actual battle. Maybe he fears there won't be another chance. That he'll end up back in that closet. Is that true, Crystal-Fire? Do you miss the thrill of fighting demonkind?"

The sword sparkled. "We have fought bravely."

"True. When we finally got the chance, we did well. But do you hold it against me, that most of our actual fights have been mock battles training Paladins? Small ones, killing lesser demons? Do you blame me for your boring existence in a scholar's blade?"

The sparkles dulled to a mere glow. "We have no choice in the sword we inhabit or the citizen we serve."

Taron glanced at Willow. "I think that's a polite way of saying I've bored him to death over the years. CrystalFire.

Your days of boredom are over. We follow the demon king right now. That final battle you warned me of will probably occur within the next couple of hours. Will you be ready?"

This time the blade flashed with a sense of true anger. "I am always ready. You, Taron of Libernus, are the one who concerns me."

For one harsh moment, Taron fought a powerful urge to throw the crystal blade against the rocks. He took a deep breath instead. "Well, thank you so much for that vote of no confidence." Disgusted, he shook his head and started to sheathe his blade. Unfortunately, he needed the light. "It's a damned good thing he makes a decent flashlight. I'm not so certain this is the one I want beside me in battle."

Willow merely sighed. "I don't blame you. It's hard to trust a weapon when you know it's got such a low opinion of you." She wrapped her fingers around his forearm. "I, on the other hand, have complete faith in you. C'mon."

They walked together up the hillside, but Taron couldn't get past what his blade had said. To be doubted by one's sentient sword had to be the gravest of insults.

He just hoped CrystalFire wasn't right.


"Bumper says we're getting close."

They'd been climbing for almost an hour and had reached the uppermost edge of the forest. Above them was snow-covered scree—the loose shale and broken rock left over from the last volcanic eruption. A trail wound through it, or the area would have been impossible to cross, but it was still going to be a difficult climb with snow covering much of the way.

The mountain's volcanic peak remained lost in darkness and clouds, but the demon had to be somewhere above them on the rugged slope. Taron raised his sword and cast light across the mountainside. Huge boulders interspersed with the occasional twisted tree barely clinging to life cast dark shadows in CrystalFire's brilliant glow.

The sword hadn't spoken since its final insult. Taron wished the damned thing's comments hadn't bothered him so much, but those few cutting words had greatly undermined his confidence.

He would be the first to admit he wasn't a warrior by nature—he was a scholar. He wasn't a brave and forceful man, not a natural leader like Alton, and he wasn't that skilled a swordsman—even Isra, a mere woman, had bested him in their mock skirmish—yet he was here, doing what had been asked of him.

He was going into war against a powerful demon, his only weapon a sword that thought he was a coward. Not an easy thing to ignore. Willow had told him not to pay the blade any attention, but that wasn't easy to do, either.

Not when he couldn't help but wonder if CrystalFire knew something Taron didn't. He'd never thought of himself as a coward, but he'd not considered himself a warrior, either. That had not been his chosen life. He had never been faced with real danger. Not until that fateful night—was it only a week ago?—when demonkind invaded Lemuria. He'd fought well that night—two demon-possessed guards at the same time. He'd been afraid—what man wouldn't have been? But he'd fought bravely. He'd come out of the battle alive, which was more than could be said for his opponents, but obviously CrystalFire hadn't been impressed.

How did a man prove his worth as a soldier when he was, by nature, not of that ilk? There'd been no battles to fight, no wars to wage all those long years when none of them had realized demonkind ruled Lemuria. Should he have sought glory, gone after demons the way Alton had?

Alton's HellFire appeared to hold Alton in high esteem, though Taron recalled it hadn't always been that way. Maybe he still had to earn CrystalFire's respect, but was that the way of a warrior? To fight, not to right an injustice or to battle evil, but to earn the respect of his sentient sword?

Somehow, that felt wrong on so many levels.

One did not fight for glory. One fought to make things right, to save a life, to preserve a society. One battled demonkind because the creatures were inherently evil—their goal was the overthrow of all that was good, and that alone made demons worthy opponents.

Taron knew he'd fought bravely when called upon, but he'd not searched for glory. Had he erred? Had he somehow failed his people, neglected his duty?

"Taron?"

Blinking, he turned and Willow was right there, mere inches away, looking up at him with obvious concern in her eyes.

Nine hells and then some, but he wanted to kiss her. Wanted to drag her into his arms, forget they hunted the demon king, forget his blade thought him less than a man—forget everything but losing himself in Willow's sweet warmth, kissing her perfect lips, inhaling her scent. Forget everything but loving her.

Instead, he let out a shuddering breath. "What?"

Willow planted her hands on those beautiful hips . . . the same hips he'd stroked earlier in the day, the same body he'd . . .

She cocked her head and raised one very expressive eyebrow. Taron corralled his roaming thoughts and focused on her mouth, but that led to even more wonderful memories.

He looked at her eyes—brilliant blue eyes, boring into him with a vast amount of impatience. He blinked. Paid attention.

"First of all," she said, "I am not snooping in your thoughts, but it's way too obvious you're agonizing over that stupid sword and what he said. Don't worry about it. Ignore him. We have bigger things that concern us."

He nodded, but couldn't keep from glancing at the damned blade. "I know you're right. But it's not easy for a man to be called a coward." He smiled and tried to make light of it. "He has insulted my manliness. That's unacceptable." When Willow smiled in return, he leaned in close and kissed her. The brief connection turned into something more, and when they finally pulled apart, Willow was breathing as hard as he was.

"What was that for?" She ran her tongue over her bottom lip, then the top. He imagined her tasting him, just as he tasted her on his mouth.

"For being right. Again," he said. "I will hereby ignore CrystalFire's insult. It appears my manliness remains intact."

"Good. It seems to be working perfectly."

She glanced down as she licked her lips and he had to turn away before the aforementioned manliness started working more than he wanted at this moment. He looked uphill at the fairly barren mountain and the trail winding through scattered snow drifts, loose scree, and old stumps. "We need a plan. We can't let him get to the portal. If the demon reaches the access to the gateways, he could go anywhere. We might never find Ed."

"I know," She turned and followed his gaze. "I don't think he's all that far. The sulfur smell is getting stronger, so we must be gaining on him. We know he doesn't like my sparkles, but he didn't truly react until we used the sparkles and your sword together. I think that might be the way to stop him."

Thunder echoed in the distance. Taron glanced at the forest just below them and the sky above. Lightning flickered in the clouds, but it was still a long way off. "He's got to know we're following him. Do you think he's actually smart enough to plan an ambush?"

Willow shook her head. "Don't doubt his intelligence. I think he's a lot smarter than we give him credit for. He went for Bumper originally because he knew Eddy and Dax would do anything to save the dog, and he figured she'd be easier to control than a human. When that didn't work, he was still able to make the adjustment and take over Ed's body. It takes a very powerful, very intelligent creature to take control of a human, especially one with as strong a will as Ed."

"He knows we're following him. There's no way he can miss seeing this." Taron lowered his sword, thought about it a moment, and then sheathed the blade.

Immediately plunged into darkness, he gazed about and wondered how they'd find their way without light.

"Give your eyes a minute. They should adjust."

He nodded and they both waited. The darkness made the sounds of the night louder, the gentle breeze colder. All of his senses seemed to grow more acute. He heard Willow's soft breathing, and an owl in the distance. Thunder rumbled once again, a distant sound warning of more to come.

A different noise intruded. He was almost certain he heard rocks clattering on the trail above them. The demon moving up the mountain? It was hard to tell, but he focused his hearing and concentrated on the trail ahead.

Nothing. The darkness eased as his eyes took in what little light there was. Where a moment ago, he'd not even been able to see Willow's shape, he could now make out the sparkle in her eyes and the glint of teeth as she smiled.

Taron grabbed her hand and squeezed. "I can see you now," he said. Then he leaned over and kissed her nose. "Willow, I can't imagine doing this without you. I'm so glad you're here with me." He thought of the silent sword in his scabbard, and realized that, without Willow, he'd be totally alone on this quest. The same quest his damned blade had ordered him to make. "I'm . . ." He sighed. "You empower me, Willow. Only you."

"Thank you." Softly, thoughtfully, she ran her fingers along the line of his jaw. Then she gave him a cheeky grin. "I'm glad I'm here, too. In more ways than you can imagine." She laughed. "Not that I don't love Bumper, but I love having a real body, one that's almost all mine." She leaned in close and kissed him. "And most of all, I love having you love me. C'mon." Willow flashed a brilliant smile at him and started up the hill, but she didn't turn loose of his hand.

He tightened his hold on her. The connection gave him the confidence his sword had so easily undermined, but he couldn't help but wonder how fragile that confidence truly was. Not good, when a battle loomed. Not good at all.

# Chapter 21

The trail was rough, but the longer they walked, the easier it was to see. Though lightning still flashed in the distance and thunder rumbled, the clouds directly overhead had parted a bit and a waning moon cast its pale glow across the mountain. There was more snow along the trail than Taron had expected, and what little moonlight there was, reflected off the glistening ice.

The snow and ice made the hike more treacherous—the rocks were slippery, and puddles had frozen over and added to the danger. He'd heard about the unexpected storm the week before that dumped unseasonably heavy snow. Eddy'd been convinced it was sent by demonkind, but for whatever reason, the next few days had been warm enough to melt a lot of the snow away.

But the cold nights added a frozen crust and icy puddles. Taron was most definitely grateful for the shoes and socks he wore. The hike down in sandals hadn't been pleasant. Of course, he hadn't had Willow beside him. He still held on to Willow's hand.

She stopped and put a finger to her lips. *Bumper senses something.*

He nodded and listened carefully. The pervasive stink of

sulfur was all around, though it wasn't all that strong. They'd noted the occasional footprint in the snow and knew the demon had come this way, but the night was silent and there was no sense of movement nearby.

Taron let go of Willow's hand and stepped to one side. *Move off the trail,* he said. *We don't want to give him an easy target.*

*I wish we could use CrystalFire. Most swords can sense demonkind.*

*CrystalFire? Can you douse your light if I pull you out of the scabbard? We don't want to give away our location.*

*I am not a fool, Taron.*

*Neither am I, sword. But I'm growing tired of your attitude. Are you with me or do you intend to continue giving me more trouble than you're worth?*

There was no answer from his sword as he quietly pulled the dark blade from his scabbard. Even with a weapon he didn't trust, he felt better going against the demon armed.

They continued on up the trail. He didn't think the portal was too far away, but it was difficult to tell in the ever-changing light. Clouds blew in and out and swirled about the mountain's rugged peak, first obscuring the moon and then parting and allowing streaks of moonlight through.

He heard Willow moving quietly off to his left and did his best to muffle his own steps, but the snow crunched and an occasional rock clattered against its neighbor. His anxiety grew, a sense of danger he couldn't ignore. The demon had to be nearby. He thought of that blast they'd seen earlier.

And wondered what kind of weapons the demon had. He felt woefully unprepared. Now, if this were a debate, he'd be in fine form—there were very few battles of words that Taron of Libernus could lose.

A lot of good that did. Damned sword. He'd feel more confident with a blade that worked with him, not against him. He'd never heard of anything like this. Of course, it had been so long since any of them had actually spoken that the whole concept of the blades' sentience had become more folklore than actual knowledge. How could he know what stories were true and what were merely legend?

Now that the blades had been awakened, their warrior souls were once again ready for battle. At least most of them were. Why not his? He knew the blades talked among themselves and shared knowledge, and the sentience in each was the true mind and heart of an actual warrior from long ago. That knowledge of battle lore was something that should be shared with the new warrior, the one who carried the blade.

That was knowledge CrystalFire should be sharing with him. His weapon could be instructing him even now on what to watch for, how to protect himself, and even more important, how to protect Willow.

Again he wondered about CrystalFire. He'd never heard of a case like this, a situation where the blade refused to acknowledge its owner's ability.

He thought of Isra and her sword. FrostFire was proud of the woman who carried her, but maybe that was because Isra had acted in a way to deserve that pride.

He tightened his grasp on the silver hilt and forced himself back into the present. There was nothing he had done that he would change. He was who he was—a flawed man, but a good man who tried to do the right thing. He could be no more than the person he was meant to be, no matter how much that man might disappoint his crystal blade.

End of argument. He had other things to worry about. Things he might actually have the power to change. He turned his thoughts to Ed and wondered how he was holding up, if the man was even aware of the physical discomfort his body had to be enduring. Ed's plight made Taron's worries seem less than petty. This was no time for self-doubt, no time to wonder if he deserved to carry crystal. This was a time where a split-second decision could mean the difference between life and . . .

A blast of fire shot from above and to the right. Taron raised his sword and threw himself in front of Willow. The crystal blade deflected most of the flames as he rolled through the snow and shot back to his feet. Willow shrieked, a cry of outrage as she pointed toward the source of the blast and fired a powerful shot of blue sparkles.

Sparkles? Nine hells! There was nothing sparkling about that sizzling tongue of blue flames that roared out of her fingertips and smashed into a pile of rocks off to the right of the trail.

Splinters of rock flew into the air. Light flashed and the afterburn left him blinded, but Taron rushed the demon's hiding place with his sword raised. He had no idea how long it would take the demon to recharge his power, but Taron knew he'd damned well better hurry. Willow was right behind him as he went over the first of the rocks.

CrystalFire burst to life with a brilliant flash of light, but there was nothing here. No sign of Ed—merely a spot in the snow that was beaten down where he'd crouched in cover.

"Gods be damned, he's gone!" Taron pointed the blade like a spotlight and swung the brilliant beam across the mountainside. Tracks appeared as dark shadows in the pristine snow, headed at an angle that would catch the trail just above them.

"C'mon." With Willow on his heels, Taron took off after the demon. The tracks disappeared when they hit a bare patch of ground. Taron and Willow slipped behind a boulder, using it for cover while they continued to search.

Rocks clattered just beyond the burst of swordlight. Taron pointed the blade. A dark shadow ducked down behind a tangle of snow-covered brush. Grasping his sword in his hand, Taron raced across the snow, cutting at an angle that would put him above his target.

Without saying a word, Willow circled below, moving as quickly as Taron until they had the demon between them. Suddenly Ed rose up from behind his cover, pointed his fingers and shot fire at Willow.

She ducked and rolled as coiling flames boiled harmlessly over her head, but Taron used that moment to cross the open ground and take a position just above the demon's hiding place.

The demon stood once again and turned toward Taron. He raised his hands as Taron aimed his sword. Flames burst out of Ed's fingertips, a burst of power roaring across the snow with a thunderous noise. Taron called on CrystalFire, but his foot hit a patch of ice and he tumbled forward, directly into the path of the flames.

Willow screamed. CrystalFire blasted a shot of blue-white fire at the demon. Taron tumbled through the blast of demonfire and rolled out on the other side.

Incredible pain sliced into him. Pain and a sense of indescribable evil as he slid through the snow and slammed into a boulder.

His sword was knocked from his hand and he scrambled on hands and knees through the snow, searching for his weapon. Adrenaline fueled his search as he grappled for the hilt with his left hand. He sensed the demon coming close. Willow screamed a cry of pure rage.

Blue fire flashed and practically blinded him. A banshee shriek echoed off the hillside as his fingers closed around CrystalFire's hilt. He turned and leapt to his feet, spinning about to face his opponent. The world kept spinning as he raised his weapon to attack. He was still searching when the demon twisted away from another of Willow's blasts and raced across the hillside.

He ran with a lumbering gait, as if the man was no longer capable of the speed the demon pushed him to. Taron wondered if Ed were still alive. Had the demon resorted to animating Ed's body in order to stay in this dimension?

He couldn't tell, though he watched until the creature Ed had become disappeared into the darkness. Gasping for air, Taron looked down at the hand clasping his sword. He'd grabbed his weapon with his left hand, though he usually fought with his right. Now he stared dumbly as CrystalFire fell from numb fingers. He continued staring at the blade lying in the snow.

Then he leaned over with his hands on his knees, intending to reach for his weapon, but everything began a slow spin with his shimmering blade at the middle. Without a bit of warning, Taron toppled over and fell face first into the snow. Smoke and steam rose from his scorched sleeve where the demon's fire had struck.

He lay there a moment, stunned and only partially conscious. Then the world seemed to settle. He twisted his body and tried to see how much damage there was on his shoulder. At first, it looked as if the heavy coat had absorbed the main force of the demon's blast.

Alton was going to be so pissed. There was a huge hole in the shoulder of his beautiful leather jacket. Taron shoved himself into a sitting position with his right hand and then grabbed CrystalFire. It seemed wrong to leave the shimmering blade lying in the snow even if the damned thing was acting like a total prick. At least the sword worked when it had to.

He picked it up and stared at the sword, mesmerized by the steadily pulsing light.

Willow reached him seconds later. She knelt in the snow beside him. "Give me your sword. I need the light."

He handed over CrystalFire, concentrating on the steadily increasing, screaming pain in his shoulder. He watched

Willow's slim fingers wrap around CrystalFire's hilt. Taron thought he should warn her, but she already had a firm grasp on the weapon.

How could that be, that she could hold his sword without danger? Instead of striking out, the blade merely offered up its light as Willow held it near Taron's wound.

"This is bad, Taron. Good gods . . . it's burned through the muscle. I can see bone." She sat back on her heels and stared at him. Her blue eyes were huge, glowing in CrystalFire's brilliant light. "Well, the good thing, I guess, is that it's not bleeding. The demon's fire cauterized the wound."

He chuckled even as he gasped for breath. The pain was suddenly intense, blinding, even, and his breaths hissed in and out between his lips in short, jagged pants. "It hurts more, given your description," he said. "I think I was better not knowing."

She kissed his cheek. "I'm sorry. Then you'd better not look at it. Hold the sword in your right hand. Dear gods," she mumbled, more as if she were talking to herself instead of to him. "I hope I can still heal wounds."

"I didn't know you could do that." He turned his head and gazed at her. Her eyes were huge dark shadows flickering with crystal light mere inches from his, her mouth too close to ignore. He practically fell against her as he kissed her. She pressed a hand to his chest, steadying him, and kissed him back.

It was nothing more than a quick touch of their lips, but it grounded him and somehow eased the pain. His heart settled down from its frantic pounding; his breathing slowed.

She pulled away from his kiss and frowned. "Let me concentrate. I don't want to make it worse."

"Kissing can't possibly make it worse." He'd started shivering though, and knew he must be going into shock, but he still managed to give her a quick grin that felt more like a grimace. Willow rolled her eyes. Then she focused entirely on his injury. She stared intently at his shoulder, and Taron could swear the pain lessened. Slowly she raised her hands and held them over the wound. Tiny blue sparkles flowed gently from her fingertips and disappeared into the blackened hole that had been his shoulder.

As fascinating as it was, he had to look away.

She was right. He really shouldn't look at the damage. It was beyond awful. The demon had actually blasted away a large portion of his shoulder and arm. He should be dead, not sitting here in the snow more interested in the gorgeous woman than the damage to his body.

He could still see Willow's sparkles from the corner of his eye, and he experienced a most amazing sensation, as if she brushed a cooling balm over his burned flesh wherever the sparkles touched.

The tiny flashes of light held him in thrall, as did the arch of Willow's eyebrows, the intense look of concentration on her face, the way she pursed her lips as she worked over his injury. At some point, he realized that one of them needed to pay attention in case the demon returned, so he forced himself to look away from the captivating tilt of her chin and the wisps of blond hair escaping from her cap. He concentrated instead on the hillside above them.

It was easier to remain focused when Willow's safety was at stake. He tuned out the odd sensation of knitting flesh and buzzing sparkles and scanned the shadows and ridges above them where the demon had disappeared.

He wasn't certain how long he kept guard while Willow worked on his shoulder, but he remained alert and there was no sign of the demon. After a while Taron realized his shivering had eased, and before very long, the pain was mostly gone.

Slowly he turned his head when Willow sat back on her heels. "That should do it," she said, but her face was drawn and she moved as if the effort to remain upright was almost too much for her. She slowly shoved an errant strand of hair out of her eyes and ran her fingers over his newly healed skin. "I wasn't certain I could still heal injuries."

Taron carefully stretched his arm out and back. He'd lost track of time, but what Willow had accomplished seemed absolutely impossible. He stuck his hand through the burned hole in the leather jacket and ran his fingers over fresh, pink skin that only a short time ago had been entirely burned away. There was some tenderness, but it looked almost normal.

Willow, however, slumped over as if she were ready to collapse. He put an arm around her and tugged her onto his lap so he could reach the small pack she'd fastened around her waist. He unzipped it and pulled out a water bottle and an energy bar. "Eat this. Drink some water. You need to replenish what you've lost."

She nodded, but just stared at the water and the bar until Taron tipped the bottle to her lips. She swallowed slowly, as if she were too tired to really think about what she was doing, but when he unwrapped the bar, she took a bite without any argument. Taron fed her, made her drink, and watched as the light slowly returned to her eyes. Then he set her on a flat rock beside them, stood up and stretched his newly mended arm. It felt fine. A little tender, the joint a bit stiff, but it was almost as good as new.

And way too close to his heart. He'd not realized how close he'd come to dying. If Willow hadn't been here to help, he probably wouldn't have survived. Almost immortal he might be, but Lemurians still could be killed. Scholars tended to live longer than warriors, and right now, though he thought himself a scholar, he was taking a warrior's risks.

The knowledge sobered him. It was a vivid reminder of the reality of their situation.

Willow had saved his life. If anything happened to her, who would help Willow? He had no medical ability to heal her if she were injured, though he would fight to the death to protect her. If he died, Taron knew Willow would continue on without him, no matter the risk to her own safety. If she were to die, he would do the same, but nine hells, he did not want anything like that.

They were in this together—a team. He needed her and he hoped she needed him. At the same time, he worried what would happen should one of them not survive. He had no intention of leaving Willow to fight this battle alone, but the demon's attack had been a very graphic reminder of just how dangerous the night had become.

Artigos the Just had done his best to remain physically active during all those long years of captivity, but it hadn't prepared him for the bone-aching weariness of sharing his life force to help build a new body for a living, breathing woman.

He was, quite literally, running out of steam.

The final steps to the main levels of Lemuria were almost his undoing. He might have blamed it on age, but the youngsters were having every bit as much trouble as he was.

At least Dax had his beloved Eddy back, and watching the two of them together, the love they so obviously shared, did his heart good. No more so than the joy he found in his grandson Alton's love for his lady. Ginny was truly a match for any Lemurian—a bold, intelligent, and beautiful woman who had accepted her unexpected life as both warrior and Lemurian without question. Artigos could not have chosen a more worthy mate for Alton if he'd tried.

And then there was Dawson. He'd learned very quickly not to underestimate the quiet, unassuming human. Dawson had hidden strengths and a love for Selyn that brought out the young woman's sparkle and her joy for life—a joy that had survived in spite of a lifetime of slavery and abuse. The adoration in her eyes when she gazed upon her human mate was a tribute to both her capacity for love, and Dawson's amazing inner strength. Only a very strong and loving man

would be able to capture the heart of a Paladin. There could
be no doubt Selyn's was all his.

*As it should be.* Artigos drew strength from each of the
young couples, but love was like that. It gave you the power
to succeed when success seemed an impossibility. It brought
joy to life, fed the soul, and strengthened the heart. He
envied each of them, sharing in their love for one another,
finding strength and the courage to place one foot in front
of the other no matter how difficult the journey.

And yet, he wondered, would he ever experience a love
like that again? Would he ever know that joy in another's
touch, that sense of completion a man knew when he'd
found his true mate?

The love of his youth had died so long ago that her
memory had grown faded with time. Alton's grandmother
had been a wonderful woman, but she'd been gone so long
now that another had taken her place in his heart. It was difficult, though, to imagine love without an image to hold, or
a real face to recall.

Ah, the meanderings of an old brain. At least his thoughts
took his mind off the agony of cramping legs and labored
breathing. It also helped his male ego to know he wasn't
alone dragging up this final bank of stairs—all of them were
ready to fall into bed and sleep the clock around.

Finally they reached the residential level. Artigos leaned
against the wall, gasping for breath with the others. They'd
each be going off to their rooms—Dax and Eddy had taken
over Alton's old quarters, while Alton had moved into his
father's rooms, now that Artigos the Younger was back with
his wife. Selyn and Dawson would retire to their small but
comfortable apartment in the Paladin's new quarters, while
Artigos himself had taken over rooms recently made available
following the death of Drago, one of the demon-possessed
council members.

Drago had truly loved his creature comforts. The thought

of that big bed waiting for him had Artigos shoving himself away from the wall. Somehow, he would find the strength to make it the final few steps to his doorway.

Eddy stopped him. She stood in front of him and took his right hand in both of hers. "My lord, thank you. I would not be here without your generosity. There are no words . . ."

Her eyes were the color of bittersweet chocolate and they sparkled now with tears. She was his daughter now, every bit as much a part of him as was his grandson, if not more. His life force was part of Eddy Marks. All he could think was how proud he was to have helped save such a worthy young woman.

He brushed his left hand through her short, dark hair. "You were willing to give your life for the future of Lemuria. I am proud to have had a part in your rebirth, my dear. Now go. Sleep. When all of us are rested, we'll free your father."

Eddy stood on her toes and kissed his cheek. Then she grabbed Dax's hand and stood beside him. Artigos's gaze fell on each of the six in turn, until finally he focused on his grandson. Gods-be-damned, but he was proud of the boy, though he spoke to all of them as equals. "We will all be tested in the days to come. Eat, sleep, and recharge. Meet with me when you are rested, and not before."

He turned his attention to Eddy. "I know you're worried about your father. You have every right to be, but you must try to rest. Mother Crystal is correct—we are all sorely depleted and would be worthless in battle. I'll contact Roland of Kronus and have him go through the portal to see if he can reach Taron. We'll find out what's happening in Earth's dimension, specifically in Evergreen. Possibly we can send Mari and Darius to help with your father's rescue. Go now. All of you. Rest and make yourselves ready to fight the good fight once again."

Eddy, Dax, Selyn, and Dawson left. Ginny and Alton stayed behind. Alton stood before him with that direct gaze

Artigos so admired, and said, very softly, "Thank you, Grandfather."

Artigos pulled Alton into a tight hug. "Thank you. I owe you more than I can ever repay."

Alton returned his hug, but when he stepped back, he shook his head. The powerful sense of conviction in his voice sent chills over his grandfather's spine. "You owe me nothing," he said. "What I have done has been for Lemuria. You, Grandfather, are the best thing for this world. I will do anything for you. Whenever you need it, whatever it is. Anything at all."

He glanced at Ginny and then once more looked Artigos directly in the eye. "I love you, Grandfather. It's so good to have you back. Be well."

Before Artigos could respond, Alton and Ginny had turned and headed to their rooms. Artigos stood there for a long, long time with Alton's heartfelt words lodged firmly in his heart.

*I love you, Grandfather.*

"As I love you, Alton. More than you will ever know." He turned away, then, and made his way to his apartment.

# Chapter 22

After such an amazing night, after so much emotion, so many unbelievable experiences, Artigos never expected the wave of depression that swamped him when he stepped into his beautiful apartment. Even with his favorite chair and beloved artwork, his books and his personal treasures, it seemed lonelier than usual.

He wished there was someone to share the night with, to talk about all he'd seen and everything he'd done, but these magnificent rooms were even lonelier than the cell he'd been held in for so many years.

He'd had everything brought here. His comfortable chairs, his well-read books. The pictures on the walls, the trinkets in the display cases and on the shelves, many brought to this world from their ancient homeland so many thousands of years ago.

He walked over to one of the display cases and looked at bits of jewelry his grandmother had worn on the original world of Lemuria long before they'd ever dreamed of a life on Earth.

So many years gone by. So many lives now passed beyond the veil. He'd missed too damned much. So many things had happened since his son, already demon-possessed, had caught him alone in his office on that fateful day. He'd been gathering important papers he would need in this new Lemuria when he'd been taken prisoner. He'd languished for many thousands of years in those silent rooms near the mines, locked away from life.

So many changes he'd not been part of, other than as a silent witness through the eyes of Mother Crystal. He sighed and sat heavily on the arm of the sofa. He'd tried not to think of her since leaving the caves, but it was impossible.

She'd been in his thoughts far too long for him to ever successfully drive her from his mind. Dear gods but he loved the woman. He chuckled, thinking of the look in Alton's eyes when he'd said he wanted Mother Crystal in his bed. He'd not been kidding. It mattered not what she looked like. He'd fallen in love with her brilliant mind, her wit, her compassion, the crystal clarity of her laughter.

He reached into the display case and picked up a necklace made of precious crystals, perfect stones his grandmother had worn, a beautiful piece of jewelry from another world. He held it in his palm and felt the warmth from the stones, and he wondered what life would have been like if their original birthplace had survived, if they'd never come to this planet.

He might never have become a ruler, would most likely not have spent millennia imprisoned in a cell deep inside a mountain. And if that hadn't happened, he would never have met the woman who would forever fill his dreams.

He wondered if she'd ever walked the Earth or any world as a living female, if she had a name other than Mother Crystal. When he thought of her, it was as Crystal, the woman of his dreams. Legend said she'd come with the huge ship that had landed on Earth so long ago, that his people so revered the spirits of their world, they'd brought many of them along rather than leave them to a dying planet.

Was Crystal truly from the world that had spawned the

first Lemurians? She'd never divulged any of her past. If it were true, she was, at the very least, a demigoddess, yet she'd taken the time to befriend him when he was held prisoner. She'd supplied him with scrolls and then books to keep him informed, had engaged him in lively debates that kept his mind sharp and his tongue nimble. She'd laughed with him, flirted outrageously and made him smile when he could so easily have chosen to cross over the veil and leave his hopeless existence behind.

He'd never seen her—had no idea if she even had a feminine form, but her crystal clear voice, her beautiful laughter— even her temper—enthralled him. He raised his head and stared at his spacious but lonely rooms, and knew he'd give anything to have her here with him now.

And not merely for tonight, but for all nights.

"Damned old fool." He chuckled and headed into the kitchen area. He was weak as a kitten and ready to drop, and yet he was growing aroused, thinking of an imaginary lover he was too tired even to attempt to woo should the opportunity exist.

He searched through the cold case and found some leftovers that looked moderately appetizing, quickly heated them and took his meal to the table. Food was the last thing he wanted, but he knew he'd not regain his strength without it.

He ate quickly and cleaned up the mess, then headed to the bathing room. As tired as he was, a quick shower made more sense, but he chose the heated pool instead, a beautiful stone grotto stretching a full eight feet across at its widest point, carved into shimmering green and black serpentine. A natural hot spring fed the pool, and the bubbling water flowed in from one side and out the other, always warm enough to give him pause when he first entered.

Stripping off his tunic and pants, he stepped into the steaming water and, groaning with a hedonist's pleasure, lowered himself all the way in until the water lapped at his chin. He settled into a curved bench seat that held him near natural vents, and let the soothing mineral-laden water work its magic.

He must have dozed off. Water splashing his face and slapping over the sides of the pool brought him to full alertness. *Earthquake?* Blinking rapidly, he charged up out of the seat and stood shoulder-deep in the steaming water.

Blinking rapidly to clear the drops from his eyes, he realized he wasn't alone.

A woman was treading water in the middle of his pool. She gazed at him out of eyes of brilliant aquamarine and her long, silvery white hair flowed out behind her as she slowly moved her arms beneath the water, holding herself in one spot, watching him.

Her face was ageless and yet so perfect she might have been carved by a master sculptor. So regal she could easily have looked cold and hard, but for the tiny laugh lines at the corners of her eyes. Her full lips were much too lush to speak of anything other than a lust for life and a most passionate nature.

He couldn't stop staring. He'd never seen her before. He couldn't take his eyes off her, and yet, in his heart of hearts, Artigos knew her. Knew her, and realized he'd not imagined his feelings. He had always loved her.

He pushed away from the bottom of the pool and met her in the middle. His feet touched the bottom but the water was deep here and almost covered his shoulders.

She smiled at him, but she didn't speak.

"Tell me," he said, and he tilted his head as he looked at her. "Tell me you're not a dream. That you really are my beloved Crystal."

She laughed, and it was the laugh he knew, the one that had kept him alive and hopeful for so long. "I'm glad you didn't preface it with 'Mother,'" she said.

He chuckled, but his throat felt tight and his body surged with need. "For what it's worth, I've never thought of you as my mother." He laughed softly. Touched her cheek with his fingertips. "You're beautiful. More beautiful than I could possibly imagine, so I know you must be real. Even I couldn't come up with perfection like this."

Again she laughed. Her lips parted, her eyes sparkled, and he wanted to kiss her so badly he ached.

"I always knew you were a smooth talker," she said. "But I never got the chance to find out if you were smooth at other things as well."

He shook his head, remembering so many thousands of lonely nights. "Why not? You would have made an old man's life much easier."

She reached out and wrapped her arms around his shoulders. Her palms were smooth sliding over his skin and her fingers tightened against his back. Her long legs circled his waist and he felt her ankles hook at the small of his back. Tilting her head, she smiled sadly at him. "The time was not right. There was so much to do, so many lives in the balance."

He wrapped his arms around her and cupped her smooth bottom with his hands. She floated closer until her breasts pressed against his chest and the curve of her belly molded perfectly to his. "There are just as many lives in the balance now," he said. "Why tonight? Why now?"

She leaned close and kissed him. He didn't hesitate, kissing her with all the fervor of a young buck. Her taste was ambrosia, like nothing he'd ever experienced, her lips firm beneath his, her breath sweet. He could have spent the rest of his life kissing her, but he was the one to end it.

He pulled away slowly, even though he was rising hot and hard against her feminine folds and his desire for her body was much stronger than his need for answers.

Yet he felt her need to explain, and so he waited.

She rested her head in the curve between his shoulder and

his neck. Her hair swirled about them in the steaming water, and her voice, as pure as crystal, was barely above a whisper.

"Much lies in the balance tonight. A battle will be fought, a most important battle with unusual warriors—a powerful demon, a Lemurian scholar, and a woman who was constructed from swamp gas and dreams. They are the ones who have been chosen as the final contestants in a war none of us really wanted."

"Why them? Why not our finest warriors against demonkind? Why a scholar? It's Taron, right? A young man who freely claims he's not a fighter but a man of words."

She turned her face against his throat and sighed. "We had no choice. None at all. This is the way it is fated to happen, this battle between good and evil. It's been building for many thousands of years, but it will all end tonight. Without Dax, without Alton or Dawson or their women. While they make love and then sleep, the fate of all worlds will rest on a single battle over which we have no control."

"I've sent Roland to help."

She shook her head. "He'll not be able to reach them. The portals have all been sealed and no one can pass out of Lemuria. The demon cannot return to Abyss. Taron and Willow cannot escape to Lemuria or even Sedona. It is all as it should be."

"So . . . what now?"

"We make love, Artigos the Just. We spend what could very well be our last night in this world as we have always known and loved it, making love. We will do something selfish and wonderful for ourselves, because it's too late to change what will happen, but it's not too late to experience what could very well be our final chance at happiness." She kissed him, just a quick, teasing peck of her lips against his. "I have wanted you all these years, and I've run out of patience."

He sighed and held her close. This was not how he'd imagined making love to this woman. Not at all. Now he thought of his grandson and Ginny, of Gaia and her newfound love with her husband after years of demon possession. His mind went to the others who loved so freely and to those twelve baby boys that had finally found mothers to give them a second shot at life.

Was it all going to come to nothing?

If the demon prevailed and Abyss ruled, life as they knew it would end. Eden would fall, and Lemuria and Earth. Even Atlantis might finally bow to the evil of Abyss.

He thought of that desperate race against a sun gone nova when his grandparents' generation had made their fearful escape, and it saddened him to think it could all end here, not because of some terrible natural disaster, but merely because evil had finally won.

Then he thought of the woman in his arms, of the love he felt for her and he knew that this was his way to claim victory, no matter how brief. He held her close against his body and walked to the stairs cut into the side of the pool. Holding her in his arms, he climbed out of the water. Once they'd left the pool, he let her slide from his embrace until her toes touched the ground. She was much tinier than he'd realized and the top of her head reached only halfway up his chest.

He chuckled as he leaned down and kissed her. "You're not nearly as big as I imagined. This could call for a bit of creativity in our bed."

She kissed him again. "It's been a long, long time for me. You'll have to remind me how these things work."

He flashed her a cocky grin, feeling more like a young man than an ancient. Then he reached for one of the warm towels hanging on the wall, and wrapped her carefully in its soft folds. He grabbed another one and tied it around his waist.

"If we make love tonight and the world doesn't end, I hope you realize I'm never letting you go." He leaned down and kissed her again, and felt her smile against his lips.

"I had hoped you would say something like that." Twining

her fingers in his, she led him out of the bathing room. Then Artigos took the lead and she followed him into the bedroom.

He'd dreamed of her in his bed for so long that it felt perfectly natural to pull back the blankets, tug the towel off of her body, and lay her down on the clean sheets.

She was beautiful, she was his lady love, and he'd be damned if all of this was going to end tonight. As he crawled in beside her, Artigos fervently and with hope promised Crystal forever.


"What's that?"

Taron pulled Willow closer against his side and leaned over to whisper in her ear. "Nothing," he said, but he managed to fill his lungs with the scent of the vanilla shampoo she'd used and her own sweet perfume. The familiar scents he would always associate with Willow calmed his racing heart. He kissed her cheek. "It's just the wind. You need to rest."

She shivered and snuggled even closer. "It's not easy. Not when I know he's up there, somewhere."

What really hurt was knowing her fear was for him, not herself. He sighed. "You know I'll watch over you." Her cap had slipped back from her face, freeing a mass of her thick hair. He brushed the tangled strands away from her forehead and dropped a light kiss amid the curls. "You have to rest. If you don't recharge, we can't go after him. I need you, Willow. I can't fight him on my own. Just a little longer. Close your eyes." He pulled the cap back into position and tucked the escaping strands beneath the soft knit.

She glanced at him with eyes of midnight blue. "I'm trying, but it's hard. Now that I know how dangerous he can be . . . what if he hurts you again? What if . . . ?"

"He won't. Trust me. Now that I know what he's capable of, I'll be extra careful." He kissed her forehead. "I'll watch over you, Willow. So will Bumper. I promise we won't let him near."

*I'm awake, Willow. I'm listening. You can sleep. Taron's right. We'll stand watch.*

Willow tilted her chin and gazed into his eyes. "I do trust you, Taron." She sighed. "And you, too, Bumper. Okay. For a few minutes."

She snuggled close, and in less than a minute he felt her tense muscles relax and heard the steady cadence of her breathing. Healing him had taken a huge toll on her reserves. He hadn't realized how much until they'd started up the hill after the demon king and Willow'd been stumbling over her own feet from exhaustion.

She wasn't going to tell him. He'd been angry at her, at the foolish decisions she made, and then he realized she might not have even known how exhausted she was. She was like a tiny child in so many ways, still learning how this body worked.

He wanted her to have this form forever, to grow comfortable in her woman's skin. He wanted her safe and the demon gone. He had no idea how long it was going to take her to regain her strength, but he hadn't been kidding—he needed Willow beside him if he hoped for any chance at all against the demon. His crystal sword—attitude included—wasn't enough on its own to overpower the demon king. It was going to take the three of them, working together. Four, if he counted Bumper, and it was impossible to discount the dog. So, four of them, and a whole lot of luck.

Holding Willow close, Taron stared at the lightning flickering in the distance and thought of the last few days. He'd lived more, experienced more since stepping through the portal into Earth's dimension less than three days ago than in all his years prior.

He didn't want what he'd found here, in this dimension, to end. No. Somehow, he and Willow had to come through this alive, not only to protect their friends and the innocent inhabitants of Earth and Lemuria and even of Eden, but because he was selfish enough to want time with Willow. A chance to experience love, to finally live after so many years of merely existing.

He glanced overhead at the pale moonlight filtering through the clouds. The storm was moving in, the clouds and the flickering lightning covering the entire western horizon. They were protected here in this tumble of boulders, hidden from the wind on two sides with a view toward the hillside above, but if it started raining again, they were going to end up getting soaked.

It was hard to judge how much time they had before the storm hit. The clouds were to the south and the wind coming out of the north—by all rights, the storm should be moving away from them. Taron had been watching the flashes of lightning for the past twenty minutes or so since they'd taken shelter amid this small pile of boulders. The huge thunderheads and the lightning were definitely coming closer, moving against the wind.

They had no storms in Lemuria—not deep within the volcano—but Taron remembered weather from his childhood. Remembered watching the clouds boiling across the rising waves and rushing toward their home by the sea.

Clouds moved with the wind. The wind brought the storms, and when it blew offshore, it blew the storms out to sea.

This was wrong. Entirely against the laws of nature. If the demon king had enough power to control the weather, he and Willow were in a lot more trouble than he'd feared. He'd been hoping the gods-be-damned demon was running out of energy—those blasts of power had to have taken something out of the creature. Unless . . . he stared at the storm, at the jagged streaks of lightning cutting through the clouds.

What if . . . ? No. If the demon king were able to draw power from the lightning, he and Willow didn't have a prayer.

*Nine hells and then some.* How were they going to fight this thing? He leaned his head against the rock behind him, but the scabbard strapped across his back made for an uncomfortable pillow.

The damned blade was an even more uncomfortable comrade in arms. What a joke! He and CrystalFire needed to work out their issues before the next fight with the demon, or there'd be no chance of surviving the coming battle.

Carefully, without waking Willow, Taron slipped CrystalFire from his scabbard and lay the sword on the ground beside his outstretched legs. *CrystalFire? No light. Keep it dark and quiet. We need to talk.*

*I'm listening.*

The blade remained dark, but the familiar voice was perfectly clear. And, so far at least, without attitude.

*I need some information from you.*

Pale light rippled the length of the blade.

*Do you know if the demon can control the weather? Can he call the storm closer, maybe draw power from the lightning?*

A flash of silver, barely visible in the darkness, pulsed along the blade. *I've not heard of such a thing. The Dark Lord has some control of the weather, but he remains in Abyss. If this demon can bring the lightning near, he wields unfamiliar powers.*

*Can you sense where he is right now?*

*He is on the flank of the hill above us, attempting to enter the vortex. For some reason, the gateway is closed to him.*

*Does he have the power to create a new one?*

*Possibly. When he controls his anger. He is furious, railing against the Dark Lord as well as cursing you and Willow.*

*Great. Just what we need, get him pissed off more than he already is. Why do you think the portal is closed?*

The glow dimmed and then began to race up and down the blade, a pale indication of the entity's thoughts. Taron waited for what felt like forever before CrystalFire spoke again.

His voice was hesitant. The attitude was gone entirely—Taron was sure he sensed the entity's uncertainty.

*Something has changed. Very unexpected . . . very. It appears fate demands a final battle without interference. A contest between Abyss and Lemuria, to take place here, tonight. You are the chosen one, the champion who will stand for Lemuria. You and Willow, and, it appears, me.*

Taron wasn't sure he'd heard that correctly. *What do you mean, we're the champions? Champions of what?*

The blade pulsed, though he kept the glow very pale. Taron waited. He wasn't sure if CrystalFire was thinking or maybe trying to connect with other blades. Willow slept beside him, her body a warm and living presence. The storm slowly drew closer. The continuous yet still distant rumble of thunder was like the roar of waves crashing against the shore.

Taron's anxiety levels ramped up another notch or three. He stared at the sword, and waited.

Finally the pulsing ceased. *I have reached EarthFire, the sword of Darius of Kronus. They are still near the ocean—Darius, Mari, and her parents. Their vehicle refuses to start and the road is blocked on either side, preventing their escape.*

Taron swallowed back a curse. *Alton told me Mari can use magic to move from one place to another. Any way they can spell themselves here? We could use the help.*

*I asked. Mari's magic is not working. Some things are inevitable. This battle is one of them. Only the outcome is subject to change, and that will depend on our ability to best the demon king. We must fight alone, without aid from others.*

Taron stared at the softly shimmering blade for a long, silent moment. How had it come to this, that he should be the one to fight the demon? He had no real experience in battle. He was not a highly skilled warrior. He was an average guy, a man who loved learning. A man who'd hardly tasted what life had to offer.

He tightened his arm around Willow and realized that there were times a man had to face things whether he was ready or not, but it never hurt to be as prepared as he could possibly make himself.

One of his greatest weaknesses was the blade lying on the ground beside him. *CrystalFire? I have no idea what your problems with me are, but there's no time for personal issues, not with so much at stake. You and I must function as a team if we're to have any chance at success. Will you work with me? I cannot hope to win a battle carrying a weapon I don't trust. One that doesn't trust me.*

The blade dimmed, went entirely dark, and Taron held his breath. Then a shaft of blue light ran the length of the blade. *It is not easy for me to admit I was wrong, Taron of Libernus. I was. I beg your forgiveness. I was holding you, a scholar, to an unrealistic standard. You have shown nothing but bravery in every conflict. My words to you earlier were without merit. I was unfair.*

No snark, no attitude. Just a very sincere apology. Taron took a deep breath, let it out slowly. *Thank you,* he said. And though his mind was filled with questions, he put them behind him. There was too much at stake, and too little time left. *What can we do to insure that we are victorious in this final battle?*

*Fight with only one acceptable outcome—winning. Once Willow is rested, we hunt. Listen carefully—you should be able to hear the demon who would be king. He's on the hill above and to the south of us, cursing the failed portal into the vortex.*

Taron listened, and he realized the sound he heard wasn't the wind, it was the steady litany of curses as the demon tried to reopen the portal. Now would be the time to attack, while his attention was focused on the solid rock in front of him.

Willow stirred. She raised her head, blinking. He knew the moment she came fully awake by the soft smile on her lips. "I slept," she said. "I didn't think I would." She arched her back and rubbed her face against his shoulder.

And then she looked at him with such a powerful sense of trust in her eyes that something inside Taron seemed to splinter and break free. The sensation was so precise he paused a moment to dissect it, but it made no sense. The only thing in his life that did make sense right now was the woman beside him, the one smiling at him as if he'd hung the stars.

"I'm glad you got some rest." How did he tell her that his fear had fled? That the anxiety that had been a constant companion ever since the demon's attack, was gone? He was ready. Willow was awake, she looked rested, and it was time.

In a minute.

He pulled Willow into his lap, held her close, and kissed her. Her lips were cool against his, but they quickly warmed as the kiss deepened. Her fingers tangled in his hair as she turned and pressed her body against his.

Fat raindrops fell, spattering against the rocks around them. CrystalFire flashed. Together, Taron and Willow ended the kiss. Her eyes were huge blue pools when she slipped out of his lap and stood beside him.

Taron wrapped his fingers around the silver pommel, stood up, and carefully sheathed his blade. He brushed his hand over Willow's black cap and cupped the side of her face in his palm. "Are you ready?"

She shrugged and smiled at him. "As ready as I'll ever be." She glanced at his shoulder, at the huge burn through the leather and his exposed but healed wound, and then her gaze slid to his right shoulder and the hilt of his sword protruding above his scabbard.

Obviously she wondered—and worried—about his blade.

He reached back and caressed the jeweled hilt. "Crystal-Fire appears to have misjudged me." He winked at Willow. "It seems I'm not a coward after all."

She laughed, and then slapped her hand over her mouth to hide the sound. "You never were, Taron. Never will be. I'm glad your blade finally figured that out."

"So am I. He apologized like a true gentleman."

She opened her mouth to reply. Rocks clattered up ahead, near the spot where the portal had been. Willow clamped her jaws shut and her eyes went wide.

Taron stared in the direction of the noise. There was no doubt the demon was close. Just as obvious he was locked out of the portal, or he'd be gone by now. It wasn't merely his escape to Abyss—it was their link to Lemuria, to the other demonslayers who might have been able to help them.

Except the combatants had already been determined by fate. He thought of telling Willow what he'd learned, but decided against it. There was no need to frighten her further about something that could not be changed. It was what it was, and they were as ready as they could hope to be.

The wind shifted, and the scent of sulfur drifted around them before it dissipated and was gone. Taron stared toward the portal, listening carefully.

For a moment, the only sound was the spatter of rain on rocks, and then even that ended. The dull rumble of thunder rolled across the mountain. An occasional drop still fell, and it was obvious this tiny shower was a precursor to a much larger storm.

It was time. Shrugging off the last, lingering frisson of fear, Taron climbed around the side of the boulders. He reached back, grabbed Willow's hand and easily tugged her over the tumbled rocks.

On this side of their shelter, they could hear the demon's curses. Taron glanced at Willow. "You ready?"

The look she gave him was pure fire and heat. He sensed her anger and resolve when she nodded. "I am."

Taron glanced toward the dark trail and drew his sword. The blade remained dark, but CrystalFire pulsed in Taron's hand. Together, following the sound of the demon's guttural voice, they headed up the side of the mountain toward the closed portal.

# Chapter 23

It was the same dream he'd had, over and over again on so many nights of his long captivity. He awakened with the taste of her on his tongue, his body sated from release, his heart pounding out a rhythm that grew slower in the waning rush of sexual climax. He lay there, loathe to give up the sense of peace, the pure beauty of post-orgasmic bliss.

The freedom of his dreams had always been such an amazing counterpoint to the reality of his interminable imprisonment.

Warm lips covered his. His eyelids popped open.

In the pale glow of a single small lamp, Crystal smiled around her kiss. "I do hope that sigh was for me, my love."

"Crystal?" Artigos shoved himself into a sitting position as the cobwebs of sleep fluttered away from his mind. "You're real?" He reached out to touch her long, silvery hair, but she twisted upright and sat beside him, knees akimbo.

"I certainly hope so." She grabbed his hand, kissed his palm, and held it to the side of her face. "I'd hate to think I imagined this delicious sense of fulfillment."

She laughed, and it was the crystalline sound of her joy that brought him out of the dream and into the real world, though he still couldn't seem to get his thoughts in order. His memories of the hours past were too much the stuff of fantasy, this beautiful woman in his bed the one he'd dreamed of for all those years.

"I thought I dreamed you," he said. Her cheek was warm and alive beneath his palm. He reached out with his free hand, stroked her shoulder, and ran his fingers through the long, sleek fall of silvery hair that covered her arms, draped over her breasts, and pooled beside her on the rumpled sheets.

She leaned into his touch. "No, Artigos. Dreams should have only happy endings, and this ending is an unknown. I am fearful of the outcome, but the battle begins. I find I cannot sleep when our future lies in so few hands."

"Should we call the others?" He leaned close and kissed her, and in his mind's eye recalled where all those other kisses had led just a few short hours ago.

She ended the kiss and nodded. "Though there's nothing any of us can do, we all have a stake in this. I think we may be allowed to observe as the fight unfolds. Call the others. Have them come to the great plaza."

He pulled Crystal into his arms first, kissed her soundly and held her close. She fit his embrace so perfectly that it was difficult to let her go, but she was right. So many had given so much in this terrible fight. If it was at all possible to share the final chapter, they had to be there, to see what their future held.

Would they witness an ending to all they held dear, or possibly a new beginning? The next hours would tell. He sent out the call—to Roland and the Lemurian Guard, to the Paladins, once their Forgotten Ones. He called Alton and Ginny, his son Artigos II and Gaia, his wife, Dawson Buck and Selyn, and Dax and Eddy.

And then he pulled Crystal into his arms and made love to her once again. If the world as they knew it was about to fall, he wanted to end his days with the taste of Crystal on his lips.

\* \* \*

Alton and Ginny arrived at almost the same time as Alton's mother and father. They nodded without speaking, and went in search of seats. Dawson and Selyn showed up a few seconds later, and then the others began to straggle in. A few of the guardsmen had been on patrol when the call from Artigos had reached them, and they were busy setting up row after row of long benches for the citizens of Lemuria. Those men were alert and awake, but just about everyone else had obviously been awakened from a sound sleep.

"Any idea why your grandfather called us here?" Eddy yawned and stretched her arms over her head. She looked better than she had a few hours earlier, but she probably could have slept the clock around. Dax didn't look much better, hovering over Eddy as if he feared losing her again.

Alton shook his head. "Not sure, but he said it was urgent. Let's get seats up front." He headed toward an aisle that would give them access to the front rows. "I wonder where Grandfather is?"

"Nine hells and then some." Ginny's soft curse reminded Alton of Taron, but before he could worry about his friend, he followed Ginny's stunned gaze and almost choked.

"Who the hell is that?"

His grandfather walked beside an absolutely stunning woman. Both wore traditional Lemurian robes of senior office—brilliant white edged in gold and precious gems— but it was the rapt expression on Artigos's face that left Alton speechless.

The man looked as if he walked beside a goddess, and if the woman actually was who Alton suspected, he nearly did. "Mother Crystal?" he whispered, nudging Ginny.

She nodded. "That's what DarkFire says. Take a look at your sword."

He glanced over his shoulder at the scabbard holding

HellFire. The blade rippled with shimmering color—not just the clear blue-white fire of diamonds, but every shade of every crystal from the crystal caves below. When he checked out the swords of the others around him, those belonging to the Paladins and guardsmen as well as his companions, the rainbow of colors was almost blinding.

Artigos led his companion up the few short steps to the main stage, where the two of them stood quietly until everyone in the plaza had taken a seat. He looked out over the crowd, and then he focused on Alton, smiled and nodded.

Alton gave him a "thumbs up" and squeezed Ginny a little tighter. His grandfather had looked exhausted when they parted only a few hours earlier. Now he looked like one of Alton's contemporaries—the sparkle in his eyes belied the gray in his hair. Alton could hardly contain his curiosity—he wanted to know more about the woman standing so majestically beside Artigos.

Artigos raised his hand and the room fell silent. "I apologize for calling so many of you from your beds at this hour, but events are unfolding that cannot wait—events that members of a democratic society need to be aware of. For those of you who were with me in the caverns just a few short hours ago, please accept my sincere apologies. I know how exhausted you are."

He chuckled softly and his arm slipped easily around the woman standing next to him. It was such an unconscious gesture, yet so comfortable, so intrinsically *right*. Alton nudged Ginny and she flashed a huge, understanding smile his way.

*All right, Grandfather.*

Artigos obviously heard him, but he didn't miss a beat. "All of you are aware of the crisis that has been building within our world, the fact we have been at war with demonkind for thousands of years, even when we thought that war long ended.

The attack within our walls just a little over a week ago brought that truth home to us in a most unnerving fashion."

He slanted a quick glance at the woman on his right, and there was no doubting his feelings for her. He tightened his arm around her waist and grasped her right hand with his left. She raised her head and smiled at him, and her expression was one of timeless, endless love.

Artigos stared into her eyes for a long, emotion-laden time. Then he raised his head and cleared his throat, almost as if this most controlled of men struggled for composure. "I want to introduce someone who is not only special to me, but to everyone in Lemuria. This woman has been a silent warrior for all the years Lemurians have inhabited this planet. I know that the full story of our past has made the rounds, so it should be no surprise to any of you when I mention the fact we are from a world far from this one. Nor should it be surprising that our ancestors, those brave souls who traveled to this world in a desperate attempt to escape a dying planet would bring what spirits they could, their beloved gods and goddesses—those few spirits willing to travel into an unknown future—with them.

"Mother Crystal is one of those spirits, a demigoddess, to be exact. She is from our long-lost home world of Lemuria, she was with us on our island continent before the great move, and she is here with us now. Crystal is the keeper of the souls of our sentient swords, our link with the spirit world and one of our last links to our home world. She has joined with me, as my friend—the one who kept me going all those long years of captivity under demon rule—and as my consort, to stand beside me as we once again face uncertain times."

His grandfather's sigh was audible. Ginny's hands tightened around Alton's arm. He leaned close and kissed her. "It'll be okay," he said, wishing he believed himself. He didn't like the discouraged tone in his grandfather's words. The man was usually a lot more upbeat, more optimistic. The optimism was sorely lacking in this speech.

"In a matter of minutes," Artigos said, "in Earth's dimension, a battle will be waged for our future as a free and honorable society. The war between Lemurian and demon, between those who stand on the side of all that is good, those who exist in this dimension, in Eden's and in Earth's, and those whose rule is rooted in evil, those denizens of Abyss . . . that war will end with only one side victorious. We have one man who represents all of us, one Lemurian who has been chosen as our champion. Not chosen by any single one of us, not by a committee or even our own Lemurian Guard—he has been chosen by fate. Many of you know him—Taron of Libernus. He is not a warrior, but he is an honorable and brave man."

Artigos shook his head. Alton wanted to leap up and yell at him, tell him not to be discouraged, to have faith in the scholar with a warrior's heart.

But Artigos was still speaking. "Taron will fight the one known as the demon king. Once a child of Eden who chose evil, he is a canny and powerful warrior in his own right. The victor will determine our future. If the demon wins, he will have the power to open the gates of Abyss and give demonkind power over all worlds. It is more than a battle between a Lemurian and a demon. This is a fight that will determine the future for our very souls."

There wasn't a sound to be heard in the huge plaza. As if collectively they held a single breath, and waited. Artigos's expression was grave when he gazed down at his consort. He released her hand and stepped aside, giving her the floor.

Crystal stepped forward. Her voice rang with such perfect clarity the sound sent chills along Alton's spine. She held her hands high, as if proclaiming a benediction; however, her message was anything but. "Something I must add to what my beloved Artigos has told you. Much of what happens is determined by fate—some things can be changed, others are immutable. For whatever reason, the choice of a champion is not always ours to make—Eden sent Dax to fight demonkind. It was their choice to call on an ex-demon as their champion, and he fought honorably and bravely, but his was not to be the final battle."

She smiled at Dax, and then turned and gazed at Eddy. "Eddy was chosen, a woman of Earth who had never carried a weapon until she carried crystal, and then Alton of Lemuria, and Ginny Jones, a human descended of Lemurians." She turned her smile from Eddy to Alton and Ginny and finally to Dawson and Selyn. "Then a gentle healer from Earth and the enslaved daughter of a woman warrior were chosen as our champions, and once again they prevailed, but their brave efforts did not end the fight. There are others, brave souls all, who most certainly did not wake up in the morning and say, 'I think I'm going to battle demons today.' That's not the way it happens, unfortunately."

She laughed, and the audience laughed with her. And they waited. What else did she have to say? Crystal turned with her hands clasped in front of her and gazed at Artigos. The emotion passing between the two of them drew a soft sigh from those watching. Artigos looped both hands over her shoulders and drew her close. In front of the citizens of Lemuria, he embraced her.

She was small, barely rising past the middle of his chest, but Alton sensed great power in her. He felt her love as well, and thought how bittersweet, that his grandfather had finally found someone to share his life, when life as all of them had grown to know it could be facing a horrible change.

He glanced around the huge plaza and recognized so many faces. Roland, once a sergeant, now the new Captain of the Lemurian Guard, sat with his wife, Chara, and their son. Former slave Isra sat beside Nica—the two Paladins were surrounded by their fellow warriors, some of whom had been slaves, others their wardens—all now serving Lemuria.

His world was on the cusp of so much that was good! Alton sent a silent prayer to the gods, praying for Taron's victory.

Crystal stepped out of Artigos's embrace. "Though this battle is between a Lemurian and a demon, it is being fought in Earth's dimension. For whatever reason, Earth has long been the chosen battleground, its citizens more often the ones who are caught between the age-old struggle between good and evil, yet with very little say in the outcome. Earth's people are unaware of the war being waged on their soil, but we in Lemuria will, with the help of the gods, have the opportunity to observe. This is why you've been brought here, as witnesses to this terrible fight."

She turned and held her hands high, and the room above the stage was filled with misty shapes, spinning and circling. Alton recognized them—they were the spirits of fallen warriors. As they spun and danced, a wall of purest crystal began to grow, like a huge, shimmering window across the entire back of the stage.

Artigos watched for a moment, and then turned and faced the crowd, which had continued to increase as more and more citizens made it from their apartments to the great plaza. "Many of you are probably wondering why we don't take a force of soldiers and meet the demon in battle. Surely we would have the strength to stop one demon, right?" He shook his head. "The portals are closed. We are trapped here, for however long. The battle will take place without our intervention, without interference of any kind. However, with Crystal's magic and the grace of the gods, we should be able to watch this final battle as it takes place."

He stepped back, and waved his hand toward the huge sheet of crystal behind him. "I have no idea what is happening, who we will see, or what the status of the combatants is. All we know is that we will be allowed to watch as our fate unfolds."

The huge cavern grew dark. Crystal joined Artigos. He took her hand and walked her down the steps to seats that had been saved for them near Alton and Ginny, where they could easily see the massive screen.

For that, Alton realized, was exactly what Crystal and her spirits had built—the Lemurian version of a movie screen, essentially turning the great plaza into a huge theater.

As the citizens of Lemuria watched, the snow-covered flank of Mount Shasta came into view. Clouds boiled about the upper reaches. Jagged bursts of lightning shot out of the clouds and thunder rumbled, so real and lifelike that it echoed within the huge cavern. And there, standing at the portal that was now closed, was Eddy's father. Or what had once been Eddy's father.

"No!" Eddy screamed and burst into sobs as the broken and bloody figure of Ed Marks turned and gazed out of demonic eyes at whatever lens transmitted this image.

Dax caught Eddy in his arms and held her close. She pressed her face into his shirt, muffling her sobs against his broad chest.

Ginny went absolutely still beside Alton. He took her hand and held on tight. "Poor Ed." Ginny slowly shook her head back and forth, in obvious denial of what they watched. "Is he still alive?"

Alton couldn't tell. But he held Ginny close, and his heart stuttered in his chest as he watched the screen and wondered when Taron would appear.

# Chapter 24

"If we can trap him in the middle, between your blue sparkles and my swordfire, we should have a better chance of separating the demon from Ed."

Taron slipped down behind the fallen log where he and Willow had taken cover. The demon was still at the closed portal, cursing the unresponsive boulder that he'd hoped to pass through, oblivious to anyone watching him.

Willow nodded. "I think Bumper and I can get to that pile of rocks just on the other side. If we go down and circle behind him . . ."

Taron shook his head. "Why don't you slip behind that boulder . . ." He pointed to a large rock just a couple hundred feet beyond the spot where they were now, "and I'll make it over to the pile."

She leaned over and kissed him. "Quit trying to protect me. It's easier for me. I'm smaller and lighter on my feet. I can move more quietly than you and blend in to the shadows better. Plus, I've got Bumper to keep an eye on things. You'll be all by yourself."

He glared at her. She just grinned and kissed the end of his nose. He was still trying to figure out how to convince Willow to take the safer hiding spot when she slipped out from behind their cover and totally disappeared into the shadows.

Headed for the tumble of boulders on the far side of the demon. *Nine hells and then some . . . deliver me from hard-headed women.* But he couldn't help but appreciate her speed and stealth as she silently raced along the hillside below the demon. She literally disappeared into the shadows.

A few minutes later, her voice tripped confidently into his mind. *I'm here. I've got a really good shot at him. Let me know as soon as you get into position.*

He hadn't realized she could move that quickly. Then he wondered if he could get to his spot as quietly as Willow. Holding CrystalFire, Taron crawled over the log and inched his way across the open hillside to the large boulder just this side of the demon.

He wished he could tell what the creature was doing. It stayed put, right in front of the massive rock where the portal had been, and he wasn't sure if the damned thing was trying to open a new gateway or just venting his frustration on the situation in general.

Suddenly the demon paused. Taron ducked low and hit the ground hard, but he did it without a sound and didn't move. He had no idea how good the demon's night vision was—the creature was working within the limitations of a human body, but those glowing demon orbs behind Ed's human eyes might have perfect demon night-vision, for all he knew.

He'd landed belly-first in snow, and it was damned cold, but he didn't budge. Rocks clattered nearby as the demon moved away from the dead portal, and from the sounds he heard, Taron knew the creature came closer to him with each step. The stench of sulfur was almost suffocating, the shuffling scrape of Ed's labored steps growing louder by the second, but Taron couldn't see a thing from this position, had no idea if the demon knew he was there or if the creature was just blindly wandering.

"Hey, demon. Whatcha doin' over there? Come 'n get me, if you can!"

*Holy nine hells, Willow. What kind of stunt are you pulling?*

*Saving your butt, sweetheart. He's almost on top of you. Don't move.*

Stones rolled by him as the demon quickly turned and headed toward Willow. Taron leapt to his feet with Crystal-Fire drawn, but the creature moved quickly, considering Ed's condition. He looked like hell, but he was headed straight for Willow.

Racing across the snow-covered hillside just below the demon, Taron ran past him, dodging behind what small bits of cover he could find. He hoped the rumble of thunder would mask whatever sounds he made.

He sensed Willow moving nearby and ducked around a waist-high boulder. She waited on the other side, crouched down low, eyes sparkling and hands ready. He felt the energy pulling close around her and knew she'd been drawing what she could from the charged atmosphere.

He wondered if the electrical storm, growing closer by the second, added to the energy Willow was drawing, but now probably wasn't a good time to ask. He heard the demon, breath rasping in Ed's lungs, feet stumbling over the loose shale covering the mountain. It was heading right for them.

Thunder rumbled, closer this time. Lightning flashed, throwing everything in stark relief. More thunder, and this time the lightning struck close enough to send shards of broken rock flying in Taron and Willow's direction.

*Duck, Willow. Oooh . . . I hate thunderstorms. Hide, Willow. They're scary!*

*Calm down, Bumper. We don't have time for this. Taron? I think the demon's calling the lightning. Don't let him see you.*

*Crap. I thought it was getting awfully close.*

*Follow me.* Willow bent low and raced along the hillside, keeping to the shadows. Taron stayed right behind her. When had she taken charge of this operation? She moved like a well-trained warrior as they slipped from rock to fallen tree, to burned out stump, to rock, using whatever they could find for cover.

Taron realized he had no problem following Willow's lead. She made her decisions with confidence, without any need to argue both sides of a situation.

Unlike his own manner of handling things. He would do well to pay attention.

Besides, following Willow kept him close, within striking distance, so he could be there to protect her. By the gods, she was beautiful, brash, and brave as any warrior, moving like quicksilver across the rugged hillside, each step so carefully planted she flew like a soundless wraith, her body a lithe shadow slipping from cover to cover.

He could do far worse than follow one like Willow.

The demon stood above them, searching the darkness. Thunder pounded all around. It was continuous now, a steady drumbeat vibrating deep inside Taron's skull. He spotted a boulder just above the demon and pointed it out to Willow. She nodded, and they took off, slipping around to the demon's left while he stared off to the right where the two of them had been hiding only moments before.

Taron scrabbled about in the loose rock, grabbed a piece of shale shaped like a large dinner plate and flung it toward their last hiding place. The spinning disk disappeared in the darkness. It traveled even farther than he'd expected and actually hit the target he'd aimed for, crashing and clattering off the boulder where they'd last hidden. The demon screamed and shoved his fists into the air, shouted a curse in his own demonic language and pointed at the rock.

Thunder exploded all about. A massive bolt of lightning

ripped the air and struck the boulder with a resounding crack. The huge black rock split into pieces and splinters of stone flew in all directions. One massive chunk of boulder rolled down the mountainside, gathering speed and disappearing into the darkness.

The demon raced for the pile of broken rock and screamed again when it was obvious his targets had already fled.

He turned and walked steadily up the hill, moving ever closer to the place where Willow and Taron hid. Taron glanced at Willow. "You ready? Be careful. We can't kill Ed."

"No kidding. He doesn't need any more power than he's already got." She let out a shaky breath and nodded. "Let's go!"

Together they leapt to their feet. Willow pointed at the startled demon and shot a wall of blue sparkles his way. Taron aimed CrystalFire and a brilliant blast of flames met Willow's sparkles—the two streams of energy combined and flowed around the demon, tapping and teasing him with flashes and tiny explosions. He screamed and hunched over, batting at the swarming energy as if he fought a thousand stinging bees.

Then he stood, wavering back and forth on unsteady legs. Willow pointed her fingers. Taron raised his blade. The demon held up one hand, palm out, as if to hold them back.

"Stop!" Willow shoved CrystalFire down. "It's Ed."

She ran closer but kept a large boulder between herself and Eddy's dad. "Ed? It's me, Willow. Can you force the demon out? We can't kill him if he's in you."

Breathing in harsh, jagged gasps, Ed shook his head. "Kill me. It's the only way. Too strong. Must die so the demon will go."

Willow shook her head, and reached out, pleading with Ed. "Ed, we can't. It's not just because we love you. If we kill you, the demon will steal what's left of your life force. It'll make him even stronger. You have to force him out. It's up to you. Fight him, Ed. If he wins, we lose everything. You have to fight him!"

Ed's eyes went demon-red and he shrieked. Raising his hands to the clouds, he screamed out a strange sentence that even Taron's Lemurian language skills couldn't decipher.

But the clouds knew. Whatever he shouted brought the storm even closer. Dark clouds boiled and churned. Thunder echoed off the mountainside.

"Willow! Move!" Taron rolled behind a boulder in the opposite direction of Willow. She dove over another pile of rocks and ducked down behind them as lightning blasted the spot where she'd just been standing.

Steam sizzled from melting snow and the demon called yet another bolt, and another. The sky was alight with fire and the afterburn that left eyes blinded, but Willow was staying just out of reach. So was Taron.

He shot another blast toward Ed. He was confident the sword wouldn't harm the man, but swordfire appeared at least to rattle the demon. Willow popped up from behind her cover of tumbled rock and blasted a thick stream of blue sparkles. The air was filled with the stink of sulfur and the thick bite of ozone.

Shrieking and screaming, with spittle flying from his bleeding lips, the demon swung his head from side to side in total frustration, forced back another step with each blast of swordfire and sparkles. CrystalFire glowed as brilliantly as the lightning, and Willow pulled even more energy from the powerful storm.

Attacking together, they finally backed the demon against a wall of solid stone—the site of the now closed portal. Willow pushed even harder and so did Taron, but it wasn't enough to force the demon out of Ed.

Lightning blasted nearby. CrystalFire shouted a warning and Taron dove out of the way of the strike. Willow shot another blast of sparkles; Taron aimed the sword at the rock just above Ed and blasted that with swordfire, showering the demon with shards of stone. They kept it up for what felt like hours, attacking from both sides until the sky was as bright as daylight and energy crackled all around them.

But it wasn't enough.

Not nearly enough.

Willow was beginning to tire. Taron could see it in the size of her blasts, the fact that her attacks were becoming sluggish, her escapes even slower. He feared for her life, for the moment when she couldn't escape in time, but they couldn't quit. Their lives meant nothing—not when worlds were at stake.

Again the demon called the lightning. A massive bolt shot straight at Willow.

She screamed. Taron's heart turned to lead. "Willow!"

Silence. Even the thunder stilled.

*I'm down, but I'm okay. My foot's trapped. Maybe he'll think I'm dead.*

Taron raced across the open space between them, holding CrystalFire in his left hand, blasting swordfire at the demon the entire time. He jumped over the pile of boulders and landed almost on top of Willow.

She lay there with her leg caught between two boulders. A huge slab of rock had fallen over the top, effectively caging her, holding her prisoner.

Taron heard the demon's shuffling footsteps, the clatter of rocks as the creature drew closer, but he set his blade aside and grabbed the piece of rock covering Willow's thigh. Wrapping his hands beneath the rough edge, he pulled at the massive plate of stone until he thought his bones might break and tendons snap. He put everything he had into moving the damned thing off of her. When that wasn't enough strength, he dug deeper and found more.

Finally the huge stone shifted. Willow scrambled backwards, freed her leg and rolled to one side just as Ed leaned over the boulder and stared at her with demonic eyes.

Taron cursed, grabbed his sword and pointed CrystalFire. Ed backed off, snarling and growling like a wild animal, but in that brief instant, Taron realized the demon's eyes were flashing, changing from glowing red to chocolate brown and back to red. Ed was fighting the demon!

Sword in hand, Taron leapt over the boulder and faced the demon. Eyes the same chocolate brown as Eddy's looked back at him. Ed held his arms wide, silently begging Taron to strike him with CrystalFire. Instead, Willow stepped out from behind the boulder and stood beside Taron, held her hands out and blasted him with blue sparkles. Taron had no idea what the sparkles were or how they did what they did, but this time, instead of batting them away as the demon had done, Ed seemed to gain strength from the tiny lights as they circled his body, glowing like tiny blue fireworks all around.

He drew them in, absorbing them into his skin. Then Ed turned and gazed at Willow with eyes as clear and as brown as his daughter's. His face was ravaged with all he'd been through, his voice almost impossible to understand, but he held out a hand as if begging for release.

"Tell Eddy I love her."

His eyes flashed red and he reached for the clouds, once again screaming that demonic chant. Taron shot a quick glance at Willow. She stared at him, eyes wide, lips parted, and he felt a change in pressure as she drew in massive amounts of energy—energy that she delivered straight to his blade.

CrystalFire practically vibrated in Taron's grasp as Willow sent more power his way. They knew. Without saying a word to one another, Taron and Willow both knew.

Somehow Ed must have understood a sacrifice made for the good of all could not be used for evil. The demon raised his arms and called the lightning. The clouds boiled, lightning flashed, but it was Ed who stepped into the path of the bolt.

Willow was already in motion. Throwing herself into the

blast, she reached for Ed even as she continued throwing energy to CrystalFire.

"No!" *Not Willow. Dear gods, not Willow!* Taron lunged forward with CrystalFire, shoving his blade straight into the shimmering bolt of energy as Ed stepped into the strike and Willow shoved him aside.

In the final split second before impact, the demon must have realized what Ed planned. With a horrific scream, it burst out of the man's body and went straight for Taron.

Taron's blade, charged with Willow's power and the power of the lightning, cut through the demon, slicing into the thick, oily mist, turning it to shards of something black and foul that burned with incandescent fire. The final flames turned to sparks in every color of the rainbow.

The loud crack of lightning and booming thunder ended as quickly as the lightning had struck and the night went deathly silent. The storm dissipated within seconds; the clouds scattered.

Taron turned away from the bits of ash and tiny sparks still fluttering to the ground. He saw Ed lying in the dirt a few yards away. He couldn't tell if the man was dead or alive.

"Willow? Willow!" He screamed her name, but with the end of the storm, darkness descended on the mountainside. Frantic, Taron shouted at his sword. "CrystalFire. More light."

The blade flashed and blue light spread out over the hill-side. There, not far from Ed, something hidden in shadow. He raced across the rugged ground, spotted her hair, first. Long, straight blond hair, like a tangled halo of spun gold spilled all around her. She'd been thrown by the power of the blast and lay in the filthy slush of snow melted by lightning. Her face was unmarked, but a dark scorch ran from Willow's left shoulder to her right thigh.

"No. Dear gods, no." This couldn't be. He wouldn't let it

be. Not Willow, but he fell to his knees beside her, touched his hands to her throat and felt for a pulse.

*Nothing.*

A cold fist tightened around his chest, encased his heart, stopped the breath in his lungs.

He couldn't leave her here. Not lying in the wet and filthy snow. Carefully he slipped his hands beneath Willow's lifeless body—that perfect woman's body she'd been so proud of—and carried her to a small patch of relatively dry sand. He lay her down and knelt beside her. Brushed the long, sleek hair from her eyes and wondered where the curls had gone.

Where Bumper had gone? Did the dog's spirit die with Willow's? But how could Willow die? How could someone as filled with life, as full of dreams as Willow, ever die?

He stared at her for the longest time, unwilling to accept what was right there in front of him. That it was over. That Willow was over. He could talk his way into or out of just about anything, but there were no words for this. No words that could possibly describe the pain of losing what he'd only just found.

No words at all. Once again he slipped his hands beneath her body, lifted her in his arms and held her close against his chest. He kissed her lips. They were already cold. Unresponsive.

Proof she was truly gone. He settled her close with her head upon his shoulder and, oblivious to the temperatures falling steadily as the night wore on, Taron bowed his head and wept.


All was silent in the great plaza. Dax held Eddy while she cried, but she wept without sound, her loss so profound there was no way to express what she felt, what she'd seen. All that kept her from screaming was the strength of Dax's arms, the power of his unwavering love.

They'd been blinded by the brilliance of the lightning, but it looked as if it had gone right through her father. Even if the lightning hadn't killed him, there was no way his body could recover from the terrible ravages of the demon's possession. Her father looked near death even before the strike. Lightning had delivered the killing blow.

The screen still showed the mountainside, bathed now in the light from CrystalFire. The sword lay on the ground where Taron had left it, but Taron was off to one side, cradling Willow's still form. He sat on the ground, his body hunched protectively over hers as he quietly wept, poignantly lost in grief. Eddy's dad's twisted body was barely visible, lying in the shadows nearby.

The demon king was dead. They should be celebrating. There should be parades and cheering in the streets. Taron was a hero, but Willow was dead, and Dad . . . all Eddy could feel was loss.

Artigos the Just knelt beside her. "Dry your eyes, my dear. We don't know that your father is gone. Until we confirm his death, I choose to believe he lives. Crystal thinks, now the battle has ended, the portal might be open." He glanced at Dax. "Bring Eddy. Her father will need his daughter. And Alton? Dear grandson . . . I believe Taron will need his dearest friend."

Alton was already standing and helping Ginny to her feet. Roland remained behind to keep order and explain to the populace more of the details of what had transpired over the past month, and what the outcome of this pivotal battle really meant to each of them as Lemurians. Eight of them—Crystal, Artigos, Dawson, Selyn, Alton, Ginny, Dax, and Eddy—walked down the long passage to the portal.

Somehow, all of the portals appeared to be functioning. All except the one to Abyss. It was not merely sealed shut—the wall was smooth, as if the portal had never existed. Eddy stared at it for a moment. She found it hard to believe that this battle was truly the end of it. The Dark Lord didn't sound like one who gave in easily, no matter what fate decreed.

Feeling slightly nauseous, unable to truly comprehend how much they might have lost, but how very much those losses had gained, Eddy turned away from the sealed portal. Blinking back tears, she glanced up and realized the others were waiting on her. Clutching Dax's hand, she took a deep breath and walked toward the gateway. Then she stepped through the portal, out onto the same snow-covered flank of Mount Shasta she'd just been watching on the crystal screen.

Blue-white swordlight illuminated the entire area. Eddy's hand was over her mouth before she realized she'd stopped her own scream, but the scene was so much worse in real life. The rotten-egg stench of sulfur filled the air, and the harsh sound of a man weeping.

Swordlight cast everything in sharp relief—Willow's grown-up body caught in Taron's embrace, shattered and scorched boulders scattered all about, and there, not far from Taron and Willow, her father's familiar figure, lying in the snow like a toy that has been cast aside.

Bloodied and broken, he lay still as death.

With Dax holding tightly to her hand, Eddy raced past Taron and Willow, praying to whatever gods might hear that her father still lived.

# Chapter 25

Willow blinked. Black spots and flashes of light, the remnants of the lightning burst, still blinded her. It took a minute or two for her vision to clear. Something cold and wet nudged her fingers, forcing her to focus. She glanced down at Bumper, wriggling and bouncing in her own familiar doggy body.

Willow slipped out of the chair—*Chair? Where'd the chair come from?*—and knelt on the cold, marble floor. Her head was still reeling and spots still flashed in front of her eyes, but she held out her arms for the wriggling, bouncing bundle of curly-haired beast that almost knocked her over with typical boundless enthusiasm. "Bumper! How? What happened?"

*I'm me, I'm me, I'm a dog again. I love you Willow, but you're no fun. You're too much like a grown-up in that body. I love being me!*

"I love it when you're you, too, Bumper. But . . . ?" She raised her head and choked back a gasp. She was kneeling somewhere without walls or boundaries of any kind. Kneeling on a slick marble floor that seemed to go on forever, beside a long table. Robed figures sat along each side and the one at the head was lost in a golden glow.

Swallowing, she shot a quick glance at Bumper. *Somehow I don't think we're on Mount Shasta anymore, are we?*

Bumper flattened herself against the floor, ears down, nose against the deck, though she couldn't seem to control that curly tail. It still thumped a staccato beat against the floor. *Uh, Willow? It's sort of like . . .*

*Don't worry, sweetie. Good girl. Now stay.* She patted Bumper's curly head, slowly stood up and forced the butterflies suddenly bursting to life in her belly to settle down. Remembering her manners, she bowed her head in a show of respect.

She'd been here before, in what was truly another life, when she'd still been tiny and innocent to the world outside. She wasn't all that innocent anymore, and these people owed her an explanation.

She folded her arms across her chest and stared pointedly at the glowing figure at the far end. And waited.

The voice came from everywhere and nowhere at once. "She's certainly not the same wisp of swamp gas we recruited for this operation, is she?"

Soft laughter. Willow listened for a sense of ridicule, a feeling that they laughed at her, but it was nothing like that. Nothing at all.

She focused on the one at the end. She had no idea who he was, though he was obviously *somebody important* and this was certainly Eden, which meant . . .

Sighing, Willow accepted the truth she'd been trying to ignore—obviously, she'd died. And Bumper, too.

She glanced at the dog leaning against her leg with her typical doggy grin. Damn! She gazed once again at the robed figures. And waited.

Dear gods, she hoped the demon had died as well, that Taron and Ed survived. She hated to think she'd thrown away her shot at a real life for nothing. Really didn't want to imagine eternity without Taron. Especially if they'd failed. She took a deep breath, let it out. "What happened?"

"More than we ever could have hoped for."

The one at the end stood and walked around the long table. As he drew close, she saw he was a man—just a regular, albeit beautiful, man. He wasn't at all scary. In fact, he sort of reminded her of Artigos the Just, with that same air of command that seemed to be inborn in some people.

At least he was smiling when he stopped in front of her. He leaned over and patted Bumper on the head, and, of course, the stupid dog rolled over to get her belly rubbed.

He laughed, knelt in front of Willow and did exactly what Bumper wanted and tickled his fingers over the dog's pink tummy. Bumper sighed and her eyes slid closed. There was nothing she loved more than a good belly rub, something Willow had found horribly demeaning when she'd shared the dog's body.

Didn't Bumper have any pride at all?

The man stood, but he was still concentrating on Bumper. Then he passed his hand over the dog. She disappeared.

"Bumper!" Willow stared at the empty spot on the floor and glared at the man. "What did you do to Bumper? Where is she?"

There was a soft gasp from the others along the table. The man shook his head and smiled at Willow, but he held up one hand to still any further comments from the others. "She's on the side of Mount Shasta, waking up and looking for Eddy. Don't worry. She'll find her in a moment."

"Good." Willow let out a jagged breath. "That's good. She doesn't deserve to die."

"And you do?" He wasn't smiling now. His face looked quite serious.

Shaking her head with complete conviction, Willow said, "No. I don't deserve to die, either."

He folded his arms across his chest and stared at her with the oddest little half smile on his face. "Why not?"

She shrugged and wondered why he found her so funny. "I don't want to make Taron grieve, and he will. He says he loves me, and I believe him. He would never lie. Besides, I love him. That's the most important reason, because he's a good man and he deserves to be happy. I can make him happy. I was doing a good job of it, and I'd really hate to think that stupid fortune teller was right."

The more she thought about it, the angrier she got. "I didn't ask for any of this, but I still did everything I could to help Dax when I was a sprite, I did my best when I was stuck inside Bumper, and when I was a woman, I gave everything I had to help Taron. I always did the best I could."

He didn't say a word. Just looked at her as if he was really listening, but then she remembered the most important thing, even more than how she felt about Taron and what he thought of her. "Did we win? Is the demon gone?"

He slowly nodded his head. "He is gone. Your sacrifice and Ed's, Taron's bravery, and even CrystalFire's understanding and free admission of his own flaws—all of this together was more than evil could overcome. The good in all of you definitely outweighed the evil in the dark one. The one who would be the demon king is gone forever. The Dark Lord survives, but his existence—like mine—keeps the balance intact."

She gave a short, sharp jerk of her head. "Good. That's good. Demonkind was growing too powerful. It had to be stopped."

"It did. Without you, Willow of the swamp, demonkind might easily have won. Those seated at this table, the ones judging you . . ." He waved his hand to encompass the robed men, "might have been demons instead of a council of citizens of Eden."

Willow hugged herself, suddenly chilled. They'd come so

close to failure. But what now? They were judging her? Crap. "What of me?" she asked, wondering if it really mattered without Taron. "What will you do with me?"

She really, really didn't want to go back to the swamp. In fact, there was only one place she wanted to be, but it was too late for that. She'd already died.

"That is a big question. What do we do with you?" He was smiling at her, so it couldn't be all bad. "We are willing to offer you a spot in Paradise, not as you were, but as you are now."

She thought about that, thought about something Dax had said when he'd turned down that same offer. He said he'd found his paradise with Eddy. He was so right. She thought of the way she'd felt in Taron's arms. Even something as simple as sitting across the table from him, sharing a meal, had been its own kind of paradise.

"With all due regards, sir, eternity in Paradise without Taron would be the same as condemning me to another death."

He glanced over his shoulder and grinned at the men seated along the table. "What did I say?"

She heard a few grumbles and what even sounded like a snort of laughter. Frowning, Willow glared at the one in front of her. "What?"

"A little bet, my dear. For what it's worth, I won." He reached out then and ran his fingers over her long *straight* hair. "You shall have your wish, on one condition."

Her wish? She hadn't actually wished for anything, but if he could read what was in her heart, then . . . "What? What kind of condition?"

"That you become one of our small band of immortal demonslayers, charged with protecting all worlds from the threat of demonkind. The one who would be the demon king is gone, but another will rise in his place. And if that one is vanquished, another will rise, and then another. It is the way of things, to constantly test that precarious balance holding all worlds in a state of equilibrium. With your addition to this surprisingly resilient and very unexpected band of demon-slayers, that equilibrium might actually be maintained.

"I want you to agree to be one of our soldiers on the front lines, to remain vigilant always."

He seemed to waver in place, and it took Willow a moment to realize she was seeing him through her tears. "I accept." She grabbed his hands and squeezed them in hers, and there was so much joy in her heart that she stood on her toes and kissed his cheek.

The last thing she saw was his somewhat stunned smile as he pressed a hand to cover the kiss. Then she heard laughter and what sounded like a sigh of relief from those at the long table.

But it drifted away until not even the echo remained, and she was spinning—spinning through night and day and night again, through a rainbow of colors and a shimmering cloud of blue sparkles.

Spinning until she'd lost all sense of up or down, left or right, night or day. The only thing familiar was the steady beat of a heart, the powerful crush of arms holding her close, the salty taste of tears on her lips.

Blinking slowly, she opened her eyes. Raised her hand, touched her palm to Taron's tear-streaked face, and said the first thing that came to her.

"I'm back," she whispered. "And they're letting me keep the big girl body."


Eddy knelt beside her poor father's battered body. He looked as if he'd shrunk, as if the strong, healthy man she'd hugged just days ago had aged by dozens of years. She touched her fingers to his throat and felt the slightest flutter-ing pulse, but she held them there a moment longer. Her hands shook so badly, she had to be sure it wasn't her own trembling she felt.

Then his eyes blinked, fluttered a moment and stayed open. His lips parted. Voice dry and raspy, he whispered, "Eddy?"

She could barely hear him, but there was no denying he was alive. "Dad? Daddy!" She turned frantically to call for help, and Dax was right there beside her. "He needs help. Who . . . ?"

Crystal knelt on Ed's other side, going down on her knees in the filthy snow, regardless of the pristine white gown she wore. "Let me," she said, lightly holding her fingertips to Ed's temples.

Eddy wrapped her fingers around her father's. His were limp and barely responsive, but she felt the slightest pressure as he tried to return her squeeze. She sat back and leaned against Dax. His left arm was like a steel band around her waist, keeping her close.

Light flashed off to their left. Eddy flinched, then stared, blinking, as Mari and Darius suddenly strode across the rocky ground. Mari knelt beside Ed. "We just got back. We've been trapped over at the coast for the past few days, but as we drove in, we could see the battle from town. Lightning flashing, huge flares of fire in the sky. It looked like the volcano had erupted, there was so much going on up here. We knew it had to be one hell of a fight. Is he . . . ?"

Crystal answered. "The demon king is dead, but Eddy's father is alive. We have to get him to Lemuria. Our healers can help him." She raised her head. "Artigos? Over here, my love. Get Dawson. We need him, too."

Within seconds Artigos and Dawson were kneeling next to Ed. Daws checked his pulse and nodded to Eddy. "We have to hurry. He's terribly dehydrated. Crystal? M'lord? Can your healers help with injuries like this?"

Artigos was the one to slip his hands beneath Ed's fragile

body and carefully lift him. "They can. But we'll have to hurry. We've got to clear the area. Darius said there are townspeople heading this way. The battle was visible to everyone around. We all have to get out of here before others arrive."

Holding Ed against his chest, Artigos headed toward the portal with Crystal and Dawson beside him. Selyn and Ginny waited by the gateway, ready to slip back into the vortex.

Eddy and Dax rushed after them, until two sounds caught Eddy's attention—the steady drone of a helicopter drawing close, and the sharp yip of a dog.

One particular dog. "Bumper? Where are you, girl?"

She turned around just in time to kneel down and catch the furry body as Bumper launched herself into Eddy's arms.

Laughing, crying, she stood up, still hanging on to a wriggling, licking, yipping Bumper.

"Hurry." Dax grabbed her elbow and rushed her toward the portal. The others had gone through already. Mari and Darius were just ahead of them. The only ones left on the mountain were Taron, Alton, and Willow.

"Go on with the others. I'll get them." Dax planted a fast, hard kiss on her mouth. Eddy hung on to the wriggling dog. The sound of the chopper drew closer as she ducked through the portal and followed her father and the others into the vortex.


Willow clung to him as if she'd never let go, but it didn't matter, because Taron had a grip on her that was even tighter. He was still trying to comprehend the fact that she was actually alive when Dax grabbed him by the arm and shoved CrystalFire into the sheath on his back.

Alton took his other arm, both men lifted, and Taron was suddenly on his feet still holding Willow tightly against his chest.

"Hang on to your woman and hurry," Dax said. Taron stumbled in his attempt to keep up, but then he got his feet under him and, holding Willow close, allowed Alton and Dax to rush him toward the portal.

He wasn't sure what the rush was all about until Alton yelled, "Down!"

They all ducked behind a boulder as the brilliant beam of a spotlight slashed across the mountainside.

"Nine hells but that was close." Alton was up and had all of them moving again the moment the aircraft passed them by.

"I can walk," Willow said.

"Not now." Taron hung on even tighter. No way was he letting her go. Not until they were safe. They reached the portal and slipped through mere seconds ahead of the next pass by that aircraft he knew was called a helicopter.

Any other time, he'd be out there gawking at the thing, trying to figure out how it stayed aloft, what kind of motor powered it, how the aerodynamics functioned. He'd heard of them but had never seen one before . . . but now was not the time.

Willow was alive. He still couldn't believe he held a live woman in his arms. She'd been dead. He was certain she'd died. He'd searched for a pulse, tried to find a heartbeat, kissed lips as cold as ice.

Now she was warm and alive and already giving him grief.

"Let me walk, Taron." She glared at him.

He just grinned right back. Then he kissed her, and this time her lips were warm and alive, and kissing him back. "Later," he said, when they finally broke apart. "There's no way I'm turning you loose. Not yet."

She smiled at him and cupped his jaw in her palm. "Okay."

He frowned as they passed through the main portal into Lemuria and headed down the tunnel to the golden veil.

"Okay? That's all you're going to say? No argument? Just okay?"

"Uh huh."

"Oh." He grinned and tightened his hold on her. She looped her arms around his neck and settled her head on his shoulder.

Alton walked beside him with a huge, sappy grin on his face. Taron glanced his way. Then he glared at him. "What?"

Alton just laughed. Taron shook his head and kept walking, but he couldn't stop grinning, either. In fact, he felt as if his face might split wide open if he grinned any wider.

He had Willow in his arms, the demon was dead, and . . . and . . . Damn. He had Willow in his arms. It just didn't get any better.


They met late the next morning, almost all of those who'd been involved in the past month's events, including the ones who'd been on the mountainside for the final battle, all of them gathering in Artigos's chambers. Crystal, looking more like a lovely housewife than a demigoddess with her hair in a crown of braids around her head and wearing a comfortable tunic and loose pants, passed around a tray of sweet rolls and hot drinks.

Taron found a comfortable spot on a long, low couch and looped his arms around Willow's waist as she settled herself on his lap. Mari and Darius stepped through the portal and took a seat next to Taron and Willow.

Willow leaned against his chest. He took a deep breath, filling his lungs with her sweet scent and tightened his grasp around her. She tilted her head back and looked at him upside down. "I'm not going anywhere."

"Just making sure."

Mari laughed. "Did anyone warn you that Lemurian men are sort of possessive?"

Selyn plopped down on the couch beside Mari and Darius. Dawson sat next to her. "No more than Lemurian women," he said.

Selyn jabbed him in the ribs.

He doubled over, groaning dramatically. "Just sayin'."

Dax and Eddy, with Bumper bouncing alongside, came in, supporting Ed between them. He was already looking more like himself, though he'd obviously had a rough few days.

Willow twisted so she could see them. "Eddy? Did you get a chance to check on Mr. Puccini?"

Eddy helped settle her dad in a chair, told Bumper to sit and stay, and walked across the room. "I slipped out through the portal and called another neighbor this morning. He's doing better. Still in the hospital, but they expect to discharge him in a day or two."

Taron thought of the old man, lying so still and lifeless on the ground. "Does he remember what happened?"

She sighed. "No. Not a thing. He doesn't even remember going outside, and his blood pressure was so low when they found him that that's what they're treating him for. He'll be fine, but it sounds as if the demon almost killed him."

She wrapped her fingers around Dax's hand as he stepped up beside her. "He didn't mention you or Willow or anything about Ed, so that's good. There were four other similar cases—forgotten memories, very low blood pressure. It'll keep doctors busy searching for a common cause."

Willow nodded. "We knew the demon had taken the life force from more people, but we were afraid he might have killed them."

"For some reason, he didn't take everything. He left them alive." Dax leaned over and kissed Eddy's cheek. "I'm going to go sit with your dad. He's still pretty shaky."

He and Darius walked back to stand beside Ed's seat. Eddy

glanced their way but then she turned and smiled at Taron and Willow. "Me, too. But Taron . . . Willow? Thank you both. The easy way out would have been to kill the avatar. Thank you for being so careful with Dad. You saved his life."

Willow took Eddy's hand and squeezed. "We love your dad, Eddy. He's one of the good guys."

"Yeah." Eddy grinned. "He is, isn't he? Damn, Willow! Am I ever going to get used to seeing you as a real woman? This is just freaky, but you're so gorgeous! Wow!"

Taron held Willow even closer. "Gorgeous is a given and 'wow' is an understatement."

Laughing, Eddy leaned over, planted a big kiss on Taron and then walked back to join Dax and her father.

The large room filled with people. Roland and Chara and their son and Artigos II and Gaia, Ginny, and Alton stood at the far side, talking to Crystal. Nica and Isra had entered together and sat on another couch across from Selyn and Dawson. Mari joined Darius near Eddy, Dax, and Ed.

A few other Paladins, a couple of guardsmen and some of the new members of the council arrived. After a few minutes while everyone milled about talking and laughing, filling the room with scattered bits and pieces of the amazing events they'd all been part of, Artigos the Just walked over to stand beside his grandson. He clapped his hands, drawing everyone's attention.

Taron thought he could probably have gotten the same effect by merely standing quietly in one spot for a moment. The man definitely had presence. Then Taron found his gaze shifting to his dearest friend. Alton had the same charisma, the same natural qualities as his grandfather. Someday, he and Ginny would make as formidable a ruling couple as Artigos and Crystal did today.

But that was something yet to come, and Artigos was speaking of the here and now. He gazed out over the room as if he spoke before the entire population of Lemuria, every bit their ruler, and yet he was the same man who'd carried a badly wounded human to safety just hours ago.

A leader anyone would be proud to follow. Taron glanced about the gathering and realized how much he had changed in just a few short days. Where he'd admired Artigos the Just before, he now saw the man through new eyes—saw him as a fellow soldier as much as his leader. It was something to think about—a reminder of his own new reality as a man.

He was not merely one thing or another. Not limited to scholar or philosopher or that most surprising discovery, passionate beast. He was so much more than a mere scholar. Somewhere, somehow, over the past few days, another side of his nature had been set free, a wild side he'd not even known existed. It was there now, a part of him for all time. It was going to be an interesting journey, watching the two—scholar and beast—learn to cohabit peacefully.

But since Willow seemed quite fond of the wild side, he knew he'd figure it out. With that thought in mind, Taron focused on their leader.

Artigos smiled at Crystal and then turned again to the gathering. "Thank you, all of you, for coming this morning. You've been invited because each of you has had a personal role to play in the events just past. Events that will change Lemuria for all time to come. Just a few short days ago, our council was ruled by demonkind, an entire generation of young women were enslaved in the mines below, and I was still a prisoner without hope of ever knowing freedom again."

He glanced about the room, somehow managing to make eye contact with every single person there. "Today we are facing a future none of us ever imagined—a chance for the people of Lemuria to go forward without fear of demonkind, a chance to once again reclaim the heritage we lost so many thousands of years ago. We have that future because of you. All of you in this room have had a part in saving our world from a terrible fate. Giving us all a chance to build a stronger civilization, one free to grow as it is meant to grow."

He put an arm around Alton and hugged him close. "Much is due to my dear grandson. Alton was willing to take risks few of his peers might have attempted."

Blushing, Alton returned the hug and then reached almost frantically for Ginny's hand. Where he might have once laughed at his friend's discomfort, Taron realized he felt highly sympathetic. There was something about the strength of a woman standing beside a man. Illogical but undeniable.

And absolutely wonderful.

But Artigos was still speaking, and Taron focused on their leader once again. "Dax, you were thrown into this battle, as were so many others. Offered a choice to run or fight, you chose to fight for a world you'd never known. Eddy, Ginny, Dawson, Mari—your courage is why we succeeded. Humans willing to risk your lives for Lemuria. Selyn, you, Nica, and Isra were treated abominably by your own people, and yet you took up arms to fight demonkind and protect the same world that turned its back on you. There is no greater example of selfless courage. Ed? I understand you've long believed we existed in spite of facts saying otherwise. I commend you." He chuckled softly when Eddy raised her eyebrows and made a face at her father.

"I also must thank you—your willingness to sacrifice yourself rather than do the demon's bidding is a large part of our victory. Evil has a difficult time fighting such a pure and good intention."

Then he stepped across the room and stood in front of Taron and Willow. "And you two!" He shook his head, laughing. "When I realized our champion, the only man standing between good and evil was one simple scholar, Taron of Libernus, I must admit I was sorely discouraged. You've done all of Lemuria proud, my boy."

Taron chuckled. "Thank you, but believe me, m'lord. You

weren't alone. I was every bit as discouraged. But none of us, myself included, counted on Willow."

She jerked her head around and stared at him, wide-eyed. "What do you mean?"

"Willow, do you honestly think I could have beaten the demon king on my own?" He shook his head. "No way."

She stood up and planted her hands on her hips and actually glared at him.

He opened his mouth to say something, but he totally forgot what he intended to say. Instead, he was trapped in the beauty of her, in the fact she was still here, still his. He'd not had time yet to process all that had happened, all that waited for him—for them. They'd only had time for a few hours of much needed sleep and a quick shower before meeting here this morning, but that was it. They'd been too tired even to make love.

He almost laughed out loud. That was definitely *too tired*.

Willow had put on the only clean clothes available—one of the traditional Lemurian robes. She looked like an angel with her blond hair falling in shimmering waves over her shoulders, and like a man possessed, he lost himself in her, running his fingers through the strands that fell almost to her waist.

"It's longer without the curls," he said, grasping for something simple, something he could understand, but he was caught in a rush of emotion he really couldn't explain.

Her gentle laughter had him looking up and seeing only Willow. It took a moment before he realized the room had gone quiet, that everyone looked their way.

Heat spread over his face. "I mean . . ."

Suddenly Alton was beside him, and he planted one firm hand on Taron's shoulder. "I know exactly what you mean."

Artigos laughed softly. "I think we all do."

Taron glanced from Alton to Ginny, from Artigos to Crystal, who stood close beside him, and then back at his friend. "I guess you do. And I know that you Alton, of all of us, understand what it's like for a man who expected to live his life alone, to discover there is so much more when it's shared."

Alton reached for Ginny's hand and tugged her close. "I do." He kissed Ginny and wrapped an arm around her, pulling her close. "And Willow, for what it's worth, Taron couldn't have done it without you, just as I could not have succeeded without Ginny or Dax without Eddy." He laughed. "In fact, Dax couldn't have succeeded without you, either, Willow. You were an amazingly effective will-o'-the-wisp." He glanced around the room. "Imagine Darius fighting demons without Mari, or Dawson without Selyn."

His father stood up and tugged Gaia to her feet. "Me without your mother."

Taron tugged Willow's hand and she settled in his lap once again. He glanced at the others in the room and realized how many of them were paired, including their new leader and his demigoddess. "He's right, you know. We all needed our mates beside us, leading us." He raised his head. "I freely admit that Willow can sneak across a mountainside with much greater stealth than I'll ever achieve."

Willow snuggled close and kissed his throat. "Here's hoping we don't have to do it again too soon."

Artigos raised his glass. "To all of you who have fought the good fight—we are at peace because of your efforts. Our children and their children are safe because of you. I raise my glass to Lemuria, to peace, to a future where we can grow and prosper as our ancestors first hoped when they came to this world. In peace, and in sunlight."

Every glass was lifted, and each one in the room paused before drinking.

"How, Grandfather?"

"A truth that demonkind hid from us all these long years. We exist in a separate dimension. We are inside the volcano, but not really *in the volcano*. It is merely the physical presence we see. Crystal explained it to me."

"When we finally got around to talking," she added.

Taron noticed this time it was Artigos who blushed. "Yes, well . . ." he said, then he smiled at the petite woman beside him. "It really is your story. You explain it."

She glanced at him and then, in a heartbeat, her power seemed to shine through. "You live within caverns because your demonic rulers wanted you here, apart from life-giving sunlight. Demons crave the darkness, but Lemurians thrive beneath the sun. Your island continent exists still, not far from here. The buildings are damaged, the terrain much over-grown, but the land itself is available through portals long closed by demonkind. We should have them open and func-tioning within the week. Just as you pass between Evergreen and this world, you will be able to step through into the trop-ical paradise Lemurians left so long ago. It's going to take a lot of hard work to rebuild, but we are not a static society. Not afraid of work. Not any longer."

Artigos raised his glass once again. "And now will you toast with me? To our future—our future as a nation and as a people. And most especially to those brave souls who made this happen, to our demonslayers."

Bumper ran around in circles and barked. Every other soul in the room drank to their leader's heartfelt salute. As Taron tipped his cup to his lips, he caught Willow's steady blue-eyed gaze. *I'm not nearly as tired as I was,* he said.

She laughed. He held her close, and together they dreamed of a future bathed in sunlight beneath blue skies.

# Chapter 26

Willow stood just inside the portal to Taron's apartment and clasped her hands over her belly. For some reason she was nervous as all get out. It didn't make any sense, not after all she'd been through over the past month, not to mention the past four days.

She wondered if she'd ever adjust to this life, a life she'd never, not in her wildest dreams, imagined. Taron stepped into the room, carrying CrystalFire. They'd gone unarmed to the gathering this morning. Maybe not the smartest move, but it had felt good to be in a room of friends and not be worried about an attack.

Of course, she still had her sparkles, and Dax was armed with ice and fire and other things he said he still hadn't figured out. And the gods only knew what Crystal could do.

"Come." Taron grabbed her fingers and tugged her close. "I have something to show you." He pulled the sword from its scabbard and set the blade on the table. Light glimmered along the faceted surface, rolling up and down in a mesmerizing pattern that Willow figured she'd always find fascinating.

"What?" She ran her fingers along the blade. "Crystal-Fire? Do you have something to say to us?"

"I do. I have already admitted I erred in underestimating

Taron's skills as a warrior. I saw naught but the philosopher and neglected the strength he hid beneath the skin of a scholar. I made the same mistake with you, Willow of Eden. I saw you as a simple construct, not as a real warrior. I was wrong. You are, in many ways, the best of all of them, brave and fearless."

She shot a quick glance at Taron. He just sat there and grinned at her. She practically snarled under her breath. *You're not much help!*

*I love you.*

*I love you too, but you're still not much help. What's this all about?*

*Just wait.*

CrystalFire flashed, a light so bright it brought tears to her eyes and she turned her head away. "What was that?"

"Take a look."

She stared at the sword, but she was still so blinded by the flash, she saw double. Blinking to focus, Willow looked again.

Still two.

Except, one of them had a blade of brilliant blue.

The same sapphire blue as her blue sparkles. She jerked her head up and stared at Taron, but he was grinning like an idiot.

"You're not helping," she said.

Then she looked again and, drawn by a power she couldn't explain, passed her fingers over the blade.

The blue crystal pulsed with life, inviting her to pick the sword up, to hold it, and watch the light shimmer along its faceted surface.

The silver hilt fit her hand as if it had been made for her. Which, obviously, it had.

"For me?" Wide-eyed, she dragged her gaze away from the perfect sword in her hand and stared at Taron. "But why?"

Taron shook his head. "I don't know. CrystalFire said he had something for you. I guess this is it."

She couldn't speak, couldn't have explained the feeling she got just holding on to the weapon, but there was a powerful sense that it somehow anchored her, held her to this world in a way nothing else could.

She didn't merely look like a woman, she was a woman—a woman warrior. A demonslayer. "What's your name?" she asked, not really expecting an answer. Taron's blade had taken thousands of years before it finally spoke, so she couldn't really expect this brand new sword to . . .

"I am SunStorm, a blade who will take you into the new future of Lemuria, a new life for you, Willow of the Swamps."

Willow sat down next to Taron. Hard. But her sword was still talking, a strong, feminine voice that projected power with every word. "From your existence as an element of nature, to your new life as a woman of Lemuria, a life you will live beneath sunshine and storms, I will be your companion. Blessings on you, Willow."

Taron wrapped an arm around her and hugged her close against his side. "She will be your companion, but I'm going to be your mate. Agreed?"

She carefully set the sword on the table next to Crystal-Fire, turned in Taron's arms and cupped his beloved face in her hands. "I've been your mate from the moment I first saw you, Taron of Libernus. I love you."

He leaned over and kissed the end of her nose. "In sickness and in health?"

"In sunshine and shadows, good times and bad times, and all the times in between." She stood up, took his hand and tugged. The bedroom was just a few short steps away. "No demons to fight, no crisis to deal with. No new world to start building."

He leaned in close and kissed her. "I guess we've got time."

"All the time in the world." Hanging tightly to his hand, she followed him into the bedroom. Stopping next to the big bed, she turned to kiss him once again, whispering against his lips.

"I hope you remembered to invite the beast."

If you enjoyed *CrystalFire*,
see how the DemonSlayers got their start in


# **DEMONFIRE**.


Turn the page for a special excerpt!


A Zebra mass-market paperback on sale now!

*Sunday night*

He struggled out of the darkness, confused, disoriented . . . recalling fire and pain and the soothing voices of men he couldn't see. Voices promising everlasting life, a chance to move beyond hell, beyond all he'd ever known. He remembered his final, fateful decision to take a chance, to search for something else.

For life beyond the hell that was Abyss.

A search that brought him full circle, back to a world of pain—to this world, wherever it might be. He frowned and tried to focus. This body was unfamiliar, the skin unprotected by scales or bone. He'd never been so helpless, so vulnerable.

His chest burned. The demon's fireshot, while not immediately fatal, would have deadly consequences. Hot blood flowed sluggishly from wounds across his ribs and spread over the filthy stone floor beneath his naked hip. The burn on his chest felt as if it were filled with acid. Struggling for each breath, he raised his head and stared into the glaring yellow eyes of an impossible creature holding him at bay.

Four sharp spears affixed to a long pole were aimed directly at his chest. The thing had already stabbed him once, and the bleeding holes in his side hurt like the blazes. With a heartfelt groan, Dax tried to rise, but he had no strength left.

He fell back against the cold stones, and his world faded once more to black.


"You're effing kidding me! I leave for one frickin' weekend, and all hell breaks loose. You're positive? Old Mrs. Abernathy really thinks it ate her cat?" Eddy Marks took another sip of her iced caffé mocha whip and stared at Ginny. "Lord, I hope my father hasn't heard about it. He'll blame it on the Lemurians."

Ginny laughed so hard she almost snorted her latte. "Your dad's not still hung up on that silly legend, is he? Like there's really an advanced society of humanoids living inside Mount Shasta? I don't think so."

"Don't try and tell Dad they don't exist. He's convinced he actually saw one of their golden castles in the moonlight. Of course, it was gone by morning." Eddy frowned at Ginny and changed the subject. She was admittedly touchy about her dad's gullible nature. "Mrs. Abernathy's not serious, is she?"

"I dunno." Ginny shook her head. "She was really upset. Enough that she called nine-one-one. I was on dispatch at Shasta Communications that shift and took the call. Shascom sent an officer out because she was hysterical, not because they actually believed Mr. Pollard's ceramic garden gnome ate Twinkles." Ginny ran her finger around the inside of her cup, chasing the last drops of her iced latte. "I heard there was an awful lot of blood on her back deck, along with tufts of suspiciously Twinkles-colored hair."

"Probably a coyote or a fox." Eddy finished the last of her drink and wished she'd had a shot of brandy to add to it. It would have been the perfect finish to the first vacation she'd had in months—two glorious days hiking and camping on Mount Shasta with only her dog for company . . . and not a single killer garden gnome in sight. She grinned at Ginny. "Killer garden gnomes aren't usually a major threat around here."

Ginny laughed. "Generally, no. Lemurians either, in spite of what your dad and half the tourists think, but for once, Eddy, don't be such a stick in the mud. Let your imagination go a little."

"What? And start spouting off about Lemurians? I don't think so. Someone has to be the grown-up! So what else happened while I was out communing with nature?"

"Well . . . it might have been the full moon, but there was a report that the one remaining stone gargoyle launched itself off the northwest corner of the old library building, circled the downtown area, and flew away into the night. And . . ." Ginny paused dramatically, ". . . another that the bronze statue of General Humphreys and his horse trotted out of the park. I didn't check on the gargoyle, but I went down to see the statue. It's not there. Looks like it walked right off the pedestal. That thing weighs over two tons." She set her empty cup down, folded her arms, and, with one dark eyebrow raised, stared at Eddy.

"A big bronze statue like that would bring in a pretty penny at the recyclers. Somebody probably hauled it off with a truck, but it's a great visual, isn't it?" Eddy leaned back in her chair. "I can just see that big horse with the general, sword held high and covered in pigeon poop, trotting along Front Street. Maybe a little detour through the cemetery."

"Is it worth a story by ace reporter Edwina Marks?"

Eddy glared at her. "Do not call me Edwina." She ran her finger through the condensation on the scarred wooden table top before looking up at Ginny and grinning. "Maybe a column about weird rumors and how they get started. I'll cite you as Ground Zero, but I doubt it's cutting edge enough for the front page of the *Record*."

Ginny grabbed her purse and pulled out a lipstick. "Yeah, like that rag's going to cover real news."

"Hey, we do our best, and we stay away from the tabloid stuff—you know, the garbage you like to read?" Laughing, Eddy stood up. "Well, I'm always complaining that nothing exciting ever happens around here. I guess flying gargoyles, runaway statues, and killer garden gnomes are better than nothing." She tossed some change on the table for a tip and waved at the girl working behind the counter. "Gotta go, Gin. I need to get home. Have to let Bumper out."

"Bumper? Who's that? Don't tell me you brought home another homeless mutt from the shelter."

"And if I did?"

Ginny waved the lipstick at her like a pointer. "Eddy, the last time you had to give up a fostered pup, you bawled for a week. Why do you do this to yourself?"

She'd be lucky if she only bawled for a week when it was time for Bumper to leave. They'd bonded almost immediately, but she really didn't want a dog. Not for keeps. "They were gonna put her down if no one took her," she mumbled.

Ginny shook her head. "Don't say I didn't warn you. One of these days you're going to take in a stray that'll really break your heart."

Eddy heard Bumper when she was still half a block from home. She'd only left the dog inside the house while she went to town for coffee, but it appeared the walls weren't thick enough to mute her deep-throated growling and barking.

Thank goodness it wasn't nine yet. Any later and she'd probably have one of the neighbors filing a complaint. Eddy picked up her pace and ran the last hundred yards home, digging for her house keys as she raced up the front walk.

"Bumper, you idiot. I only left you for an hour. I hope you haven't been going on like this the whole time I've been gone."

She got the key in the lock and swung the front door open. Bumper didn't even pause to greet her. Instead, she practically knocked Eddy on her butt as she raced out the front door, skidded through the open gate to the side yard, and disappeared around the back of the house.

"Shit. Stupid dog." Eddy threw her keys in her bag, slung her purse over her shoulder, and took off after the dog. It was almost completely dark away from the street light, and Eddy stumbled on one of the uneven paving stones by the gate. Bumper's deep bark turned absolutely frantic, accompanied by the added racket from her clawing and scratching at the wooden door to Eddy's potting shed.

"If you've got a skunk cornered in there, you stupid dog, I swear I'm taking you back to the shelter."

Bumper stopped barking, now that she knew she had Eddy's attention. She whined and sniffed at the door, still scratching at the rough wood. Eddy fumbled in her bag for her keychain and the miniature flashlight hanging from the ring. The beam was next to worthless, but better than nothing.

She scooted Bumper out of the way with her leg and un-latched the door just enough to peer in through a crack. Bumper whapped her nose against Eddy's leg. Shoving fran-tically with her broad head, she tried to force her way inside.

"Get back." Eddy glared at the dog. Bumper flattened her ears against her curly head and immediately backed off, looking as pathetic as she had last week at the shelter when Eddy'd realized she couldn't leave a blond pit bull crossed with a standard poodle to the whims of fate.

She aimed her tiny flashlight through the narrow opening. Blinked. Told herself she was really glad she'd been drink-ing coffee and not that brandy she'd wanted tonight, because otherwise she wouldn't believe what she saw.

Maybe Mrs. Abernathy wasn't nuts after all. Eddy grabbed

a shovel leaning against the outside wall of the shed and threw the door open wide.

The garden gnome that should have been stationed in the rose garden out in front held a pitchfork in its stubby little hands like a weapon, ready to stab what appeared to be a person lying in the shadows. When the door creaked open, the gnome turned its head, glared at Eddy through yellow eyes, bared unbelievably sharp teeth, and screamed at her like an avenging banshee.

Bumper's claws scrabbled against the stone pathway. Eddy swung the shovel. The crunch of metal connecting with ceramic seemed unnaturally loud. The scream stopped as the garden gnome shattered into a thousand pieces. The pitchfork clattered to the ground, and a dark, evil-smelling mist gathered in the air above the pile of dust. It swirled a moment and then suddenly whooshed over Eddy's shoulder and out the open door.

A tiny blue light pulsed and flickered, followed the mist as far as the doorway, and then returned to hover over the figure in the shadows. Bumper paused long enough to sniff the remnants of the garden gnome and growl, before turning her attention to whatever lay on the stone floor. Eddy stared at the shovel in her hands and took one deep breath after another. This was not happening. She *had not seen* a garden gnome in attack mode.

One with glowing yellow eyes and razor-sharp teeth.

*Impossible.*

Heart pounding, arms and legs shaking, she slowly pivoted in place and focused on whoever it was that Bumper seemed so pleased to see.

The mutt whined, but her curly tail was wagging a million miles a minute. She'd been right about the gnome. Eddy figured she'd have to trust the dog's instincts about whoever or whatever had found such dubious sanctuary in her potting shed.

Eddy squinted and tried to focus on the flickering light

that flitted in the air over Bumper's head, but it was jerking around so quickly she couldn't tell what it was. She still had her key ring clutched in her fingers. She wasn't quite ready to put the shovel down, but she managed to shine the narrow beam of light toward the lump on the floor.

Green light reflected back from Bumper's eyes. Eddy swung wider with the flashlight. She saw a muscular arm, a thick shoulder, and the broad expanse of a masculine chest. Blood trickled from four perfectly spaced pitchfork-sized holes across the man's ribs and pooled beneath his body. There appeared to be a deep wound on his chest, though it wasn't bleeding.

In fact, it looked almost as if it had been cauterized. A burn? Eddy swept the light his full length. Her eyes grew wider with each inch of skin she exposed. He was marked with a colorful tattoo that ran from his thigh, across his groin to his chest, but other than the art, he was naked. Very naked, all the way from his long, narrow feet, up those perfectly formed, hairy legs to . . . Eddy quickly jerked the light back toward his head.

When she reached his face, the narrow beam glinted off dark eyes looking directly into hers. Beautiful, soul-searching dark brown eyes shrouded in thick, black lashes. He was gorgeous. Even with a smear of dirt across one cheek and several days' growth of dark beard, he looked as if he should be on the cover of *People* as the sexiest man alive.

Breathing hard, her body still shaking from the adrenaline coursing through her system, Eddy dragged herself back to the situation at hand. Whatever it was. He hadn't said a word. She'd thought he was unconscious. He wasn't. He was injured . . . not necessarily helpless. She squatted down beside him, and, reassured by Bumper's acceptance and the fact the man didn't look strong enough to sit up, much less harm her, Eddy set the shovel aside.

She touched his shoulder and grimaced at the deep wound

on his chest, the bloody stab wounds in his side. Made a point not to look below his waist. "What happened? Are you okay? Well, obviously not with all those injuries." Rattled, she took a deep breath. "Who are you?"

He blinked and turned his head. She quickly tilted the light away from his eyes. "I'm sorry. I . . ."

He shook his head. His voice was deep and sort of raspy. "No. It's all right." He glanced up at the flickering light dancing overhead, frowned, and then nodded.

She could tell he was in pain, but he took a deep breath and turned his focus back to Eddy.

"I am Dax. Thank you."

"I'm Eddy. Eddy Marks." Why she'd felt compelled to give her full name made no sense. None of this did. She couldn't place his accent, and he wasn't from around here. She would have recognized any of the locals. She started to rise. "I'll call nine-one-one. You're injured."

His arm snaked out, and he grabbed her forearm, trapping her with surprising strength. "No. No one. Don't call anyone."

Eddy looked down at the broad hand, the powerful fingers wrapped entirely around her arm, just below her elbow. She should have been terrified. Should have been screaming in fear, but something in those eyes, in the expression on his face . . .

Immediately, he loosened his grasp. "I'm sorry. Please forgive me, but no one must know I'm here. If you can't help me, please let me leave. I have so little time . . ." He tried to prop himself up on one arm, but his body trembled with the effort.

Eddy rubbed her arm. It tingled where he'd touched her. "What's going on? How'd you get here? Where are your clothes?"

The flickering light came closer, hovered just in front of his chest, pulsed with a brilliant blue glow that spread out in a pale arc until it touched him, appeared to soak into his flesh, and then dimmed. Before Eddy could figure out what she was seeing, Dax took a deep breath. He seemed to gather strength—from the blue light?

He shoved himself upright, glanced at the light, and nodded. "Thank you, Willow."

Then he stood up, as if his injuries didn't affect him at all. Obviously, neither did the fact he wasn't wearing a stitch of clothes. Towering over Eddy, he held out his hand to help her to her feet. "I will go now. I'm sorry to have . . ."

Eddy swallowed. She looked up at him as he fumbled for words, realized she was almost eye level with his . . . *oh crap*! She jerked her head to one side and stared at his hand for a moment. Shifted her eyes and blinked at the blue light, now hovering in the air not six inches from her face. What in the hell was going on?

Slowly, she looked back at Dax, placed her hand in his, and, with a slight tug from him, rose to her feet. The light followed her. "What is that thing?" Tilting her head, she focused on the bit of fluff glowing in the air between them, and let out a whoosh of breath.

"Holy Moses." It was a woman. A tiny, flickering fairy-like woman with gossamer wings and long blond hair. "It's frickin' Tinkerbelle!" Eddy turned and stared at Dax. "That's impossible."

He shrugged. "So are garden gnomes armed with pitchforks. At least in your world. So am I, for that matter."

Eddy snapped her gaze away from the flickering fairy and stared at Dax. "What do you mean, you're impossible? Why? Who are you? What are you?"

Again, he shrugged. "I'm a mercenary, now. A hired soldier, if you will. However, before the Edenites found me, before they gave me this body, I was a demon. Cast out of Abyss, but a demon nonetheless."